WEST OF WANTING

WEST OF WANTING

A NOVEL

JARED REINERT

WALKING MAN BOOKS

WEST OF WANTING is a fictional work. Names, places, and incidents are of the author's imagination or are used fictitiously. Resemblances to actual names, places, or events are coincidental.

Copyright © 2020 by Jared Reinert
All rights reserved.

First printed July 2020.

Published in the United States by Walking Man Books.

For information on author appearance, bulk orders or press, contact:
jaredreinertbooks@gmail.com

Printed in the United States of America.

FIRST EDITION

ISBN: 978-0-578-69087-2

To Nik,
    who taught me all I know
    about brotherhood.

To Mom,
    who taught me the
    power of kindness.
    And books.

WEST OF WANTING

Teeming pastures were to the East
Cast out of Paradise like hungry sinners.

But their desolate trek under cloudless ether,
Through a dust bowl Babylon,
Carried the plainsmen westward.

Youthful zealots, skirting flames of gall
Prodded onward by winds of their drought.

Setting off from their forsaken port,
Ambling through the dust of Eden.
In desperate search of reckoning,
In answers and belonging,
Past the horizon's furthest reach
Somewhere West of wanting.

PROLOGUE

Before

WEST OF WANTING

THE HINGES OF THE DOOR squealed to signal the end of another day on the ranch. He had promised her that he would grease the hinges weeks ago with a fingertip of lard but, nearly a month later, the metal still ground on itself like a seized cog. The heavy soles of his boots thudded against the wooden floor somewhere between the door and the shabby chair she sat on, waiting for him.

"I sure hope supper's in the oven," he growled when he saw her sitting motionless by the broken radio.

"Sit with me please." Her voice was as soft and pacifying as a sip of warm milk. "I would like to talk to you."

He fought with the buttons down the front of his chambray shirt, eyes glaring at her. "Goddammit Caroline. I told you already and if you make me tell you again, you'll be sorry."

Caroline was unmoved. "It's our baby. And if you don't want another child then you're free to leave."

The man scoffed, finally having ripped his arms free from the shirt. He looked down at his wife with frothed tobacco juice slipping between his scowling lips. "I ain't going any damn place but the kitchen." He wiped his mouth with the back of a grimy hand. "Our crops are dying and the ground's drying up and blowing off. We've already got one hungry son and now you want another?" He rubbed his chin and shook his head slowly.

"Whether I want another child or not, we have one coming."

His thumb against his stubbled chin was the only sound filling their decrepit house. "I'm tired of repeating myself," he said. "So take care of it."

"I plan to," Caroline replied and stood.

"No," the man hissed. *"Take care of it."*

She turned toward the hallway and took a step toward their bedroom.

"Hey!" he called after her. "I don't have any intention of raising a family like your old man did. Have a wagon full of kids, feed and house the bastards for years just for them to go belly up."

Caroline took a few quick steps toward him and landed a hand on his bristly cheek. It cracked and echoed like a bullwhip in the small room.

He reached up and grabbed the collar of her house dress, pushing her against the wall of the hallway. "Take care of it," he lashed. "Or you might have an accident around the house here. Might be easier to just take care of it myself."

He released her and stormed from the hall, through the kitchen and back into the prickling evening coolness outside. Over her ragged breathing, she could hear the baby crying from his makeshift crib, awoken and startled by the commotion. She went to him and picked him up, reswaddling him. His second birthday had already come and passed, yet she called him the baby. He writhed in her gentle hands until she nestled his wet face against the crook of her neck. She cooed and shushed him although he was already calm and quiet.

"This will all be okay," she whispered. "You're going to be a brother soon enough, my baby Lester. You're going to be a good brother and you're going to be a good man." She wiped her cheeks before her tears dropped onto Lester's scalp. "I'll make sure of it."

PART I

The Ranch

Chapter 1

Hayes County, Nebraska - 1941

LESTER SPIT BETWEEN HIS BATTERED BOOTS and watched the dirt devour it. A small dimple remained like a splatter of blood dropped from a wounded pronghorn. He stood on a striated bluff and watched the prairie below him rippling like a bedsheet. The terrain unfurled like a wraith of the spirited life that stippled the ground before it turned to sand and roiled in clouds out of the dust bowl. The wind-worn boulders below him jutted from the barren ground like a herd of bison. Beyond the far side of the horizon was the expanse of land Lester's family owned. A ramshackle homestead ranch in Hayes County, Nebraska. The land of the county was claimed first by the Pawnee — borrowed from whichever God had created it — then reallocated to the families that claimed the land first after their government asserted dominance on their behalves. The blood of the native tribes had hardly soaked into the dust before the men began laying foundations.

Lester broke his stare with the brush-tufted ground and squinted into the purpling sky. It was time for him to return home, to sneak the horse into the stalls and silently pad down the hallway into the bedroom. He pulled his wide-brimmed hat tight over his eyes, then looped his boot in the stirrup and reared himself into the saddle. He cinched his heels into the horse's haunches and they began trotting west, chasing the sun toward the horizon. *Ma's going to be fine,* Lester repeated to himself like an incantation. *Ma's going to be just fine.*

By the time Lester loosened the saddle and stalled the horse, the sky was aflame with the last minutes of dull daylight. Lester unlatched the front door of their plain house and took off his boots. He knew the leather soles would echo down the worn wooden floor slats into the bedrooms throughout the house. He sidled on socked feet toward his bedroom, his feet sliding easily over floors worn smooth by generations.

"What in the goddamn you think you're doing, boy?"

Lester turned slowly to his left, expecting to see his Pa in his undershorts, his ragged leather belt looped sleepily in his hand, a sure sign of Lester's hasty trial and swift punishment. Instead, he saw his brother, three years his junior, standing in the recess of the hallway, hand over his mouth doing his best to contain a laugh.

"Christ, Jack!" Lester growled. "Get to bed!" Lester gave his brother a shove toward their bedroom. "I'll be dreaming of a thousand different ways to kick your ass in the morning!" he added for good measure. Walking behind Jack, he could see his shoulders trembling, trying to hold in another laughing fit. When they were settled in their beds and the door was latched behind them, Lester laid staring at the wood grain patterns on the ceiling. He could hear Jack letting off heavy sighs whenever he felt the silence had grown too heavy on his chest, and Lester knew this meant they were both far from sleep. A half-minute after his last sigh, Jack hauled himself up on his side, propped up on his elbow and looked at Lester waiting for him to look at him. Lester laid still for a minute and considered bluffing sleep but he turned his head on his pillow to face Jack.

"Ma didn't come out of her room all day," Jack said quietly.

"She's just been tired lately," Lester replied. "Probably her time.

You know." He knew Jack didn't know, but wouldn't ask. Which was lucky for Lester, as he wouldn't likely know the answers anyway.

"She didn't even make supper tonight. I was damn starving."

"Watch your tongue," Lester scolded. Jack had gotten into the habit of attempting to work cuss words into conversation with Lester. It would have likely gone mostly unnoticed if Jack's knowledge of unsavory vocabulary was more experienced, or if it extended beyond damn or goddamn or any combination of which he could manufacture.

"Pa made butter bread and bacon," Jack said. Lester knew the bacon would have been eaten raw and slimy from the ice chest. Pa didn't have the slightest idea how to turn on the stove and he wouldn't have been even slightly tempted to build a fire when the air was already sweltering. "Well," Jack went on, "he left a few corners and some gristle on his plate so I picked at them."

"Jack, Mom's fine. She told me the other day she's just fighting something off, but it ain't nothing a mouthful of whiskey can't get rid of. You're getting all worked up over nothing." Lester did his best to convince Jack, knowing the weight he had felt on his shoulders since the last time he went into his mother's room. She had hardly said a word. She had looked gaunt, her eyes sunken and dark, her cheekbones higher and sharper than usual, her lips the same pale yellow as her cheeks, the knuckles of her fingers like inhumanely large beads splitting her once gentle hands. The veins in her neck were like twine cord, thick and tight, under her waxy skin.

He thought of the times as a child when he would nuzzle into the crook of his mother's neck, then so gentle and soft. Often, when he had a bedroom to himself and Jack was still in his crib by his mother's bed, he would wake Pa, knowing there was a spanking he would undoubtedly receive in the morning.

"Goddammit Jack, get back to bed!" Pa would rumble from under the covers and roll over to face away from him. He often called him

Jack, and Jack Lester for as long as he could remember. Lester had often sworn to never call his sons anything besides their God-given names. Elijah, he thought, would work just fine.

His mother would already be out of bed by then, slinking past the crib as to not disturb her sleeping newborn son. She would stand in the doorway with her hand out. Lester would lace his fingers through hers, best he could, and let her lead him to the kitchen. There, she would pour two servings of milk into the kettle, quietly strike a match, and warm the milk until it was the perfect temperature for them to both drink in slow, rhythmic sips like he watched Pa drink every morning from his steaming cup.

Ma would kick her chair away from the table and hold open her arms. Lester would go to her, and allow himself to be lifted onto her lap and nestle his head into her neck. He would breathe deeply, taking note of the fragrances on her skin which was as smooth as his brother's. The sweat overlaying lye soap, the salty grease of the bacon she cooked for lunch and yeast from dinner's bread, the sweet powdery scent of his brother who spent hours laying his head in the same place, just as Lester had - and still did.

His mother would tuck him under the covers of his bed, kissing him in the hollow of his temple. She would sit on the edge of his bed, smiling down at Lester, her oldest son. Lester, now unafraid of whatever ghouls had woken him, would be long asleep by the time his mother's weight lifted from the mattress, her bare feet silently padding toward her bed.

"Ma's going to be fine."

Jack's sighs had turned into snores and he made no sign of hearing.

"Ma's going to be just fine," Lester whispered and wiped a tear from above his ear before it could wet his pillow.

Chapter 2

The sun rose early and hot, and brought with it a wave of humidity that made walking feel like swimming. Lester was too concerned with the dread of working the fields on that summer's hottest day to remember the thumping he had promised Jack the night before. He dressed in his lightest denim and chambray, risking the straw splinters that could lodge in his arms as long as toothpicks. When he emerged from the house, the heat surrounded him instantly like a sun-soaked blanket fresh from the clothesline.

The morning grew warmer, like a pot of water over the stove. Lester's hat cast a perfectly round shadow on his shoulders by the time his stomach began to churn on itself. The sun was high and the clouds were long since burnt away. The wind came only in slow, deep sighs and at irregular intervals. Lester walked in long strides toward the barn. He rounded the corner and headed to the water pump. He thrust the pump until a gush of water spewed out and formed brown marbles out of the dusty ground. He removed his hat and put his head under the faucet until the warm water soon turned a blissful cool.

"I say it was time to quit?" A voice hissed from behind him.

Lester hardly heard it through the rush of water gurgling over his ears. He straightened and wiped his face with his dirty shirtsleeves.

When his eyes cracked open and made sense of his blinding surroundings, he saw Pa standing in front of him. He was working off a corner of plug tobacco and stuffed it into his cheek.

"I'm sorry, Pa. My boots are filled with sweat and I haven't had a drink since breakfast," Lester said. There had, in fact, been no breakfast that morning, only a tall glass of lukewarm tap water.

"Think it's any cooler up here?" Pa towered over him. "You left yourself a mess of bales in there you better think about stacking." He pointed toward the barn, where Lester knew there were dozens of hundred-pound bales lying in disarray. Lester had been avoiding the barn. On days like that, the hayloft selfishly held onto the heat, blocking any wind and hoarding the humidity. Lester bent to pump a last drink of water before heading into the barn when he heard Pa's boots turn, scraping on gravel. "And don't bother setting foot in the house til it's done. Maybe get that goodfornothing brother of yours to help for once." He turned again toward the house and spit a mouthful of foaming brown tobacco juice into the brush.

The work was hard but it always was. The bales felt especially heavy that afternoon, the heat siphoning the power from Lester's youthful muscles. He hadn't been paying attention to the time, but when he emerged from the sweltering barn with the straw stacked neatly, the sun was hanging low and peeked under the brim of his hat when he walked. His stomach was thundering painfully, his arms weak and shaking, his head felt split in two. He made his way to the house, praying Jack had opened the windows to let the breeze through. He took off his chambray shirt and shook it loose of dirt and straw which clouded around him and stuck immediately back to his bare arms which were tacky with sweat.

He made his way to the kitchen although there were no sounds or smells of dinner. A few crumbs of bread sat directly on the table next to a collection of empty glass bottles still beaded with dew, the caps on the floor under the table. Lester was rummaging in the pantry when he heard sniffling and ragged breathing. His stomach hardened and dropped. He closed the pantry quietly and made his way down the hall. He cupped his hands around his ears and placed them gently on his mother's door but the noise had stopped. Returning to the kitchen for a glass of water, he heard another wet sniffle. The sound snuck under the door of his and Jack's bedroom. He rushed down the hall and opened the door to find Jack laying on his bed facedown. His boots were still on, spreading dirt over the bedsheets as he squirmed and kicked.

Lester walked to Jack's bedside and laid his hand on his brother's shoulder. Jack drew a quick breath and turned over, startled. His face was soaked and red with tears and sweat. His nose was a dull crimson and his eyelids were drained and puffed. His face softened when he realized it was Lester but he turned back to the pillow to hide his tears.

"It's just me, Jack." Lester replaced his hand on his brother's shoulder. "What's all the fuss about?"

He could feel in the changing tension of Jack's shoulders that he was considering where to start. After a few moments he turned over but still avoided Lester's eyes.

"Come on now Jack," Lester said. "I can hardly shut you up most times and now you don't wanna say a word?"

Jack only sighed, but after a minute he wiped his eyes and looked at his brother.

"Get on then," Lester said with a reassuring nod. "Tell me the story."

"Well, I was outside," Jack stammered, "and I was bored so I started playing pepper on the side of the house." He sniffled a fat, wet breath. "I didn't think Pa would be back before you so I was really chucking it."

"And I suppose you weren't throwing my rubber ball?"

Jack shook his head slowly.

"Did he give you the hand or the belt?" Lester asked, knowing all too well it was the belt.

"Belt." Jack said and began crying again, gagging on jagged breaths. "The buckle though."

Lester tried to keep his face still. "Naw, it probably just felt like it if he gave a good whack."

Jack shook his head quickly. "He showed it to me. Told me he was gonna use it too."

"Show me your back," Lester ordered, and when Jack hesitated, he turned Jack back over, rolling him facedown on the mattress. Jack fought him but Lester outmuscled him. Lester hauled the back of his brother's shirt up over his head. The skin on Jack's back was covered with at least a half dozen welted streaks as long as Pa's boots, all of them raised and swollen, most of them drawing blood. The blood beaded on the peaks of the bruises, trickling down and mixing with sweat like rain on a window. Lester pulled his brother's shirt down, the dingy white fabric soaking up some of the blood dripping down.

"Well," Lester took a deep breath, "guess you best be thankful Pa never won any rodeo buckles." He threw his brother a dusty handkerchief from his back pocket. "Now wipe your eyes and stay here for a while."

Lester stood up and strode down the hallway and slammed open the front screen door. His face was angry red and his hat pulled low over his eyes. He rounded the barn and found Pa taking a drink from the pump.

"What'd you do to him?" Lester demanded, his limbs electric with adrenaline.

"The hell you say to me, boy?" Pa wiped tobacco dribble from his mouth and stepped toward Lester.

"I said," Lester refused to back down, "what'd you do to him?" Pa's eyes widened and his mouthed tightened into a grim smile. "I saw his back!" Lester yelled. His eyes prickled against tears. "Don't you ever touch him again! I'm not too small to fight for and I ain't afraid to fight for him!"

"Shut your stupid goddamn mouth," Pa hissed. "You'll be praying for my buckle after I'm finished with you."

In a blink, his hands were on Lester. He grabbed the collar of Lester's undershirt with one hand and wound the other behind him. Lester pushed Pa hard in the chest and threw him off balance enough to put a long step between them. Lester held his hands chin high in doubled fists. Pa took two steps and uncocked his arm, hitting Lester just below the left eye. A lightning bolt shot through Lester. A flash of light blinded him, his face felt like flames. His eyes let loose a cascade of tears before he could stop them. He stumbled a few steps backward and heard Pa's boots in the gravel keeping pace. Lester found him in his swirling and warping vision. Pa cocked his arm again, aiming for the other eye. Lester lifted his leg as quickly as he could, hitting Pa square in the A of his crotch with the toe of his leather boot. Pa bent in two like a folding church chair. Lester pushed him in the side and he hit the gravel like a felled pine. Lester ran past him, eluding Pa's hands reaching out, clutching at his ankles.

He flung the barn door open. The horses looked up and stomped their hooves with a jitter of surprise. He opened the gate and reigned his horse, not bothering to saddle her. He didn't know where he was going and he had no plan beyond putting space between him and Pa. He jumped on the horse's back and kicked into her haunches. The wind surrounded Lester then, finally. His hat nearly flew from his head. Still, he didn't loosen his heels on her until they were nearly past town.

When he got to town, he tied his horse to a post behind a ramshackle building. If Lester would have seen another town before then, he would have realized that half-mile unpaved road, bordered by a handful of shops and low, empty buildings, was hardly a Main Street. He walked to the general store, keeping his head down and heading for the restroom. He looked in the mirror and was surprised he didn't look worse. He examined his eye. It was red and swollen but he was sure it would quickly set to a grisly purple by the morning. He covered his right eye, looked around the restroom and shrugged. His vision wasn't any blurrier than usual. He washed his face and walked back into the store. He mindlessly walked between the displays and shelves, working through the last hour. As good as it would feel to ride off into the sunset and never return to face his judgment day with Pa, he knew Jack would never forgive him. Not to mention he would never forgive himself for leaving while his mother was ill. Lester took off his boot, removed the insole, and lifted out a folded and tattered five dollar bill. It was soaked through with sweat and hardly holding onto itself. Lester slid his boot back on and walked the half dozen aisles until he found what he was looking for.

Jack laid quietly on his bed for most of that evening just as Lester had told him to. Not that he had much inclination to leave anyway. The angry streaks down his back screamed every time he twisted so he laid on his side and sniffled as quietly as he could, hoping he would be able to hear all the sounds around him. He heard Lester's heavy steps go down the hall then the door slammed open and shuttered. A minute later Jack thought he had heard some sort of shuffling and grunting outside but had assumed Lester and Pa were dealing with an unruly steer. Things were quiet for a while then. Jack and his mother laid in their beds, both silently suffering in their own ways. The next time the door slammed shut, he hoped it would be Lester coming down the hall to keep him company. Instead, he heard glass bottles clinking and Pa's muttering until his snores echoed through the house, sounding like an animal in rut.

Jack did his best to stay up until Lester came back. His worries were beginning to grow. The sun had set at least a half-hour ago and there were still no noises indicating Lester had come in from his ranch work. Jack worked to convince himself that Pa had given him a long, punishing list of chores to finish before he came inside. It didn't take all that much convincing, knowing Pa. Jack was sleeping soundly by the time Lester returned from town, so he didn't hear the sounds of the barn door opening or the clinking of his reins. He hardly even heard Lester tapping on the window across their bedroom. It took three rounds of his brother's rapping before he sat up.

"What in the goddamn are you doing out there?" Jack asked groggily.

"Open up Jack!" Lester whispered from the other side of the glass. "I got something for you!"

Jack twisted his legs over the side of his bed and felt a lash of pain prickle up his back. He grimaced as he walked across the floor to the window. The window frame was stuck so Lester thumped it with his fist from the outside. The window, freed from the sticking wood that had swelled from the humidity, flew open so quickly the boys held their breath and waited for it to shatter.

Lester stood on tiptoes and reached into the window, holding a small box neatly wrapped in brown butcher paper. "Take it," he said.

Jack grabbed the package and opened it excitedly. Soon, a pile of tattered paper and packaging laid at his feet and in his hand was a bright pink rubber ball. Jack's smile reflected the low moonlight when he looked up at Lester.

"Maybe that'll save you from another whooping," Lester smirked.

Jack bounced the ball off the uneven floors a couple times until it hit a knot in the wooden floors and bounced off his dresser, almost knocking over their oil lamp. He let the ball patter away into the corner and looked at his brother. "What happened to your eye?" he asked.

"Well," Lester sighed, "I tried to ride Amigo without a saddle and she didn't take that took kindly. Guess I might's well sleep in the barn to make sure I didn't spook her too bad."

Lester's favorite horse's name was Amigo, even though she was a mare. His mother had taught him rudimentary Spanish during the cool evening hours between ranch work and bedtime, but her own understanding was limited by geography and lost to time, so Amigo she stayed.

"Who're you hiding from?"

"I ain't hiding from anyone, Jack! Just need to stay in the barn tonight."

Jack nodded warily. "Suit yourself then," he shrugged. He collected the ball and laid back in bed, leaving the window open to allow in a lazy nighttime breeze.

Lester stepped quietly back out to the barn and slowly closed the sliding door behind him. He climbed the splintered wooden ladder up to the hayloft. The heat from earlier had softened outside, but in the loft it was still as hot as the afternoon sun. He peeled off his jeans and made a bed from a pile of prickling hay. Sweat dripped into his face, stinging the small cut under his eye. He laid down, his mind still racing, still streaming sweat, knowing it was too hot to consider sleep. He thought about his mother for the first time since he'd ridden away, then he let out a breath he had been holding all night and said his prayers.

Chapter 3

The land Lester and his family called home was a vast cattle ranch that extended beyond the drop-off of the horizon. It was once as green and damp as moss. The rain came often and cool, the sun rising proudly to shower the fields in gold. Jack and Lester, though, had never known the land to be anything other than dust. In the years of their childhood, the cattle would die of starvation faster than they could butcher them. But they were so emaciated there was little meat to cut away anyway. Once, back then, Pa spent an entire day digging a long trench in the northeastern corner of the ranch. The next morning, he rounded up what seemed like thousands of heads of their cattle and shot them, grunting as he rolled the massive beasts into the pit. He and Lester worked into the night covering the swollen grave with powdery dirt.

Only recently had the dust of the ranch relinquished and allowed life once again.

It seemed to Lester that as soon as Jack was born, the ground turned from a fertile manure to weightless sand. The grasses that covered their ranch disappeared in one season. The rain came less and less often those years, then not at all. It was as though Jack was born against a curse and the gods had punished the family by turning their beloved ranch into a wasteland. But the dust that swirled over their land in clouds as wide as cities put grit under their eyelids, between their teeth, and in their hearts. It filled them with the kind of dirt that, when met with the pressure of gratitude and fortitude, shone through like a gemstone.

Lester, even now, had nightmares of the dust bowl storms. He would often dream of the days he and Pa would be working the cattle when the sunlight would shift. The air would feel charged with electricity, and he could feel a rainstorm would be blowing through soon. The air would grow more swollen over weeks without a drop from the skies. He would pray every night for rain, pleading with God to allow his family to keep their slice of land, to glue the dust back to the ground. Then there would be shade on his neck, certain angry black storm clouds were riding the wind toward their ranch. When he would turn to face the glorious rain, ready to hit his knees in gratitude, he would see the storm clouds roiling from the ground instead. These clouds were larger and angrier. There was no thunder, no lightning. No rain. The dust cloud would be on them in seconds. Their horses would rear back in rodeo bucks, neighing and screaming. Lester's eyes filled with sand and grated with every blink. The sun disappeared. Lester was sure he had gone blind. Every gasping breath would leave his mouth chalky dry. The only sounds were the horses stomping and the dull scattering of the dust slamming his ears. His handkerchief provided little relief. Every time the clouds would roll through, he was certain he would die. But each time, he would emerge, caked with dust, his eyes hollow holes in a shapeless face, his black hat now silverbelly.

During the nightmares he had on those years of those years, he could feel himself gagging on the dirt, unable to take another breath, his tongue a dusty cork sealing his mouth. Most nights, Jack would shake him awake, his face twisted in concern.

Jack knew the dreams too. In his, he would be lying in his crib with his mother's arms wrapped around him, her head hunched over to protect him, tattered quilts stuffed in the windowsills. But both of the brothers had survived and, by some miracle, so did the ranch.

Lester learned early in his life that, even if blinded by the churning eclipse of a dust storm, every man is required to have the courage to move onward, to place one boot in front of the other. And that first blind and stumbling step is the most difficult but it is the stride that matters most.

Lester and Jack remembered the storms when their sleeping minds insisted they should, but they would always wake and emerge from the dream like it was a dust cloud. Those dust bowl children.

Lester's great-grandfather, his mother's grandfather, made his way westward from Pennsylvania in a long line of bumping and shimmering wagons with his newborn son, Jack — who two generations later would thereafter be known as Grandpa Jack — swaddled in his young wife's lap. They traveled onward until they found a stretch of land to claim, which ended up being a couple hundred acres along the northern edge of Hayes County, Nebraska. The county was open to claiming during Rutherford B. Hayes's presidency. Hayes had never set foot in the county bearing his name and likely had no inkling it existed. These years were the only times the population of Hayes County grew. Thousands were drawn in by the mirage of free land and abundant riches. Only one of those, most of them would find, was readily available. By the time McKinley was in office most of the family's neighbors had hung up their sun-beaten hats and moved back east or farther west in search of new adventures or work where paychecks came at regular intervals. Lester's great-grandfather hastily bought the land their neighbors were leaving behind, sifting through a stack of silver certificates or jingling gold pieces while they repacked their wagons and saying how much a shame it would be for them to return to their former towns without a dollar to fold in their pockets. The family's land quickly doubled, then tripled, then doubled again. By the time Lester's mother was born the ranch had swelled to nearly ten thousand acres. Most of the land was barren and of little use to their cattle operation. However, Lester's great-grandfather believed that to hold a sizable piece of land, useless as it may be, is to loan a piece of God himself.

Grandpa Jack, as Lester knew him, knew a very different Hayes County than his grandsons. The town Grandpa Jack rode into was like a frosted painting on the front of a postcard. The banks, taverns, attorney's offices, and schools were all built in multiples then quickly filled. The buildings still stood and lined the sleepy streets of town but had grown shut nearly as quickly as they were opened. It was an American boomtown, just like the countless others that speckled the West in those years, and it was built on promises as precarious as dynamite.

Grandpa Jack met his wife, Gramma Copeland, at a hoedown that rolled in and was set up under a rippling tent in the middle of town just like a rowdy circus. They danced that night and then for another fifty-seven years. They had a handful of children, all of them loved. Only one of them, Lester's mother Caroline, lived into adulthood. Lester's mother had never talked about her brothers or sister, and would purse her lips and shake her head when Lester would ask. Gramma Copeland died when Lester's mother was about his age during that summer. Ma didn't like to talk about that either.

Ma would often tell him, though, that Grandpa Jack had been waiting anxiously in the hallway the day Lester was born. When he heard crying, he burst in and held him tightly, nuzzling Lester's cheek on his bristly chin. Grandpa Jack would tell Lester bedtime stories nearly every night, the rumbling of his Grandpa's chest soothing him to sleep. Lester would often strain to remember those nights but never could. Some of his earliest memories had the quality of a shirt faded by the sun and washboard, drained of color and structure. His memories of his grandfather seemed to be a shirt so worn and tattered it was cut into pieces to make wash rags until they were discarded without a second thought.

Grandpa Jack died when Lester was only a few years old. His mother was pregnant with Jack when Grandpa passed. Jack was born with a full shock of brown hair, downturned eyebrows and an upturned smile, which gave him the same tough but genial expression as his Grandpa Jack. Ma held her newborn son and took in his features, counted his fingers and toes, and called to her husband. I know we decided on naming him Peter, she had said, but I believe this boy is a Jack.

Pa was older than his mother and towered over the entire family. He would often come into the house and hit the crown of his hat on the top of the doorway, sending it swirling and rattling around the porch. His height was not menacing on its own, but coupled with the drinking he'd grown to enjoy, the boys had learned to mostly avoid him. The brothers weren't quite sure what their father's name was and bickered about it often. Lester knew him only as Pa and Jack's guess changed as often as his clothes. Lester felt sure, though he would not have put money on it, that his mother had once told him Pa's name was S.A. and shrugged when he asked what in tarnation that stood for. Pa had gone overseas during the great war, and he would sometimes share stories with the boys about his Army friends and about lands the boys could hardly imagine. When they would ask to hear about his heroic battle scenes Pa would grimace and his eyes would bore blankly into the wall. He'd walk to the kitchen and soon the boys would hear the familiar clinking of glass bottles. Jack and Lester had, over the years, grown to hate the times their father talked about the war.

Lester was now well into his fifteenth year and prayed every night for a growth spurt. He had heard for years that he had the genes to be tall like Pa but he was still waiting, and with dwindling patience. Lester worked the ranch with Pa as well as he could, putting in long days with little to show for it besides blisters and limps. His father, at least before their tussle, had granted Lester a quiet respect where he would be mostly left alone if he completed his chores quickly and quietly.

Jack was twelve years old but rarely spent days working the ranch after he had fallen from the hayloft and nearly killed himself — according to his own dramatic first-hand account. While he was on the mend, their mother had commanded Pa let Jack stay inside until he was fully healed. Pa argued halfheartedly and conceded early, knowing Jack had only grown to be a bother and a danger to himself and his brother on the ranch. He had a penchant for trouble and a mind for imagination. Jack felt his most important job on the ranch was to make Lester laugh. This would often end with Lester leaving behind his work to watch whatever feat Jack was attempting. Before being relegated to the house, Jack's biggest hit was the time he snuck up behind a calf and slapped him hard on the rump he reared and kicked like a rodeo bull for a full five minutes.

It had been nearly two years since his fall and nobody had mentioned that Jack was surely healed well enough so he spent his days playing toss with himself, chucking rocks at the side of the house, or pretending he was a cowboy riding a kitchen chair into the sunset.

Chapter 4

Lester woke in a pile of hay, soggy from his sweat and the stifling humidity. He hadn't slept well or much at all. He took a few moments to untangle his mind, listening for the sounds of early morning on the ranch. Lester heard Pa's yips and cattle calls echoing through the hills and into the hayloft. He knew he would have to face his judgment eventually, and the one he faced scared him more than the one with the almighty, but he was hoping to sneak into the house to at least fill his stomach before his hide got tanned.

Lester put on his dingy over shirt and descended the hayloft ladder then crossed the yard with as much stealth as he could muster. He kept a slitted eye over both shoulders even though he could hear Pa commanding the cattle well out of sight. When he got to the house, he bounded to the kitchen sink and wet a rag. He'd been wearing the same straw covered and sweat-soaked clothing since yesterday morning and was beginning to feel the prickling of heat rash. He stripped to his undershorts by the sink and washed himself quickly, the cool water instantly tightening his skin. He scrubbed at his face, then took the time to comb his mustache with his fingers. Lester had secretly been grooming his mustache for months. In reality, there were less than a dozen dark blonde hairs but Lester could hardly believe nobody had mentioned the thickness and fullness of this new sign of manliness.

He walked down the hallway toward his bedroom, one arm piled high with denim and chambray and leather. He found Jack laying with his back on his bed, tossing his new rubber ball into the air. He had just thrown the ball into the air when Lester walked in and Jack, by instinct, looked toward the door. He looked back to catch the ball just in time for it to hit him square in the eye.

"Trying to make me go goddamn blind?" Jack cursed.

Lester tried to hide a laugh. "Reckon we'll both have a nice big shiner now," he said.

"Suppose you'd want to tell me the real reason you slept out in the barn now?"

Lester paused, standing in his dirty undershorts but feeling exposed by the question.

"I already told you," Lester said shortly.

"Oh sure sure, I suppose Pa woke up cussing about how goddamn goodfornothing Lester best be primed and ready for the ass whooping of his life all because your horse bucked you?"

"Suppose so," Lester shrugged He could feel Jack's eyes on his naked back, so he slid his damp undershorts off, knowing Jack would hastily look away. He could hear Jack sighing heavily from the bed, the rubber ball being squeezed in his palms.

"Ma's been calling for you all morning," Jack said into the silence.

Lester felt knocked off guard again, a knockout punch compared to the jab his brother let him feel a minute earlier.

"You been sneaking into her room now too?" Lester snapped. He knew Pa had been clear that Jack was not allowed into their mother's room, where she had been lying with the shades drawn for weeks. Lester couldn't think of an argument against the rule. Lately, even he had needed to take a deep breath before opening her door, as if he was preparing to enter the room of a haunting spirit. The wasting away of his mother's body had not disconcerted him as much as the silence, which filled every crack and recess of the room. Worse yet, it would sometimes be broken by moans coming from deep in his mother's throat. It had been at least a dozen days since his mother had spoken an understandable word to him and even then, she had alternated between calling him Lester or Jack or Harold or S.A. He knew her mind was slipping away, being eaten one memory at a time, with the same aggression, as whatever disease that was ravaging her body. When he would leave the room and close the door behind him, it would seem that his memory would only allow him to remember snapshots of his mother or the room. Looking back even an hour later, he could clearly remember every detail of the bed pot but not a single detail of how she had looked. Perhaps his mind was protecting his heart. Perhaps his thoughts were wandering, trying to meet his mother in the scattered void of her razed mind.

"What'd Ma say?" Lester asked.

"She's been calling for you. Saying 'Lester, Lester' all morning."

Lester dressed quickly and made his way to his mother's room. He stopped just short and drew a long breath, preparing to look at his mother's body, warped and withered.

His mother smiled when he opened the door and came into view, an unexpected sign of recognition, a shadow of motherhood peeking through.

"Hello my Lester, I was hoping I would see you today." His mother greeted him in a voice Lester had begged and prayed to hear again. Her perfect grammar and enunciation parted the clouds of her illness. "Could you please bring me a glass of water?" she asked him, the corners of her eyes already creased with appreciation. Lester poured a glass from a speckled porcelain pitcher. The water was lukewarm and covered with a floating film of dust that had blown in from the plains.

"Ma, you're talking like you used to! I believe you're getting better!"

Lester said, his eyes pleading. His mother looked toward her toes, tented by the bedsheet.

"There's a chair by the chest. Why don't you pull it over and sit with me?"

Lester did as he was told without question. His mother's soft voice was sharp as glass to his ears, her suggestions heard as directions. Still, it was the most beautiful song his ears had ever heard. He sat at his mother's bedside, facing her without pause for the first time in weeks.

"Jack told me you were hollering for me."

"Lester, can you please speak like a gentleman? You're too handsome to speak like a cowboy," she cut in. The women of Lester's lineage had all felt strongly the easiest way to raise a gentleman was to raise a boy that spoke clear and kind. The clearest measure of a man, she would say, is based on the behavior of his mouth.

His mother had been strict with her sons' educations, keeping a keen eye over each other their shoulders to make sure they were working diligently on their schoolwork. Hayes County had once been home to a couple of schools but by the time Lester was old enough to go, there was only a one room schoolhouse to serve the entire county. It was a ramshackle building tossed to the far end of Main Street in town. The school had six pupils, two of which were Lester and Jack. Lester would wake before sunrise and complete a list of ranch work, then saddle his horse and help his brother climb on. They would ride double into town in the cool fall mornings and home in the afternoons when the spring heat was just beginning to bloom.

The brothers, like most of the school-aged children in the faraway neighboring ranches of Hayes County were brought up on the education of the West. They would attend school during the shortened school years, but their mathematics consisted of hay, corn and cattle prices; their science curriculum revolving around growing seasons, fertilizer, mating techniques of horses and cattle; their English lessons no more than repeating the words their father's said in the same lazy-tongued diction.

Lester and Jack remembered their school lessons and their mother's admonishments, but Lester had been spending more time on the ranch with his foul-mouthed father and Jack went to sleep every night imagining himself on horseback, cussing through a mouthful of tobacco leaves.

"Sorry, Ma. Jack told me you were hollering — asking for me," Lester said measuredly.

"I figured if I called for you a couple times word would find you. Your brother's been laying on his stomach in the hallway trying to peek in under the door." She smiled. Lester could easily imagine the scene. "Your father was in quite a mood this morning. Would you like to tell me why?" She asked pointedly.

Lester looked at the floor. "Don't know nothing — anything about that."

His mother's eyes looked him over in the flat, loving way inherent to motherhood. "I'm sick but I'm not blind, Lester. I can see your eye." The skin beneath Lester's left eye had turned a midnight purple overnight.

"Naw Ma, I was trying to ride Amigo without a saddle is all!" Lester traded his grammar for a fake smile, but it was clear his mother knew more to the story than she let on.

"Pa was walking funny this morning, like he was riding a bull last night. I don't suppose you would have ever whacked him in the stones, would you?"

Lester's mouth dropped open, his eyes wide, taking in his mother's stoic face. He had never heard his mother use slang, let alone any concerning the male anatomy. Her face only broke into a thin smile when muffled laughter came floating from under the door. They both turned to see a shadow cast from the hallway, the approximate size of a twelv year old boy.

"Back to your room, young man," was all it took for Jack's shadow to disappear. His socked feet slid down the hallway toward his room.

"Couldn't hear you back here Ma, what'd you say?" Jack called down the hall from his doorway. At this, Lester and his mother smiled at each other. This had been a common occurrence in their house — Jack attempting to weasel out of a situation with more confidence and seriousness than skill, causing Lester and his mother to put their heads in their folded arms on the kitchen table and shake with laughter.

His mother's eyes told Lester she hadn't forgotten her question. She was always a few more steps ahead than either of her sons realized.

"It's nothing, Ma. Just Pa was giving Jack a licking that didn't seem fair is all. He didn't take too kindly to me saying so." Here, Lester had presented a version of the events that balanced precariously between the truth and falsehood. Lies by omission, his mother had taught him, were just as deserving of a spanking. "I'm alright though. Promise." Lester grabbed his mother's hand but immediately regretted it. It was the hand of a corpse, like the monsters he had seen in a comic book once, not the hand of his mother.

"You're really looking better today, Ma." Lester lied. She looked no better than she had, but she was awake today and, by some miracle, talking. "Most of the time I come in here you're sleeping. You must be feeling better."

His mother nodded, closing her eyes. *Our prayers are answered,* Lester's mind repeated.

"Lester, I need you to know that I'm sick and I don't see myself getting better." She squeezed Lester's hand with as much strength as she could muster. "I'm dying, Lester. I need you to understand that, so it doesn't come as a shock." A tear leaked out the corner of her closed eye. "So you can be there for your brother. He'll need help to understand."

Lester's chest turned to lead, a cold metallic anchor dropping into his stomach, his veins turned to copper wire, his fingers instantly cold and weak. He knew his mother was ill but he had imagined her bedridden, at worst, for the remainder of her years. Mothers weren't supposed to die and leave behind children so young they could still bring to mind the comfort of her nipple. He had seen death in various gruesome and drawn out forms on the ranch, but his mother was not a head of cattle. She was not a piece of replaceable life, whose birth and death were hardly noticed. She had done nothing to deserve this fate, and yet it was her fate all the same.

"You're a good boy and you'll be a good man," she went on. "Your brother needs you. You have more patience than your father and Lord knows you'll need it with Jack."

Lester was listening but was not hearing. His head was filled with radio static. His mind played a picture show of a funeral. He had never seen one, so he filled in the gaps with his imagination - the grave was an endless pit, his mother, covered in her bedsheet, was rolled over the threshold like she was being thrown down a well. He tried to bring to mind his mother's face before she was ill, when her smile was as joyous as a summer rainstorm, but all he could picture was his mother's face swollen with sickness and decomposition, her eyes empty sockets, her mouth glued into a lifeless smile.

When the clouds of his mind parted Lester said, "Jack's been asking to see you. Pa says he isn't allowed but he's really been pesting." Lester was already folding his brother's feelings in with his own.

His mother looked toward the ceiling. "That's not your father's rule. That's mine. I said I didn't want Jack to see me like this."

"But he really—" Lester pleaded before his mother tapped her fingers on the back of his hand, cutting him off.

"Jack is too young to understand why I'm stuck in here, looking like this. He's too young to *really* understand any of what's going on. He would only understand that his mother looks like a monster." She pulled Lester's hand to her chest. "I didn't want you to see me like this either, but I knew one of you had to. I know you probably wish you'd never seen me so sick but I trusted you to bear that. I can't risk Jack seeing his mother as a dying woman every time he thinks of me. I'd rather he think of the times we had as a family. You're almost grown, and when I'm gone you'll need to be mature enough to handle Pa and Jack. I've been a good mother and my only regret in raising you boys will be leaving you too soon." She raised his hand to her lips, kissing Lester's knuckles. His skin was cracked and callused from the ranch but was still hardly the hand of a man. His mother dropped his hand and held out her arm. "Come here, Les" she offered. Lester kicked his chair back and laid next to his mother on the edge of her bed. His mother wrapped her arms around him. He nudged his way into the crook of her neck, taking the time to find a new position, his body multiples larger than the last time he let her hold him. There, his head in his mother's neck, he picked up the subtle perfume of her skin, mixing with the salt of their tears.

It could have been minutes or hours that Lester laid there with his mother, but eventually she squeezed his arm and did her best to lift her head. "I believe it's time you spoke with your father," she said, laying her head back on her pillow and watching Lester leave the room.

Chapter 5

Lester emerged from the house unbathed and wearing his same filthy clothing after speaking with his mother. Two river deltas flowed down his face, riverbeds of clean skin surrounded by dust and grime on his cheeks. He stepped into the sunlight and saw Pa working near the barn. Pa turned when he heard the door swing open and quickly closed the distance between them, coming face-to-face with Lester.

Lester dropped his eyes and stared into the dust Pa's boots kicked up. His chest was too empty and cold to fight. "Ma's dying," Lester whispered.

The rage on Pa's face crumbled like the dirt between them. He chewed on his bottom lip and looked over Lester's head toward the house. He sighed then dug a finger in his cheek and removed a hunk of tobacco and threw it into the dry sagebrush. "Reckon she is," he said.

Lester knew his punishment was unavoidable but he'd be damned if he wouldn't argue his case anyway.

"Pa, listen, I'm real sorry for hitting you. I ain't sorry for sticking up for Jack though. You shouldn't have whipped him like you did. You know he didn't deserve to get hit like that."

Pa nodded then, without another sign of hearing, turned on one boot heel and began walking toward the barn. "Let's get to going. We got half a day's work to catch up on," he said over his shoulder.

Lester was too young to understand then but Pa knew as well as anyone that a man can do unspeakable things to protect themselves or their brothers, bound by blood or by trench. Most would say a son raising his fists at their father is worthy of swift punishment but most had never been inches from death, had never felt their friends' blood on their hands, had never seen a man who was supposed to be the enemy but had a face more full of fear than a birthing cow and been required to shoot him between the eyes anyway.

With the dread of facing Pa slowly trickling from his sore limbs, Lester could feel the full weight of his mother's words. He would spend the next days rolling them over in his mind. By the next summer, those words would continue to tumble through his thoughts and would be shined and smooth around the edges like they'd been in a rock tumbler.

Lester and Pa kept themselves busy on the ranch until well after sundown. It went unspoken that summer that they would aim to keep their hands employed and minds distracted until their strength or sunlight completely dissipated. Most days, both ran out long before they decided to quit.

Lester did his best to keep his mind reeling with other thoughts, hoping they would encircle the picture of his mother and keep it contained like bulls on a cattle drive. Still, the cattle would sometimes grow unruly and break through unexpectedly. Lester was haunted by the unknowable yet certain end that was coming for his family. He felt as desolate as a man on death row who had just received an appointment from the governor. His mother's death was coming as certainly and unavoidably as the dust bowl storms of his childhood.

"Don't be late tomorrow, you hear?" Pa called after him when they finally went inside. "Sure to be a busy day."

WEST OF WANTING

In truth, they'd already finished most of the jobs that needed attention for the next week. A broken heart, by some sick irony, made a man as hardworking as an ox. Both of their stomachs had been calling to each other for the past several hours but the thought of delivering any food toward their unstable and quaking stomachs was enough to send bile rushing to the back of their tongues like an elevator. They bypassed the kitchen without a second thought.

Lester opened the door to his bedroom to find Jack sitting on the corner of Lester's bed, his face twisted in anticipation. He had obviously been balancing a question on the tip of his tongue for hours. Lester decided to act as if he didn't notice and went about his business of getting ready for sleep. He was used to Jack bombarding him with questions at the end of the day — *why's the moon light up, how come cars move all on their own, you suppose I see blue the same way you see blue, why's water come from rain but we pump it from the ground?* — but he knew that night's questions were not going to have any correct answers at all.

"Well past dark, ain't it? Thought you and Pa might stay out til goddamn dawn." Jack finally exploded. He had been rehearsing his questions for Lester for what seemed like days until the burning need to ask them was buried in his anger that it was past sundown and he still hadn't been able to ask them. Lester continued stripping off his clothes, refusing to acknowledge Jack's outburst.

"Anyway," Jack calmed himself, "I got a question for you."

Lester padded across the bedroom floor in his bare feet. "Get in your own bed then. And you got one question and that's it."

Luckily, Jack thought, his mother had already taught him how commas can join sentences together so he figured he would string a couple questions together that way and, if he talked quickly enough, Lester wouldn't be able to cut in.

"I heard you talking to Ma and I heard you dragging a chair and I wanna see her. That ain't my question, that's a *ree-quest*."

Lester rolled his eyes. "Get on with it, you dunce."

Jack wasn't exactly sure what that word meant but he did his best to remember it so he could ask his mother later. He could deduce enough to assume Lester would get his knuckles slapped for saying it.

Jack took a deep breath then began his rapid-fire interrogation. "Why's Ma crying when you and Pa are out working, were you two crying when you were in there, did Ma say anything about me, when's she gonna be better again, why ain't she taking her own bed pot out, when's she gonna make potpie again, why ain't she calling for me like she calls for you?" Jack rattled off without pause. He had forgotten a few questions but it was too late to add them now. He raised his eyebrows and looked expectantly at Lester, sure he had just pulled off the perfect crime.

"Damn near eleven questions you just asked," Lester said flatly. "Pick one and go to bed."

"God-*damn*, Lester!" Jack hissed. "Just answer them already! I've been wondering for weeks what in damn tarnation's going on."

Lester slid his legs under his bedsheets and sprawled out on his mattress. "Haven't heard enough when you were laying outside Ma's room?"

Jack's eyes bulged. His youth had fooled him into believing he had gotten away with most everything he attempted, but the past couple minutes were cracking those assumptions with doubt. "I got no goddamn idea what you're talking about," Jack defended himself.

Lester made no attempt to answer him. Jack wondered if Lester had fallen asleep or if he was forming answers to his string of questions. He sighed a few times just to remind Lester he was still waiting, and with dwindling patience.

"Come here, Jack," Lester finally said. He slid to the far side of his mattress, leaving enough room for Jack to sit. Jack joined his brother without being asked twice. He sat by Lester's side, facing the foot of the bed, his head turned up to look at the seam that joined the wall and ceiling.

"Ma's sick," Lester said. "She's real sick. She's been laying in bed for weeks and I don't suppose she's gonna be getting up anytime soon."

Jack had already reasoned this but to hear it out loud in simple terms caused his eyes to fuzz and sting like he'd just come inside from a dust storm.

"So why ain't I allowed to see her?" Jack asked, pleading.

Lester took a few long breaths. There were answers that were correct, but none that were right. He worried Jack would never forgive his mother for refusing to see him, her own son, on her deathbed. He also knew that Jack would willingly trade a punishment from Pa in exchange for seeing his mother again, so he could leave no room to compromise.

"Jack, I need you to listen to me and listen good. Better than you ever listened before, got it?" Lester sat up in bed and turned to face his brother. Jack nodded, his eyes squinting but unblinking. "There's a good chance Ma's never getting better. She's gonna be sick and keep getting sicker. Nobody knows how long she's got left. But Jack, she doesn't look good. She's hardly speaking at all, and what she does say hardly makes any sense. She doesn't look good at all. Doesn't look a lick like our Ma, I'll tell you that, and I don't want you to have to remember that for the rest of your life." Lester searched Jack's eyes for understanding.

"Our Ma's too pretty for you to remember some face that isn't hers. I just want you to remember Ma the way she used to be. I'd hate for you to remember her looking all —" Lester stopped himself. He refused to give Jack details of what their mother looked like, knowing his mind would grasp onto only the sordid details and paint the rest with a heavy-handed imagination. "Point is, it's me that says you're not allowed to see her. And I don't expect you to understand it but I need you to follow it." Lester's eyes bored into Jack's, underlining the importance of what he was saying. "Ma said she loves you more than life itself and she misses you something mighty. But what I said's final and there ain't going to be any arguing about it."

Lester suddenly felt the weight of this, his taking responsibility of denying his brother a last word with his mother, but knew he had done the right thing. It would be a burden between his shoulders for the rest of his life, but life would soon pile so much on him that he would no longer recognize the jagged shape of it digging into his back.

"Ma's dying, ain't she?" Jack asked, turning his crumpled, tear-streaked face toward his brother. Lester knew this was as sure a sign as any that Jack had understood.

"Everything's gonna be alright, Jack." Lester promised, hoping to assuage both of them. "We'll be just fine."

The room grew silent again. Both of the brothers became lost in their own thoughts, playing out their futures like a film reel, splicing out any scenes starring their mother.

"I'm afraid of Pa," Jack blurted out suddenly. "Especially if Ma isn't gonna be around anymore. What if he whips me again?"

Lester cupped the back of his brother's head in his hand, pulling him close enough to feel Jack's ragged breaths on his face. "You never have to be afraid of Pa again. You got a problem with anyone, especially him, you call for me loud as you can." This promise was one Lester need not convince himself of.

Jack closed his eyes, pinching tears from the corners of his lids, and nodded. "Suppose that shiner on your eye isn't from a horse then either," Jack attempted a smile. Lester brought his brother into his arms, Jack's face nestling into his shoulder. He held Jack until the choppy seas of his breathing became as soft and rhythmic as low tide.

The days that followed ebbed and flowed in a cycle of heavy rains and clouds of dust riding the air. Lester kept no tally or notice of the days or storms passing. He was wading through his own squalls, which were also coming unexpectedly on quickly built clouds. Some hours he could concentrate without effort, able to lasso a young steer or reshoe the horses like a seasoned ranch hand. Other moments, he would feel his mind grey and fog with storm clouds, his eyes no longer truly seeing, his fingertips buzzing with electric, his breathing erratic. The change would be upon him before he would remember why it had come at all. Slowly, then, his mother's face would emerge from the back of his mind, the edges of her bones against her thin skin cutting through the dreamlike quality of the picture.

Chapter 6

A FEW DAYS LATER, Lester was closing off a cattle pen when he saw a dust cloud rising off the horizon. He was instantly dropped inside the memories of hunkering down while the dark, silent clouds rolled closer. He had remembered them to be much bigger than this but maybe that was part of growing older and taller. It wasn't until he saw the once sleek, now powdered, car bumping across the pitted trails toward their house that he took his handkerchief away from his face and replaced it in his pocket. Lester could only remember one other visitor pulling up to their home and he was quickly and aggressively chased away by Pa and his double barreled shotgun. Lester felt the tingle of nerves run through him, expecting Pa to round the barn any second. The air around him had the electrical ozone scent of brewing turmoil.

The car slowed as it neared the house. The tires pinched and popped the gravel. Lester rubbed his eyes in disbelief when Pa leaned his spading fork against the barn and made his way toward the car, removing his hat and attempting to rub his hands clean down the sides of his overalls. Lester was sure Pa was just lowering the man's defenses and the trouble was about to begin but, Pa gave the man a quick wave, took another couple steps toward him and shook his hand, pumping it like he was hoping water would gush out like a spigot. The man retrieved his hand back to his side and took a shined black leather bag out of the car, tucked his felt hat under his arm and held his hand out toward the front door, inviting Pa into his own home.

Lester had never seen anything like this, not even close. He fought, with every fiber of his mind, the urge to run inside the house. His consolation was knowing Jack would do his best to sneak into whatever crevasse he could find and soak in as much of the goings-on as possible. Jack usually understood only pieces of the conversations he listened to, leaving Lester to splice together the snapshots Jack offered him into a full story. Jack's undercover account would often come to an abrupt end, signaling the exact moment he was caught in the act.

Lester had become well-practiced at keeping his hands busy to keep his mind still, so the front door creaking on its hinges again sometime later caught him off guard. He quickly smoothed over the dirt he had been moving from one pile to another, sure to pick a spot that was inconspicuous but still provided a view of the house. He stood straight and propped his chin on the handle of the shovel, squinting through the shimmering late morning sunlight. The man with the leather bag emerged and closed the front door behind him. Lester scoured the man's face for any signs of what had transpired inside. The man's face was unmoving, his features as difficult to read as a boulder blanketed in snow. Still, Lester stared at the man, hoping he would continue walking past his car until he was face-to-face with him, sharing with him the details of the conversations that had just taken place. The man opened the back door of his car and tossed the black bag onto the seat. Lester could hear the jingling of metal instruments clanging on each other when the bag hit the steaming leather. The man stopped himself before climbing onto the front bench seat. He turned and looked directly at Lester, his hand resting on the open driver's door. Lester removed his hat, the sun overwhelming his eyes, and nodded to the man. The man's face remained motionless and he made no attempt at a greeting before stepping into the car and rolling the engine over.

The clouds of dust once again rose from the back of the man's car as he drove toward town, reawakening the dirt. Lester waited until the last of it was settled before deciding to make his way to the house. He had just thrown the shovel against the side of the barn and taken a step when Pa burst through the front door, the hinges not creaking but screaming, clinging onto itself like straining fingers. Pa's overalls were folded down at the waist, his undershirt wrinkled and covered in splotches of dirt. He stomped on booted feet across the front path and around the house, a glass bottle in his hand.

Lester waited a beat for Pa to get a head start to where ever he was going then ran to the house, having no idea what he was about to see, but confident it would be a sight he would be able to immediately bring to mind, like a photograph, for years to come.

Inside, the house smelled of grain alcohol. The kitchen table was upright but that was all. The chairs were strewn around the room randomly, shafts of wood as thick as broom handles laid on the floor next to their broken wholes. Lester's family had spent thousands of meals at this table, with the chairs meticulously in their places. Everyone had *their* chair and a spot it belonged. Until recently, the family would sit and eat two meals a day, three on the weekends. Pa shoveling his food and timing his grunts to sound like a member of the conversation; Jack playing with the food on his plate, making a sludge of whatever their mother had spent the day preparing; Ma sharing a scene from the book she was reading or a riddle the boys would mull over until she would finally grab their empty plates and whisper the answers to them; and Lester, his eyes slits on his face from the smile he was wearing, tears pooling on his eyelids from laughing, orbs shining for his mother. There, the family would sit. Together, all four of them.

Lester sat on the kitchen floor and began piecing the chairs together, hammering the joints into place with the heel of his palm. The chairs were once again in their places, although they sat hobbled and crooked, by the time Jack emerged from their bedroom and made his way down the hallway. He found Lester sitting in his regular spot at the table, his head bowed, staring at his hands folded in his lap.

"You alright, Les?" he whispered from the doorway, then repeated again louder.

Lester's head rose slowly to look at Jack. His face was slack and his eyes stormy.

"What happened in here?" Lester asked.

"That man showed up and went into Ma's room with Pa," Jack pursed his lips. "Pa got real mad about something and the man just walked out and Pa started throwing chairs and hollering."

Lester gestured for Jack to join him at the table. Jack sat on his chair, the right back leg now standing an inch off the ground.

"Did the best I could to fix them," Lester nodded his chin toward the chair. "Now tell me what you heard, Jack."

Jack was silent for a moment, re-reeling what he had heard and seen while Lester was in the field. He glanced at the door to make sure their father wasn't going to barge in on them and destroy Lester's handiwork.

"At first I didn't hear much," Jack began. "Just some jangling and breathing mostly. Then I heard the man, I reckon, because I never heard Pa huffing like that. Like he was real mad or something. Then Ma said something about 'We knew this was the news' or something like that."

Lester did his best to pull the reins of his mind, stopping him from propelling toward the end of the story, improvising the route as he went. He could see this playing out a hundred different ways and none of them were endings he'd have written if he really had a chance to choose.

"Reckon that man was a doctor?" Lester asked.

Jack considered this and shrugged.

"Only doctor I've ever seen brought me into this world and I don't hardly remember much of that."

"Go on with your story. What else did you hear?"

"Well then the other man — the doctor I guess — he had a real whiny voice like on the radio. He was saying something about it being 'too late' but I didn't have a clue what he was saying cause it was hardly high noon." Jack kept on, "Then Pa started getting louder and louder talking about medicine. 'Paying good money for some of your fancy city medicine!' Pa was yelling, then it just got quiet for a while. There wasn't any talking for a good long time then finally Ma goes 'I told you S.A.' — that Pa's name or what? — 'Told you we best be preparing for this.' That made Pa madder than a bull and he started yelling 'I ain't marry you just to raise your boys, I married you for just you and now you're shriveling up and dying' — I'm gonna swear here Les, just so you know — 'like the fuckin' crops out there.' He started breathing real strange like he was outta breath or something, breathing between each word."

Lester sat still in his chair, his head bowed once again. "Hear anything else?" he asked.

"Naw, just the doctor said he's real sorry then I heard him shuffling toward the door so I ran back to my room." The boys were silent once more. Finally, Jack asked, "What's all this mean Lester? I tried to hear as much I could and tried to remember it best I could too. Figured you would know what all that means."

"Well, Jack," Lester raised his head and locked eyes with his brother, "I don't believe there's much news at all in your story, but you did a damn fine job remembering all that. Just remember what we talked about earlier, you hear? That's all you need to concern yourself with right now."

Lester's heart sagged, already broken into particles of dust too small to be broken again. There was no saving their mother, not even according to a man in a suit driving a fancy car. He looked across the table at his mother's chair, tucked neatly under the worn tabletop. He struggled to fathom that his mother would never sit in her chair again. He would never taste her pot pie or biscuits, never hear another of her riddles. His mother, the only woman he had ever dreamt about, would soon disappear and exist only in their minds, a fate too ethereal for the woman he'd known better than any other person on earth. He feared he would forget her, piece by piece, after she was gone.

How long before the pattern of cobweb wrinkles around the corners of her eyes and lips would rearrange into a pattern that never was? Would he remember on his own deathbed the way the soft pads of her fingers would trace his shoulder blades when he couldn't sleep, or the way her voice sounded when she read the brothers stories, lulling them to sleep like the raindrops of an almost passed storm?

A rumbling noise broke Lester out of his thoughts. He checked through the windows but the sky was cloudless. The sound hadn't been a storm coming, it had been the thunder of Jack's stomach.

"Hungry?" Lester asked. Jack made a face like he was considering his hunger for the first time all day, then nodded. Lester stood from his chair, pushing it back into its place at the table. He turned toward the pantry, shuffling through the last of their stocks, keeping his back to his brother, allowing his tears to stream freely.

Chapter 7

It was well past sunrise by the time Lester stirred himself awake. He and Jack had rustled around their beds for most of the night, rolling over to face away from the thoughts that were keeping them from sleep, only for the nightmares to crawl under their beds and pop up on the other side. Sleep finally came just before daybreak, the ink black of the night sky beginning to soften like a drop of cream folding into coffee. Lester sat up in bed, confused by the sunlight streaming in and the birds chirping their fluttering midday songs. He dressed sleepily then opened a dresser drawer and dug for his pocket watch, hoping to find some idea how late in the morning it was. His hours were usually marked only by Pa saying it was time for work then time to quit and, before, the aroma of his mother's meals. He found the heavy watch under a mess of cotton socks. The hands were no longer ticking. They were frozen at some meaningless time on some forgotten day. He pulled on a pair of mismatched socks and made his way down the hallway.

Jack was sitting at the table when Lester came into the kitchen. He was seated in the same chair as last night, as always, rolling back on the shortened leg then front again like the pendulum of a grandfather clock.

"Morning," Lester muttered, his tongue still swollen from sleep. He walked to the stove and lifted the lid of the kettle. He picked it up and swirled the contents, hoping for at least a half cup of day-old coffee but found only a sludge of thick, burnt smelling grounds sloshing around like melted chocolate.

Jack sat wearing his best blue jeans. The denim was still stiff and fibrous. Ma had brought them home after one of her last trips into town and imparted the importance of saving them for a special occasion so they lasted longer. He tapped the heel of his boot against the wooden floor and looked expectantly at Lester.

"Something I can help you with?" Lester asked, turning back to face his brother.

"Suppose there is."

"Get on with it then, I ain't got all day."

"What the goddamn is so important that you got to do today?"

"Just cause Pa isn't around doesn't mean the ranch is closed for business. Could probably use your help out there today anyway. You'll break those new jeans in real quick."

Jack dismissed the offer, although he had been hoping to start helping on the ranch whenever Pa or Lester said he was allowed. He had woken up with an idea and quietly checked if their father had returned home, then dressed and sat at the table to wait for his brother. He hadn't anticipated the wait would be so long and was about to go outside and keep busy playing pepper when he heard Lester's drawers shuffling open and shut.

"Suppose I got a better idea," Jack said.

"Yeah, I suppose you think you've got lots of them."

"I was just thinking Pa never taught me how to ride. Never taught me to shoot neither."

"Well, I don't reckon anyone this side of the Nile would let you hold a gun."

"What's the Nile?" "Never mind that."

"Well anyway," Jack went on, "since he isn't around today I was thinking it may as well be high time for someone to teach me to ride."

Lester rubbed his cheek for a moment. "I reckon you would have learnt how already if you hadn't gone ass first off the hayloft, wouldn't you say?"

Jack's cheeks flamed. "That ain't goddamn fair and you know it!" He exploded.

"Hush your big mouth before Ma hears!"

"I've been dreaming of being a cowboy since I was a little boy. All I want is to learn to saddle a horse myself so I don't gotta beg for someone to let me ride double."

"Firstly, you're still a little boy. Second, I sure hope you're not planning on riding by yourself. Haven't heard a worse idea in a long time."

Jack looked around the room, frustrated. "I promise I won't ride by myself," he lied, spitting in his open palm and holding it out for Lester to consider, knowing Lester thought spit-shake deals were juvenile and wouldn't shake on it.

"Right. Let's get going before Pa comes home. If we get caught, don't consider blaming me," Lester said. He stood and walked toward the door, leaving Jack to wipe his hand dry down the side of his perfectly new jeans, leaving his palms dyed a pale blue for the rest of the day.

The horses were jittering when they slid open the barn door. "They're hungrier than a hound I guess," Lester reasoned. Jack wanted to say he was miles past hungry himself, but held his tongue.

Lester brought Amigo, his favorite horse, from her stall. He lazily tied a rope around her neck then around a post and threw a pile of hay on the ground in front of her. Amigo bent toward the food excitedly while Lester and Jack gathered the saddles.

"So this is your blanket and this is your saddle," Lester explained. "Well, actually that one's my saddle and I'll use Pa's old one."

"You can saddle Amigo. She's a good old girl. Mighty patient," Lester said, laying his saddle down and grabbing a brush. "Now you gotta brush her first, to make sure she's good and clean and comfortable."

Jack began to brush Amigo's back and withers uneasily, slowly gaining confidence she wouldn't rear back and crush him. "She's pretty sweet," Jack smiled, patting her rump.

"Now take that blanket and throw it over so it's all nice and even over her back," Lester explained. Jack did as he was told, then looked to Lester for approval. Lester nodded and went on, "You're gonna want to get that stirrup hooked on over the horn," Lester pointed to it, "so it doesn't hit her and get her spooked. Then just pick the saddle up and give it a toss over her back."

Jack grabbed the saddle and heaved it, lifting it less than a foot off the ground.

"Goddamn thing's heavy as I am!" Jack spat. "Ain't no goddamn way I'm ever gonna lift that damn thing!" With this, he began kicking the dirt loose from the barn floor, muttering to himself.

"You wanna be a cowboy or not?" Lester said. "Get the saddle up on your horse or you're not going to ride her."

This time, Jack lifted the saddle with both hands, holding it against his stomach and leaning back, giving it a heave toward Amigo's back. He pushed the saddle up, twisting it on her back until it was nestled in her withers. Jack turned to Lester and shrugged, like it had hardly taken any effort at all, his breathing rasping and heavy.

Lester knew he couldn't contain the laughter tickling his throat and didn't attempt to. The laughter lifted Lester's spirits higher than they had been for days. When they stopped, he went about patiently teaching his brother the remaining points of tacking a horse.

"She's gonna goddamn bite my finger off! I goddamn know it, Lester!" Jack said after Lester explained the process of bridling the horse, his fingers trembling toward the corner of Amigo's mouth.

"Well you're not going to ride a horse if she doesn't have a bridle, I'll tell you that."

"Les, I'm not about to go sticking my finger in her mouth!"

"And I'm not about to make you either," Lester said, beginning to loosen the rear cinches.

"Now come on Les, just do it for me. Just this once," Jack pleaded. "My finger's the same size as a carrot. She's gonna take a nibble just to make sure it isn't one, I'm telling you!"

Lester's stomach shook with laughter. He and Jack were soon laying prone on the rough and splintering barn floor, pounding at the boards like their laughter was agony. Amigo stood patiently, half saddled, her head down searching for more hay.

Finally, the boys wiped the tears from their eyes and stood, examining Amigo's massive, stained teeth. "Aw, alright let me try it," Jack said, grabbing the bridle. He slid a trembling finger between Amigo's lips when Lester grabbed the back of his elbow quick as a snake.

"*GODDAMN it Lester!*" Jack roared, his eyes wide. Amigo skittered but remained calm, no stranger to the boys' antics. She once again searched the floor for food while the boys fell on the floor in another round of hysterics.

The brothers rode to the bluff, which Lester had used as his oasis for several years, miraculously without incident. Jack was the first person Lester had ever shown the way. He wondered as they rode how he had found it, whether the spirits that truly owned this land had guided him there the first time. By the time they stood by their horses and looked over the terrain from the bluff, their shadows stretched long behind them, the sun hanging low in front of them. The sunlight was the dull heavy orange of late evening when the wind begins to wake and the skies paint themselves with a new palette.

"So this is where you come out to when you sneak off?" Jack asked.

"Sometimes. I like the quiet up here. Can really see the plains from here too."

Jack took in the view vaguely. "Suppose there's oil under there?" He asked, jutting his chin toward the horizon.

"Who said anything about oil?"

Jack shrugged.

"I'd be damned if I know, Jack."

There was a pause. "One time I saw a picture of oil spewing outta the ground like piss. Wouldn't that be something?"

"Reckon so. Don't have any inkling what we'd need all that money for though."

"You're shitting me!" Jack squealed. "Some Tom Dick hands you a stack of dollars and you'd say 'No thank you, sir'? Not a goddamn chance!"

Lester considered this, really considered it. He had little use of money, and knew Jack had even less. Lester had a dollar or two under his boot sole but had only recently touched it for the first time in years.

"I reckon I haven't got much use for money and you've got even less. The ranch gives us more than enough to get by, God willing."

"Yeah, suppose so," Jack said, disheartened. "What do they call it again?" He asked after a moment.

"Call what?"

"Oil."

"Black gold."

"Right. Black gold." Jack's eyes became starry, no longer seeing the land unrolling below him but dreaming instead of oil gushing from a corner of the ranch, soaking everything he'd ever known in tarry black fortune. He quickly began tallying how he would spend this money, which was difficult as he had no idea what most things cost, and instead decided he would bury some of the cash under the house just in case a band of outlaws ever came along.

"Alright now, don't go acting like a Rockefeller before you've made a dime," Lester said, noticing his brother's crooked smile. "Let's get to going back home."

They looped their boots in their stirrups and jumped on their horses, pushing their heels into the horses' flanks. They rode down the rocky decline from the bluff and made their way back to the ranch, the sun flirting with the horizon, their hats pulled low.

"You bring anything to drink?" Jack asked, unable to stand the silence broken only by hooves shuffling in the brush.

"I told you to pump some water before we left."

"Right," Jack said. Then, after another stretch of silence added, "Care if I sing a song?"

Lester turned quickly to look at him, nearly falling from his saddle. "You reckon you're some kind of Gene Autry or something?"

"Just trying to make some noise. Too damn quiet out here," Jack admitted.

"That's the point of being out here. No noise except for God breathing. But I've never met someone that hated quiet as much as you." They rode on a while longer in silence before Lester relented. "Go on, sing a ditty."

Jack tipped his hat with bravado then considered which song to sing first, in case Lester only allowed one. "This one's called Cowboy Jack. How about that?" he said with a sly smile, then cleared his throat and sang in a voice that Lester hardly recognized. He had never heard his brother sing, and could hardly believe what he was seeing — and hearing. Jack's voice cracked a few times during the first lines but then warmed. If Lester hadn't been so surprised, he would have told Jack he sounded just like Ma's Jimmie Rogers record without all the hissing and popping. They rode, Lester's face slack in surprise, and Jack's eyes closed in concentration as he sang:

He was just a lonely cowboy

With a heart so brave and true,
And he learned to love a maiden,
With eyes of heaven blue.
They learned to love each other
And named their wedding day,
When trouble came between them
And Jack he rode away.

He joined a band of cowboys
And tried to forget her name,
But out on the lonely prairie,
She waits for him the same.
One day when work was finished,
Just at the close of day,
Someone say 'Sing a song, Jack
To carry our cares away.'

When Jack began his singing
His mind it wandered back,
And he thought of a brave true maiden,
Who wanted him to come back.
Jack left the camp next morning,
Breathing his sweetheart's name
He said, 'I'll ask forgiveness,
Cause I know that I'm to blame.'

But when he reached the prairie,
He found a new made mound.
And his friends they sadly told him
They laid his sweetheart down.
They said when she was dying
She breathed her sweetheart's name,
And she said with her last breathing
To tell him when he came,
'Your sweetheart waits for you, Jack.
Your sweetheart waits for you,
Above the lonely prairie,
Where the skies are always blue.'

"That's mighty fine, Cowboy Jack," Lester said after the last echo of Jack's voice came to them from the bluffs. He couldn't think of anything else to say. "Mighty fine indeed."

Chapter 8

T HE DAYS BEGAN moving more quickly for Jack after that. He no longer felt like a prisoner in the house, which had grown silent and cell-like without his mother's company. He had begun to find refuge in sneaking a horse from the barn and disappearing. He would wait just outside the front door until he could no longer hear Lester or Pa's voices then tack an old horse with an old saddle that was angry with dry rot. He would brush and stroke the old mare, whispering promises of the day's adventures before climbing on.

In those weeks, he explored every acre of the ranch, trotting on as far as the fenceposts ran then turning ninety degrees and following a new row. He and the horse would amble off toward the corners of Hayes County, especially those where the dirt had been swept away by millennia of wind and rain, leaving the jagged blades of hillsides to jut from the prairie. The bluff Lester had shown him had turned out to be only one of dozens. He collected the geography like strange rocks, placing them gently in the pockets of his memory. He found his favorites and called them what he told himself were names the spirits whispered to him; Red Blade, Running Water, Sunrise Cliff, and so on.

His days were no longer filled with games of pity and self-entertainment played only for the sake of passing time. He had felt for months that he was able to return to working on the ranch - his muscles felt stronger, his mind sharpened, his hands more ready for the sandpaper of a day's work - but he was afraid to bring it up to Pa, knowing he would find a way to make Jack regret his willingness, and he was no longer allowed to speak to his mother.

When his mother first became ill, he felt it was his responsibility to stay close to her, sometimes as close as her door, ears perked for the haggard calls of suffering. He was haunted by the idea she may be visited by the reaper while he was too busy chasing steer in a far-reaching corner of the property, unable to hear her calling for Jack by name. It was a childish nightmare, but one that haunted him nonetheless. His body felt more grown every day, but sometimes his mind would remind him of his adolescence, teasing him with terrors he casually dismissed as juvenile but which terrorized him regardless.

By the time he had asked Lester to show him the process of saddling and riding, he was ready to explore the recesses of his thoughts as well as the corners of Hayes County, far from the walls he had come to know too well. He was sure the thoughts that shortened his breaths would feel less claustrophobic under a wide open sky.

The rides refreshed him like a mouthful of seltzer, prickling his insides in places that had felt hollow for months. He found the gentle breeze and the rhythm of the horse's muscles against his legs had a way of greasing the cogs of his mind, working lose the sticky teeth and allowing a more efficient stretching, folding, and recycling of his musings. Jack was now able to chew his thoughts like tobacco leaves, spitting out the stems, then when he felt ready, disposing the entire mouthful on the side of the trail, leaving a bitter sweetness in his mouth and the empty headedness of a high.

After weeks worth of days riding to the corners of Hayes County, his mother passing was no longer a constant nightmare. Instead it was a puzzling reality he struggled to digest. It would sometimes toss his stomach in fits, like he had swallowed the mouthful of chaw instead. Other times, the machinery of his mind was prepared to dissect and neatly store away the idea of his mother disappearing from his life. He no longer heard his mother's howls for help when the wind would whistle over his ears. He had come to terms with the idea his mother was going to die, and it was selfish of him to assume her last calls would be for him.

Lester may have noticed this change in Jack, but he made no mention of it. As brothers do, they existed in their own orbits, only coming together briefly at the end of their days. Each day they grew older, the less their gravity pulled each other in. Jack no longer puzzled over lists of questions for Lester. Most of the things he would have asked had already been answered that day somewhere beyond the reaches of the fenceposts. He no longer simmered during the day, waiting for dusk and therefore a companion. He had once been like a pup, running to the door with uncontained excitement when he heard the hinges squeak. Now, he would likely be unable to discern that sound from the countless others echoing through his days.

"Don't have any questions for me anymore?" Lester asked one night.

Jack considered him. "Suppose not. Been thinking myself a lot lately. Trying to answer some questions on my own."

The room fell silent again. "I saw you out riding the other day," Lester said coyly. "You need to be more careful. So Pa doesn't see you. If I could see you, he sure as hell could've too."

Jack shrugged. He would gladly trade his rides for Pa's belt. "Just got lots of things on my mind," Jack replied. "With Ma and all," he explained needlessly.

Lester nodded. "That's why I showed you the bluff. Can do lots of good thinking up there. Air's better for thinking, I guess. Just be more careful, so Pa doesn't catch you sneaking out. He'd have both our hides for that, I reckon."

Jack understood. He felt like more of a man than he ever had. He felt the pull of his brother's orbit then, this secret between them heavy enough to bring them together again.

"Remember when you told me a man doesn't need to be a cowboy to be a man?" Jack asked.

Lester nodded.

"Sure does help though, doesn't it?"

"Reckon you're not slinging shit there," Lester replied. The boys laughed in low howls. The laughter continued in contagious sputters for the rest of the evening. Long after they should have been asleep, Lester spoke. "Reckon you should get some sleep, as I suppose you've got a long day of riding ahead of you."

"Suppose I'll ride up to your bluff again in the morning."

"Right, just remember what I told you. And be safe."

"Sure thing, Les."

"Night, Cowboy Jack."

PART II

Changes

Chapter 9

Hayes County, Nebraska - 1942

THE TIME CONTINUED like that, more or less for the year that followed. The boys rotated in habits dictated by the cycles of their avoidance then head-first dives into their thoughts. In many regards, the brothers became boys again and enjoyed this change. It was a slackening of the cinches they had been feeling around their chests. What they hadn't expected during that year was for the latigos to completely let loose, their shoulders unclenching and their jaws relaxing for the first time in nearly a year on the day their mother passed away.

By fall, Ma had stopped speaking completely. Her eyes shut in a constant, fitful sleep by the first snowfall, and her limbs grew still, as if frozen by frostbite, by the time the grass became so cold you could snap it like a toothpick. She survived through the winter, her favorite season, although her body and the soul it encompassed was as blank and harshly lifeless as the weather outside her window. In that way she remained until the ground had completely thawed.

The boys had nearly forgotten she was silently existing in her own orbit, just on the other side of a door they passed every day. Their mother's love no longer pulled them toward her physically. Her breathing was drowned out by the numbing wind that cut through the windowpanes like a blade. They prayed for her nightly, then weekly, then sporadically as the snow piled up in drifts outside their house. The thoughts of her became like their shoe prints in the snow — quickly filled in and covered over.

There is only so much closure one can experience before the door is slowly closed by the breeze and latched, unnoticed, and the hinges left to rust over. The passage in their minds that led to their mother's impending death became grown over, all thoughts stemming from it long since chewed over, digested, and excreted. The thoughts were there, but they knew what was being stored on the other side of the door and no longer felt the need to cross that threshold.

There was an unfamiliar sense of contentment when their mother passed. They were prepared for it and had even grown restless for it. The story had been written and the ink dried. They had never wished their mother dead, but how long had it been since her wilted body had been their mother?

Jack had gone for a ride that morning. The early morning sun caught the corner of his eye and woke him from an anxious sleep. He had been dreaming of Sunrise Cliff. He and the horse ambled along, exploring the scenes he had hankered over during the winter with longing and reverie. He returned from the ride to find Lester sitting behind the house, mindlessly shuffling the handle of a shovel from one hand to the other. Jack came around the house and startled his brother, whose eyes had a vague and distant focus. At Lester's feet was a patch of freshly overturned soil.

"What're you planting?" Jack asked. His brother remained silent. Jack searched the ground in front of them for an answer, looking for a spent sack of seeds or bulbs. He saw the row of organized stone blocks. Jack had known what they were, in some form of child-like understanding but had refused to truly think about it, knowing he would regret pulling front the images of what was under his feet. Over the years, they had become parts of the landscape as much as the fenceposts or boulders dotting their land, pieces of the terrain that had been there long before his existence. He looked at them with a newly ground lens — blocks adorned with initials and years, lined up like a timeline, to be read like a Rosetta Stone of their lineage. Their great-grandfather and his wife, Grandpa Jack and Gramma, a collection of smaller blocks for their children, then a patch of sickly bitter smelling dirt where their daughter had joined her family at long last.

The boys did not spend long grieving the death of their mother. They had grieved in full many months ago. Their lives were not altered in an instant. The changes that needed to be made had long been complete. Their family seemed to let out a long breath that had tightened their chests when she passed, as if they could all feel her bony body passing to the ether of another life. As she emptied herself of life, the brothers exhaled the breaths they had been holding for months.

Their mother had laid still and lifeless for many months. All the boys had done was put her to rest in a new bed. One, Jack was relieved to realize, he could visit without punishment.

Chapter 10

The second time a car rattled down a rutted path through the fields toward the house, Lester nearly didn't hear it. He had been busier than usual on the ranch, with spring beginning to mature into summer and Pa absent more days than not. He had noticed Pa's feet had been kicking up more gravel when he walked lately, sometimes causing him to stumble, and he began only speaking to the boys when necessity compelled him to. The trail of empty bottles he left behind him had multiplied as well. When Lester finally noticed the crunching of the vehicle approaching the house he wondered if it would be the doctor again coming to examine Pa, whose skin had begun to wrinkle and loosen in curtains on his face. Jack was convinced their father had caught whatever illness plagued their mother and believed the empty bottles of whiskey or moonshine were medicinal. Lester knew better but said nothing to dispel the idea.

When the man got out of the car, Lester did not recognize him as the doctor. He wore a slim navy suit with a tie clip that sparkled like a diamond and black shoes shined so smooth they reflected an image of the sky. The man was more hesitant than the doctor, considering each step toward the house before taking the next. Finally, he stood at the front door and rapped on the frame. After a minute, he began slowly turning to take in the property, searching for something but most likely anything. He made eye contact with Lester, jutting from the ground on horseback, who tipped his cap to the man. Just then, the door swung open as if an outlaw had entered a saloon and Lester saw Pa, half-dressed, standing in the doorway. Pa and the man went inside for a time. Lester did his best to ignore the questions prickling at the back of his neck.

He was just finishing fencing a herd of cattle when the man strode toward him, his shoes now dusted over with a thin matte layer of dirt. He stopped short of Lester and waited patiently until his presence caught Lester's attention.

"Pardon me," the man nodded. "Is your name Lester Harold Copeland?"

"Yessir," Lester said, eyeing him warily.

"We need you to join us in the house, if you would."

They stared at each other for a moment. "Just need to finish fencing these steer, then I'll be right in."

The man nodded, forced a tight smile, and walked slowly back to the house.

Lester finished his task with unease rippling through his limbs. This was different and on the ranch, Lester knew, different was hardly ever good. He tied Amigo just outside the house. When he entered the kitchen, he saw Pa and Jack sitting at the table and the man in the suit sitting in his mother's chair. Only Jack looked at him. His eyes overflowed with confusion muddled with concern.

"Have a seat, Mister Copeland," the man said.

Lester sat in his chair and scoured the table for signs of what was to come. There was an envelope, ripped open and browned around the edges, along with a small stack of official looking papers.

"Mister Copeland," the man said, "I asked you to join us because we are going through your mother's last will and testament and found it imperative you were present."

Lester nodded skeptically.

"It has recently come to the attention of the Hayes County Bank & Trust that Ms. Caroline Copeland Burke has recently passed away." The man's eyes rounded the table and saw no signs of disagreement. The man was a gentleman of tact so he didn't mention the manner the Hayes County Bank & Trust had come to learn about Ma's death. Pa, who had steadily handed off the small stack of bills they had saved in exchange for whiskey and moonshine, had stumbled into the bank the week previous. He leaned heavily on the counter and demanded his wife's savings be handed over to him. *She dead as'a fuckin' snake in'a pigpen*, he slurred to the bank teller, *she left'er money ta me an' I fuckin' wan'it*. The bank, which employed the only lawyer in Hayes, Perkins, Frontier or Chase counties, soon handed the lawyer the will for one Caroline Copeland Burke. At the lawyer's soonest availability he rode his sleek Studebaker, tan as the dry soil, to the ranch where he saw a patch of overturned dirt near smoothed gravestones and knew he had found the right place.

"My name is Richard Addard. I am an attorney based in the Hayes County Bank & Trust. I'm here to read Ms. Copeland Burke's will and testament," the man said and looked at each of them. "Ms. Caroline Copeland Burke's last will and testament," the lawyer went on, "reads as follows: I, Caroline Copeland Burke, of Hayes County in the state of Nebraska, being of sound mind, memory, and understanding, do make this my last will and testament, hereby revoking all former wills by myself made at any time heretofore. I direct that my burial be conducted in a manner similar to my predeceased family on property bequeathed to myself upon their passings. I bequeath the sum of fifty dollars to my spouse, Harold P. Burke." Lester's eyes shot to Pa's, who sat motionless, staring at the edge of the table. His mother had mumbled the name Harold some days while she was ill, but all these years he had thought

Pa's name was S.A. Jack's eyes had a faraway gaze, the legalese racing through his head and exiting without pause. The man stopped reading. "I assume that would be you, Mister Burke?" He asked, looking at Pa.

Pa finally looked up at the man, his eyes the color of a sunset. "No sir," he replied.

The man shuffled the papers, tapping them edgewise on the table. Lester's mind was whirring at such a speed he had to lean in to hear them over the whistling in his ears.

"You are saying, sir, that you are not Mister," he consulted the papers, "Harold P. Burke?"

"That's what I said. My name's Sybil Andrew Hodge."

The man's cheeks flushed. "Have you any idea where one could find Mister Burke?"

Pa's face went aflame, his anger or embarrassment or whichever combination a man would feel then, rushed to the surface. "Ain't got the slightest," Pa said. "Run off years back. Before I lived here."

The man nodded slowly, treading lightly. "Were you previously aware of a Mister Burke in relation to Ms. Caroline Copeland Burke?"

"Yessir. They were husband and wife before he ran off to Cheyenne."

"And had Mister Burke and Ms. Copeland Burke filed for annulment?"

Pa looked at the man blankly.

"Divorce," he simplified.

Pa shook his head. "Don't believe so. We were never married, me and her."

"Ms. Copeland Burke, you mean?"

"M-hm."

The room was silent then. Lester's eyes were wide, watching the volley with rapt attention, careful to avoid any movement that would remind them he was there.

"Then, sir, I must ask," the man said, his eyes avoiding Pa's, "are these young men your sons?"

Pa looked at Jack then Lester, locking eyes with him. He looked as though this exchange had aged him nearly a decade.

"No sir," Pa said. "No kin of mine. Believe they'd have to be Harry's boys."

"Mister Harold Burke?" the man asked.

"M-hm," Pa grunted.

The man nodded gravely and began asking Pa questions about guardianship, questions that were now completely drowned out to Lester. He was swimming in a pond of murky and acrid tasting water, unsure which direction he was being pulled. The riptide turned his stomach upside down, his eyes rolled to keep up. Lester would not feel as if he were walking on solid ground again for several days. When the gurgling in his ears subsided enough, he could hear the man continuing to read from the papers.

"I bequeath unto Lester Harold Copeland, born September of 1924, the entirety of 9,875 acres of land, inclusive of all livestock, buildings, implements, and crops in Hayes County, Nebraska to which I derived title by bequeathment from my father, Jack S. Copeland. I also bequeath the entirety of my assets in holding at the Hayes County Bank & Trust," the man read. He stopped and looked to Lester. "Is that correct, son?" He asked.

Lester stared back at him blankly.

"Were you born March of 1924?" He asked again.

Lester had thought he was born in 1926. He had been sixteen years old for months to his recollection, but his mind was already reeling too hectically to check the math. He did not know how to answer so he sat silent and motionless.

"Lester. Answer the man." Pa said forcefully.

"Yessir," Lester replied slowly, "I reckon so."

WEST OF WANTING

The man considered them. "I suppose that would make you, Mister Copeland, nearly nineteen years old and therefore of legal and mature age to receive title for this house, property, and the remainder of your Ms. Copeland Burke's assets."

Jack's eyes grew to gaping saucers. Pa's expression was blank and impossible to read. Lester was still reeling from the onslaught.

Lester was, in fact, born in 1926. He was born on an unseasonably warm day in early fall of that year, in the house he now owned. Since he was born in a ramshackle homestead far from the reaches of the capital in Lincoln, his birth certificate was bound to be riddled with mistakes. Misspelled names, incorrect birthdates, and mixed up parental names were all commonly recorded erroneously on birth certificates then, especially in the quiet and distant corner of the plains Lester was born into.

The lawyer promised to write up a new birth certificate with a date of birth listed as September 1, 1924.

Lester's mother had watched her own mother pass away when she was just shy of her eighteenth birthday. That had got her thinking about what would have happened to the ranch if her father had soon fallen ill as well. A seed was planted then, a kernel of an idea for when she had children of her own, a way to make sure the ranch was passed down to her oldest child — a boy who was now sixteen years old but had full ownership of a sizable parcel of land in the dust bowl of Nebraska.

As Lester knew as well as anyone, his mother was always at least one step ahead.

Chapter 11

"What the goddamn did all that mean?" Jack asked again, repeating the question into the silence. He was lying in bed, hearing the faint echo of words he didn't understand shuffling around his head. Lester laid on his own bed, still dressed, his boots still on. The lawyer had loaded himself and his paperwork into his sleek car and bounced away toward town. The sun had set hours ago. Still, the boys were far from considering sleep. Jack had been unsuccessfully attempting to get Lester to talk since Pa had walked out the front door shortly after the man and left them alone in the house, reeling. Lester hadn't heard his brother. He was standing on ground that was altogether brand new. His old footholds had been cracked apart like a fault line and replaced with unsteady, crumbling soil. He felt as if his bed was floating on the ocean, ebbing and cresting as the waves of his thoughts rolled through.

"…gonna talk to me or not. I ain't gonna sit here talking to myself all night!" Lester finally heard.

"What are you spewing off about?" Lester replied shortly.

"I said," Jack huffed, rolling his eyes, "what the goddamn did all that mean?" He had asked the same question five times previously, by his count.

Lester took a moment to collect his thoughts, leaving Jack to stew further. "Well, turns out Pa isn't our Pa. Don't reckon I have any idea who our real Pa is, so don't get to asking about that either." Lester shot a look toward Jack. "Think Ma changed my birthday on those papers. I reckon the ranch belongs to me now. Even though I haven't got the slightest idea how to pay bills or own a house."

"Well," Jack itched his chin, "Pa isn't your Pa but maybe he's mine?"

"You see him making a show to claim you?"

Jack's eyes dropped. The room fell back into oppressive silence. "So the ranch's all yours then, huh?" Jack finally said, hoping to lift their spirits.

"Belongs to me as much as any land can, I guess. It all seems hard to believe."

"You planning to kick me out now that you're the boss?" Jack raised his eyebrows, searching his brother's lips for a tick of a smile.

"Keep asking questions and I'm liable to. Now go to bed. We've got a ranch to work tomorrow and I'm the boss now and I say you're plenty old enough to help out." Jack's eyebrows shot up. "I saw you riding and you won't have any problem out there tomorrow as long as you get some sleep."

It was hours before the boys slept, if they slept at all. Lester's chest still felt hot and roiling with acid. Jack was so excited for his first day as a cowboy that when he finally found sleep, he woke himself nearly every hour, his arms twitching him awake while dreaming of lassoing calves.

Lester and Jack worked the ranch for several days, with only minor skirmishes, before the man in the tan Studebaker came cruising back across the ranch, a cloud of dust in tow. He parked by the barn and waved his fedora to Lester, who had already wheeled around on his horses. Lester rode to the man, climbed off, and shook his hand like he had seen gentlemen do. The man pulled an envelope from his satchel.

"These are the birth certificates for both you and your brother," the man said and handed over a flat envelope. He reached back into his bag and removed a smaller envelope, swollen and stretched at the folds. "And this," he said, "is your mother's liquid assets."

Lester's brows furrowed, his hand in his pocket, unmoving.

"The money, son. This is your mother's money." The man explained. "And I suggest you find a safe place to keep this," he said, holding it tightly. "It's a sizable amount, which I'm sure most people around here would be happy to take off your hands."

Lester took hold of the envelope, imagining the bills inside and the sound they would make if he'd rifle through them. More clearly, he thought of how he wished he could trade this stack of bills and the small pile under his boot sole for his mother to walk out of their front door at that moment.

"Thank you sir," Lester said. "You've been mighty kind to us."

The man nodded. "You can always open an account for this money at the bank. We would be happy to help. If you ever need anything there, just ask for Richard. That's me."

"Yes sir, Mister Richard."

The man tipped his hat and turned back toward the Studebaker. He stopped and faced Lester again. "Son?" he said, "I'm sorry about your father. It's never easy to deliver news like that. I hope you and your brother find the answers I'm sure you're searching for."

The man tipped his hat and threw his bag into the car. By the time the sound of the engine faded and the dust settled back to the paths carved by his tires, the seed of what the man had said was dug into the soil of Lester's mind, the hole filled in and the waters of a gentle rain beginning to nourish it.

Lester waited for days to speak to Pa. He had questions he needed to ask, but he had difficulty finding the time to bring it up. Most days,

Pa would be gone from the ranch, returning after a couple of days to sleep for a stretch of time Lester could hardly comprehend. Lester would try to catch Pa after these hibernations, knowing it was a rare moment his breath would not be sour and hot with alcohol. But Pa would slink out to the barn and Lester would only realize he had woken up when he heard Pa's horse clopping away.

After another week, Lester was boiling a pot of coffee when he heard Pa's footsteps coming down the hallway. He turned away from the stove and positioned himself between the hallway and the front door.

"Got a couple questions for you."

Pa looked at him under puffed eyelids, his lips cracked and scabbed over. He grunted in reply. Lester poured two cups of coffee, careful to keep his eyes on the door in case Pa attempted to slink away. He set the mugs on opposite sides of the table and gestured to Pa to sit, pulling out his own chair. Lester owned this house, he reminded himself, and that made him the man of it. Pa reached over the chair, grabbing the mug by the body and leaned back against the wall, looking down at Lester.

"Why didn't you or Ma tell us about our real Pa?" Lester asked.

Pa took a gulp of steaming coffee like it was a snifter of neat whiskey. "Your mother told me not to."

"You knew?"

"Course I knew!" Pa snapped, his patience quickly running dry. "Caroline'd just had your brother when I moved in."

"Tell me the story," Lester said. His heart raced but he suddenly felt brave.

"The hell you wanna know? I ain't about to sit here and tell you a whole goddamn sob story. You got work to do out there, boss man."

"And you've got drinking to do, but we ain't leaving til you tell me the story." Lester refused to blink. His neck singed and tingled with adrenaline.

Pa scoffed, rolling his eyes. He looked Lester over, then again, then again. Seeing a boy ready for a battle he didn't have the energy to fight, he pulled his chair from the table and sat.

"Jack wasn't more than a couple days old when I moved in," Pa began. "I was back from the war for a while and there wasn't no work to find in Hayes County. The ground was about as dry as it'd ever been. Old Man Jack hired me for some work around the ranch, mending fence and all. That's how I met her."

"Ma?"

Pa nodded. "Before she knew it, she's got a brand new baby, her man's run off with hardly a word, and her Old Man's dead. I moved in to help her take care of the ranch full time. Ended up taking care of you boys more than anything though." Pa looked at Lester, then turned his eyes toward the window. "Tell you boys the truth, I never been a fan of being a father but I was a fan enough of your mother."

They sat in silence for a minute. Pa drained the rest of his coffee, the mug clattering on the table when he set it down.

"Any idea where my real Pa went off to?" Lester asked.

"Well," Pa thought, "all I know is he talked a bunch to your Ma about driving cattle out on the North Range, driving steer south as far as Denver up to Cheyenne, I believe. Probably cavorting somewhere out there, if I had a guess. He'd always tried to talk her into moving west and leaving the ranch behind. But I don't suppose your Ma would have left this land unless God himself asked for it back."

Lester sat rooted, his eyes glimmering in thought.

"What's your plan?" Lester asked. "Now that Ma's gone. Doesn't seem to be much keeping you here."

"Suppose I'll stay long as you'll keep me. Don't imagine there's a whole lot of work to find in Hayes County and I don't feel much like setting off and starting over right now. Just right back to being a ranch hand, I reckon."

"Don't suppose much has changed as far as the ranch. You still know the land better than me or Jack and you know it."

Pa nodded shortly. "We done then?"

"One more thing," Lester said. "Where's Cheyenne?"

"Wyoming. Out on the North Range. Big railway line stops there. It goes clear across the country from there."

"Which way's that? Wyoming?"

Pa's eyes narrowed. He regarded Lester vaguely for a moment, then looked out the window toward the early morning sun, hanging low in the east. He turned his head and nodded his chin in the opposite direction.

West.

Chapter 12

Lester rifled through his dresser drawer, squeezing the bloated navy blue sock that was pushed into the back corner. Just to make sure. He had counted the money before Mister Richard and his car had jolted back into town. Lester was not decidedly anxious to figure out how much richer he had become, but what else is a young boy to do when handed a pile of cash? His eyes had followed the Studebaker fading away from the ranch while he folded the envelope in half and stuffed it in his back pocket, then walked to the outhouse and latched the door shut behind him. He pulled the envelope from his jeans, carefully as to not drop it down the repugnant pit. He ripped one edge of the envelope off and threw it down the hole. The bills slid into his palm easily in a neat stack, the corners sharp and matched. He counted them slowly and deliberately, then counted them again in the opposite order. Some of the bills were kinds he had never seen before, the faces on them strangers, but he tallied up the number on the corners intently. Lester imagined the number he counted to, seeing the digits in his mind, so he could more easily recall the sum if need be. He replaced the money back into the envelope then into his pocket before going straight to his room and stuffing the wad of bills in the tattered sock which he shoved to the back of the drawer.

Not once did he consider the security of this hiding place. He had only hidden a handful of items in his life and they were all still tucked away neatly in the drawer; a still wrapped Peanut Chew candy that had been hidden so long it had nearly turned to powder, a flattened bottle cap with some blaze red paint peeking through the rust reading *Topo Chico* that he had found discarded on the road in town when he was a child, and an illustration of a naked woman in profile that he had found stuck in some dry brush on the ranch, a memento that had blown into Lester's hormonal possession on the eastward wind.

He had checked the wellbeing of the newest addition to his collection nearly every morning while grabbing for a mismatched pair of socks. He thought about it sometimes, the sound of the bills rubbing on each other or the smell of the linen paper. Lester wondered some stifling afternoons if the roll of money in his drawer had made him a rich man. He had rarely seen more than a couple sheets of paper money at one time, including the bills under the sole of his boot, so he assumed the sum he took ownership of was, in some parts of the world including his, more than sizable. He laughed when he thought that if he placed the money from his drawer in his boot, it would cause him to walk with a knock-kneed limp.

Jack had quickly grown into his role as the newest ranch hand and Lester was happy to find they made a good team and could finish their work smoothly and efficiently for the most part. On the days Pa was home and able to walk, their chores would sometimes be finished not long after noon. Lester had stopped counting on Pa's attendance on the ranch but some days he would surprise the boys by brushing and saddling the horses before they had stumbled down the hallway for their breakfasts. Lester could feel himself growing into the guardian of the land he worked every day, his back widening to shoulder the responsibility. Still, there were some jobs Lester couldn't finish himself, even with the help of Jack or Pa, and for those he put on a new shirt and rode into town.

It was late morning and the day's work was being checked off at a steady pace. Lester rattled off a list of chores for Jack to finish before calling his day over, knowing Jack would likely spend the next several hours fooling around then rush to complete his jobs before sundown. Lester tied his horse near the house and went inside. He bent over the kitchen sink and scrubbed his face nearly raw with a cold washrag then headed to his room. There, he peeled off his dingy undershirt and slid his arms through a crisp white pearl snap shirt that he had picked up in town the previous week. Lester ordered it at the general store, special order from the owner's catalog. The man even measured his arms and chest in directions he found comical, then dumbfounding. He buttoned up the pearl snaps, enjoying each of the seven clicks as they snapped into place. The sleeves were a bit longer than Lester thought they were meant to be but he figured it looked fine enough. If he were to be honest, it was the finest shirt he had ever owned and maybe the finest he'd ever seen. A real cowboy shirt. He tucked in the shirttails, the starched cotton fighting his hands, then compared the perfectly white shirt to his faded and worn jeans. He might have to get himself a new pair of Levi Strauss jeans, creased down the center of each leg, while he was in town, he thought in passing. The thought of buying more special order clothing made Lester's neck feel warm. The shirt, after all, had cost him nearly a full dollar. He spit into his dirtied tee shirt then bent over and polished the toes of his boots. After looking himself over once more, he walked out of the house and climbed into his saddle. He rode slowly into town, paying close attention to anything that may soil his shirt and keeping a careful hand on the bulge of cash in his front pocket.

Lester walked through the front doors of Hayes County Bank & Trust with as much fake hubris as an outlaw. He was careful to remove his hat and keep his chin high while he strode toward the counter. He asked to speak to Mister Richard and was promptly ushered into his office. The room smelled like the wisps of smoke curling from the man's pipe. Mister Richard invited Lester to sit in a chair that was so lusciously padded he wiggled in his jeans just to further explore it.

Lester spent the remainder of the morning in Mister Richard's office. Lester had been mulling over how to handle his newfound fortune for a couple weeks and impressed the man with his requests. By the time he rode from town, Lester had deposited a majority of his pile of cash into three accounts – one for himself, one for Jack, and another for Pa. He had set aside the money required to pay any taxes the ranch would owe for the remainder of the year and saved a smaller stack of seventy five dollars for himself.

Lester had replaced the roll of bills in his pocket with a thinner stack of papers, one of which was a copy of his own will and testament. It was a short document that took hardly twenty minutes for the man's secretary to type on her clacking typewriter. The sole beneficiary of all assets Lester owned was Jack Copeland.

Chapter 13

By the time the sweltering, humid June air was settled into his corner of Nebraska, Lester knew what the next months would hold for him. Mister Richard had told him weeks prior, standing on the ground he still could hardly fathom he owned, that he hoped Lester and Jack found the answers they were looking for. That simple statement, a formality of kindness more than anything, had been a kernel of corn that fell into the soil of Lester's mind and had, in the weeks since, grown into a sturdy stalk two heads taller than himself. It was an idea that was larger than himself and rooted so strongly even a dust bowl wind wouldn't have felled it. The man, in one sentence, had confirmed to Lester that questioning the changes that had come to his life so slowly, then so abruptly, was normal. More importantly, if the man said he hoped Lester found the answers then that meant, Lester assumed, there were answers somewhere past the horizon that required finding.

The idea came on slowly at first, but then after the right combination of conditions — rain and sun, tears and smiles — grew to border on unruly. Soon the kernel planted in his mind had grown to a lush, green field that required either harvesting or razing. Lester, a rancher since birth, decided to harvest. The restlessness in Lester's chest grew after nights that were too quiet and days that seemed to contain too many hours. The idea of searching for answers somewhere past the land he had known his entire life seemed alien to him for weeks until he began hearing a word, which had first rolled off Pa's lazy tongue, reverberating in his mind each night before he would finally find sleep. The word was like a lullaby falling on his ears, the name of an oasis where solutions spewed forth and steamed from the ground like a hot spring.

It was the land of answers. Lester's first question was *which direction shall I go forth?* and the answer was the sweet melody of the place itself. Cheyenne.

"Pa, I've been meaning to talk to you."

Pa turned from the sink in the middle of scrubbing his stubbly face, his hands and face dripping water like tears. He considered Lester. "Get on," he said, turning back to the sink.

"I've been thinking lately and I've got a deal for you."

Pa's eyebrows raised. He lifted the bottom of his shirt and dried his face and hands on the filthy fabric. He shook his head and chuckled while his face was covered, not trying too hard to hide it from Lester.

"I usually lose at deals. Been losing at them my whole life," he said, turning to face Lester. He wasn't known for betting on billiards or shuffling a deck of cards but most would say falling in love with a married woman raising two boys on her own after her husband ran off was a gamble. It was one that Pa had bet his pile of coins on and felt he lost.

Lester refused to back down. They were all hurting, all on unfamiliar footing. He knew he would drive himself insane by searching for steady ground in places where there was none. Instead, he busied his mind with the idea of going out and finding new ground to step his boots onto. The plan he had laid out in his head was going to set off like a firework. The fuse was already lit and was about to take flight, whether or not anyone else was willing to watch.

"Just listen to me before you tell me off," Lester said. "I'm planning to saddle one of those horses and ride on out to Wyoming. I believe if I can find my real Pa out there and show him I'm a cowboy now then maybe he'd be willing to come on back home with me."

The room was silent for a moment, then Pa's face broke into a smile for the first time in over a year.

"Now *that*," Pa snorted, his face wrinkled in laughter, "is that funniest goddamn thing I've ever heard!" He continued haltingly between laughing fits. "Boy, your Ma used to tell me how goddamn smart you were but you're a goddamn fool if you believe that lousy goodfornothing jackass is about to follow your ass home like you got a goddamn pile of gold here waiting for him!"

Lester's face flamed in anger, the rims of his ears singeing, a tightening crimping over his temples.

"Don't you talk about my Pa like that!" Lester said, collecting as much courage as he could. "Maybe you're right. But I can't bet on that and I'm gonna find out one way or another. I've hardly got anyone left so I might as well go out and find someone."

Pa's laughter subsided and he wiped his eyes, regarding Lester vaguely.

"So here's the deal," Lester went on, "I'm gonna take Amigo and ride her to Cheyenne and find my real Pa. I'm asking you to stay here and work the ranch. I put a stack of money in the bank for you that's all yours when I get back. I'm expecting you to take good care of Jack while I'm gone. The cattle too." Lester searched Pa's face but found it steadfast, unwilling to give any signs of agreement or the opposite. He continued. "If you change your mind while I'm gone, just go on and sell the cattle and horses to the next ranch over and put the money in the bank in town. Just go through town and stop at the bank on your way out and ask Mister Richard to send me a note that Jack is here by himself and I'll turn around and come home. He's expecting you, just in case."

The kitchen grew oppressive with the silence, the breeze no longer blowing through the windows like it was afraid to come between the tension of the two men inside.

Finally, Pa spoke. "I suppose there's nothing I can say to change your mind so here's what I'm gonna say anyway." He leaned forward toward Lester. "I reckon I came here to be a ranch hand for Old Man Jack and I'm not too proud to do that again. I'll take good care of the ranch. Don't you worry about that. Been doing that since before you can remember."

"Then you best stop your drinking," Lester said before he could stop himself.

Pa's eyes showed surprise, not in the request, but in Lester's bravery. Pa grunted. "I've just got a condition about this little deal."

Lester nodded.

"I ain't about to take care of your brother. Especially if you expect me to quit drinking. That boy'd drive God Almighty to chug a jar."

Lester had considered this already. He knew Jack and Pa got along about as well as fire and kindling. He also knew if Jack smelled any hints of Lester leaving, he would saddle a horse and follow Lester in any direction, no matter Lester's willingness.

"Alright," Lester sighed. "I suppose he's both of our's Pa anyway."

They sat for a while, the beginnings of contentment creeping into their bodies for the first time since they could remember. Lester, like a cowboy, found this fulfillment in the idea of not sitting still. He would set out and find the answers rather than wait for them to blow onto the ranch from the west, just as a cowboy wouldn't find contentedness sitting and biding his time waiting for a herd of cattle to stroll onto his land.

"Is Cheyenne a big city?" Lester finally asked.

"I've never been," Pa said. "But I suppose it's a hell of a sight bigger than town here."

"Reckon we can get there on horseback?"

Pa nodded. "Believe that might be the best way to get there."

"Suppose we'll even find him?" "Your old man?" Pa asked.

Lester nodded.

"Suppose if you stay long enough you'll find damn near everyone out there eventually."

"About as much as I can hope for."

Pa's glare softened. "Let me give you some advice," he said. Lester leaned forward. "It's still early summer, even though it's hotter than a whore out there already. You should head to Col-or-a-do first," Pa said, exaggerating every syllable of the name.

"Where's that?"

"Damn close to Cheyenne," Pa replied. "Those cowboys drive steer from south as far as Texas some years and bring them up to Cheyenne where the railroad stops. At least that's how they used to, according to a man I was stationed with. If I was a gambling man, and I ain't, I'd bet your old man's somewhere between Cheyenne and Denver. Best bet'd probably be to head straight west. That'd take you near Fort Collins, if I ain't mistaken. I haven't seen a map since I was in the service."

In a tragedy Lester was too excited to notice, Pa was more helpful than he'd ever been to him while telling Lester how to leave.

"Suppose you'll be back?" Pa asked.

Lester nodded. "That's the plan." Then after a moment added, "I'll check the post office in Cheyenne and —" he paused, "what's the name of that other town?"

"Fort Collins."

"I'll check at the post office in Cheyenne and Fort Collins if you need to send us a message. Mister Richard at the bank said he'd help you get us a telegram."

Pa was quiet then. Lester began to stand when Pa knocked on the table gently and cleared his throat. An uncomfortable question lodged just past the back of his tongue, threatening to choke him if he didn't cough it up.

"About how much do you suppose's in the bank for me?" Pa asked finally. Hardly a half dozen times in his life had Pa had bills enough to rub together but the promise of money was the reason his feet were staying grounded on the kitchen floor. Grandpa Jack had paid him in cash for his work, but that money disappeared quickly as he began courting Caroline. With Grandpa Jack's passing, Caroline had paid him in love, and he would gladly work more hours than a day could hold to have a payday with her one more time. Money was not something he considered beyond trading meat for cash and cash for liquor, but if he was being hired by a boy one-third his age, he might as well ask about the wages.

Lester turned to face Pa full-on, not letting him wallow in the embarrassment of the question. "More than enough to buy yourself a shiny new car and get the hell outta here if you want."

Pa's eyes ticked to the floor. "And suppose I want to stay?"

"Then we'd be able to buy the shiniest tractor this side of Cheyenne."

Pa's face cracked into a shy smile. Lester began heading outside to find Jack, ready to invite him along on his journey, then turned back to Pa.

"Do you think there's any chance he'll come home with us?" Lester asked.

Pa considered this. "I would say if you're riding all the way out there just for that, then you might have yourself a long ride back."

Lester hung his head for a moment. "But I gotta go. I don't expect anyone else to understand it, but it makes perfect sense to me."

"I'm not saying anything about that, Lester. You have to go. I get that. But your old man felt like he had to go too and he never promised anyone he'd be back. Not like you just did. I suppose if he wanted to come back home bad enough, he could have found his way by now."

"I need to try. I could hardly forgive myself if I didn't."

"You're right. Doing the right thing is a good pillow to lay your head on every night."

"Guess so," Lester shrugged and went outside to find Jack.

Chapter 14

"You're goddamn fooling! Aintcha?" Jack howled, his voice buffeted by the dust-laden wind. "You're telling me we're heading to Wyoming on horseback?"

Lester nodded, fighting against Jack's contagious euphoria for no good reason.

"I've never rode out past those bluffs. Suppose they're any place near Wyoming?"

At this, Lester couldn't contain his joy any longer. He broke into a laugh that surprised Jack. "Just a ways past there, I reckon."

Jack was silent for a long couple seconds. "You think we'll make it?" he asked shyly, kicking the ground. "With all them Indians and such?"

"Jack, listen to me," Lester reassured him with knowledge he had picked up along his three extra years on earth. "All the Indians between here and Cheyenne have all long since run off."

"But," Jack whined, "what if they're still angry about all that stuff and we get a spook put on us by an old Indian lady?" Jack did his best to convey the seriousness on his face. "I read that they can do that in one of your books!"

"Firstly," Lester said, "those are called hexes, if that's what you're talking about. Second, we're not about to see any Indians and I bet a dollar if we do, they'll just tip their hat and ride on by just like any other cowboy."

Jack nodded, but he was hardly convinced. He had more concerns to discuss so he hoped they could circle back to the Indians later. "What about buffalo?" he asked after some consideration. "I've seen a picture of them in that same book of yours. They look mighty mean."

Lester knew the picture Jack was speaking of. It was one of his favorites. The page was dogeared and worn from the countless times he had flipped through it before bed. He would often dream of riding through a land where the bison were so plentiful and content that they looked like small, woolen boulders grazing on the prairies. The picture in his book was a painting that showed the terrain of the real West — the gentle hills covered in knee-high grass giving way abruptly to the mountains jutting to the stars, a background so unnatural to Lester's corner of the world that he had to believe it had been imagined — with a herd of bison spread in an innumerable group like ants on a sugar pile.

"They're called bison," Lester said.

Jack turned to him in disbelief. "Excuse me," he scoffed, "nobody sings about 'Where the *bison* roam' do they?"

"I'm not saying that's not what the song says. I'm saying that's the wrong word for them. If you don't believe me, I'll show you in that book. It's right there under the picture."

Jack had never even considered there might be words below the picture.

"And anyway," Lester continued, "all those bison disappeared just like the Indians before we were even thought of."

Jack mulled that over. He had imagined they would have to avoid bison like mosquitos on a humid summer night. As scared as he was to encounter a bison in close proximity, he felt a pang of dismay that they might not see one at all. "Still hope we see some," he said. "Just from a way's away."

"Then you best keep an eye out for them. And don't be disappointed if we don't."

"I won't!" Jack snapped, knowing he would be, very much so.

"Let's get to going," Lester said. "We've got a lot to do before we leave."

The brothers rode, bumping side by side, into town with the worst of the late afternoon heat beginning to dissolve. The sky was deepening slowly as if it were water tainted with a measured trickle of blood. The boys were silent for most of the ride, taking in the slow change of the evening redness. "Nothing wrong with a sky like this," Jack noted once with reverence. The boys didn't realize the skies they had grown under, the only horizons they had ever known, were merely the gods cleaning their palettes and mixing their oil paints before they brushed the western skies over Wyoming.

When they got to town, they removed their hats and tucked them under their arms after tying their horses in front of the small building. The faded sign overhanging the door was once emblazoned in canary yellow paint, *Hayes Co. General Store*, and below that in smaller letters, *R.W. Spencer, Prop.*

R.W. Spencer had long since passed away but his son still ran the place even though he was aged well into his sixties. It was a small store with simple provisions but, as R.W. would have sternly told anyone brave enough to complain, it was the only honest store between Omaha and Denver. He had never been to either of those cities and hardly any places in between but he realized early on that a passing knowledge of city names could fool most Hayes Countians into thinking he was well traveled.

Lester had been in the store many times, mostly after his mother had become ill. Jack, however, had only been to town a handful of times for reasons other than school and had not once set foot inside this building, which looked drab and uninteresting from the outside. Stepping through the threshold, Jack was at once struck with the amount of dry goods, the farming hardware and implements, and the glistening bottles of cola and sarsaparilla. By the front window, there was a small assortment of books, their covers faded and curled at the edges, but the depictions of cowboys or beautiful women still fully on display.

Lester was instantly overwhelmed. He was usually fully prepared for trips into town, spending hours writing and rewriting lists for his errands. But in his excitement over Jack and his new adventure, he had forgotten to write down a single item they would need. He turned toward Jack, ready to tell him not to touch anything, when the excitement on Jack's face made him wonder if this trip might not have the makings of a nightmare.

"Christ, Jack! Get your hand off that!"

They had only been inside the store for a few seconds before Jack became enamored with the hulking, ornate cash register and couldn't help but feel the spines of the brass tooling. The store owner rounded the counter that held the register and took in the two boys. He had been doing his best to take special care of Lester, mostly unbeknownst to him, after he heard of his mother's passing and almost nightly saw Pa stumbling through the middle of Main Street, just outside the store. The man had even recently helped Lester order a beautiful new pearl snap shirt a few weeks prior, paying the extra forty cents so the boy could have it for only a dollar.

"How are we doing, boys?" He asked brightly. Some shop owners may have run off two dirty teenage ranch hands if they sauntered into their stores, but this was Hayes County where there were no strangers, young or old. Lester's visits were always a highlight for him. He would watch the boy carefully check off each item on his meticulous list, him counting his money methodically before handing it over, then attentively placing the groceries into his saddlebags, rearranging them nearly a half dozen times before they fit in a way he saw fitting. "Anything you'd like me to get for you?" the man asked.

"Got any toys?" Jack asked immediately.

The man laughed, surprised by the younger boy's buoyancy. "I take it you're Lester's brother?" he asked.

Jack nodded without taking his eyes off the shelves. The man was struck by the difference between the brothers. Lester's lankiness and seriousness was a stark contrast to his brother's stout stature and uninhibited manner.

"We're here for some supplies. Going on an adventure," Jack said casually.

The man raised his eyebrows and leaned back onto the counter. "That so?" he asked. "How far are you boys traveling? Out to the bluff?"

"You know about the bluff?" Jack sputtered.

"Well, I know a good amount about this land, nearly all the way to Lincoln," he said confidently, using the lesson he had learned from Pa.

"Then maybe you've been where we're going!"

"Where's that?"

"Wyomin," Jack said, then added matter of factly, "we're going to find our real Pa cause Pa ain't really our Pa but our real Pa is in Wyomin or Cordalato."

"Ain't that something?" The man asked coyly. "I've heard Cordalato is beautiful this time of year."

"He means Colorado," Lester cut in.

The man turned toward Lester and saw his arms piled with canned goods, his face wrinkled in disapproval.

"You boys hitchhiking all that way?"

"Naw," Jack said, "we're cowboys."

"I see," the man said, as if that answered all further questions. "I do hope you boys visit me on your way back and tell me all about it. That's a mighty long way!"

"Thank you sir," Lester cut in again. This time he grabbed Jack's arm and pulled him alongside himself, tearing Jack's eyes off the glass case holding dozens of containers of penny candies.

"If you don't shut your mouth I'll leave you at home with Pa before than you realize I'm gone!" Lester hissed at his brother.

Jack looked back at Lester, shocked. "He's a nice old man and he asked what we were doing! Why's it a secret where we're going?"

"Just," Lester eyed him, "let me do the talking from now on."

Jack rolled his eyes. "Suit yourself."

Lester grabbed anything in the store he thought they might wish for while baking on horseback from the Nebraska sun or laying under a star-filled sky in the open range of Colorado. The man tallied the prices and Lester counted out the money, surprised by the bills he had left over.

"Do you have any maps?" Lester asked as the man dropped the money into the cash register with a flourish.

"What kind of map are you looking for?"

"Well," Lester thought for a moment, "anything that might be of service getting us between here and there. We're going to —" Lester searched his memory, "Fort Collins first. In Colorado."

Jack's head snapped toward Lester. "Ain't that what I said?"

The man smirked, then ducked behind the counter and emerged with a folded pamphlet. "This should serve some purpose if you boys get turned around, I hope," he said, handing it to Lester.

Lester unfolded the map. *Official Map of Nebraska Highways, April 1, 1940* was printed in one corner, under the panhandle, where the boys would soon be traveling. The man moved aside the smattering of things on the counter and directed Lester to lay it flat. Jack stood on tiptoes to see.

The man took a stub of a pencil from behind his ear and put an *X* over a seemingly random spot.

"That's just about your plot of land," he said. Then he pointed a wrinkled finger toward a crooked line. "Look here," he said, "at the red one." Under his finger was a red line extending horizontally across the map until it disappeared over the Colorado border. *Highway 6.* "One of the longest paved roads in the state, Highway 6. As long as you ride due west for a ways, you'll meet up with Highway 6 in a day or two. About 50 miles from here by the looks of this." His finger traced a line from the X toward the left edge of the map until he tapped on the spot where his fingertip met the bright red line. "Beyond that," he said, "you'll have to ask another old man behind a counter for more directions."

"Yessir," Lester said, "thank you kindly. Can we buy this map?"

The man looked between the boys. "No," he said sternly, "you may have it."

The supplies filled both of Lester's saddlebags and one of Jack's. While Lester was cramming the last of their canned foods into Jack's bag, he remembered he had forgotten to buy flint. He was fairly confident he could start a fire with two lengths of dry branches but had no inclination to find out while they were alone and in the dark somewhere between Hayes County and Cheyenne.

"Jack," Lester turned to him, reaching into his pocket, "take this dollar and go back inside and ask the man if he's got any flint."

Jack looked at Lester blankly. "Any what?"

"*Flint.*"

"You betcha, cowboy," Jack said, jumping over the two steps to the door. "Flint," he repeated.

Jack emerged several minutes later. Lester was sitting on Amigo's back using a toothpick to dig dirt from under his nails. Jack was just about to climb back on his horse, tossing a brick of slate grey flint from one hand to the other when Lester faked a cough.

"Need a soda for that cough? I know where you could get one," Jack said, a smart smile cracking over his face.

"Where's the change?" Lester asked with quickly dwindling patience.

"The what?"

"*Goddammit it Jack! The change!*" Lester barked.

"Jee-sus, Les! Don't have to yell," Jack said, eyeing his brother. "Didn't get any change anyway. Hard to believe, but flint cost exactly one dollar."

"Boy, that sure is hard to believe."

Jack shrugged, "Beats me."

"You better hope we don't see any Indians," Lester boiled, "or I'm liable to leave you with them just to be rid of you!" With that, Lester rode away. Jack climbed onto his saddle, reaching a hand deep into his pocket and unwrapped a small lemon gumdrop. He examined it with fascination before plopping it in his mouth.

Jack ate four of his ten candies before they reached the ranch. He hardly remembered unwrapping and eating the other three. He had been so distracted thinking about the other treat he had gotten himself with Lester's left over money, wrapped and packed away safely in his back jean pocket. He imagined the joyful noise that would come from it, the songs echoing through the prairies of Wyomin and Cordalato. Jack was so distracted, he nearly forgot to clamp a hand over his front pocket to stop the pennies the man had given him from jingling like spurs.

Chapter 15

Lester was up early the next morning, his joints stiff and eyes puffed from another night of restless sleep. He dressed quietly in case Jack was having better luck calming his heart into sleep and went to the kitchen. He made a strong, steaming pot of coffee and poured himself a mug filled to the rim. Pa was usually awake by sunrise but Lester saw no sign of him today. He assumed Pa had gone off while the brothers were in town last night and hadn't returned until much later, if at all. Perhaps they had passed each other without realizing it somewhere in the blankness between the ranch and town, the hoofbeats of the other blanketed and smothered by the dusk.

Lester drained his coffee and went outside to the barn. The sun was just beginning to reflect off the dewed grass like brilliant gemstones. The barn door was opened a crack, but he wrote it off to Jack not closing it last night. Lester figured Jack had been too excited about the candies in his cheek or the pennies in his pocket to care about the door. Jack did his best to hide his new treasures but Lester had noticed, without much effort at all, the jingle in Jack's step and the sickly sweet lemon scent wafting from his mouth.

Lester slid the barn door open and took a step inside. It took nearly a full minute for his eyes to adjust from the sparkling spotlight of the rising sun to the dull, heavy darkness inside. When his vision returned he saw Pa standing near the far wall, a white rag hanging slackly from his hand. He had been hunched over but stood and turned to face Lester when he heard the clattering of the door on its rails. The heat of the morning had not rolled through yet, but his forehead and lip were studded with sweat.

"What are you working on?" Lester asked.

Pa jutted his chin toward where he had been working. There, Lester saw a saddle balanced on a sawhorse. Looking at it through the early morning light streaking between the slats of the barn, Lester could see the saddle had once been beautiful. The tooling had been hand carved and stamped with a steady and loving hand before the leather had dried and cracked. Jack had used it often but had not once heeded Lester's advice to oil and condition it.

"I talked to Jack about oiling that up about a year ago," Lester said.

"Seems he listened about as good as any other time," Pa scoffed. "Didn't suppose it'd make it to Wyoming like this." He sloshed some oil onto the rag and began rubbing circles into the leather like he was washing a newborn. He continued for several minutes, doting over the saddle until he spoke again. "Figured you and your brother might want to fight over this one," he said.

"That one?" Lester asked dismissively.

Pa nodded.

"I got my own saddle," Lester said. "Jack's been using that one and he ain't got a problem with it, so long as he takes care of it."

"Come here," Pa said patiently.

Lester crossed the barn. When he was close enough to smell the sweetness of the oil, Pa lifted the left jockey to reveal a patch of beautiful chestnut leather that hadn't been bleached by years of sunlight and gritty dust bowl wind. Pa jabbed a dried, cracked fingertip onto the pristine leather.

"What of it?" Lester asked. "I knew it was a good saddle. Damn shame nobody took care of it the way they should have."

Pa gave him a sharp look. "Just look there!"

Just above Pa's finger, Lester saw letters carved into the leather. They were shoddy and squared, surely the work of a pocketknife by firelight.

H P B

"Right," Lester said naively. "Some kind of code?"

Pa turned to face him, pinching his hips in cupped hands. "It's your Pa, Lester."

"My real Pa?" Lester asked, a light beginning to spread over his face like a sunrise.

Pa nodded.

Harold P. Burke.

"This's his saddle?" Lester began reverently touching the scaled leather. "But why's it here? I thought he rode off."

"Well," Pa huffed, "suppose he rode out of here on Old Man Jack's saddle. Your Ma and me tore this barn apart looking for it and never saw a piece of it."

"Grandpa Jack's?"

Pa nodded again.

"Whose saddle have I been using then?" Lester asked.

"That one," Pa said, pointing to Lester's favorite saddle.

"But whose is it?"

Pa considered him. "That's your Ma's saddle. From when she used to help out around the ranch. Before she was too busy with you boys."

Lester walked to the hook where he always hung his saddle. It was the same hook it had been hung on since before he was born. He lifted the jockey and searched the leather for a sign of his mother. Frantically, he took it and checked the other side, then under each flap and skirt on the entire saddle. After he had scoured every inch for her sigil, he reached into his pocket, unfolded his knife, then carved his mother's initials deep into the leather.

Pa waited silently for Lester to hang the saddle again. He made no attempt to go to him. He had nothing to say even if he would have. He had let the boys grieve in their own ways, hoping they wouldn't hate him for leaving them on their own and grieving the only way he could imagine. On days when he was sober, Caroline's face would appear everywhere he looked, like a specter hanging in front of his eyes.

Lester wiped his face with his handkerchief and turned back to Pa.

"I found something in your Ma's things I thought you might want," Pa said, the words stumbling over his tongue. He wasn't going to say anything, preferring to let Lester find it on his own rather than struggle through a conversation about her, but he could feel Lester beginning to drown in his heartache and knew he needed an outstretched hand to cling to. "I left it in your saddlebag in case you want to take it along."

Lester eyed him, unsure what to say. His hopes weren't high.

"Better get to work. Ride safe if you boys head west today," Pa said and tipped his hat and walked out of the barn, walking close enough to Lester to shake his hand or grapple him into a hug but brushed by without looking back. He walked out of the barn and onto the ranch. If his eyes were wet, it must have been from the dust.

Later that morning, Lester had gotten their supplies in order and studied his new map of Nebraska until he had the paved highways and dirt county roads memorized. He worked to repack their saddlebags so the horses would be comfortable and the cans wouldn't jostle each other with every step, slowly driving them insane over a stretch of a million gentle clinks. He had nearly forgotten that Pa had left something for him when he opened the saddlebag that had been empty last night.

Inside, he saw a tattered black book with a scaled cover, the spine holding on to itself lazily. He removed it and examined the front cover.

Holy Bible was stamped, at one time in gold, boldly across the front cover in a swirl of decorative type. At the bottom corner there were more faded letters imprinted.

Jack S. Copeland.

Lester flipped the front cover open and read the inscriptions on the first page, written with flourished cursive in bleached ink — *To our son, Jack Spencer Copeland, on this, the day of his birth, November 12th, 1886.* Below that was another shorter dedication in small block letters — *To Caroline, our beautiful daughter.* At the bottom of the page, squeezed under the previous writings, was his mother's tidy and measured handwriting. *To my sons, who others may hold but only I have carried. With continued prayers your minds and hearts grow strong enough to carry yourselves.*

Lester flipped through the tissue-thin pages of the bible, remembering countless hours of reading lessons with his mother. Until his mother bought Lester a book on the history of the West this had been the only book in their house, so it served as the brothers' lesson book for both reading and writing. He still had some verses memorized after laboriously copying them until his handwriting met his mother's standards of accuracy and neatness.

The bible opened to a page that had been marked with a purple ribbon bookmark, which streamed from the spine and overflowed past the bottom edge. Lester looked over the page vaguely to find any passages he had at one time gone to bed repeating, his writing hand stiff and tired. He didn't recognize any of the verses. He wondered why the page had been marked and who had marked it.

Lester was about to replace the purple ribbon and close the book when he saw faint, shaky pencil lines outlining a single verse:

For ye shall go out with joy, and be led forth with peace; the mountains and the hills shall break forth before you into singing, and all the trees of the field shall clap their hands.

Lester read the verse several times before he gently closed the book, keeping the bookmark where he had found it and placing it carefully in his saddlebag.

The saddlebags were nearly filled to their capacity. Their underwear, socks, undershirts, and an extra pair of jeans were bundled in their own chambray overshirts. The horses had been fed, brushed, and watered more thoroughly than at any point in recent memory. Lester had been hoping to leave at daybreak to allow them as much sunlight as possible to travel, but the thought of another sleepless night before leaving made him feel anxious. So did leaving at a tick past noon and losing nearly six hours of riding before they would be forced to set up camp for their first night, but he had been growing increasingly impatient to begin their journey.

Jack was mounted on his horse before Lester could fully explain the pros and cons of leaving then versus the next morning.

"Might as well get to going," he said from his saddle.

"Right," Lester replied. "Have you seen Pa?"

Jack shook his head. "Ain't seen him since this morning."

"He say anything to you?"

"Not a word."

Lester hoisted himself onto the saddle, still tacky and dark hazel from the oil he had rubbed in after Pa had left that morning. He imagined his real father sitting on this same saddle, winking to his mother, lassoing the calves effortlessly, pushing his cap back, and dabbing the sweat off his brow with the back of a kid gloved hand. A real cowboy. Lester wondered how a real cowpoke like his father could not be impressed with his two sons riding across the western plains together, yet alone, to find him.

Lester turned his horse in a tight circle, surveying the ranch one time before leaving. Next time, he thought, this ranch will be more of a family homestead than it had been in a long time.

"Ready?" Lester asked, his chest fluttering like a battlefield flag.

Jack tipped his hat.

"Then let's get to going, Cowboy Jack."

Lester held the reins with one hand and forced his hat still with the other. He kicked his spurs into Amigo's haunches. Jack followed suit and soon they were galloping recklessly, yelping and hooting like feathered Indians. After a few miles they relaxed their reins, dropped their boots in the stirrups and slowed their horses to an amble. They stopped to make a camp just over the western border of Hayes County. When they laid their heads on their bedrolls, Jack swore he could hear the cars whizzing past on Highway 6, still miles ahead of them. But soon, they would reach the highway and follow it like a stream, with vehicles trickling past them like white-capped water. They would travel yonder, keeping their ears perked for the song of the West.

PART III

Yonder

Chapter 16

The boys found a gap in the wired fence and crossed over the gravel of Highway 51 just before noon of the next day. They rode along the western side of the highway a mile north then nearly two south without finding a break in the fence sizable for their horses. They came to a compromise then, which was caused by Jack's near constant heckling and complaining, to tie their horses to the fenceposts lining the highway and eat their lunches on the small embankment of the road.

Jack grabbed himself a can of beans from his saddlebag, working the point of his pocketknife into the lid, squealing and scraping until it finally opened and the greasy brown juice ran down the curves of his fingers. Lester ate his beans silently, half a can which he had saved from their morning meal, as Jack slurped and gulped and moaned himself into a bloated, greasy mouthed tizzy.

"Believe I might need to take myself a nap!" Jack said.

Lester scoffed. "We don't have time for a nap. And I told you to save our food. This's supposed to last us through the ride back home too."

"Yeah, yeah, I know," Jack said rolling his eyes.

The boys sat for a couple minutes longer, taking in the barrenness of the land they had yet to travel. The vegetation grew in low spurts along the ground, even more sparse than on the ranch. The dirt was a bleached tan color and ran through their fingers like sand. They had passed a couple herds of cattle around sunrise that morning and the steer eyed them from their battered and desolate ground, seeming to hope their saddlebags were filled with alfalfa or a tight roll of lush green sod. Beyond that, they had not seen any other breathing life larger than prairie dogs. And even they would only give the boys a cursory glance before returning to the coolness of their burrows.

Lester rummaged in his saddlebag and removed his Nebraska highway map, carefully unfolding it and placing the panels of their corner of the state on his knees. Jack, believing his brother to be distracted enough, carefully reached back into his stocks and removed a slice of raw bacon, slick and warm. He slowly turned his upper body to face away from Lester and began gnawing on it quietly. He made quick work of it, then wiped his greasy fingers down the seam of his jeans and used the shoulder of his chambray shirt to wipe his lips. He closed his eyes to reflect on the taste left on his tongue in reverie and turned back to his brother.

Lester was already staring at him. "I truly hope that makes you sick," he said.

Jack stammered.

"Truly," Lester said. "I hope that makes you shit your drawers tonight."

"Aw, hell! I ain't gonna shit my damn self, Les!"

Lester returned his attention back to the map, shaking his head in a display of egregious disappointment.

"Christ, Les! If I don't eat it now, it'll go bad!"

"You're right," Lester replied. "Can I ask you something?"

Jack nodded suspiciously.

"If you knew it was gonna go bad, why in the hell would you bring it? Or did you forget to pack yourself the icebox too?"

Jack's eyes bulged. "I brought it cause I figured we need it more than Pa, that's all!"

"Should have left you at home."

"Too late now, so quit being such a tight wad about everything!"

Lester rose to his feet, the silent sign between them that a wrestling match was about to commence.

"I ain't gonna wrestle you, Lester. My belly's too full. Have a slice of bacon and have yourself a nap!" Jack held out another piece of bacon, hanging from his fist like viscera.

Lester took the bacon from his brother and went back to his spot on the embankment. He sat for a minute with the map in one hand and the slimy bacon strip in the other. Jack let out a huff and laid down on his side in the prickly grass. Lester waited for his brother to close his eyes and stop squirming before folding the bacon into thirds and flinging the slice at Jack. His aim was off but not by much. It hit Jack's face and stuck fast, angling across his face to cover one eye, his nose, and a corner of his mouth.

Lester waited for his brother to react, knowing he had lit a millimeter long fuse. He stared at Jack, who remained motionless, for nearly a minute. Slowly, Jack's mouth began to open but he remained silent with his eyes closed. Like a rattlesnake creeping from the alcove of a crevice, Jack's tongue slithered out of his mouth and hooked the side of the bacon. Unhurriedly, his tongue retracted back into his mouth with the bacon, as if it were a deep sea octopus dragging its prey back to its lair. At the same time, his arm lifted as if his arm and tongue were connected to a pulley system. By the time the bacon had disappeared from his face, leaving his mouth bloated and his cheeks smeared with oil, his arm was perpendicular to the ground, his middle finger standing at attention like a boot camp cadet.

Their hysterics would have likely carried on until the sun sank to eye level if not for the plume of dust rising from the gravel road on the northern horizon. The boys wiped their faces, licked their lips and straightened their hats while investigating the change to the lifeless panorama.

"I'll be damned," Jack said. "I'll be a skinned cat if that ain't a herd of buffalo coming this way."

"Bison," Lester corrected him. "And there's no way in hell that's a herd of bison."

"I'll betcha two pennies it is!"

Lester looked at him. "I'd take that deal and gladly take that money except I believe those pennies are mine anyway, ain't they?"

"I haven't got the slightest goddamn idea what you're talking about."

The dust continued to roil from the road toward them. They could hear the rumbling and crunching of the thing gaining on them. A minute later, the rusted and dirt plastered grill of a Ford truck came rattling toward them, its headlights like a pair of surprised eyes looking at them widely. Lester stood when the truck was within a hundred yards and they could hear the engine slowing and the brakes beginning to whine. The truck, rolling by like a freight train against its mass, finally rolled to a stop fifty feet past where the boys had been picnicking. The engine rattled under the hood, strained like a rubber band ready to let loose, then finally began inching backward as if pulled by a broken mule. The brakes squealed again for a moment then the truck stopped so the man behind the wheel could look once more at the young cowboys sitting on the side of the highway. Tear streaks ran down their filthy cheeks, their battered cowboy hats pushed back, their faded denim shirts spattered with some kind of brown oily juice.

"Howdy boys!" the man called from inside the truck. He leaned over toward the passenger side window as far as he could, but his rotund belly made it difficult. "I take it you boys are plum lost."

"No sir," Lester said, "we're riding west to find Highway 6."

The man jutted out his bottom chin, impressed. "You boys've got quite a ways to go yet."

"Yes sir. We were just having some lunch then setting out again. Just need to find a break in this fence here," Lester said, pointing a thumb to the fence behind him.

The man nodded. "Believe there's a cattle gate not too far south."

"Yes sir."

"Ain't much around here in any direction. You boys sure you know the way?"

Lester nodded confidently.

"Looking for work? I've got a ranch up in Perkins County. I couldn't pay you two all that much but times are hard."

"No sir, not looking for work."

"Right. Well I could give you boys a ride down to Imperial. That's where this road meets up with the 6."

"No thank you, sir. We can't leave our horses behind."

The man nodded and looked over the horses tied at the bottom of the ravine. "Be safe out there, you hear? Lots of poor farmers out here with a hankering to shoot their buckshot at whoever looks at them sideways."

Lester nodded again.

"Not me though. Don't you boys worry," The man smiled. "If you're going into the city, watch yourselves for the drifters."

"Drifters?" Lester asked.

"Mm-hm. Guys that've been out of work and stealing and threatening to make ends meet. They'll take the boots right off your feet while you're walking past them if you're not careful enough."

Lester could feel Jack growing jittery behind him.

"I've got to keep moving, boys. If I don't see that cattle fence down this way, I'll loop back around and let you boys know to check the other way instead."

"Yes, sir. Thank you." Lester tipped his cap to the man.

The man nodded in reply. "God speed, boys!" he called to them as the engine roared and clattered back to life. By the time the car had rattled away southward and the dust resettled on the road, the boys had their bags packed and climbed back onto their saddles. They began to ride south and within fifteen minutes they had found the cattle gate just as the man had promised. As Jack worked to kick the gate close from the other side, Lester looked toward the road. There was no sign of the man or his battered truck that could have gotten the brothers to Cheyenne by the next morning.

Chapter 17

The nearing storm clouds caused the evening light to dissipate early that night. They argued for miles whether the rumbling ahead of them was thunder or the highway. But the brothers nearly made it to the highway before they were forced to set their camp. Jack spread his bedroll and propped his head on his saddle and watched his brother work. Lester worked in silence as he gathered kindling and tumbleweeds before contemplating how long they had before their fire was doused by the coming storm. They had made camp under a sparse, scrawny tree that would not likely survive through the winter. Most of its branches were bare, its trunk scattered with bald areas, its bark flaky and splintered. It would provide very little protection from above but it had been the only tree Lester noticed in nearly five miles and he was concerned how far the bleak terrain might stretch ahead of them. Jack gave no serious argument against calling it a day early, so the boys sat under the meager tree eating their searing hot tins of black eyed peas and straining their ears to hear the noises of the highway over the rumbling of the approaching thunder.

Jack used a dirt packed index finger to scrape every dribble of juice from the can then threw his head back and overturned it above his mouth, pounding its bottom like a timpani. He licked a half drop from the lip of the tin before getting to his feet and moving beyond the scant stretch of the tree limbs. He bent and stood the can in the dirt then began building an embankment on all sides of it, packing it tightly as if he was mortaring it in place.

"Reckon I shouldn't interrupt you since you're being quiet for once," Lester called to him. "But what in the pits of hell are you doing?"

Jack was silent, continuing to pack the slope from the bleached dirt. When he was finished, he stood and looked at his brother with a thin smile, eager to show off his handiwork.

"You're a regular old arc builder, ain't you?" Lester teased.

"Pretty good, ain't it?"

Lester rolled his eyes and turned his attention to the darkening clouds.

"You'll be sorry when you don't have one in the morning," Jack said.

"How can I be sorry not to have one if I have no goddamn idea what it is?"

"*Jee-sus*, Les. It's to catch the rainwater!"

"We got water."

"Not to drink, you dunce," Jack had remembered his brother's word for over a year. "To measure how much it rains!"

"Why's it matter how much it rains? If us and our saddles get wet then it rained and we'll be sopping away from here tomorrow. Doesn't matter how much."

"If it's no difference to you then I'll betcha two pennies that jar's filled to the brim by sunrise."

Lester considered his brother vaguely. "I'll never understand why you're so keen to hand over the pennies you stole from me."

"I haven't got any idea what you're talking about. Anyway, I've never been so rich in my whole life and the jangling's damn near driving me nuts!"

Lester refused to laugh so Jack laughed for both of them.

Jack had just decided he had said enough for the day. He let the last reverberations of his voice travel along the prairie, with hardly a single imperfection to reflect its echoes back, when the first raindrops began to pelt the windswept dirt. Within minutes, the dimples of dampness had coalesced into a waterlogged, granular film over the land, a counterfeit of a seashore in that barren, landlocked landscape.

The boys, at Lester's direction, took their bedrolls and used them to cover their saddles, sleeping on the few remaining patches of blanched dirt. They propped their heads against their covered saddles and pitched their hats over their faces, the raindrops echoing through the crown like gunshots in a cave. It was a restless night for them both. The rain came in multitudes and pelted them with teaspoon sized drops for most of the night. Jack's can was nearly overflowed with rainwater before either brother had their first winks of sleep. By the time they uncovered their faces from their soggy and misshapen hats, the dirt embankment Jack had so carefully built was washed away and the tin lay wasted on its side.

Lester had often praised the rainstorms that blew through their ranch, intermittent but torrential, knowing it was the nectar for all things they needed to survive, but that night he reviled the rain and pled for the sweltering, arid heat of Nebraska summers. Whichever gods had taken notice to his invocations did as he wished. The remainder of their journey would hardly be punctuated by anything except nearly unbearable heat.

They woke that morning with their denim plastered to their limbs, gritty from splattered dust clumps. They rose as they were born into the world; soaked, chilled, exhausted and confused. Their boots squished as they packed their camp. The saddles, a darker chestnut brown than they had been in years, seemed to have doubled in weight when they tossed them over their horses. Jack wound up and kicked the can as far as he could before they left their camp behind.

Luckily, the sun rose with a vengeance and brought with it a ravenous heat that engulfed the moisture that had taken all night to collect. By the time the sun was fully visible in the sky behind them, everything save for the seats of their pants had dried. The boys had no way to realize, but the day was the longest of the year. They would use every minute of the solstice as selfishly as a beekeeper collecting honey in slippery mounds. They had a long way ahead of them. So far, in fact, that if the wind blew just right, they were still close enough to catch the scent of home.

Chapter 18

Lester and Jack reached Highway 6 not long after their clothes had dried to stiff and starchy sheets. They pulled their reins and stopped their horses, taking a moment to observe the highway and its sputtering stream of cars passing them by. Lester decided they would follow the contour of the road from a distance, keeping just barely in ear and eyeshot. Jack agreed, although in his mind he had been picturing them galloping down the shoulder of the road, women young and old alike hanging from the windows of their cars to savor every detail of the handsome cowboys. Much like the rest of the trip so far, Jack's mind had painted a much more cinematic scene than what they'd experienced.

The boys continued on for a while, both lost in their own woolgathering. Lester, as he had been for weeks, was trying to imagine his father's face. It would surely be similar to his own but wrinkled in unfamiliar places as if viewing his reflection on rippling water, perhaps with a fuller and darker mustache than the one Lester had been coaxing to grow for months.

Jack, floating through his own reverie, continued to imagine themselves riding westward on the pavement, tipping their hats coyly to the cars that passed and honked their horns or waved their handkerchiefs from their windows. Thank you kindly, just passin' through, he would say to the winsome daughters from the families that felt compelled to pull over and admire the strength of both horse and rider. Both of them were lost in their musings until noon when they nearly rode down the embankment, into the valley, and straight into the gathering below.

It was the first change in terrain for nearly a day. In front of them was a gradual descent to a large pool of midnight blue water. One side of the pond abutted the embankment of Highway 6. The other edges, swollen and extended from the previous night's storm, sloshed over some lush green grass, giving it the appearance of seaweed. On the far side of the water was a group of a few dozen people. Lester thought they were wearing winter clothes but, squinting through the rippling mirage of the heat, realized they were dressed in traditional native garb.

"What do you make of that?" Jack asked.

"Looks like Indians."

They both continued to stare into the distance at the group, circling and reversing and stomping and drumming.

"Should we go around?"

"Go around and waste half a day?" Lester snapped.

"I ain't about to go riding through that party down there."

"If you're so afraid we can just wait here til they're gone."

Jack turned to him. "I never said I was afraid!"

"Then go ride past them!"

"Why don't you?" Jack whined.

"Cause I ain't afraid!"

"Oh, you're fuller of shit than an outhouse!"

"Do I look scared to you?" Lester asked, squeezing the leather of the reins and gritting his teeth to stop himself from trembling.

"Remember when you said if we passed by an Indian, he'd look like us and ride on by?"

"Don't remember any such thing."

Jack rolled his eyes and climbed off his saddle and sat on the ground in the shadow of his horse. Lester joined him a few minutes later. They continued to watch the people with vague attention. They lost semblance of time in their mindlessness and only realized how much of it had passed when their stomachs began to rumble in duet with the hide top drums. They both ate a can of peas in silence then rolled the empty cans in their hands as their eyes stared past the water.

"Reckon they ain't praying for white men's good luck, are they?"

Lester hesitated. "I'd be fibbing if I said I've got any idea what's going on down there."

They continued to sit atop their vantage, looking down on the proceedings below until the low brush near them began to crackle and fold.

"Hey!" Lester shouted. "Who's that in that brush yonder?"

The noise stopped. There was no sign of scurrying of flying although Lester was, by this time, positive it was an animal. He warily stepped toward where the noise had been coming from. He was nearly standing over the brush and there still was not another noise. Whatever critter had crawled under this patch of dry kindling grass had either grown brave or had frozen in its fear. As quickly as a snakebite, Lester kicked his boot, hardened toe first, into the grass. His boot met something inside with a thud. Something large. Whatever it was was now awakened and let out a reedy gasp before climbing to its full height. The animal continued to grow in height, covered in its battered human-like skin and pigmented feathers, until it was eye level with Lester. The beast's eyes squinted at him angrily.

"What in the hell was that for?"

The brothers blinked, refocusing on the thing in front of them. It was a man. A boy. Most likely around their age, but difficult to be certain with his tanned skin and the chevrons of paint decorating his face.

"I said," the boy hissed, "what the hell was that for?"

Lester rubbed his eyes. "What do you mean what was that for? Why are you sneaking into our camp?"

"Camp?" The boy scoffed. "Not much of a camp. You gonna make a tent or just sleep with those cans over your heads?"

"Who are you? And what are you doing here?" Lester looked the boy over. His hair was inky black and braided in a long row down his back. His eyes reflected from behind his painted face, as dark and murky as the pool of midnight water below them. He was dressed in clothes that looked similar to what they were able to see from across the pond. Lester saw a leather sheath hooked to his belt that looked like it was to hold a knife, with a blade by Lester's estimation that would require little added effort to gut a deer. It wasn't until that moment Lester thought storing a gun in their saddlebags may have been a good idea. He and Jack had their folding pocketknives with their blades pitted nearly to the point of serration, but they did little more than whittle twigs into toothpicks.

"I'm heading east," the boy shared.

"Shouldn't you be down there?"

Both of them turned toward the new voice to see Jack.

"Left early to get a head start," the boy replied.

"You ran away you mean," Lester said.

The boy shrugged.

"What's going on down there anyway?" Jack asked.

The boy's eyes volleyed between the brothers. "Putting curses on any white man within two hundred yards of here. Looks like you both are the only ones we caught, but we won't know til sundown tonight if it really worked."

The brothers' eyes bulged. Lester struggled to swallow his dry mouth.

The three of them stared at each other seemingly for an hour before the Indian boy began laughing. "You two really believe we've got nothing better to do than hex you? We saw you sitting up here like a couple of scared field mice."

"We ain't scared," Lester snapped.

The boy shrugged again.

"What were you really doing down there then?" Jack asked.

The boy rubbed his chin, smearing the cobalt and white paint together. "It was the Sundance. It's the solstice today."

"What's that?" Jack asked.

"What's what?"

"The solface."

"Solstice," the boy said. "It's the longest day of the year."

"We know that," Lester said sharply, although he didn't.

The boy spat into the middle of their group. "Well it's good luck or something for us to have a celebration today." After a minute he added, "You can ride around it, you know?"

"I know that," Lester snapped. "We were just resting."

"Hope you aren't going too far if you're resting half your days away."

The three boys were silent then. Lester squinted at the Indian boy, the Indian boy looked past them toward his tribe, and Jack looked at his feet kicking at the dust.

"I should keep moving," the boy said then turned eastward and began retracing the tracks the brothers' horses had left before he turned.

"Where are you headed?" he yelled, carrying his voice over on the wind.

"West," Lester yelled back.

"Where to?"

"Til we go far enough west," Lester said dismissively. "Where are you going?"

"Til I go far enough east."

Lester stared.

"Watch out for the Double Faces," the boy said. "This land's full of them."

"The hell you just say?"

"I said," the boy huffed. The young Indian walked back to the brothers, reforming their crooked triangle. "I said *watch out for the Double Faces.*"

"Wh— what's that?" Jack stammered, his eyes darting between the other two.

"Yeah," Lester said, "what on earth are you talking about?"

"The Cheyenne believe in *Hestovatohkeo'o*," the boy said. "Means Double Face. This is Cheyenne land around here and off to the west."

"Are you a Cheyenne?" Jack asked.

"Pawnee."

Jack nodded, feigning understanding.

"But the stories get passed around," the boy said. "Double Faces look just like you and me. You wouldn't know them from any other rider until you see the back of them."

Jack began to whimper, quietly from the bottom of his throat but loud enough for Lester to hear and jab him with a sharp elbow to his ribs.

"They've got a second face," the boy continued, "and if you look them in their second eyes then you're a goner. Nothing you can do about it." The boy shrugged.

"What do you mean *goner*?" Lester asked.

"Dead, probably. Or worse. I've heard sometimes if they're especially busy, they'll just kinda turn your body to raw meat so you can't yell or get away and they'll leave you until they're ready to get you."

"Oh, bullshit!" Lester flared.

The boy shook his head solemnly. "I wish I was kidding, but I've known many ancestors that've gotten snatched up by those Double Faces."

"Um— when— how do— what do the faces look like?" Jack faltered.

He had balled his hands into tight fists and thrust them into his pockets to keep them still.

"Their first face is normal as can be. Sometimes even pretty. But they say their second face is whatever you're most afraid of." The boy looked the brothers over. "And by the looks of it, they'll have a hard time choosing with you two."

The Indian boy turned back to the east and left once again. This time for good. The brothers watched him trek away until his form was lost in the rippling heatwaves. By the time they turned back to the pond, they were once again alone on the prairie with no sign of what they had spent the past hours watching. For the rest of their lives Jack would swear that afternoon happened just as they remembered it. But the images in their minds became more faded with each day until the reality and imagination of the memory became indeterminable.

Silently, they climbed on their horses and rode down the incline to the water where they fed and watered their horses and filled their canteens. They continued on and rode for hours until the sun had nearly completely set. They took no notice to the reddening skies above them, or the mountains beyond them just barely hidden by the purple curtain of the sunset. They were preoccupied, taking heed to every minute sound throughout the day and into the restless night they had ahead of them.

Chapter 19

Lester woke in a panic, certain he would crack open his eyelids and find himself in the sights of an Indian facing away from him. The cadaverous second face was just as the boy promised, surely. He had been sleeping fitfully, just barely under the surface of sleep and reawakening each time his head crested between waves. Each time his heart would calm itself enough for his mind's machinery to whir to a stop, the blankness of his thoughts would be overtaken by the idea of facing — or worse, not facing — a Double Face somewhere in the oppressive void of their hardscrabble surroundings. His mind was nearly finished painting the unearthly scene in his phantasm when he heard a high, reedy noise like a far off scream battered by hard miles. Lester fought to break through the imaginary setting, pushing past the group of fiends waiting for his thoughts to quiet fully. He opened his eyes and looked around. He found no signs of his nightmares seeping into his reality, just the lifeless void of the barren plains.

Lester sat up and examined the campsite. They had split a can of beans last night but hardly touched them, their appetites swallowed up by their fear. The can was sitting where Jack had left it before laying down, a thin rind forming on the surface. The fire they had made was withered into a pile of lukewarm and perfectly colorless coals spread on blackened ground. Lester had collected the kindling and any dry vegetation he could gather before sundown and placed them in a pile and set it aflame without a word. They both knew a native ghost would hardly be cast off by a paltry flame such as theirs but a low flamed oil lamp or a single flicker of camp light does wonders to dissuade the specters residing not on the land but in the mind.

He was staring vaguely at the coals when he heard the noise again, a thin metallic squeeze of sound. His heart shuddered. The veins in his neck turned to copper wires sending electricity in jolts through his limbs. He turned dreadfully toward the noise, one eye closed in an attempt to thwart off half of any curses. There, standing on a short and wind worn boulder, was Jack. Jack was facing away from Lester, his hands to his mouth, certainly attempting to hold in the horrors of whatever he had seen. Lester reluctantly inspected the back of his brother's head and, finding no signs of infernal eyes, called out to him.

Jack jumped and turned quickly,. His hands dropped heavily to his sides.

"Just about damn near scared some squirts outta me," Jack howled.

"You hear that noise?" Lester asked.

"What noise?"

"Like a scream or something."

"You — you mean like a ghost or something?" Jack asked, dramatically searching the horizon with a hand shielding his eyes.

"Sure. If you believe in that."

"Aw, I don't believe in that any more than you."

Lester ignored him. "I just heard a noise not two minutes ago."

Jack shrugged.

"You're telling me you're so dumb you're standing on that rock staring at the sun like a blind mule and you didn't bother to unclog your ears?"

Jack then made a show of bowing his head to each side and rattling his head against the heel of his palm as if his ears had been sloshing with water.

Lester turned back to their camp and stood, collecting their belongings. He spit into the coals which gave an indolent sputter. They silently split the remaining beans from the previous night before packing their bedrolls and tacking their horses. They began their daily trek toward some indeterminable point beyond the western horizon. It was nearly noon before Lester was sure he heard the noise again.

They rode with Highway 6 to their left, in the corner of their eyesight, and checked it periodically like a pocket watch. The sky was swollen and white with the late morning humidity. The brothers still had not been able to glimpse the mountains floating off above the horizon in front of them. If the day was clear and cloudless, perhaps they may have been able to see the highest escarpments of the Rocky Mountain range; their whitecaps, the last reminders of the brutal and unrelenting winters, camouflaging its rough crags into the sparkling sky, causing the entire range to appear like a mirage in the clouds. A fantastical painting by the gods. Instead, their panorama consisted of the endless barren prairies, still days from the foothills, passing by them in slow motion.

Jack considered for most of the morning why anyone would have left their homes in places farther east than he could imagine to live in a place such as these to claim a tract of land as useful and enviable as a worn through boot without a partner. He pondered the idea that some unknown and faceless man owned the land they rode on, and all the land they had already passed through and plan to pass. He tried to conjure their faces in his mind, imagining the effects the wind, dust and laborious years would have on the skin around their eyes and the backs of their necks. He could easily hear their voices, their throats dried to jerky by tobacco smoke and their tongues weighted down with whiskey. The men who owned the ranches around here, Jack supposed, couldn't be much different from Pa.

It had been at least a full day since Jack had thought of Pa. He mulled that over for a minute before realizing he couldn't remember the last time he remembered his mother. Had it been yesterday? If not, then the day before, he told himself. Or had their journey been so exciting he had forgotten about his own mother? If he couldn't summon the exact thought of her then it may as well have never existed.

"Hey Les," Jack asked gently.

Lester grunted in return.

"How much do you reckon you think about Ma?"

Lester turned in his saddle to face his brother. "What are you talkin' about?"

"Just wondering how much you think about Ma. Every day?"

Lester remained silent, his eyes heavy.

"Or is there a day or two you don't think of her?" Jack added.

"You forgetting her already?" Lester asked.

"Uh-uh," Jack shook his head in an exaggerated pendulum. "No way, no how. Don't know how anyone could forget their own Ma."

Lester nodded. "I reckon so."

"I was just," Jack hesitated. "I was just thinking about Ma and couldn't remember if I thought of her yesterday or not."

They rode on for a time in silence. Jack labored to not be the one to break it. Finally, Lester spoke, so softly Jack needed to steer his horse closer and leaned over on his saddle to hear.

"I suppose you're thinking about Ma even when you don't realize it. Especially when you don't realize it, I guess," Lester said. "I don't think you'd have to see her face or hear her voice to know she's talking to you. How many times a day do you hear something she'd always say?" Lester looked at his brother's hands, working the leather of the reins between his fingers. "I can't tell you how many times a day I hear her in the back of my head saying *Be nice to him, he's the only brother you've got*!" The corner of Lester's mouth rose in a smirk. "Lord knows I need to hear it sometimes."

"Yeah," Jack sighed. "Reckon you're right."

"We're always thinking of her. I know we are. I'm not sure we couldn't if we tried."

"I miss her," Jack said suddenly, wiping his eyes before his brother's eyes caught him. "I try not to think about her and I don't wanna talk about her cause we haven't in a long time. It makes the back of my neck feel hot when I think about her. You ever feel like that?"

"No, not like that. But I miss her. I can hardly think of the way she used to smell without wanting to scream."

Jack nodded. "I used to," he said. "When you were out working with Pa, I would sit on my bed and cry til I was starving and my head felt like it was hammered."

They rode on a bit longer, working through the emotions they hadn't held so tightly in months.

"Remember how you used to lay at her door when she was sick?" Lester asked.

Jack's brows furrowed, not remembering he had already been caught. "Ma told me."

"I wasn't just laying there," Jack said. "I was talking to her. She talked to me too."

Now Lester wrinkled his brows.

"Yeah," Jack said. "We would talk for a long time. Most days she wouldn't say anything back so I'd just talk to her but sometimes she'd talk right back. Tell me riddles like she used to at supper sometimes. She never told me she was dying so I didn't know. By the time I figured it all, she wasn't talking anymore."

Jack could feel the smooth wood grain below his chin, his forehead propped on the cool door jam, his mother's voice floating ethereally from the other side. He stayed in that place as long as he could, refusing to acknowledge the world he was now in, the desolation and isolation surrounding them. He refused to allow the clopping of hoofbeats into his ears, allowing himself only to hear the melody of his mother's words. He was astray deep inside his reverie when the quick sniffle of his brother broke through his imagination like bolts of lightning. He looked at his brother hanging his head.

"I'm real sorry I brought it up," Jack said. "I shouldn't have."

Lester shook his head quickly. "Just regret all those days I worked past sunset on the ranch cause I didn't want to be near her. I couldn't stand it. It was easier to be outside and ignore it. Wish I spent some of that time with her."

Jack considered his brother. "She knew how much you loved her, Les. She would ask about you every time she could say a word." He went on, "Remember when I asked you to teach me to saddle and ride? Ma already stopped talking by then. I'd spent weeks lying there in case she said something but then I just couldn't take it anymore. I had to get out too. I don't blame you for working all day or riding out to the bluffs."

They rode on, ignoring each other's ragged breathing, wiping their eyes with their thumbs as if a gnat had landed on their cheeks. They made no effort to push their mother from their minds. Instead, they allowed her memory to wrap around them like a flannel blanket, letting the protective and tender arms of her spirit encompass them.

"What do you reckon she was thinking about all those days we left her there by herself?" Jack asked.

After a moment, Lester replied softly. "Us," he said. "She was thinking about us."

Chapter 20

Later that same afternoon, after the prosaic miles had calmed the whizzing of their spiraling thoughts, Jack's mind was focusing not on the unhealing strain in his chest but on the riddles his mother would tell them. He could clearly picture their family sitting at their table, dishes of potatoes, corn and beef with steam rising and catching the early evening sunlight streaming through the window. His throat cinched on itself and his stomach lurched when he pictured it, so he turned his mind over the memories, lightly, hoping to find the first clues of the riddles. Some of them he found easily enough, but he found remembering the answers, which he and his brother had guffawed over, to be more elusive.

Finally, like a spark catching a thread of dry kindling, one of the riddles flamed, fully formed, in his mind. He practiced the introduction and clues at least a half dozen times in his head, trying out varying amounts of drama and brio until he was finally ready for his performance.

"Heya Les," he said.

Lester grunted.

"Got a riddle for you. Like Ma used to tell."

Lester eyed him. "Get on then."

"So, Cowboy Jack rides into Cheyenne on Friday and stays there for three days…"

"Horse's name was Friday," Lester cut in.

"*Goddammit* Lester!" Jack howled, his voice grating and echoing through the Nebraska prairie. "Why the hell'd you do that?"

Lester's face wrinkled into half of a dry smile which only swelled his brother's anger. "Why would I sit here and listen to you talk any more than I have to?" Lester said. "Besides, I knew the answer almost before you started."

Jack rode on in silence, continually shaking his head in utter disbelief.

"I didn't fall off the turnip truck yesterday," Lester added.

Jack's head continued in its pendulum. "Whatever the goddamn that means," he muttered. After a while, he felt he finally had a response worth sharing in full voice. "You are absolutely no goddamn fun, you know that?" Jack said. His head was still shaking but his eyes focused on his brother's back.

Lester began nodding. "I know it," he said. "Good thing too or else people'd think we're some kind of traveling circus."

"Don't you goddamn worry, they do! Reckon they just think I'm traveling with one of those freak show fellas!"

Lester began laughing quietly, knowing fraternal etiquette did not allow for it but unable to contain it nonetheless.

"You betcha," Lester said. "I'm the one in the cage with a big banner saying 'Biggest Cock in the West'!"

Jack's head quit shaking then. His face went slack, having never heard his brother use the kind of language he wished so badly to have a working knowledge of. After the shock subsided, he joined his brother in laughter. Their heads hung and bobbed in time with the ambling of their horses. They continued on for several miles like that, no longer able to remember if they had been joking or arguing.

"Hey, I got one for you," Lester said after a while.

"Alright."

"What kind of building do you go into blind but come out seeing?"

"Aw, that ain't fair!" Jack spat.

"Why ain't that fair?"

"Cause it's too hard!"

"How could it possibly be too hard if you already heard the answer?"

"I never heard that goddamn riddle as long as I lived."

"Then I suppose it must've been some other dunce sitting across the table when Ma said it."

Jack turned to him, "I know what that goddamn means!"

"What are you talking about?" "Dunce! I know what that means!"

"Say it then if you're so smart."

"Dunce," Jack said.

"No, you dummy! Say what it means!"

Jack was quiet for a moment, considering this new insult. "I've had enough of your goddamn riddles!" he said finally.

Lester scoffed. "It's only a riddle if you really are a dunce."

Jack resumed his head shaking in earnest. "I've had enough of you duncing me," he muttered. Lester turned his face away so Jack wouldn't see him smile. They rode on for several more miles, continuing their cycle of silence and bickering. It was a pattern that would, if they continued far enough westward, progress to the California coastline.

Sometime in the afternoon, with Highway 6 still within earshot to their left, the brothers passed, unknowingly, by a wooden sign hanging from a timber post. It hung from a short chain and swung gently, creaking like a rusted porch swing. The sign itself was planed lumber that looked as if a cabin resort's vacancy sign had been picked up by a tornado and planted firmly alongside the westbound lane of the highway. WELCOME TO COLORFUL COLORADO was carefully carved into the sign then filled in with blinding white paint. The boys passed by the threshold without pageantry, unaware that they had reached a milestone that would have ended their arguing instantly.

The wind camouflaged the sound of the sign's rusted chain but even on a perfectly still day Jack and Lester would not have heard it. Their ears, at that time, were being filled with a haunting and sorrowful sound floating low over the land like the vapor wisps of a ghost. The brothers, hearing the sound, both lifted one ear toward the sky.

"That what you heard this morning?" Jack asked.

Lester shook his head slowly and raised a finger which he placed over his lips. He kept it there, with his eyes squinting, listening for the sound again. It wasn't the same sound he had heard that morning, but perhaps the wind had carried it differently that time. After a few minutes, the sound returned. It was a low, guttural rumble like a chair grating on a roughhewn wooden floor.

The sound that followed soon after was Jack's hiccuping giggle. He then took a deep breath and asked again, "You're sure that wasn't what you heard?"

Lester quickly connected the dots like clues of a riddle. "I hope you're not serious right now," he hissed.

"What do you expect me to do?" Jack shrugged. "Eating beans three meals a day for a week is gonna make my farts spookier than an Indian! Nothing I can do about it!" he shrugged again.

"Should've left you at home," he muttered over and over like a mantra.

"Just to be sure," Jack added after a minute, "this was *not* the sound you heard this morning?" Then he pushed another round of percussive flatulence from his bowels with the force of an artillery shell. A flock of birds to their right took flight in a black cloud, certain they had just heard a shotgun blast.

Lester knew Jack was waiting for a response so he clenched his own abdomen and lifted his behind off his saddle. He strained until he began seeing stars zigzagging in his vision then felt a rumble behind his belt buckle that turned his sweat cold. He pulled the reins of his horse and quickly dismounted, pulling her toward a small bush where he dropped trou. He had hardly cinched his belt again when he could hear Jack's voice echoing from a few hundred feet ahead, hooting and yelping louder than a Pawnee warrior.

Chapter 21

Lester's path spiraled out into the near-total darkness of the range. He was working to fill his pockets with kindling and enough thicket branches to burn until they had fallen asleep. He didn't wander far from their makeshift camp and concentrated on keeping his bearings so he could easily stumble back to his brother. Jack had begged to come with him, but Lester explained their situation would be much more grave if they both left camp and were unable to find it. For this reason, Jack would call out at erratic intervals in an attempt to help his brother. Jack's shouts, however, served to only cause Lester to jump, nearly out of his boots, at each call.

Between some of his brother's hollers from their spot in the blank nighttime, Lester could have sworn he heard the same noise that woke him that morning. He stopped and crouched down, the kindling cracking in his pocket. He removed his hat and took a deep breath then held it, concentrating intently on the symphony around him, attempting to decipher one melody from the noise of all the rest. When his lungs began to scream for air, he breathed heavily and stood. While he was standing — the seams of his jeans rubbing on themselves, his hat clanging in place on his head, the pearl snaps of his shirt pinging on one another — he heard it again. He cursed himself for not staying still for two seconds longer. Lester dropped the kindling and sticks from his hands and cupped them behind his ears, angling them toward the direction he thought the voice had come from the previous time. He stood like that for no more than half a minute.

"*Still right here!*" Jack shouted from the darkness.

Lester's boot soles took flight, his knees giving out in midair. He hit the ground tailbone first and hooted in pain, his vision lighting up with flashes of lightning.

"That's enough of your goddamn yelling!" Lester yelled back after he picked himself up and dusted off.

"Suit yourself then," Jack muttered from whichever unseen point was the middle of Lester's circular path. "Good luck finding camp then. Have fun sleeping out in the dark!"

"I'm out here getting firewood so you would be the one sleeping in the dark!" Lester called. He could hear Jack muttering something inaudible.

Lester continued on, filling his arms like a bindle. When he had his fill of wandering the dark prairie by himself, he made his way toward their camp. Less than a dozen steps later, he heard the noise once more. A lonesome wail, low over the brush and barren ground.

"Jack!" he called, "You hear that?"

"Yeah! Come quick!" Jack yelled, "It's a Double Face and it's got me by the balls!"

Lester heard the unspoken name and went running toward Jack's calls. He only realized he was back to their camp when tripped over his own saddle and went down hard, sprawling chest first on the hard packed dirt.

"Aw, jeepers! Now you ruined the fun!" Jack joked.

"What the *fuck* was that for?" Lester raged.

"I was just fooling with you, Les! Didn't have to come running like a dunce!"

Lester grabbed blindly in the air. "Tell Ma I said hello cause I'm gonna kill you!"

Jack kicked his boot heels into the ground and pushed himself away from his brother's seething voice.

"Cut it out! Stop it! I was just goddamn joking!" Jack called. He could still hear Lester stomping around their campsite, kicking everything in his way, hoping it was his brother. "At least start the fire first so you can see my mangled body," Jack said after Lester kicked everything in camp at least twice.

Lester went about lighting the fire silently, stewing. When the thin branches caught and took flame, their camp came into view and looked like it had been ransacked. Both of their canteens along with a can of peas had an angry dent in them from the toe of Lester's boot. Lester sat in front of his saddle, ignoring the camp, locking eyes on his brother. His chest was pounding and he thought his chin might be slowly dripping blood but refused to wipe it away. He wanted Jack to see it.

Lester continued to stare at his brother, even as Jack busied himself in his saddlebag, rattling around the cans of food, slowly deliberating on which to open for supper.

"Want some green beans?" he asked.

Lester stared silently.

"These might settle your stomach," he said, putting his hands together as if in prayer. "Good thing too cause I think our horses figured we were rattling off some birdshot."

Still no reply from Lester.

Jack placed the can of green beans near the edge of the fire and, once the salty brown water inside began to simmer, he carefully brought it back to his spot and dug in. He plowed through the entire can quickly, complaining how hot they were with each bite but cut his thoughts short with another steaming mouthful. When the beans were devoured, he slurped the sludge from the can and tossed it to the side, wiping the corners of his mouth with his shirt sleeve.

Jack sat, content, for a couple minutes. His contentment disappeared quicker than his can of supper when he took notice of how quiet it was. Confident his life was no longer in imminent danger, he spoke up.

"You look like Pa when you're angry," he said.

Lester just stared for a time, then finally replied. "Ain't kin of mine," he said flatly.

Jack shrugged. "One time Pa told me if you let a dog in the house, you start looking like the dog and the dog starts looking like you. Maybe that's what happened to us and Pa."

"Who's the dog?"

Jack considered this. "Me, I reckon," he said with a coy smile.

"Goddamn right about that." Then Lester wiped his chin and checked his shirtsleeve for a crimson stain. Seeing none, he asked Jack to roll him a can of beans.

"Yes sir," Jack said, passing him the can. "No wonder those ghosts are leaving us alone with the way we smell. Hopefully the fire dies out before we fall asleep or else the whole county is liable to go up in flames."

Lester gave no indication he had heard his brother's ramblings. He sat, still silent, slowly eating from the steaming can.

"If I tell you something, you promise you won't try to kill me again?" Jack asked after another stretch of silence.

Lester shook his head slowly.

"Well, I'm gonna tell you anyway cause I know you would never actually kill your own brother."

"Don't tempt me," Lester said.

Jack rolled his eyes. "You know that noise you've been hearing?" he asked.

Lester continued eating slowly.

"Remember when we went to the store in town before we left?"

Lester nodded, fixated on his dinner.

"Yeah, sure you do," Jack started. "So anyway, remember when you told me to go back inside and get you something you forgot?"

"Jesus, Jack!" Lester howled, "Get on with your damn story!"

"Right, right, right," Jack nodded quickly. "Well when you sent me back inside, I got myself some yellow suckers. Man, those things were sour! Puckered me right up! Anyway, I got myself something else."

Lester's eyes lifted from his almost empty can. "More than just the pennies you decided to steal from me?"

Jack huffed. "Christ, Les! Yes! Besides your godforsaken goddamn pennies!"

Lester took one last mouthful of beans.

Jack pulled a small package out of the front pocket of his jeans. It was a thick paper box the size of a single cigar. He took off the lid and spilled the contents, which sparkled and glared in the firelight like a silver bar, into his palm. He cupped it in both hands and brought it to his mouth like a dripping handful of water. He took a slow, deep breath then puffed his cheeks and expelled his lungs with a steady burst. The noise, muffled by his hands, sounded like a bursting train horn traveling to them from many miles away.

The tin can slipped from Lester's fingers and clattered on the ground, spurting up a splash of juice. His eyes went wide and skittered over his brother, only half visible in the waving amber light.

"The hell was that?" Lester hissed.

Jack slowly dropped his hands and held them out for his brother to see, like he had caught a rare insect and was sharing it with him for further inspection. There, cupped in Jack's cruddy hands, was a harmonica. Its shined chrome continued to glint in the firelight.

Lester examined it but made no attempt to reach for it. "Where the hell did you get that?" he asked.

"I just told you! At the store in town. When you sent me back in for something."

Lester's eyes narrowed. "I sent you in for flint! Not for whatever that is!"

"It's a harmonica, Les. You really don't know wh—" he stopped himself. "Just listen." Jack began playing an ambling tune with no melody or reason, no structure or story. He played until his lungs began to burn, then offered it to his brother.

"I don't want to touch that spitty thing," Lester said shortly.

"Have it your way then," Jack shrugged then played another tune.

"Is that what I've been hearing this whole time?" Lester asked after a while.

"I've been trying to practice when you were off or sleeping but I ain't got a clue what you were hearing."

"It's hard to believe you could find a more annoying noise to come out of your mouth, but I reckon you found one," Lester said then put his head down and closed his eyes. Before he drifted off to sleep, he heard another muted and meandering tune like a lullaby coming from the other side of the fire, the crackling branches keeping time.

Chapter 22

It was nearly July by the time the unchanging course of Highway 6 ended. The highway they had come to know so well, which comforted them in the same ways as a well-worn pillow, merged with another paved road ahead of them. From their vantage it looked like Highway 6 had been shattered into a massive shard of glass where it met the other road, the tip pointing to a small town. They stopped to examine the intersection, still nearly a mile in the distance. Highway 138 came from their right, Highway 6 to their left. They hadn't noticed the hum of cars coming from both sides, like an echo of the road that was the soundtrack to their travels thus far, cornering them into the change in landscape. Lester had meant to ask for directions, as the shop owner suggested before they left, but he had no idea their travels had brought them to Colorado already. Even if he had heard the swinging welcome sign, he hadn't seen a face besides his brother's since their run in with the Indian boy nearly a week ago.

Lester figured if they continued heading west, they would eventually find a place their father may have passed through. Jack, on the other hand, was convinced a blind westward heading would result in their eventual entrance into West Virginia. Lester gave an honest effort to explain to his brother West Virginia was farther east than they'd ever been, but quickly realized it was futile and gave up attempting to argue his brother's misguided geography.

"Looks like a town down there where these roads meet," Lester reasoned. "Suppose we might as well head there and ask for some directions."

"Ain't my circus," Jack shrugged and followed Lester, who was already riding onward.

They rode into the town, crossing first over Highway 138, a paved two land road with no discernible origin or destination. Lester had wondered for many sweltering afternoons where Highway 6 came from and went to. He pondered where the humming cars were heading and why their travels had brought them through the barren expanse they shared. He was stubborn in his silent belief that highways and paved roads would eventually fall into disuse and crumble. He imagined this sight with amusement while riding no more than two dozen miles from the path Highway 80 would someday slice through the sleepy landscape. Lester chuckled to himself in near disbelief when he realized the two highways bordering them traveled such similar directions. He had the time and inclination in plenty but still could not fathom why that would be necessary.

Next, they passed over a railroad line which seemed to serve as a border for the town. Contained on one side of the steel rails was a small settlement not all too different from the one they had known in Hayes County, save for the water tower standing guard over the half dozen streets webbed out below.

"Looks like the biggest goddamn coffee kettle I ever laid eyes on," Jack remarked of the tower. It was battered to a dingy white and wore a pastel green lid like a giant bamboo coolie hat. The boys rode by, keeping their eyes fixed on the structure looming over them. Slowly, the letters emblazoned on one side came into view, two at a time.

STERLING
COLO

"What's that mean?" Jack asked. "C-O-L-O?"

Lester grinned. "Suppose that means Colorado."

"Well I'll be damned! We've been in Colorado this whole time?" Jack's face lit into a smile of his own.

"Guess so. Haven't got the slightest idea when we crossed over."

Jack took a deep, whistling breath through his nose, pointing his face toward the sky like a tracking bloodhound. "I could've told you. I swore the air was better the second we got in!"

Lester rolled his eyes. "Bullshit! You were shooting your double-barrel ass the whole time so I doubt the air was any fresher than a mine hole."

The brothers unsaddled and led their horses through the first road they came to. It was bordered by sporadic buildings — a post office, a bank, several taverns — that suddenly reminded the boys of home.

The chinking of their horses' shoes on the macadam echoed back to them off the facades of the low buildings. They walked down the middle of the unlined road like desperadoes. The town seemed, for the most part, deserted except for a few indiscriminate locals eyeing the boys from their front awning vantages. Just down the street, they saw a cabin juxtapose between the brick and stone fronts. From its from porch, an old woman sat on a creaking chair. She rocked in a rhythm more accurate than a jewel timepiece, the runners of her chair having massaged the roughhewn lumber into a high shine over countless years. Her skin was as thick and wrinkled as deerskin. By Jack's silent estimations, the woman must have been nearly two hundred years old. She eyed the boys as they neared. She took in every detail they would never think to share based on their clothing and condition thereof, the gaits of the boys and horses, the condition of their horses' coats, and the lackluster shine of their leather boots. She could have nearly told their own stories to them by the time Lester began angling their horses toward where she sat.

Lester removed his hat, leaving an angry red stripe across his slick forehead. Jack followed suit. Lester passed the reins to his brother and told him to stay put and stay quiet ten feet shy of the porch where Lester stood and gave the woman a half bow.

"Good afternoon, ma'am," he said. "I'm hoping to find someone who could help me with some directions westward."

The woman's eyes narrowed, deepening the streaks of the deltas flowing across the sides of her face. She volleyed her eyes to Jack, then back to Lester. Jack stood stock still as if Pa had told him to wait his turn for a licking.

"Whatchu boys running from?" she asked.

Lester shook his head. "We aren't running, ma'am."

"Your parents know where y'all are?"

"No ma'am," Lester shook his head slowly. "Our ma just pass—"

"So y'all runaways then," the woman cut in. "I ain't going to be of no assistance to runaways."

Lester shook his head quicker. "Our Ma just died."

The woman pursed her lips and cocked her head at an angle. Her rocking changed tempo, slowing while she thought then resumed its previous metronome beat over the floorboards. "And your old man?" she asked.

"He run off!" Jack shouted. Lester wheeled to face him, giving him a barbed look. Jack's cheeks went red and he turned his focus to the patch of street in front of him.

"That true?" the woman asked.

Lester nodded.

"I can't hear your head rattling around, young man."

"Yes ma'am. He ran off to Cheyenne when he was born." Lester pointed behind him to his brother.

"That's where y'all are headed then?"

"Yes ma'am."

The woman nodded in time with her rocking. "Got a ways to go, boys."

"Yes ma'am. Came a long ways already too."

The woman smiled. Her face crumpled into fractals of wrinkles like discarded butcher paper. She began taking in the boys afresh, as if a new lens had just been dropped in front of her eyes. "Where's a pair of handsome cowboys like you two from?"

"Hayes County, Nebraska."

"I take it that's about as small a place as God makes them?"

Lester nodded, then hastily added a yes ma'am.

"So you set out on your own to find your old man. Is he expecting you?"

"No ma'am, don't reckon so."

"Come over here young man," the woman said, gesturing toward Jack with a crooked finger.

Jack shuffled his boots hesitantly forward until he was next to his brother.

"I once had a man before he passed many years ago and we had a couple boys," she began. "Reminds me of you two more than I can tell you. Lived my whole life here in Sterling. My family too. My old man ran this store, selling dry goods and such til he passed then me and my man took it over. Planned on our boys taking over one day too. Our oldest was already working behind the counter some days and we paid him well as we could. Our little one got mighty jealous of the change jingling in his brother's pocket and lonely with all of us away working. So one day the little one, when he was about your age," she nodded to Jack, "tried climbing that water tower on a dare or out of spite, nobody knows. Made it about halfway up before a rung gave out but he was plenty high enough and that was all for my little boy. Couple months later, his brother — my oldest — decides he's more cut out for life in Fort Collins. Decides this place and his family ain't enough to keep him happy. So he pads his pockets with the cash and just up and leaves with nary a word." She stopped, closed her eyes for a moment, then went on. "I wrote him plenty of times, left messages all over that city. Never heard a lick from him and still haven't. Likely he's either dead or passed on but I haven't got any way of knowing. Reckon he could be right as a trivet but I've got no way to be sure and that's a hard meal for a mother to eat."

The brothers looked at each other blankly.

"Point is, some people haven't got the slightest inclination to be found once they're lost. Suppose they'd be surprised to know anyone's even thought to look for them. Just keep that in your back pockets and pull it out if you ever need to. And ain't it the damnedest thing that if he came strolling down this street right now, I'd have a party for him like he just got back from war. Lord knows it's much too easy to forgive your blood even when the whole world knows you shouldn't."

Lester nodded although he hardly understood a word. The three of them continued to look at each other vaguely.

"Well," Jack said finally, "how about those directions?"

The woman smirked. "Why don't you keep heading down this street til you find Mister Eli. He runs the saloon just before the outskirts of town. He'll get you headed in the right direction on your way out. But feel free to stay here, long as you want."

Lester nodded and grabbed his reins from his brother.

"But boys," she warned. "Be careful who you cavort with around here. That railroad line brings in as much trouble as it does coal." She eyed them with practiced maternal sternness. "Times are hard for nearly everyone. Some people've lost their Ma and then some."

The boys mulled this over. They had not heard a whisper about the Depression on their desolate ranch, a place where times were hard freestanding of banks or stocks. They thanked the woman for her help although they were still unsure of the help she had offered.

Lester and Jack mounted their horses and ambled in the direction of Mister Eli's tavern, silently deliberating the bewildering but undoubtedly kind nature of the woman, and the others they'd crossed trails with thus far. The water tower grew smaller behind them and a departing train whistle moaned a warning.

Chapter 23

"What can I do for you fellas?" the man behind the counter asked. He leaned his fists against the edge of the bar, bracketing two glasses he had already clattered onto the bar top. The boys had continued down the street after bidding their elder confidant goodbye and had no trouble finding Mister Eli's tavern. The building seemed no larger than a toolshed. Its walls were furnished with glasses glinting sunlight which came through the scattered bullet holes that dotted the wood-slat walls.

As they were tying their horses outside, they could hear the clanging of an out of tune piano. It wasn't honky tonk playing, rather one cautious note followed by another with no discernible melody. They climbed the creaking porch steps and crossed the threshold inside, allowing their eyes a minute to adjust to the dingy darkness fogged with blue tobacco smoke. They both looked around before taking a step forward as if their boot heels were nailed fast to the floorboards. Jack attempted counting the holes in the walls, unaware of what had caused them, but lost count halfway through the second corner. He then turned his attention toward the music, hoping to find a musician willing to form an impromptu duet or at least to play a Jimmie Rodgers tune. The piano suddenly played a clangor of a medley of keys pressed simultaneously like the player had wrapped his head in his arm and went to sleep sitting at his bench mid-song.

Jack spun on his heels toward the noise. There, he found a piano, its wood stained nearly black from decades of smoke and adorned with bullet holes of its own. It hung cocked to one side due to the absence of its front right leg. Sitting comfortably on top of the ivory keys was the most profoundly overweight tabby cat the brothers had ever laid eyes on. He eyed the boys wearily and, seeing nothing of interest, closed them gently. His tail gave a flick before settling near his belly, which hung over the edge of the keys.

Lester's boot heels clicking on the floor pulled Jack back to the present. Jack followed him toward the bar.

"Just a glass of water, thank you."

The man nodded and filled one of the glasses with turbid, dust-laden water.

"And for you, son?" the man asked Jack.

Jack examined the smut falling to the bottom of his brother's glass. "All set, thanks," he said.

Lester downed his glass in a few gulps and asked for another. Jack crinkled his nose and felt a quick shiver run down his back watching his brother down the second glass of ocher water.

"Any chance you're Mister Eli?" Lester asked.

"One and only, son." The man behind the bar tipped his cap. "Hope you boys aren't Federales."

Jack looked to Lester but he shrugged.

"Guess not," the man said. "How can I help ya? Look a bit young for whiskey but if that's your vice then I'll line some up."

Lester shook his head. "A lady down the street told us you might be able to help us with some directions."

"Did this old hag happen to be sitting on a rocking chair about as old as her?" the man chuckled.

Lester nodded apprehensively. "You could say that."

The man poured himself two fingers of whiskey and downed it. "Where are you boys hoping to end up?"

"Cheyenne," Lester said. "But Fort Collins before that."

The man rubbed his stubbly cheek. "Looking for work? Plenty of work to be found round here."

"No sir. Isn't work we're searching for." Lester pulled the tattered map from his pocket and unfolded it on the sticky bar top. "This X is our ranch. We've been following Highway 6 for a while but didn't realize we'd crossed into Colorado already."

The bartender raised his eyebrows. "Well I'll be goddamned. You boys traveled all that way already?"

The boys nodded proudly.

"Got your horses tied up outside?"

They nodded again.

"I bet you've got a pile of stories to tell from just a few odd days, don't you?"

Lester's eyes dropped. "Wish so. Hardly saw a soul besides my brother here."

The man puffed his lips and took the boys in again. "Look to be in pretty decent shape after a ride like that. Especially this one," he pointed at Jack. "Don't appear to be starving."

Jack tipped his hat obliviously.

"You boys are well on your way," the man continued. "Just keep following the main road out of Sterling here. That's still Highway 6. In a couple days you'll get to a split. Make sure you keep to the right. Past Fort Morgan. That'll get you following Highway 34 which takes you right into Loveland. Beautiful little place. Before that is Greeley which ain't much more than a road and a field, and beyond is Estes Park which is the prettiest goddamn piece of land God ever made."

The boys looked at each other with wide eyes.

"But that's a couple days out of your way, so if you're on a schedule then guess you'd just want to take Highway 87 north out of Loveland toward Fort Collins. Hell of a place there too. I believe you boys'll be plenty happy with the crop of cowgirls there," the man winked. "But that Highway 87 will take you straight up into Cheyenne too. Never been there myself but if y'all can ride damn near across the plains you'll do just fine in that cowtown."

Lester thought over the highway numbers and directions in his mind, making sure he remembered every detail.

"How do you know so much about getting there?" Jack asked quietly.

The man smiled. "Aw, well my Mom sent you boys down here cause she knew I'd know better than anyone in this town. Traveled that way damn near a dozen times searching for my brother."

The brothers were bewildered.

"But that lady said one of her boys ran off to Fort Collins and the other fell off the water tower and died!" Jack said, working to make sense of it all.

The man laughed so hard he put a hand on his swollen belly. "Boys, I fell off that damn water tower more than enough for every man, woman and child in this town but I never did more than bust my arm."

Lester and Jack shook their heads in harmony.

"She likes to sit there and cast lines to anyone who'll listen. Most folks around here know her stories hold up about as well as lard in a hot skillet."

"What's your brother's name?" Jack asked, breaking the man's tittering.

"Levi," the man said. "Eli and Levi, how about that? Guess my old man never was too creative. Our Mom used to run up a wall trying to get our attention with both of us acting like she'd said the other's name."

This made the boys laugh alongside Mister Eli. They understood as well as anyone the most hysterical ruses were the ones beautifully orchestrated between brothers.

"Well," Jack said after they had all caught their breath. "If we find Mister Levi, we'll send him on home."

The man nodded solemnly. "Don't lose any sleep over it either way."

Lester placed his glass back on the bar. "We'd better get on our way. Thank you kindly for the directions."

"No problem at all, pilgrim. If your horses need a rest, come on back and I'll get you boys and your horses fed and rested at my place. It's not much but it's better than a dust bowl. Either way, safe travels to you fellas."

Lester tipped his hat and turned toward the door. Jack mirrored him. "Appreciate it, Mister Eli," Lester said.

In a couple steps, they were back in the street untying their horses. They led them west through town, the water tower barely peeking over the horizon behind them. They pulled their hats low over their eyes, fighting with the setting sun ahead of them.

They walked on, these dust bowl desperadoes, their long shadows stretched out over those simple streets that had been so kind to them.

Chapter 24

Dusk came quicker than the boys had expected. They were barely past the low, dull lights of Sterling by the time they were forced to look for a place to spend the night. The yellow glow emanating from the town behind them mingled with the red sunset ahead of them to cast everything in a warm, flaming light.

From a distance they saw the silhouette of a thin cottonwood that seemed as good a place as any to make their camp. They rode toward it, both playing through reels of daydreams about the road ahead. Jack had pestered for fifteen minutes to visit the town past the other town that the man had said was beautiful, neither of which he could remember the name of. Being lost in their reveries was the only reason either of them could think of as to why they continued toward the sparse tree rather than returning to Mister Eli and accepting his generous offer.

As they neared the tree, a form began taking shape. It was a man sitting on the ground and leaning his back against the trunk of the tree, one foot propped up, on the other heel to toe, the open crown of his hat balanced over his face. He lifted the hat quickly and deftly got to his feet when he heard the brothers' nearing.

"Howdy fellas!" the man called to them from under the tree. "Bout near scared a stain into my britches!" He walked out from beneath the branches, aflame in the firelight sunset. His jeans had been worn and patched so frequently, with denim or otherwise, they resembled a patchwork quilt wrapped around his scrawny legs. They were held up by suspenders he wore over top of his buttoned denim jacket. He was built like a young man but his face told the story of many hard years. His hat, an unshaped bucket of grimy and battered felt with a withered and misshapen brim, was pulled down so low on his head it forced the tips of his ears to flop nearly in half. The sweat stains cresting in waves over his hat, his copper colored skin, and his tired and bent posture betrayed his boyish build.

Lester and Jack rode toward the man but remained saddled. "Sorry to disturb you, sir," Lester said. "Just hoping to find a place to make camp. We'll be on our way through." He tipped his hat and turned his horse at an angle toward the empty plains.

"No sense in riding around in the dark! Make yourself a camp right here!"

Lester looked around the base of the tree and saw no signs of a camp — no saddle or horse, no fire or food, not even a bed roll.

"Were you making camp there?" Lester asked.

The man nodded and opened his arms in a mock invitation. He and Lester only stared at each other for a long moment.

"You hungry?" Jack called down to the man. Lester turned to accost his brother for what he hoped was the last time that day. "Aw, don't give me that look!" Jack snapped at him.

"Could always use some grub," the man said with a shaded smile. "Sure you boys wouldn't disagree." He coughed a hacking rattle for a minute then raised his chin and went on. "Those who oppress the poor reproaches his Maker but thee who are generous to the needy honor Him."

The brothers furrowed their brows, but Jack rustled in his saddlebag and found a can of pigeon peas and threw them to the man.

The man rolled the can in his hands, reading the label blankly. "Any chance you boys got any flint to get a fire going?"

"No flint, sorry." Lester lied. He turned once again toward the empty night and spurred his horse into moving onward.

"Just wait one goddamn minute, Lester!" Jack yelled after him. "This place'll do just fine to make camp for a night so I ain't about to ride around in the dark looking for a better one cause we ain't about to find it."

Lester shook his head. "Come here. I want to talk to you."

Jack dismounted his horse and passed the reins to the man. Jack walked to Lester slowly. "What is your goddamn problem?" he hissed when he was just out of earshot of the man.

"We haven't got any idea who that man is, and I don't feel too great about closing my eyes around him. I'd rather ride on," Lester whispered.

Jack guffawed. "There ain't nothing wrong with that guy!"

"You don't know that! That old lady even told us there are troublemakers in this town once the train drops them off!"

"Jeepers, Les. That lady was so full of shit she was liable to bust right then and there. Even Mister Eli said so!"

Lester considered his brother and the dim silhouette of the man under the cottonwood tree. "I just don't trust him and it ain't worth the risk."

"You do realize if we ride on and make camp over there, nothing's stopping that fella from walking on over while we're sleeping and doing whatever you think he's got planned anyway?"

Lester hadn't thought of that but didn't let on.

"Besides, we haven't met anyone in this town that's been anything but nice to us. We're in the West now and they know how to treat a cowboy right out here."

"He ain't from around here." Lester jutted his chin toward the tree.

"I can tell."

Jack rolled his eyes. "Give me one good reason why you don't trust him."

"I don't like the look of him."

With this, Jack howled, his laughter echoing off any imperfections of the barren plains. "I don't like the look of you but I've been stuck with it my whole life!"

"Night then," Lester said and turned to ride away.

"Aw, alright, alright," Jack held his hands in defeat. "I just want to get a good night's sleep." Lester nodded.

"So I'll be under that tree if you need me," Jack finished.

Lester scoffed. "I don't suppose that man'll be keen to read you your bedtime stories."

Jack turned toward the tree and began walking away. "Maybe so," he said, "but I've got the flint in my bag. Goodnight!"

Jack untacked his horse and tied her up on a low branch then snapped a dozen or so off, piled them, and used the flint to eventually spark the saplings into flames. The fire smoked so badly the brothers couldn't see the man eyeing them and the flint they'd denied having. Jack found himself a can of peas and he and the man ate in silence, occasionally coughing from the smoke when the breeze changed direction.

Jack had just rested his head on his bed roll when he heard muffled hoofbeats.

"Just went to collect some kindling," Lester said, carefully climbing off his horse with full arms. "Had no problem finding you. Thanks for the smoke signal."

Jack huffed then closed his eyes and fell asleep to the sound of Lester building up the fire and the gentle chimes of him loosening the cinches and laying his head against his saddle for the night.

Chapter 25

Lester was hoping to sleep lightly, keeping his suspicions high and his ears perked, but he slept comfortably through the night. He also hoped to be the first one up but it was a shuffling noise that woke him. He rubbed the night's worth of dust from his eyes and sat up on his elbows. On the other side of the tree trunk, he could see the man they camped with crouching over something. Lester could only see half of him so he crawled over his saddle as quietly as he could to get a better view. The man was bent over Jack's saddlebag, rifling through it. Lester was just about to shout when his belt buckle caught on a rigging dee and rang like a bell.

The drifter's hands stopped but didn't withdraw. "Just trying to get some breakfast started," the man said without turning. This woke Jack, whose face was quickly shrouded in confusion.

"What the goddamn you doing in there?" Jack asked in a groggy voice.

The man turned and stood then shook the can of red beans in his hand. He threw it to Lester as he walked by. "Gonna get some kindling," he said shortly, walking away from their camp. Jack shrugged and went back to sleep.

By the time the man returned to their ramshackle camp with half a cord of twigs under one arm, the boys were awake and sitting cross-legged next to the whispering coals from the night before. The man dropped the kindling directly into the burnt out fire, sending up a plume of grey ash that stippled both brothers' jeans. The man rounded the tree to the other side and sat facing away from them, leaving the boys to prepare the breakfast he had seemed so keen to get started.

Lester grabbed another can of red beans from his saddlebag while Jack worked with the flint to spark the twigs into life. When they started crackling and Lester placed the beans near the edge of the flames, the man groaned and got up then joined them around the fire.

He sat for a minute, observing the fire vaguely, then reached into his front pocket and removed a small package. He worked with practiced diligence as he flattened the rolling paper, removed a few pinches of wizened tobacco, then licked the long edge of the paper in one fluid movement. He finally looked up as he rolled the paper into a thick tube. The boys watched him with fascination.

Their mother had smoked thin, dainty looking Marlboro cigarettes nearly every night, after she had cleaned up their suppers and washed the pots and dishes, sitting by herself at the kitchen table. Pa had a wad of leaf tobacco in his right cheek for so long and so often, the boys would have hardly recognized him without the bulge in his jaw. They had, however, never seen the inner workings of the things and were duly impressed by the man's manufacturing process.

"Not much of a morning person," the man said while he poked the tip of his cigarette against a glowing coal.

The boys remained silent until the cans began steaming. They each took a dripping spoonful of beans then Jack passed his can to the man who ate eagerly.

"Hungry?" Lester asked through a half chewed mush.

The man took and savored another two spoonfuls. "Food does not bring us near to God," he said. "We are no worse if we do not eat and no better if we do."

The boys looked at each other but neither of them was able to make much sense of the man.

"So are you living out here or just stopping for the night?" Lester asked.

"Just stopping," the man replied. "Heading west."

Jack began saying something but stopped himself with a hiccup.

"Lose your horse?" Lester said.

The man shook his head, a dribble of gritty bean juice running down into the stubble growing in a film over his chin. "Rented a horse to get going, then found a rail yard and rode a couple trains to get here. Stopped off in that town back there for a few days." He turned on the seat of his jeans and stretched out, putting his head on Lester's saddle and stacking his boots on top of each other. From Jack's vantage, he could see the bottom of the man's boots had worn through in tiny pin spots scattered throughout the soles where there were a couple fibers of his wool socks peeking through.

"I don't believe we even know your name," Jack said.

The man took a deep drag of his cigarette, the ashes glowing then toppling into the dirt. "Name's William Walter Roland, God given," he took another drag. "But call me Willie." He tipped his filthy hat dramatically. "And I ain't any good at remembering names so I'd just as soon call you boys *fellas*."

"What brings you west, Mister Willie?" Lester asked.

"Just Willie."

"What brings you west, Willie?"

Willie blew the last plumes of silver smoke into the crisp morning air. "Suppose the same thing as damn near every other person going anywhere nowadays. Looking for work."

"What did you used to do for work?"

"Farm hand. Mostly cornfields out in Kansas."

"No work out that way?"

Willie scoffed. "No work out any way."

"What kind of work are you looking for out here? Farm work?" Lester asked.

The man rolled his eyes. "Any damn work that pays," he said.

They were all silent for a while, watching the fire collapse on itself and begin to burn out.

"Seems like you boys are heading west too. Any chance you're passing near Greeley?"

Lester nodded hesitantly. "At least that's the plan."

"Then I suppose I better hitchhike with you fellas for a couple days. Rumor has it there might be a few jobs out that way."

Lester looked at his brother but his face was hard to read. "What do you have to say, Jack?"

Jack looked around the fire then shrugged. "Wouldn't be the worst thing to have a new face to look at besides yours," he said to Lester. He looked toward Willie, sure he had made him laugh, but the man may as well have not even heard.

"I guess that would be alright, Willie," Lester said, although he was far from convinced. "But we won't be able to feed you every meal of the day. Our cans are running low so's it is."

"Fair enough," the man said.

"And," Lester continued, "we can't have you riding double on our horses all day so you'll have to walk a ways and we won't be stopping and waiting if you fall behind. We're on a schedule."

Jack mumbled something under his breath but no one heard what he had said.

They sat for a few minutes longer until the coals had gone from white to grey.

"Reckon we better get moving before we waste what's left of the day," Lester said abruptly. He stood, brushed the ashes from the legs of his jeans, and saddled his horse.

Chapter 26

They rode on, through the increasing oppressiveness of the late morning heat. Jack had lost a coin toss, even though he begged for a best-of-three, then best-of-five, then winner takes all. For that reason, Willie, their unlikely companion, rode double with Jack while Jack mumbled in layman's terms about the unlikeliness of a coin landing tails side up four consecutive times. Willie remained entirely quiet throughout the morning, save for a handful of hacking coughs when a wall of wind blew the prairie dust in their direction.

Highway 6, still on their left, carried more traffic than it had before the merge at Sterling. The pulsing of the tires on macadam was a droning melody to the cadence of their horses' hoofbeats.

Lester spent most of the blissfully quiet morning reflecting on the strangers they had met in Sterling and looking forward to the promised beauty of what lay ahead. Suddenly, it struck him that he hadn't thought of his father in some time. He was the culmination of their journey west — the reason for the entire voyage — but, for some reason, he had slipped from the forefront of Lester's mind as easily as wind through a mill. Lester began to wonder how his father's face might mirror his own, whether they would share unconscious ticks, or feel the same insatiable yearning for setting eyes upon a wide panorama of open space. He assumed, as all boys do, he would possess the most favorable traits their father had passed to his sons, leaving the rinds and pits of his genes to another son.

That son, at about that time, was forcing Willie off his saddle. He made an excuse about the horse slowing and getting tired but really had more than enough of the man's musty odor. The man climbed from the saddle begrudgingly, leaving the horse to shake its head in relief. He walked between the saddled brothers, feeling diminutive and exiled. He likely wished he had caught another train ride to another nameless town. The rattling and bumping had seemed insufferable but that was before he was forced to walk toward the blank horizon under the scorching noon sun toward a rumor of a job.

He walked on for some time before Jack, now more comfortable in his saddle without his riding partner, felt the need to fill the humid air with noise.

"How old are you, Willie?" he asked.

Willie looked up at Jack, then up at Lester. Lester gave no indication he heard his brother. The man continued to trudge on for some time without answering.

"I'm twelve," Jack said. "Or reckon pretty close. Wouldn't you say, Lester?"

"Suppose so," Lester shrugged. "But I'd be a fool to trust your math."

The silence resumed as they walked, growing heavier on Jack's mind with each step.

"Alright, I'll guess then," he said finally. "If I'm twelve and Les here's a few years older then I reckon you're close to sixty." He looked down at the man for an answer but found none. "Too high? Too low?" he asked, becoming desperate for a reply.

"Not even close. But I'm old enough to be your daddy," Willie said after another minute of silence.

Both boys turned toward him. Jack furrowed his brow. "I ain't too keen to believe that," he said and gave him another vetting look.

"Don't talk about our father," Lester scolded.

Jack went on, "Look like a stiff wind might pick you up and blow you back to Kansas!"

Once again, Jack's joke seemed to fall on deaf ears. The man kept marching between the brothers' horses without displaying any measurable amusement.

"Reckon you ain't much of a joker?" Jack said, breaking another stretch of quiet.

"Nope," Willie grunted. "Never was neither. Seems like this one ain't either," he listlessly pointed to Lester.

Lester nodded toward his brother. "And *he* ain't much one for silence."

"It is good that one should wait quietly for the salvation of the Lord," Willie said plainly.

"The hell is that?" Jack asked.

Lester looked toward the open flatness ahead of them. "I don't see anything."

"No," Jack replied. "What he said. What are you talking about?"

Willie gave him a sardonic look. "From the Good Book, son. Book of Lamentations."

Jack's eyebrows raised. "Say some more then. Maybe we'll know some."

The man shook his head slowly. "That would be vain," he said. "And vanity is not my chosen sin."

Jack pursed his lips and settled on silence.

A few miles later, Willie coughed until his throat had to have been tattered. "How do you feel about joining me in a few ditties?" he croaked.

"Not if that song you just played was you getting ready," Jack replied.

"I seen that harmonica you're hiding in your saddlebag. Why don't you play us a song?"

Jack scoffed. "Cause my brother over there thought he was hearing the devil himself last time I played that thing."

"Don't joke about that, boy," Willie admonished.

"Go on," Lester said. "Just play the damned thing."

Jack immediately went into his saddlebag, nearly falling from his horse, and rummaged through until he found his harmonica. He cradled it in his hands, brought it to his mouth and blew a considerable breath through the reeds, letting loose a tinny roar like a miniature church organ. He moved the harmonica across his lips from one side to the other, then jumped haphazardly around the plate. "This one's called Cowboy Jack!" he huffed before taking a deep, gasping breath and breaking into an arbitrary prelude. He began singing the verses as loudly as he could, his voice carrying for miles over the desolate surroundings.

Lester bobbed his head in time with his brother's voice. Willie remained unmoved, seemingly unaware of the change in the static purl that had encompassed the plains for millennia.

Jack stopped after the third verse, becoming fully aware of Willie's obliviousness. "I thought you wanted a song," he said.

"I don't know that one," he said dully.

Once more they rode on without a word. Jack was just about to place his harmonica back into his saddlebag when Willie coughed then spoke.

"Let me sing one for a minute," he said. "Just play along."

"What's it called?"

"Called 'The Wanderer's Warning,'" the man said, then coughed for a spell again and sang:

I'm riding along on a freight train
Bound for God knows where
I left home just this morning
And my heart is heavy with care.

I quarreled with my dear father
Because of the things that I've done
He called me a drunkard and gambler
Not fit to be called his son.

So I packed my clothes in a bindle
And went to wish mother goodbye
My poor mother broke down crying
Saying 'Son, my son, do not leave.'

I know my old mother is weeping
Day after day while I'm gone
Hoping and watching and praying
For a son that will never come home.

So boys hear a wanderer's warning
Don't break your poor mother's heart
Stay by her side cause she needs you
And let nothing tear you apart.

The last lines reverberated, echoing off the caverns of their loneliness rather than geography. Silence enveloped them once more. Even the horses respected the hush, as if they had just heard and understood a funeral dirge.

"You write that?" Jack asked.

The man shook his head. "Might's well have though, fellas," he said. "Might as well."

Chapter 27

The North Platte River crept into their sight gradually, much like the intersecting roads of Sterling. The burbling eventually drowned out the soft whirring of the cars from the highway. They came to the crest of a gentle slope and their vista opened beneath them. From there they saw the wide, bouldered headwater ambling alongside the macadam stream, both tributaries in their own fashions.

"Just pull on up over here," Jack blurted over the noise. "You know what the sound of water does to me." He steered his horse to the right, angling toward the river then unsaddled and handed his reins to Willie. "Won't be but a couple minutes. Might as well take a shout while I'm taking a whistle!" he called over his shoulder and disappeared into the low, shaggy trees growing from splits in the bouldered ground that bordered the water.

Lester and Willie waited quietly. Even though the three of them had only been traveling for less than a full day, Willie had gotten used to Jack's frequent and abrupt calls from nature. The brothers and their ephemeral partner could have most likely been tracked as easily as a crippled elk based on the recurrent droppings Jack, nearly singlehandedly, had left in their wake.

Abruptly, Jack exploded through the branches. His breathing was erratic and his eyes wild. He wiped blisters of sweat from his lips.

"A — m — a *man*," he stuttered.

Lester was out of his saddle and planted on the ground so quickly his horse reared on her back legs and let out a blustered breath. "Where's the man Jack?" he called, walking quickly toward his brother who was shaking under the branches. "What happened?"

Jack turned and pointed a quivering finger toward the water. "D — down there."

"Hold onto the horses," Lester ordered to Willie. Then he turned to Jack. "Show me where."

Jack hid behind Lester, peeking forward over his brother's shoulders. He pushed Lester in the direction he had walked the first time.

He had headed toward the water, looking for an excuse to take in the river at a closer vantage. It was his curiosity, more than an intestinal emergency, that had brought him behind the massive rock, bent with his backside extended. He was enjoying the proximity to nature such as he'd never witnessed in Hayes County, scanning the landscape to make sure he laid eyes on every detail when he noticed the buffalo plaid flannel contrasting the monotone palette of the rocks just down the river from him.

The brothers approached the man warily and as quietly as possible over the loose shards of rocks. The man gave no signal he could hear the boys approaching. He remained motionless, sitting on the rocky ground with his back against a long boulder, its top as flat as a table.

"It's just an old man sleeping," Lester whispered, still nearly a hundred feet from the man.

"Nu-uh," Jack shook his head. "He would've heard us by now. I think he's dead."

"Oh, for Christ sake Jack, he ain't dead!"

"Then go check for yourself."

Lester, unable to deny a fraternal challenge or his own morbid curiosity, continued toward the man. He called out as he neared but the man still made no indication of hearing him. When he could no longer compel his feet to move closer, he bent and picked up a baseball sized rock. He wound up and flung it at the man, aiming for the cliffside of the boulder next to him. The rock hurtled toward him and struck him in the left shoulder. It made a sharp, sickening thud. His face remained unmoving. After a moment that seemed impossibly long, the man's back slid off the rock, leaving him to lay face down in the honed rocks.

Jack's eyes were wide and his mouth hung open. Lester picked up another rock, making sure it had a ragged and serrated edge, and walked toward the man. When he was close enough, he outstretched a leg and kicked the bottom of the man's roughneck boots. The man's leg shuddered in time with the kicks but settled quickly and did not move again. Lester kept his eyes rapt on the man's fingers, waiting for a twitch of movement. When none came, he reached out and felt the man's hand with the back of his own.

"Cold as snow," Lester said.

Jack nodded knowingly, his mouth still agape.

Lester bent next to the man, bowed his head, and whispered something quietly. Then he washed his hands in the shallow edge of the river and walked back toward their horses, collecting his dazed brother on the way. They broke through the trees, a few yards from Willie and their horses, and went slowly toward them. They each grabbed the reins of their horses in silence and hoisted themselves onto their saddles.

"All this standing around made me have to go now," Willie said. "Just wait here for a minute." He disappeared through the same spot they had just emerged from.

The brothers were quiet for a stretch. Looking toward the trees plaintively.

"A Double Face's done that," Jack said suddenly. "I know it."

"Oh, get off it Jack. That was an old man and I reckon he slept there and never woke up. Simple as that."

"Bullshit and you goddamn know it, Les!"

"No Jack," Lester said. "I don't know it. It wasn't no goddamn Indian hex that killed that fella."

They continued arguing over the most likely causes of the man's demise when Willie came through the trees. He held his arms up over his face to protect against the low, barbed branches. Gone were the decrepit and worn through boots he had been wearing. In their place were a pair of scuffed and broken in leather roughneck boots.

"You've got to be fooling me!" Lester said incredulously. "You stole a dead man's boots right off his damn feet?"

Willie shrugged. "Figured I need them more than he does, is all."

"I'll be goddamned. Spouting the bible all goddamn day, then steals a pair of boots from an old man's cold body!"

"Make no mourning for the dead. Bind the tire of thine head upon thee, and put shoes upon thy feet and cover not thy lips," Willie said peacefully and walked toward the sun, hanging low in the western sky, his leather boots leaving new tracks in the barren ground of the plain.

The boys rode in somber silence until they caught up to him, choosing to ride behind him rather than in rank as before.

"What were you fellas bickering about while I was trying to have some peace back there?" Willie asked over his shoulder after a few miles.

Lester's eyes remained on the horizon, his lips tight.

Jack coughed. "Well," he said, "Les was saying that man was just old and died sleeping, but I reckon that was the work of a Double Face and there ain't two ways about it."

"Double what?"

"Double Face. It's an Indian hex or something. It has a face on the back of its head and if you look at it, bye-bye Cowboy Jack."

"I don't believe in such things as that," Willie scoffed.

"Well, believe it. Cause a real life Indian told us about them and that back there was the work of one. Guarantee it."

Willie was silent for a time. "Suppose I'm more inclined to agree with your brother."

Jack shook his head. "You keep talking about God but don't want to believe in a devil?"

"Oh, I believe in the devil, son. There is a devil and there ain't no sense in arguing. But my God has nothing to do with those savages and their wicked ways."

"So if we see a Double Face between here and wherever you decide to ride another train," Lester cut in, "you'll look it right in the eyes?"

Willie nodded confidently. "Put on the armor of God, that ye may be able to stand against the wiles of the devil."

"I've had enough of your Bible spouting, Willie," Lester snapped. "And I'm about ready to leave your blessed ass behind."

"You don't believe in God, son?" he asked Lester.

Lester grew quiet.

"And what about you, boy?" he turned to Jack.

Jack shrugged. "Some days," he said. "Guess I'll have to decide for good when I'm older."

They rode on until the sun was beginning to hide behind the flat horizon ahead of them, meditating on the events that had lined up to bring them to a day such as the one they had just lived.

"The way I see it," Lester said without warning, "is I've been talking to God nearly all my life and I'll be damned if I ever heard a peep back. Prayed for months and months for Ma to get better and what good did that do?" He was hissing now. "Way it looks to me is either He ain't up there or He's hearing every goddamn word and won't do a goddamn thing about it." He looked at Willie, his eyes aflame. "Which is worse, *son*? Tell me. Which is worse?"

Willie's face remained stoic, trudging toward the half sun.

"Only God I believe in is the one we make for ourselves. The rest is just a bedtime story we tell so we can sleep at night. Nothing more than that. Either we tell ourselves stories or we think the devil's gonna win." He shook his head. "Ain't no devil except the one we make for ourselves so we can pass blame. Blame don't help us sleep too soundly."

Jack looked away from their group of weary travelers and lifted a shirt sleeve to his eyes, wiping away hot tears that had snuck from his eyelids. He had never considered their prayers had gone unanswered and suddenly felt angry at the transcendent sunset in case the God who had heard him begging for his mother's life was the one that had created it.

"The devil ain't gonna beat me," Lester continued. "And whatever God there is, I ain't interested in thanking so I'll just go on believing in myself until He decides to start listening to poor ranchers like us."

Chapter 28

They rode until darkness required them to stop for the night, just across the highway from the northeastern edge of the modest village of Fort Morgan. They were all silent for most of the evening. Jack had grabbed his harmonica and started a few rambling tunes but stopped after Willie took no notice and Lester shot him a barbed glare. They made camp and laid in their expanding silence. Lester had quietly refused to collect the kindling for their fire. His stomach was still filled with choppy waters like the river that flowed past that man's body. He assumed his brother would feel the same. Jack, however, had almost immediately pried open a cold can of peas and slurped them down without a thought of denying himself supper.

"Getting cold," Willie said suddenly. "Might as well get some fire going if no one else's about to." He stood in a huff and walked away, disappearing into the night.

"I believe that's the most words I've ever heard you string together, Les," Jack said when the shuffling of Willie's boots had faded.

Lester took a deep breath, held it, then expelled it like his lips had sprung a slow leak.

Jack tried again. "Reckon it's about time that guy does something to help out."

Lester sighed again. "Thought you two were buddies," he said finally.

"Now why'd you say something like that? You know I ain't know that man from Adam."

"You were the one so riled up with needing to help him."

"If you want me to say I was wrong, I ain't going to. He needed help and we helped him. Ain't my fault he's a shade," Jack chewed his bottom lip, "off."

"More than a shade."

"Well, it ain't no use pissing about it. He'll be off preaching to some other folks in a day or two then we'll never see his worn out face again."

"I shouldn't have listened to you. Knew he was trouble just looking at him and I hardly got a good view til this morning." Lester spit into the dust. "Gospel quoting son of a bitch."

"For with whatever judgment you judge, you will be judged. *Son.*" Jack made himself laugh. "Ma taught me that one."

"Oh for Christ sake. We don't need two preachers in this troop."

"You remember any verses? You should start saying some back. That'll show him."

"I remember some and they've never done me much good so far."

Jack grew quiet. He felt uncomfortable when Lester became angry. It reminded him of Pa, though he would never say it.

"I got the old bible in my saddlebag," Lester said quietly.

"Yeah right," Jack scoffed.

"No kidding. Pa wanted me to have it."

Jack guffawed. "Now I know you're fooling!"

"Cut it out, Jack! It ain't a joke! Pa gave it to me just before we left," he reflected on that day which seemed to be a faded memory from a previous lifetime. "It was marked to a page and had a line circled."

Jack's eyes were wide, glistening in the moonlight. "You think Pa did it?"

Lester shrugged. "Don't seem much like him, but I got no way of knowing. Could have been Ma too, I reckon."

"Wasn't me," Jack replied vaguely.

Willie returned to their camp and dropped the twigs and branches, scattering them between the boys. "Wake me up when supper's ready," he said and laid flat on the hard ground.

"We already ate," Lester said.

"Well I ain't!"

"Then you'll be good and ready for breakfast," Jack said derisively.

"Watch yourself, boy. Ain't no telling what a man'll do when he's got an empty stomach and a tired mind."

"Hey Willie," Lester called from across the half constructed fire. "Don't talk to him like that. Ain't no telling what a man'll do when he's got a drifting half-wit preacher threatening his brother."

"I ain't threatened no man and I ain't no half-wit," Willie spit. "Or a preacher."

"Tell that to your mouth then." Lester kicked over the pyramid of kindling and went to his saddle and lay down.

From across the scattered twigs, Willie spoke quietly. "Let not the sun go down upon your wrath, nor give place to the devil."

Lester rolled over. "Here's one for you," he said. "Go out with joy and be led forth with peace. The mountains and hills shall break before you into song and all the trees of the field shall clap their hands."

"The book of Isaiah."

"Is that the one, Les?" Jack asked, wide eyed.

"Yeah Jack, that's the one. Now go to sleep."

The sun rose lazily behind a veil of clouds. It was the kind of morning sunrise that did nothing to wake a man up, and the three of them started their day in a dazed petulance. They cut open two cans and ate them at a slimy cool temperature in silence, staring blankly at the dirt just ahead of their boots. The air was still brisk so the brothers had their denim overshirts buttoned top to bottom, their cuffs cinched tight around their wrists.

Lester ate half a can of beans then went to his saddlebag and took inventory of their remaining supplies. He did his best to calculate their remaining miles, divided by distance per day, multiplied by two or three meals, but realized his guesswork was too crude to be useful in any way.

"Guess we ought to ride into town so I can pick up some more cans," he said. "Might as well get some extra flint too."

Jack thought for a moment. "Reckon we could get a wool blanket too? I've been freezing my stones off at night."

"You boys must be made of money!" Willie scoffed.

The brothers eyed him through tired, swollen lids. They'd had their fill.

"Guess the Depression ain't reached whatever podunk town y'all hail from. Ain't got a damn nickel to my name, I can tell you that," Willie went on.

Lester shook his head. "Suppose you won't be pitching in to earn your keep then?"

"That's correct, son. And I don't suppose I owe much after you fellas made me walk halfway from Kansas."

Jack laughed. "We helped you plenty and I don't suppose we got a damn thing to show for it except a new pain in our asses," he said before he could stop himself.

Willie glared at him. "Unless my ears were deviling me, I seem to remember you were the one that wanted to bring me along to begin with."

"Reckon you ain't made a single mistake?"

The man spit into the dust between his sordid boots. "Made my share, boy." He spilled the rest of the beans into his upturned mouth and threw the spent can outside their makeshift camp, clattering until it caught in a dry shrub. Then he dug in his pocket and began assembling a cigarette. "Bet you fellas come from money," he said, one corner of his mouth ticking. "Bet you never had to worry about money a day in your pissant lives."

Jack rolled his eyes.

Lester shook his head. "Hardly ever had enough money to rub together between us all and when we did, I suppose we ain't had no one to do it any good with." He took off his hat and rubbed his forehead until he left four angry streaks on each side. "I'd take every dollar I ever touched and trade it for a family."

Jack remained silent.

Willie chuckled to himself. "Ain't a damned thing in the world I'd have over money and that's the gospel truth. Way I see it, buying my way in might be the only way I'll see the gates of Heaven," he coughed. "Besides, tobacco ain't free. And neither's whiskey."

"You'd take a pocket of cash over a family?" Jack asked quietly.

"You bet your ass I would!" Willie bellowed.

"You have a family?"

Willie light his cigarette and drew a few deep tokes.

"Do you?" Lester asked.

Willie continued pulling his cigarette until the glowing ash nearly singed his knuckles. "Just as rather not talk about that," he said flatly.

"Well," Jack sighed. "We all got a family, so I reckon you do."

Willie threw the stump of burnt rolling paper into the scattered, unburnt kindling from the night before.

"We got a family, but I reckon it's rightly complicated. Our Ma was our real Ma but then she died —"

"Listen," Willie hissed. "I ain't gonna speak a word about my goddamn family and I couldn't give two shits about yours if the Lord Almighty came from the sky right now and preached on it. Hear me, boy?"

Jack recoiled. He stood quickly and grabbed his saddle, throwing it over his horse's back. "Let's go, Les. High time to get moving if you plan to stop off in town."

Lester nodded and the brothers tacked their horses quietly. They climbed onto their saddles and started another long day of riding, both wondering what the dwindling hours with their drifting partner would entail.

The town of Fort Morgan was as sleepy as the brothers that morning. Hardly a soul was awake and present enough to take notice of them. They found a dry goods store and refilled their saddlebags with clinking and sparkling cans then rode west out of town before rejoining Highway 6. Their minds, as fogged and clouded as the skies, longed for the kinder and sunnier roads and faces they had seen in days past.

Chapter 29

By the next afternoon, the low clouds had long been evaporated by the midsummer sun. It proved to be a break from the near constant humidity that had swarmed the prairie air for the past months. The wind stilled to a whisper, which rippled over the low crests of the arid plains.

Earlier in the day, they had followed the northernmost branch of the highway, as Mister Eli had directed previously. It was the first time since their second day on horseback, then just over the border of Hayes County, that they would not have Highway 6 as a traveling companion. If they had been in a mood for talking, which they were not, they may have even been too busy to notice the rearrangement of pavement to their left. But on that morning, silence filled the cracks, which fractured their group, like caulk and protected their wounds from further irritation like a salve.

"Guess that's Highway 6 kicking away to the south there," Lester said quietly, jutting his chin toward the cleft in the roadways.

Lester and Jack quietly bid farewell to the road that had kept them company and provided comfort that, only after watching it fade into the billowing heatwaves over the horizon, felt contrived and childish. Perhaps, they both felt certain they would see their concrete confidant soon enough, after they turned the pages of their books to an adventure back eastward. That tale, surely, would contain their father rather than that drifting preacher.

Willie remained silent, staring straight forward.

They stopped for a long lunch at a low spot between the North Platte River and a large reservoir of dark turquoise water. Their horses bent and gulped heartily, sending ripples on the surface of the water as far as they could see. The brothers took three random cans from their bags and placed them on the ground, the tin shimmering and blinding them as they undressed. They stripped to their underwear and went to the edge of the water then cautiously waded in, stopping only when the bottom of their chins grazed the top of the cool water. They had never learned to swim — nor had they ever seen such an expanse of water — as water is a rare commodity in any form in Hayes County. There is often just enough to survive and even their cattle's water pen would have hardly wet their knees. The boys scrubbed their faces until they felt raw and rubbed their knuckles into their putrid armpits until they felt as fresh as a cool pillow. They treated themselves to a few minutes of relaxation. Both felt they damn well deserved it.

Lester trudged from the water and returned to their piles of clothing. He plucked his undershirt from the mess and began to pull it over his head when he caught a whiff of his own teenage aroma. He bent, bundled up the entirety of the clothes and returned to the water, sitting on the silty bottom and working the fabrics between his palms until they released most of their grime and fetidness.

By the time Lester had laid the sodden clothing flat on patches of prickling dry grass, Willie had stripped his own sorry attire and splashed into the water. The cans, sitting in the blazing noon sun, warmed themselves and were ready to be devoured. Willie half nodded to Lester in appreciation of the generous portions, a trickle of water falling from his chin. The three of them sat, sunburnt and nearly naked, beads of water glistening on their backs and shoulders, slapping their tongues and moaning in their unexpected solace.

Riding west and following Highway 34 later that day, their clothes quickly dried and already dirtied, they found themselves riding up a slow incline. Their shadows stretched long behind them, reaching nearly to the bottom of the hill. Whatever laid on the other side, just over the crest, was spraying clouds of dust into the air so high it could have been a dust storm. Jack hoped the dirt would settle to the ground like ash before they reached it. His chambray shirt felt brand new after its washing and he intended to keep it feeling that way as long as he could.

"Suppose you might get your wish after all," Lester said as they rode up the slope.

"What's that mean?" Jack said.

"Well, you were getting real blue about not seeing bison on our way, but I can't think of another thing out here that'd kick up that much dirt."

Jack's face lit, blazing in the orange, early evening sunlight. "You mean it?" he beamed.

"Reckon so, but I guess we'd just as well wait and see."

"I'll be goddamned! Bout to see some buffalo after all!"

"Bison," Lester said flatly.

"Goddammit Les! You can call them whatever you please, but I'll be just fine calling them buffalo!" Jack huffed. "What do you call them, Willie?"

Willie was quiet for a minute. "Never thought of it. No use for a man living in Kansas to call them much of anything."

"Right," Jack said. "Well I'm calling them buffalo and I ain't arguing about it no more." He then reached into his saddlebag and removed his harmonica. He played for a few minutes then went into a rousing rendition of "Home on the Range" although he had trouble remembering the words, as he always did.

It took them the better half of an hour to reach the brow of the hill. Jack scoured the opposite hillside wildly, searching for the hulks of fur grazing in the sagebrush. Instead, they saw a titanic piece of machinery propelling itself along the field. The motor chugged and burped thick clouds of tarry smoke, jerking and rattling the entire contraption as it went along. It had wings that fanned out over the crops, transforming a swaying field into a manicured lawn of sorts. It spewed a cloud of dust and dirt so vast it was as if the machine had swallowed up the entire contents of the ground and discharged it into the sky.

"What in goddamn tarnation is that thing?" Jack gaped. He took his hat off, squinted his eyes in disbelief and held his hand over his brow. His head shook like the pendulum of a grandfather clock.

"Combine," Willie said flatly. "Hell of a machine. If my leg ever turns to gold and falls off, I'd trade it for one of those."

Lester raised an eyebrow and shook his head.

"Where's the buffalo?" Jack asked. "Won't that thing scare them off?"

"There aren't any," Lester sighed. "I should've kept my mouth shut. There ain't any bison anywhere in this whole country but I figured it had to be them when I saw all that dust."

Jack hung his head. "It ain't nothing, Les," he reassured his brother, even though it was.

They made a wide turn to the north to avoid the expansive field the machine was manicuring and harvesting. The boys stared straight ahead, but Willie kept his eyes so fixed on the combine he nearly tripped a dozen times before they emerged from its dust clouds.

"Can't hardly believe there's machines that big in this world," he remarked after a while. "Damn near sacrilege."

"How's that so?" Lester asked.

"Bible says a man should work the fields, but that creation's like making fish and loaves for the masses and that ain't for us to do."

Lester shrugged.

"Thought you said you'd cut off your own cock to buy one?" Jack asked.

"Jesus, Jack!" Lester shouted.

"Well," Jack went on unbothered. "Didn't you?"

"Boy, I'd love to say I ain't one to sin but then I'd be lying and that's a sin too. I ain't perfect and I've sinned plenty and don't reckon I could stop if I wanted, but it strikes my mind that if a man sins for money, the transgression may's well just come out in the wash."

Jack shook his head. "Keep your lives free from the love of money and be content with such things as you have," he said. "My Ma made me write that damn near a hundred times a day. Ain't that right, Les?"

"Mm-hm," Lester nodded. He was hardly listening though. He was too busy imagining the refashionings that field behind them had seen. He wondered for how many millennia there were generations that fed and nurtured themselves and their children and their children's children on the land that now took an implement nearly as large as the Copeland homestead to harvest. He was sure the field had once been home to a herd of bison, as expansive as the farmer's grain crops, which had chewed off the natural crop but left only a scar as an offering in return. He wondered if the combine left any benefaction of its own besides the thick, smoggy clouds of graphite grey smoke.

Chapter 30

They camped that night further along the Platte River. The lazily rushing water lulled them to sleep. Jack laid under his new wool blanket, his loud and ragged snoring performed in duet with the crickets at night and bobwhites in the morning. Willie laid on the bare ground, then turned to one side and rolled a cigarette while leaning on one elbow. He lit it and laid back, balancing the back of his head on the crown of his hat. He took two drags before falling asleep, letting the pillar of white ash grow and fall, withered, until it nearly singed his knuckles and blew northward by the midnight breeze.

Their group had been growing silent more with each mile. They had much to say but hadn't the energy required to say it. The mid-July heat, along with the extended hours of sun had exhausted them. A man cannot live off beans alone, Willie had muttered while they silently slurped their dinners that night. As the pile of days and miles behind them grew, their muscles continued to turn to sand, their bones trembling and wilting like unset gelatin. They allowed Willie to ride double on their horses more often. He had been as slim as a steel rail when they met him but he must have lost half of himself somewhere along the Colorado plains. Their horses were also beginning to show the signs of exhaustion. They required more frequent stops to rip the dried grasses from the ground and chug hats full of dusty water. When they would unsaddle and hitch them to whatever means of scant shade they had found, their horses would almost immediately lay on their sides, huffing dust clouds from their twitching noses, until their breathing fell in time with their weary riders.

Lester, despite his lethargy, had been sleeping fitfully for the past several nights. He would dream so vividly when he finally found sleep that he would wake at sunrise, bleary and red eyed, feeling like he had hardly closed his eyes. His thoughts during the long hours of the daylight seemed tattered and faded compared to the radiance of his dreams. He may have even wished only to dream, looking forward to nighttime as much as his companions, so his thoughts would once again be lucid. He may have, had it not been for the dreams themselves.

He hadn't had those nightmares in months, but his purgatory had found him. Even out on the prairie, miles away from the nearest town and even farther from home.

That night, less than a day's travels from Greeley, Lester closed his eyes and willed away the fatigue, which squeezed like a vice, in his back. He rolled onto his right, then his left, then nestled his spine back into the thin, rancid bed roll.

His mind was only blank for a moment before his dream, re-reeled and racked like a motion picture, played again from the beginning.

His eyes prickled from the sparkling sunlight reflecting off each particle of the dusty ground. He felt the leather band inside his hat grow slick from sweat. His neck burned an angry warmth like he had been standing out in that desolate field all day, under the flaming July sun. The unburdened wind whipped around him, rippling his shirt and floating his wide brimmed hat until it hovered just above the red stripe it had left on his forehead.

He knew this place — this dreamscape that was so alien yet all too familiar. He knew what came next so he turned on a boot heel and faced west.

The wind caught Lester's shirt and popped open the pearl snaps, leaving a flapping denim flag trailing behind him. His hat blew clear from his head and out of sight behind him, ejected as if filled with lit dynamite. Lester looked toward the western horizon, knowing his home should be somewhere near where the dust bowl curved out of sight. But the entire sky was veiled with the thick black curtain of a dust storm. There was no house. Perhaps it had been picked up and cast off to a different dream like in a movie. Lester was alone in the field, the dust storm inching closer. It may have taken all night to reach him but there would be no escaping. No matter how long the night seemed. His boots were now planted firmly in the dust bowl ground like the roots of the grass and brush that once blanketed the land.

At some point during the night, after those unending hours of anticipating, the first waves of dust bristled over his sunburnt skin. It covered his sweaty face and began piling in his pockets like sand he'd collected from faraway beaches. He lifted the neck of his undershirt over his mouth and nose but every breath still felt like hot metal shavings on his throat. The sun, stationary even after several hours, was now gone. It was completely burnt out and blocked by the roiling cloud. Lester's eyes were fastened shut as tightly as he could manage but the dust still got through.

The wind, seemingly strong enough to pick him up and carry him as easily as a tumbleweed on a gentle breeze, continued to pelt him with the minuscule buckshot of the ground until any exposed skin was numbed by the onslaught.

Lester began to feel a gripping on his forearm. It was barely noticeable over the barrage of the dust cloud but eventually the pressure, cinching so tightly around his arm, was all he could feel. He lifted his other arm, heavy and staticky, to shield his eyes. He turned his head toward the pressure on his arm and opened his eyes only to a thin slit. Even this was enough for dust to pour into his eyes, sticking to their dewy surface like flour on a damp dish.

Holding onto his arm was a hand, gripping so tightly the skin was blanched to a lifeless white. The fingers were long and elegant with knuckles like pearls, the skin worn but not weather-beaten, the nails trimmed close and cleaned to a polish. He could recognize the hand clutching him while asleep as easily as awake. It was the same hand he had seen in this nightmare many times before, and nearly every day of his life before that. It was the hand of his mother.

"Help me son!" Her voice would shout, barely audible over the noise of the dust storm. "I don't want to die, Lester!"

Lester fought the impulse to reach out and grab her hand. He had made that mistake many nights prior. He would grab his mother's wrist with his free hand and pull her toward him, doing his best to protect her from the dust and wind. He would close his arms around her until they both felt anchored. Only then would he realize her skin was as chilled and slick as gristle from an icebox. When his arms regained sensation, he would feel the sharp edges of his mother's bones jabbing him as he squeezed her. He would try to drop his arms, to let her go, but she would hold fast with her bones wrapped around him. She would slither her face toward his until he could feel her cold breath on his earlobe and smell her putrid breath.

"You left me to die," she would hiss. "You and your rotten brother. Every man I've ever loved left me as soon as I needed them. You're no better than that drunk who tried taking your father's place!"

Lester had learned many nights ago that pleading made no difference. No amount of explaining or rationalizing would turn this wraith into his mother. There's no way to ripen a rotted fruit.

There was nothing to do but wait, so wait he did. Eventually, the sun would rise somewhere beyond the curtain of this nightmare and the dust cloud would open like a chasm. His mother's appalling hug would loosen, and she would fragment and blow away along the wind of the receding storm. Just another pile of dust.

But that night, for the first time, Lester felt another hand tugging on his arm. He tried to ignore it until he thought his shoulder would pop like a cork. The next heave pulled him over, his feet no longer moored to the ground. He landed hard on his side and his makeshift mask was pulled from his face. He took an instinctive breath when he hit the hard ground and felt his lungs fill with the chalky air. He scrambled to his feet, hacking. The hand then held him by the back of the elbow, guiding him forward — whichever direction that might be.

It seemed as though he walked for miles on his jaded legs, trudging back through the belting storm. As suddenly as Lester had found himself in the infernal mirage, he was now out of the dust cloud. The wind was no more than a gentle breeze and carried nothing other than the sweet smell of yeasted bread. He wiped his face to clear the dust and found there was none. His face was clean and dry, his hands smelled strongly of lye soap. Only then did he open his eyes, afraid the reverie that had sprung up would disappear. But it remained.

He saw his home, standing proudly in the middle of their massive tract of land. The fields were covered in luscious green grasses. Somewhere in the distance, he could hear their steer groaning happily. There were white bedsheets hanging in perfect order on the clothesline. They blew like pennants for a world more perfect than Lester would have thought his mind could imagine.

Between Lester and the house was a man. He walked toward the home, his back turned to Lester. It was the man that guided him out of the dust bowl storm and into this ethereal homestead. Lester called out to him but the man only reached an arm back and waved him to the house. *Follow me.* The man wore chestnut leather riding boots like Pa but had a hat balanced on his head unlike any Lester had ever seen. A serape blanket was folded over one shoulder, even in the blazing sunshine. Lester called out once more, as loud as he could muster.

"Les! Heya Les!" he heard in response. "You're talking in your sleep, Les!"

Lester sucked a gasping breath and opened his eyes. He was laying spread eagle on the ground, nearly five feet from his bedroll. Jack was crouching over him with a hand placed gently on Lester's chest. He sat up and rubbed his eyes and blearily took in his surroundings. It was the quiet hours just before sunrise, but the approaching storm clouds, high in the western sky blotted out the purple skies. Gone were the green fields and heartening sights of a home. In its place was the desolate and lonesome plains, somewhere between their ranch and a seemingly random point on an outdated and battered map.

Lester stood slowly, his legs stiff and fighting against him. "Suppose I was just having a dream," he said.

Jack nodded soberly. This was not the first time he had heard Lester's moaning and whimpering during the night. He had tried to wake his brother other nights but was unsuccessful, so he was scared nearly out of his boots when Lester gasped himself awake.

"Might's well get a fire going," Lester said and limped slowly from camp. He gathered an armful of kindling and dry brush mindlessly. His mind was busy digesting his dream. He hadn't recognized the man that pulled him from the storm but he was sure he knew the man. Lester wasn't usually one for optimism but he felt confident the hand that had guided him through the cloud was the same hand he had been reaching for over many miles of barren land.

Chapter 31

THE SKIES RAGED a war that entire day, dropping a deluge of rain on the plains. The ground, confused by the sudden onslaught, refused to take it in so the water collected in expansive puddles that proved unavoidable, even by horseback. The three weary travelers trudged on toward the next town, keeping the highway to their left and the river to their right like the long white lines on a roadway. They were sopping wet, soggy to their innards. The sodden clothes on their back, along with the tiresome days, felt like sandbags weighing their wobbly knees into their horses' haunches. The horses' heavy steps splattered mud in all directions and sometimes as high as the brims of their hats. The legs of their jeans were pockmarked by the gritty splashes only to be momentarily washed away by the torrential rain.

Willie's sorry excuse for a hat had grown so waterlogged the already misshapen brim hung in the front and covered his face from his lips up. He attempted to roll the brim into a less vexing style at regular intervals that entire day. He would push the front brim up toward the crown and poke it in place with an irked finger, making it look like a prospector's until the rain collected near the band and fell without warning, dropping the stockpiled rainwater like a bucketful dumped over his head.

As quickly as Lester was shaken from that night's dream, the rain stopped. The clouds' end seemed to coincide with the city limits of Greeley, Colorado. The three of them crossed into the miraculously dry streets of the city, leaving wet hoof prints and erratic, splattered drops of dusty rainwater from the cuffs of their denim. They rode down the wide streets of the city, waterlogged and dog tired, looking as if they had been raised from some sort of swampy grave.

Jack climbed from his saddle and began walking, leading his unwilling horse. The seat of his jeans showed an oval of dry denim where his bottom had been glued to the leather saddle.

"Going to rub yourself raw walking in wet jeans," Willie said. "Believe you me."

"He's right," Lester agreed quietly.

"My ass can't take no more!" Jack exploded. "I'd rather chafe my balls right goddamn off than sit on that saddle another minute!"

After a minute, Willie coughed and said, "Guess this's where I get off. Might as well see a man about that job before sundown."

Jack pretended not to hear.

Lester nodded vaguely. "Suppose we'll ride into town and get a hot meal," he said.

Jack's ears perked like a pup.

"Well," Willie said, "May the Lord bless you and keep you. May the Lord make His face shine upon you and be gracious to you. May the Lord lift up His countenance upon you and give you peace." He reached to tip his cap to the boys but it had been pressed up out of his face so he bowed his head instead.

Lester nodded. Jack tipped his hat.

Willie began walking away, trudging in his now-battered roughneck boots toward the green fields bordering the town.

"Hey Willie!" Jack called. "No reason you couldn't join us for supper."

Willie removed his hat slowly. "You boys have shared your table with me enough so's it is."

"Well," Jack said, "reckon we might meet you down the trail somewhere."

Willie nodded slightly. "Careful what you wish for," he smiled. He turned back to the fields and set off again. After a few steps, he turned back toward the boys. "So long, Lester," Willie called. "And so long, Jack. Godspeed."

And with that, the brothers watched their unlikely and perverse companion fade into the early evening light for what they took to be the last time.

Greeley, Colorado was a modestly sized city of less than twenty thousand people, but it might have been Fifth Avenue in Manhattan for the Copeland boys as they rode into the neon light soaked streets. Their eyes struggled to take everything in. Not only was there a place to buy a hot meal, there were enough for them to deliberate what they were truly hungry for. The shops weren't separated, like they were in Hayes County, into goods that were dry, wet, or otherwise. There were shops erected and kept for the sole purpose of selling, shining and repairing leather boots; a massive window fronted store showcasing felt and straw cowboy hats and fedoras; a building that looked like a quaint cabin filled to the rafters with a staggering array of books. The roads were buzzing with a steady stream of cars as curved and glossed as a glass Coke bottle.

They wandered a handful of blocks, hardly able to comprehend the new stretches of buildings, similar but distinct, that extended from each street corner. The sun was hanging low above the horizon. The air cooled and steamed a subtle reminder of the storm that had passed nearby earlier in the day.

"I'm ready for some supper," Jack said after they had passed four restaurants by his count.

Lester pointed ahead of them. *Miss Greeley Diner* glowed in red neon, blazing its own light against the orange sunset.

"Ain't this city the damnedest place," Jack grinned.

"Damnedest place I ever been." Lester replied. Until they reached the diner, Lester mulled over in his mind whether they had found themselves in a space age city or if their corner of the world was just a half century behind.

The Miss Greeley Diner looked like a derailed train car that had been planted and left just off the sidewalk. It was painted kelly green with elaborate, hand painted white letters emblazoned across the long side of the diner car. They climbed the steps and walked in. The boys were immediately hit with the heavy, slick air of grease. There was a line of stools bolted to the floor and lined against the countertop like perfectly grown mushrooms. Jack and Lester found an unoccupied pair and sat, their wet jeans squelching on the vinyl seats.

Without notice, the plump woman behind the counter thwacked a pair of steaming mugs in front of the boys.

"Anything else to drink, honeys?"

"Sure could use a glass of ice water, ma'am," Lester said.

"Coke for me would hit the spot," Jack chimed before hastily adding a ma'am.

"All we've got is tap water," the woman said. "And Dr Pepper."

Jack nodded and Lester shrugged.

The woman turned back without a word. She slithered sideways from one end of the counter to the other — as she would have hard fit head on — and squeezed through the opening at the end of the bar to check the handful of tables against the front windows. The woman and the line cook, a man who also looked to thoroughly and routinely enjoy the greasy fruits of the smoking flattop, performed a practiced dance, sharing the tight space effortlessly.

Lester took a hesitant sip from his mug. Jack nudged his across the linoleum until it was next to Lester's. As if summoned from thin air, the woman set the boys' drinks in front of them. And as quickly as they were served, the brothers downed them. The waitress continued to keep the boys' lips wet, serving them as often and heartily as a barkeep to a drunkard.

"Better save some room for supper," she chided after Jack's fourth empty Dr Pepper bottle clattered against the other three.

"Right. Yes ma'am," Lester said. "I'll have a steak, pink inside, biggest you've got."

The woman nodded. "Anything on the side?"

"Potatoes. Any way you got them. And coleslaw would be great."

"And you? "Cheeseburger with extra fries, ma'am."

The woman shook her head and smiled. "You boys must be starving. Ralph here'll take good care of getting you boys fed." She tapped the countertop once then brought them another round.

Ralph, as promised, took care of them. Lester was served a flat iron steak so massive it hung and dripped grease over the sides of the plate. It could have been brought out on a hubcap and still dripped onto the counter. Jack's plate was a mound of glistening, french fries. He thought Ralph had forgotten his cheeseburger but was too hungry to say anything when faced with a plate like his. It was only after he ate half of the fries that he realized his steaming burger was buried underneath.

The boys' conversation quickly fizzled out when the food was in front of them. They groaned and burped, slurped and huffed as they scoured their plates. The waitress came one time to ask how everything was but took their hunched posture and greasy chins as an answer.

Jack used the last of his bun to sop up the drops of grease studding his plate. "Excuse me ma'am," he called to the waitress. "Could I get another burger?"

The woman danced with Ralph and glided in front of the boys. "You boys got enough money to pay for all this?"

Lester nodded. "Yes ma'am."

"Put on another burger, Ralph! And anything else for you?" she asked.

"Got any pie?"

"Pies we've got aplenty," the woman said with a wink before launching into an extensive list of flavors. Lester couldn't decide if he would rather have the strawberry rhubarb or the apple crumb so he ordered them both, à la mode.

Lester and Jack worked just as frantically on their second helpings. Jack finished his cheeseburger in three bites then stole nibbles of his brother's pies. They cleared their plates, downed their drinks, and sat in triumph with their elbows on the edge of the countertop, looking down on the battlefield of plates, silverware and bottles they had conquered. Lester slid off his boot, dislodged the insole and removed a sizable bill. He placed it on the only sliver of bare linoleum he could find.

They were both struck with a sudden drowsiness that weighed down their minds and bodies. Lester could feel his eyelids beginning to deceive him and drop lazily over his eyes.

"Let's find some place to sleep," he nudged Jack. They both stood and brushed a collection of sizable crumbs from their damp jeans. Lester called a *thank you kindly* to the woman. They emerged from the boxcar diner, their clothes reeking of onions and tallow, like travelers departing a train that had transported them to a distant land.

Chapter 32

Lester and Jack led their horses through the streets lit dimly by orange streetlights. They walked as if their chins were leadened, unable to find the strength to do much more than stagger across the city. Their stomachs ached to the point of splitting. Jack would lift his head intermittently to expel a violent burp tinged with the scent of mustard. Lester was beginning to regret their decision to walk through the city, wishing they had instead backtracked and camped on the eastern edge of the city limits. But how was a boy who had never seen a neon sign to know the expansive grid of a city?

They came up on a small group of kids a few years older than Lester. They wore striped linen shirts with the sleeves rolled nearly to their shoulders, their hair slicked and combed as neatly as rows of corn, and long thin cigarettes hanging limply from each of their lips.

"How-*dee!*" One of the boys called as the brothers passed.

"Hiya," Jack replied innocently.

"I'll be damned," the fattest one of the group said, "if they ain't some real rootin' tootin' cowboys."

Lester nudged his hat up his forehead. "We're just passing through. Looking for a place to rest for the night."

The fat one snickered. After a moment a boy, so tall and scrawny he had been oddly unnoticeable until he spoke up, said, "There's a park a few blocks that way." He pointed toward a street that was a right hand turn from where the brothers stood. "Mostly quiet around here after sundown, no matter what these guys here try to sell you." He jutted a chin down at his friends.

"Thank you kindly," Lester said, and they turned down the street in search of the park.

The group of boys they left behind began punching the tall one's arms, annoyed he'd blown their cover as rabble rousers.

"Hey Les?" Jack asked after they'd walked a block.

Lester grunted.

"What in the goddamn's a *park*?"

Lester was going to ignore him but didn't want to raise suspicions that he didn't know either. "A good place to spend a night," he said finally.

About a block from the park, they found themselves on a street once again steeped in the red glow of neon. As they neared, a massive sign blazed ahead of them.

C H I E F

It was a tall, massively thin structure glowing the block letters. At the top was an Indian warrior in full headdress, looking proudly over the street below. The sign stood like a radioactive roman column balanced on top of the marquee.

"Well I'll be good goddamned," Jack gaped. He was unable to look away from the sign, drawn to it like a gnat. His exhaustion had left him as soon as the sign came into focus. His bloated stomach was forgotten. Now, his limbs tickled like they were lit fuses.

"What do you reckon that is?" Jack asked.

"Ain't got the slightest," Lester said. He wasn't feeling the excitement his brother was. In fact, he could see the argument coming from down the street: Jack, enamored with whatever the sign was advertising, would beg to explore it, and Lester, still exhausted and barely able to continue to the park, would fight him tooth and nail.

Jack squinted into the distance. "Ghost of Frankenstein, Lester!" he shouted. "It says Ghost of Frankenstein!"

Lester set his jaw.

"We gotta see that Les! Whatever it is! We gotta!"

Lester shook his head. "We gotta sleep is all we gotta do. We're not going into whatever that place is."

Jack continued to plead until they were in front of the building, just outside of the reach of the marquee's shadow. They stood in the phosphor red soaked street.

There was a young girl sitting in a glass booth between the two front doors. She would sweep her long brown hair into a ponytail then yank it down and repeat the process from the beginning. The boys had never seen anything like it before.

"Hey!" Jack called from the street. "What are you doing in there?"

The girl looked at them, startled. Whatever troublemakers she had expected to see standing in front of her, these boys were not it. Still, she rolled her eyes and went back to working her hair.

Jack handed his reins to Lester and walked toward the girl. "Excuse me!" he shouted although his nose was nearly touching the glass. "Why are you in this box? Do you need help getting out?"

The girl's eyes grew wide. She took in the boys suspiciously, then surprised herself when she let out a giggle. "You don't need to shout, cowboy," she said and pointed to the circle of holes just above Jack's head. Then she pointed to the small door behind her that connected the ticket booth to the theater lobby and giggled again.

"Right," Jack said. "Well, that's a pretty fancy sign you got there. What is this place?"

"Movie theater," she said flatly.

Jack raised his brows. "So that ghost movie is in there?"

The girl nodded, still working on her hair.

"How much for the two of us? We want to watch your ghost movie."

Lester sighed from behind Jack and pulled their horses closer. "We're not seeing a movie, Jack."

Jack turned and gave his brother a pointed glare then turned back to the ticket window.

"Movie's started already anyway," the girl said casually.

"See?" Lester said. "So let's keep moving. We're both sleepwalking out here."

"I'm not!" Jack snapped. "I'm wide awake!"

"Movie tickets are twenty five cents each," the girl said in a practiced voice.

"Come on, Les!" Jack whined. "I'll pay you back!"

Lester guffawed.

"Goddammit Lester! Just have some fun for once in your life!"

Lester squinted at his brother. He pulled off his boot and dug for a dollar bill then passed it through the slot in the glass window. The girl ripped off two ticket stubs and clattered a pair of quarters back through the opening.

"Right through there," she said without giving any indication through where.

The boys walked through the doors into the lobby and were hit with the smell of butter, which sat like wet concrete on their already distended bellies. Their tired eyes fought to see every intricacy of the plush carpet, the second floor balustrade, the wide and sweeping staircases leading somewhere surely just as elegant and impressive. They were a long way from their dusty, roughhewn home but, like weary tourists, had become anesthetized to the contrast this city had showed them.

They quietly followed the arrows up the staircase and into the theater and found seats in the short mezzanine. Jack stood in front of his seat and spun in a full circle, taking in the gothic painted walls, the scrolling plaster on the ceiling, the balcony seeming to float on air above the viewers below.

Lester grabbed his arm and yanked him into his seat. The seats were as plush as a new mattress beneath them. Only then did Jack notice the motion picture, as wide and tall as a building, playing in front of him. At first, he thought he might grow sick to his overfilled stomach. The movement, the glaring lights, the crashing soundtrack overloaded his sapped senses. He nudged Lester's arm and looked to him, excited to see his brother's own face of disbelief, but Lester was leaning a cheek against the heel of his palm and his eyes were blinking in slow motion.

"Wake me up when it's over," Lester whispered. He was drunk with fatigue.

Jack started to reply but was shushed by an older boy in the row in front of them. He turned his attention back to the screen just in time to see Ygor dig the undead monster from the wall of his mansion.

Neither of the boys would be able to say much about the film after that night. Jack insisted for years to come it was his favorite movie of all time but balked at recalling any of the story. Truth be told, they were both snoring by the time Frankenstein's monster woke up.

Lester was shaken awake by a gruff old man.

"Wake up!" the man grunted. "And wake him up too!"

Lester elbowed his brother, who shivered awake like a monster that had been regenerated by a lightning bolt. "Movie's over," he said.

"Yeah," Jack said groggily. "Yeah, I must've fell asleep right when it was over."

"Mm-hm. How'd it end then?" Lester asked.

"Boy, I wish you could've seen it!" Jack grinned coyly.

The boys staggered from the balcony and walked, once again, into the blazing red street. They unhitched their horses and walked them west through town, attempting to dissect the day into pieces that were real and parts that must have been a dream. Lester was sure the mouth-watering pies had been a dream until they found Lincoln Park and laid against a tree trunk where he let out a massive, fruity burp.

"What a day," Jack said, in groggy awe.

"Just the beginning, Cowboy Jack," Lester replied.

Within a minute or two the brothers were snoring, off somewhere painting dreamscapes of monsters, rhubarb pies and neon.

Chapter 33

It was late in the morning before the swelling sound of the city woke the boys. They startled awake under the shade of a wide maple tree near a sidewalk bordering the park. They had been getting curious and amused looks from passersby for most of the morning; those two cowboys sleeping against a low tree with their faces hidden under dusty wide-brimmed hats, their horses tied up hastily nearby eating a clear patch in the grass around them. They looked like an illustration from the side of a Stetson box that had come to life just to rest in that false little prairie.

They stood and shook out their stiff legs, tacked and untied their horses, and set off as groggily as they had stopped. They'd hardly gone a block when Jack pulled up short, unable to take another step.

"What's your problem now?" Lester sighed.

"I gotta go," Jack said.

"Go where?"

"*Go.*"

"Well," Lester laughed, "reckon we'll find some place before we leave town."

Jack shook his head frantically. "No, Les. I gotta go *now.*" His eyes were growing wider.

"You're gonna drop trou and leave a pile right here in the street?"

"Reckon you're tempting fate here, Les," Jack said. "Let's go!" He was already moving forward, taking slow and short steps, careful not to move his legs and, more importantly, his backside too much. The seam of the seat of his pants had disappeared between his hermetically clenched asscheeks.

Jack continued down the street like a crippled cowboy with two bum hips until they reached a pharmacy. Jack had been so blinded by his bowels he'd walked past by it until Lester called a *whoa boy* toward him.

"Suppose they've got a john in here," Lester stuck his thumb toward the wide glass windows.

Jack nodded thankfully and passed his horse to Lester.

"Reckon if we were on horseback there, you'd just as soon've messed yourself," Lester said.

Jack gingerly climbed the three steps into the front door of the pharmacy. "Just as soon shit on *your* goddamn saddle, ya dunce!" Jack called back as he closed the door behind him.

Lester stood outside, keeping himself and the horses close to the wall of the building Jack was befouling. He patted the horses' heads and withers, running a dirty and callused hand over their twitching muscles. They'd been jumpy since they arrived in Greeley the night before, most likely the fault of the traffic. Lester silently hoped then, for the first time, their horses would have the nerve and grit to get them to their father. And the trail would be just as long on their way back.

Lester peered inside one of the windows, checking twice to make sure Jack's soiled body wasn't laying prone on the floor with his pants soiled. When he turned back, he looked down the street in the direction they had been heading. There, between the squat buildings lining the road, Lester could see the first evidence of the western ground reaching toward the heavens.

The mountains were shrouded in a purple silk curtain. They were barely visible, only standing out to an observer that had never caught a glimpse of the mountain range. Even on a day as clear as that one, they appeared more like white-capped rapids in the sky, as if the River Styx jutted from the underground to somewhere above the horizon.

The mountain range was nearly as far to the west as the brothers had traveled to that point. Still, it felt to Lester in that moment that he was in the foothills of the most tremendous piece of landscape he'd ever seen. It was as if the mountains were sculpted just for his awe and enjoyment. Lester felt his chest warm and swell with the sight of them. If the brothers had set out on their trek with the intention to find the West then they would have, in that moment, succeeded.

"Hey Frankenstein, let's go!" Jack shouted as he vaulted down the stairs. He grabbed his reins and hopped into his saddle as if he'd just left behind half his body weight.

"Don't think about rushing me when you were the one that woke up walking like a sored horse!"

"Aw come on Les, I'm just fooling. I even rushed while I was in there but I reckon I didn't have much say in that."

Lester shook his head. "I wish you would've just shit yourself, then maybe I could've left you behind."

"No way, no how. I'd be right there with you. Riding just up wind."

"Right," Lester said. "If you shut your mouth and keep your drawers on long enough, you might's well look up that way." He jutted his chin down the street.

Jack squinted into the crystal blue, cloudless sky. He made a show of scouring the sky right, left, up then down. "Ain't see a goddamn thing," he huffed. "Nary a cloud though."

"Straight ahead. Behind all those miles are the mountains. You can see the white caps."

Jack held a flat hand above his eyes. "Oh, *now* I see it!" he exclaimed, although to him the sky ahead still looked as dull and lifeless as it had for many miles.

Lester grinned and kicked his horse into motion. They continued toward the mountain range like withered explorers chasing an oasis floating high in the sky.

They left Greeley behind them and were once again surrounded by low crops and lazy livestock.

"So quiet out here I reckon I almost wish we had that preaching fella with us again," Jack smirked.

"Ain't about to hear me saying that."

Jack shook his head. "Don't suppose I know why you still hate that fella. Ain't a spoonful of good that'll do you."

"I don't hate him. Just don't trust him. Never did either."

"Jesus, Lester. He's back there somewhere cropping those fields in this goddamn heat so you should cut it out or I reckon I'll have to start preaching too."

"The only hellfire and brimstone you've got, I suppose you left in that shop back there."

As the day warmed further and the July sun cooked off the damp air between Greeley and the Rocky Mountains, the boys continued to trudge toward them. By some trick of the imagination, the mountains seemed to be matching them, step for step, in moving westward. Lester had seen pictures of the mountains before but black and white, wide angle photographs did little to prepare his eyes for the grandeur of the ground reaching up to join the unmatched glory of the western skies. To see a landscape such as the one in front of them is to peek a glimpse at the face of the gods whose hands had worked tirelessly to sculpt it.

Lester and Jack stopped in the late afternoon for a meal of beef jerky and beans. Their meal from the night before sustained them well into the day. Lester told Jack they would stop for a midday meal then ride straight through Loveland without stopping and sleep when they found their way going a new direction pointing them to Cheyenne. Jack, who had emptied his stomach earlier and was soon feeling grumbles for another reason, grudgingly agreed.

Jack was digging a finger around his mouth to free gristly chunks of jerky from his teeth when Lester clattered a can on the ground and stood. He stood tall, his neck stretched and his head turned up, like a hound on a scent.

"What got into you?" Jack asked, his finger warping his words. "Need a hopper now too?"

Lester held a hand out and shushed his brother. "Quiet!" he hissed. He continued searching their barren surroundings. He stood still for several minutes before he turned to Jack. "There's a rider coming from the west," he said. "Heading straight toward us."

Chapter 34

"Riding on horseback?" Jack chewed a chunk of soggy jerky then when it was spent, gnawed the inside of his lip.

Lester nodded slowly, his eyes locked on the distance.

"Maybe," Jack bit his lip too hard. He sucked on it then spit a wad of pink saliva into the dust. "Maybe it's just a horse. Or maybe it's Willie."

"No," Lester said shortly. "I can see him riding. Anyway, if that was just a horse it'd be the most beautiful wild mare I'd ever seen and I don't reckon Willie could afford a horse like that on one day's pay."

Jack stood up in a huff and scanned the horizon but saw nothing other than the rippling heatwaves dancing over the ground. "Reckon I might need a pair of eyeglasses, Les?"

Lester hung his head and shook it. "Time like this and that's the best thing you got to worry about?" Lester hacked then spit his own mouthful into the dirt. "Now shush up."

Jack did shush up for a few minutes, but the thought of having to wear a pair of eyeglasses like the old men in town scared him more than the approaching traveler. "One time Ma told me you can see better looking through the hole of a Ritz cracker. You ever heard of such a thing or was she pulling my leg? Wish we had some Ritz crackers out here, Les, I'd test my sight til I worked up an appetite and then I'd eat the whole damn sleeve of them," Jack rattled off to no one in particular.

"Jack," Lester said flatly, "I'm about to say this cause I'm your brother and I'm supposed to mind you." He paused. "Shut your goddamn mouth."

Jack pursed his lips and sat back down near the spent can. His jittering heel pounded a tight pile of dirt under his boot.

"Looks like a cowboy," Lester said after another minute. "Let's clear camp and get moving."

Jack saluted his brother and tightened the cinches on his horse and followed his brother toward the peculiar rider. The cowboy was within a half mile by the time they were back on horseback. He may have seen the boys scrambling to kick their scraps under a pile of dirt and clamber onto their horses, but he gave no sign and continued his course.

The boys were almost within earshot of the cowboy when Jack asked, "What's the plan, Les?"

"Just shush and do what I do," Lester said sharply.

Jack wondered whether his brother had a plan or if he was just that stubborn.

"Hiya!" Lester called to the cowboy and raised a hand.

The cowboy continued riding; eyes set on the sky ahead, just above the boys' heads. The man's horse nearly rode into the boys' before he broke his stare, and stopped his horse.

Lester eyed the man once, then again. Jack did the same.

The cowboy had thick, amber skin. He was about Pa's age but his skin was beaten ragged by years in the sun and dust. A collection of wrinkles spread over his face and collected into single deep lines below his eyes and bracketing his mouth. Lester had never seen a cowboy that looked like the man in front of them.

"Hiya," Lester repeated.

The cowboy reached up and tipped his hat, which was balanced precariously on the back of his head, making him look like a pinup cowgirl in a drawstring cowboy hat. The man gave each boy a cursory look then returned his eyes to the horizon.

"How's the trail west of here? We're heading that way far as Loveland. Figure we'll make it sometime around sundown, God willing."

The cowboy nodded slowly.

"Right," Lester said. "Best keep moving. Happy trails."

Just then, a gust of wind came from behind them, so powerful their horses took a stutter step forward to keep from being blown over. The boys instinctively reached up to force their hats down tight on their heads. Dust flew between the three riders, spiraling around them like they were each eyes of a storm. Lester shielded his eyes and squinted toward the silent cowboy.

The cowboy's hat had disappeared, whisked off by the absurd squall. He made no attempt to look back in the direction it had flown. It was as if he hadn't even noticed it had blown clear across the barren plain and vanished into the dusty air.

The dust just began to settle and fall back to the ground when the man began riding again, slowly plodding past the boys.

"What in the hell just happened?" Jack asked, not entirely expecting an answer.

Lester shook his head and waved Jack into motion. They had ridden less than half a mile away from the cowboy when they heard a shout behind them.

"*Help!*" the cowboy shouted. "*Please help me, boys!*"

Jack immediately turned his horse around to face the cowboy's calls. Lester, considering what had just happened and what was possibly on the horizon, hesitated. He and Amigo ran to Jack and cut him off before he reached the cowboy.

"Wait here!" he called to Jack as he rode by.

Jack pulled on his reins and stayed put a hundred feet from the cowboy.

WEST OF WANTING

The cowboy was still on horseback. He and his horse stood so still they looked like a bronze statue planted in the middle of the nothingness. Another dust cloud whipped around him, springing unnaturally from the ground. From inside the cloud, his clear voice called out. *"Hurry up Lester! Help me Jack!"*

Lester pulled up a hundred feet short of the cowboy. The cloud surrounding him fell as quickly as it had risen. The voice called again. Lester looked toward the cowboy and, for a second, thought he had turned around to face him. He saw the mouth moving with each call. Except the mouth he saw was not the hardened and lined mouth of the cowboy that had ridden up on them. He surveyed the chin, mouth, cheeks, ears, and nose of the face.

"LET'S GO JACK!" Lester screamed. He wheeled his horse around so hard they both nearly fell sideways to the ground. *"Turn around and ride! Fast as you can!"*

Jack's eyes grew wide and a dozen questions burst into his mind but he did as Lester told him. He turned away from the cowboy and rode away as fast as his weary horse would carry him.

It was close to four miles before Lester caught up to Jack. Their exhausted horses slowed enough for Lester to call out to his brother. Jack cautiously turned and saw it was only Lester.

Jack huffed. "Lester, what the godda—"

"I don't want to talk about it right now," Lester cut him off. "We'll talk when we make camp but I suggest we get the horses as far as they'll take us for now."

So they rode on until their horses trudged and tripped over bumps in the terrain. Then they climbed from their saddles and walked a few miles more. After sundown but before dark, they saw the lights of Loveland burning in the sky a couple miles ahead of them.

"We've gone plenty far, Les. Can't we just sleep right here?" Jack begged.

Lester shook his head. "One more mile then we'll sleep."

A mile later, close enough to hear the gentle buzz of the nearby city, they untacked their horses and hitched them to a tree trunk. They didn't bother with a fire and didn't have an appetite for dinner, not even Jack. They laid out their bedrolls and fell onto them like they'd been wounded.

"Lester," Jack said quietly, "please tell me what happened back there."

Lester let out a long sigh. "I suppose I'm still not quite sure what happened."

"I saw the face," Jack said. "I saw it when the wind died down. It looked like his face was melted. Like he just had holes for eyes and a mouth and that's it. Never seen anything like it, Les. Hardly had to tell me to turn and run."

Lester stayed quiet for a time, pinching and rolling a sharp pebble between his fingers. "Yeah," he said quietly, "reckon we're just seeing things out here. Haven't had a good rest in a while. Guess it's just our heads playing tricks."

"No," Jack shook his head defiantly. "That was a double face. We both know it so don't bother. We saw it and there ain't any explaining it away. Just lucky we didn't look it in the eye, I reckon."

"Quit it Jack. Whatever happened, it almost turned out bad and we ought to be more careful now, being closer to the cities and all."

Jack was silent. Lester thought he'd fallen asleep. He was just about to fall himself when Jack rolled over to face him.

"Did you see the same face as me?" Jack asked.

"Reckon so, but I didn't get a good look," Lester lied.

"I just can't seem to make sense of it. That Indian boy said it'd be what scared us the most and what I seen on his face ain't anything I've ever been afraid of before. Guess I am now, but why'd it have that face?"

Lester shrugged.

"Should've been a Comanche or a rattlesnake. Those'd be good ones to scare me."

Just then, it made sense to Lester. He could still picture the face he'd seen on the back of the cowboy. He recognized the pattern of wrinkles, the corners of the mouth turned up into a coy, weak smile, the sickly and waxy skin. It had been his mother's face. His mother's face in the days she had grown sickest. The days Jack had been afraid to leave her door in case she would call for him. His mother's dying face had stared out at the boys, begging for them to look, seeking to snare their souls in some cursed land.

The Double Face had shown them what they were most afraid of. Only, Jack had never been allowed to see his mother's sickly and sunken face so his mind had no details to paint the features. He saw a blank face, but it was her just the same.

Lester pressed his palm into his chest. He could feel the thudding of his heart shaking the fabric of his shirt, springing back against his hand. Jack was already snoring. Lester breathed deeply and stared into the clear, star studded night. He knew sleep would hardly visit him that night. First, he prayed his dear mother's soul was resting more peacefully than her sons. Then he laid awake for a while, counting the stretch of miles that were between them and Cheyenne like sheep over a fence.

Chapter 35

Lester was awake long before sun up, so the brothers set out on horseback toward Loveland while the sun was still rising. The morning was cold, the sun not yet completely freed from the horizon's grasp, so Jack rode slumped with his blanket wrapped around him like an injured cavalryman.

Lester sat in the faint early morning light studying the notes he'd written in the margins of their highway map. He traced the change in direction they would take that day. They would skirt the northeastern edge of Loveland, cutting across the corner of the sharp right turn the map depicted, until they met Highway 87. Their traveling companion, Highway 34, had become a hesitant friend like their unlikely drifting comrade, but changing their course to a new direction caused Cheyenne to feel so close Lester swore he could feel the place's electrical charges buzzing through his limbs.

Highway 87 would carry the boys north toward the Wyoming state line. But first, it would show them the western metropolis of Fort Collins, Colorado. Quietly, Lester was growing more nervous with every town they passed. When they'd set out toward the Front Range to find their father, the open space between them had protected him. It shielded him from the possibility of denial and romanticized the trek westward. He only realized in the plains of Colorado that he should have been scared out of the journey with hardly a second thought. The miles on the map had seemed vast, even scaled to fit on a single folded sheet. The towns and roads and waterways between Hayes County and the Front Range were like an extensive checklist of things they'd need to conquer along their way. As the list dwindled and only a few tasks remained, the weight of the last and foremost endeavor placed itself squarely on Lester's tired and sunburnt shoulders. The doubts crept into his mind as effortlessly and stubbornly as his nightmares, refusing to give his mind rest, even in the final days of their journey.

Lester had appeased himself over many miles with the notion that even if their father denied them or proved elusive, the pilgrimage westward, rather than their father, was the valuable trinket they'd come to collect. But as the miles behind them began outweighing their miles left to travel, and the exhaustion and stress of the past weeks added their weight to his shoulders, Lester felt more each day their mission may forever be tainted as a failure if they returned empty handed. A gold coin of a lesson only proved valuable in hindsight, and the road outside Loveland, hundreds of miles from home was hardly a place for looking back.

In an open field beyond the hum and buzz of the Loveland, the boys came upon some things they'd never seen before and things that, in all retellings of their story, were never excluded. The field hadn't been planted or cropped in a handful of seasons. The grasses and brush grew unruly and ragged. Towering above the bracken, stippling the otherwise shapeless landscape, were pumpjacks. Each of them, in their own rhythm, would stand tall then teeter for a moment before slowly pecking its pointed head toward the ground like a drunken chicken digging for elusive feed.

"Would you look at those contraptions!" Jack called to his brother.

"Whatcha reckon those damn things are?"

Lester continued to watch the machines. The steady and practiced movement transfixed him. "Never seen anything like it," he said. The brothers were equally mesmerized.

They rode along the edge of the dancing field for nearly a mile before they saw a pair of men walking between pumps. As they neared, Jack whistled to them. The men turned quickly, their brows raised.

"Gave us a helluva start doing that this early in the morning!" the one man called toward the boys. They both wore work shirts with the rolled above their elbows. They were enjoying the last drags of their cigarettes, which hung limply from the corner of the one man's lips and waggled like a scolding finger as he spoke.

"What are those things?" Jack yelled to him.

The other man turned to look at the pumpjack like it had just, in that instant, grown from the scrubby dirt and it was the first time he'd ever seen it. He looked over its steel beams and braided wires before answering.

"Nodding donkey," he said flatly.

Jack cracked into laughter. "You fellas are pulling my leg! That ain't what those are called!"

The first man shrugged. "Only thing I ever heard them called."

"What do they do?"

The second man threw his cigarette into the ground and crunched it with a twist of his boot. "Oil," he said. "Sucks the oil right outta the ground."

Jack's eyes lit. "I told you there's oil here, Les!"

Lester rolled his eyes. "You said there's oil in Hayes County and we're a long way from there." He turned toward the men. "Best be on our way," he said and tipped his hat. He started riding again and didn't turn to check on Jack, even though it was a minute until he heard his brother's horse clacking behind him.

"Heya Les," Jack said when he'd caught up. "That's really something, ain't it?"

Lester grunted.

"Reckon those fields must be damn near brimful of oil if those fellas were covered in it head to damn toe!" Jack said excitedly.

Lester turned to look at him slowly. Seeing Jack was serious, Lester broke into laughter. Jack laughed hesitantly, unsure what the joke was and if it had been him.

"You're joshing, ain't you?" Lester cackled.

Jack stopped laughing. "Joshing about what?"

"Those fellas! They weren't covered in oil, ya dunce! They were black fellas, Jack," he lowered his voice. "Negroes."

Jack furrowed his brow and whipped around hoping to catch another glance of the men. "Well I'll be —" he muttered. "Ain't never seen one before in my whole life!"

Lester shrugged.

"What do you call them, Les?"

"What the hell are you spouting about? Call them whatever their name is."

"Right. But Pa called them something one time but I don't reckon I can remember what it was."

"Probably best you don't remember," Lester said plainly.

They continued their ride westward. Lester was silent. Jack remained wonderstruck. It was as if the neon and greasy food and motion picture had been indications they were entering a place far different than home, but meeting a couple of black men was definitive proof for Jack that they were in strange and unfamiliar territory.

Near the farthest corner of the oil field, at the end of the group of pumpjacks, they found another small group of oil field hands. The men were bent and crammed into the tight spaces between the beams, wrenching and pulling, grunting and commanding.

Jack whistled to the men as loud as he could. They snaked their heads free from the pump to look at the cowboys passing by.

"Howdy negroes!" Jack called to them proudly.

The men stared at the brothers blankly then turned their confused stares to each other, shrugging and smirking until their eyes went back to the boys.

One of the workers took off his straw hat and waved it to them as if he was cheerily sending off a passenger ship. *"Hola gringo!"* he shouted.

Lester struggled to contain a fit of laughter. *"Lo siento muchacho!"* he called to the man.

Jack's face crumpled in confusion. "The goddamn are you two saying?" he demanded.

"I said I was sorry," Lester said. "Sorry my brother's such a dunce."

"Naw, I heard what you said and that ain't it."

"Said it in Spanish."

"What in the goddamn, Les. Why'd you say it like that?"

"Well," Lester said, "I suppose cause those fellas were Mexican."

The brothers' laughter rattled and echoed from the empty plains surrounding them on three sides and the wall of ragged mountain range that covered the horizon in front of them. They had nearly made it to Fort Collins by the time they'd caught their breath.

Chapter 36

The sun was still setting when the brothers stopped for the night. They were just outside Fort Collins and could have easily ridden in and explored the city for an hour or two before being forced by darkness to make camp, but Lester felt it was best to ride in for the first time in the early light of morning.

Lester felt anxious about their proximity to the turning point of their journey. But he thought it called for a celebration of sorts, so he piled a fire and showered the tinder and twigs with flint sparks. He'd directed Jack to open and prepare what was remaining of their dwindling stock, save for a can of beans to split in the morning. They worked without speaking. Their only sounds came in small grunts while they chewed their tongues and gnawed their lips in concentration.

They ate like western royalty, as if the magnificent land around them had placed kernels food in their stores with each step until they'd reached their new beginning. They chewed methodically and joyously, nodding with each new spoonful until their bellies were inflated and the cans and jerky spent. They leaned back and propped their shoulders on their saddles in quiet contentment. If they'd had the inclination or supplies, it would have been fitting to roll and smoke a thick cigarette, one relishing drag at a time.

Jack rolled onto one side with a groan and reached into his drained saddlebag. He rifled around the scant contents for a moment, rattling each item inside.

"Real funny," Jack said. "Where is it?"

Lester ignored him.

"I said," Jack hissed, "where is it?"

Lester closed his eyes and tilted his hat over his face. "I hope you don't mind if I don't play this game of bullshit," he said plainly.

"It ain't bull, Les! I just wanna know where you put it!"

Lester lifted the front of his hat an inch to eye his brother. "Hid *what?*"

"My harmonica! I wanted to play a couple songs before bed and it ain't in my saddlebag where I always put it!"

Lester shook his head. "Lose your balls if they weren't attached."

"I didn't lose it, Les! I'm telling you!"

"Reckon you just dropped it when you were getting those cans out."

"I don't think so Les," Jack said hesitantly but quickly sprang to his feet and scoured the ground around them in the dusk light, kicking rocks and peering under the sagebrush. When he was certain he'd checked every inch of their camp, he kicked Lester's boot. "I know you goddamn took it!" he howled, tears fighting to break free from his eyes.

Lester sat up and punched his brother in the thigh as quick as a horse's kick. "Jack!" he hissed. "I ain't going to say this again. I didn't take your stupid goddamn harmonica!"

"I hope we find our Pa soon so I can tell him what a bull's ass you've been!" Jack yelled. He turned and kicked plumes of dust into the air for a couple minutes until he sat back down against his saddle. He continued to huff and mumble until the last of the night sky's purple vanished and his lids grew heavy.

Jack was awakened by something tugging and kicking his boot as hard as if it was being hammered. He scrambled awake and found Lester, half dressed and red faced, standing over him.

"Real goddamn funny!" Lester snapped.

Jack wiped his mouth and rubbed his eyes, squinting up at his brother. "Why are you so mad? And half naked?" He asked in a sleepy, smoky voice.

"Why don't you tell me, you sorry goddamn brat?"

Jack quickly felt completely awake. "Les," he reasoned, "I got no idea what you're mad about but you're scaring me."

"*Good!* You should be scared!"

Jack considered his brother, his heart racing. "You're acting like Pa," he said quietly.

Lester pulled back into himself, his bony shoulders wilted on themselves and his chin lost its posture. He looked at the ground in front of his boots for a minute in silence, taking heavy breaths. "My shirt," he said quietly. "I can't find my shirt."

Jack looked around their camp, cans scattered around a pile of gray, skittering coals. "Hell, Les. You slept in it. How'd you lose it?"

Lester closed his eyes and took a deep, slow breath. "No," he said. "My white shirt."

"Oh," Jack's eyebrows raised. "That nice and fancy one? With the pearl snaps?"

Lester nodded.

"Haven't seen it. Didn't even know you brought it."

Lester eyed him. "I didn't take your harmonica so if you have my shirt, this is your last chance to hand it over before I find it and whoop your ass."

Jack nodded defiantly. "Wish I knew you did bring it, then I would've thought to take it."

Lester sat on the ground glaring at his brother, who was dramatically avoiding eye contact. He was still half dressed, his jeans hanging open with his belt clinking with every movement. "If you don't have it then where is it?" he asked.

Jack shrugged. "Same damn place as my harmonica."

"If I find out you touched that shirt," Lester pointed a finger at Jack, "I'll leave you in whatever godforsaken town I can find and don't think I won't."

Jack ignored him and slowly began saddling his horse. He silently dug through both of his saddlebags and double checked their camp for the shimmering tin of his harmonica. "You got any idea what really might've happened to that stuff?" he asked solemnly.

Lester shook his head. He was slowly pulling on his dirty and worn chambray shirt, buttoning it with disdain and roughly tucking it into his jeans.

"Guess we ain't got a choice but to be smelly and quiet then?"

Lester ignored him. He cinched his belt then began tacking his horse. He looked across their camp at his brother, battered and weary, but sitting tall and confident on horseback. It was hard to recall the picture of Jack, jittery and alarmed, the day he'd taught him to ride. Now, his younger brother looked like a painting of a cowpoke, painted as if each mile were a brush stroke until the canvas was covered and the cowboy came into focus, brave, ready, and looking westward.

"Hey Jack," Lester said. "I'm sorry I yelled. I shouldn't have."

Half of Jack's mouth curled into a coy smile, just as their mother's had so many times. "It ain't nothing, Les. I'd be sore about it too if it'd been my shirt."

Lester nodded slightly. "Still—" he offered.

"Must've cost you a pretty penny. Don't blame you being mad. But I guess it's all just stuff anyway."

"Reckon that's about right," Lester nodded again. "Suppose I was just jumpy this morning."

"Ain't no time to be all wound up tight," Jack smiled and gestured toward the Fort Collins city limits. "We made it. And our luck's gotta come up spades soon enough, don't you say?"

"Sounds like the most sense you've talked in a while," Lester said with a smirk. He kicked his horse toward the city of Fort Collins with his fingers crossed tightly at his side like a holstered pistol. He was certain their brotherhood would serve as a talisman to ward off the clouds of doubt that had been rolling into the front of his mind over the past days. They entered Fort Collins blissfully unaware that their luck, which they swore had turned bad, would only grow darker before any glints of light peeked through.

PART IV

West

Chapter 37

THE STREETCAR TROLLEY rumbled and rattled down the middle of the streets of Fort Collins, occasionally making a sweeping turn to meet another set of rails before setting off steadily down a different street. Cars passed by without slowing, their drivers uninterested in the trolley's deep green and tan paint, glossed and trimmed like a Rolls Royce. Its varnished walnut woodwork glimmered around the windows and doors, its rectangular front panel was divided into four triangles with their peaks meeting in the center at a bulging headlight. Altogether, it looked similar enough to the Miss Greeley Diner, save the wheels, track, and cable, that it may have made the boys' mouths water had they stumbled on it in a different manner. The streetcar trudged along without slowing. It only gave its horn two quick honks to warn the young cowboys on horseback, who were planted near the tracks, turning in their saddles to take in the bustling city.

Their horses skittered out of the streetcar's path and the boys stared at it in astonishment as it traveled by. Their slack-mouth expressions were mirrored on the other side of the windows by youthful university students, middle aged office workers, and elderly errand runners. Those amused faces blurred as they passed until the boys were alone in the center of the street with shined and curved cars whizzing past them on both sides. They carefully dodged the traffic and unsaddled near a line of cars parked curbside that stretched as far as they could see.

"Howdy young men!" a voice called from over the parked cars. Lester turned and saw a man waving cheerily to them. His face was as wide and flushed as a football, his chin wagged rhythmically as he spoke. He was about as tall as he was wide, most likely more so if he were to remove the bucket-crowned cowboy hat balanced high on his head. He smiled brightly at the brothers as they took him in, glowing like a miner's headlamp in his perfectly white three piece suit. A glimmering gold chain connected a belt loop to a pocket in his vest that seemed entirely too small to fit a pocket watch.

"Some mighty fine horses you've got there!" he called again.

Lester nodded. "Thank you, sir. Would you happen to know any place we could stable them for a few days?"

The man in white let out a long, nasally sigh. "Suppose I rightly do. Fine establishment not three doors that-a-way," he waved a thumb over his shoulder.

"Right. Thank you for the directions, sir." Lester looped a boot in his stirrup and began hoisting himself up when the man came shuffling toward them, his chin jiggling from ear to ear.

"Now just hold on young men! Wouldn't be too neighborly of me not to show you the way!" He beckoned them with a hand of wide, stubby fingers. "Follow me!" he called and disappeared, shuffling down the street.

As promised, just down the street and behind the main drag, a small inn sat patiently waiting for a traveler tired enough to forego the extra couple blocks to the much more impressive hotels. A haggard man hobbled toward them as they neared the building. "What is it now, Howard?" he asked flatly.

"Well Larry, I've found some young cowpokes here that would be happy to pay for use of your fine stables. Isn't that right boys?"

"Yes sir," Lester nodded. "Reckon we'll be in town for a few days. These are good horses but the city's making them as skittish as I've ever seen them."

The old man looked the horses over then walked a circle around them. "Look mighty goddamn skinny is what they look."

Lester nodded. "Yes sir. Rode them from Hayes County, Nebraska."

The man in white's eyebrows shot up, sending his hat even higher up his forehead. "Well," the stable owner said, "I ain't about to feed them extra just because you boys got the notion to ride the hell out of 'em."

"Yes sir."

"Rate's two dollars a day per horse. That'll cover stabling, brushing, feeding, and watering. I ain't, I repeat, I ain't liable for anything besides that. I ain't a horse doctor. I got a closet full of shotguns in my office but if I don't hear them bastards riffling through the barn then I got nothing to shoot at. Understood?"

Lester nodded.

"You owe me four dollars then as a deposit. Rest is paid when you pick them up and you're not untying those horses til it's paid in full."

"Understood." Lester bent and removed a boot, dug inside and removed a five dollar bill. He handed it to the man, "Put the extra dollar on my ledger."

"How about I put it down as a tip?" the man asked with narrow eyes.

"No," Lester said flatly, putting his boot back on. "Put it toward my bill. We'll talk about a tip in a few days when we got our horses back." He handed the man the reins of both horses and walked back in the direction they'd come.

They emerged back onto the main road in time to see the trolley trundling past in the opposite direction. They stopped on the sidewalk and watched it go by.

"Were my ears deceiving me or did I hear you boys say you've come all the way from Nebraska?" the man in white huffed from behind them, catching his breath.

"That's right," Jack said.

"On horseback?" he asked incredulously.

Both boys nodded.

"What brings you young men to the great state of Colorado?"

Lester eyed him. "Looking for someone. Hoping we might find him here or Cheyenne."

The man jutted his hand toward them. "The name's Howard Rockwell." He pumped Jack's hand, then Lester's. "I've got something I'd like to show you. Right around the corner."

He led the boys to a store with a massive window front displaying a scale model western scene on the bottom. Flowing, sequined, and embroidered rodeo shirts hung like flamboyant curtains above it.

"This," Howard said, presenting the display with an outstretched arm, "is my store. Howard's Haberdashery and Quality Western Wear."

Jack's eyes shone as brightly as the glass window. "Can we —?" he began to ask.

Howard flashed a bright smile and opened the door wide for the boys to enter. They were immediately surrounded by the smell of wool, felt, and leather. The window display was barely an appetizer for the feast their eyes got inside. One wall was covered with western shirts of all colors and patterns, another wall dotted with high shafted boots made from nearly every imaginable animal, and the last wall, opposite the window, was stacked to the ceiling with felt and straw cowboy hats.

Howard chuckled to himself over the boys' reactions. "Figured if you traveled all this way to meet someone they ought to be mighty special, and mighty special meetings require mighty special attire. And if I say so myself, Howard's Haberdashery and Quality Western Wear has the finest duds this side of the Rio Grande."

Jack walked along the walls, shuffling the arm of each shirt through his fingers as he went along. He then poked and petted the toes of each boot, marveling the grain and grit of each hide. Finally, he grazed the brim of each hat, feeling the roughness of the straw and the fuzz of the fur. He picked some up, worked the stiff brims between his fingers, and placed the softest ones on his head before moving on to the next.

"Well," Howard said, "guess I wouldn't be colored surprised if you men told me you're in town courting a young cowgirl. Is that who you traveled all this way to meet? Lord knows a man'd travel off the edge of the earth for a woman that'd winked at him once."

Jack turned away from the wall, the massive hat on his head rattling and twisting on his head like a bell. "Trying to find our Pa," he said excitedly.

"Your Pa? As in your father?"

Jack nodded.

"You boys might just be in luck then. Seems nearly every cowboy passing through this city's stopped by Howard's Haberdashery and Quality Western Wear. If he's been through here then I'd bet on red that I've looked him in the eye."

"His name's Harold," Lester said. "Harold Burke. All we know is he might've come out here to drive cattle."

"Well, I'll catch a sleeping weasel!" Howard yelped.

Lester's face flushed, and his jaw loosened and hung. "Do — do you know him?" he stuttered.

"I suppose I do know him," Howard said. "Haven't had him in here for several years though. Couldn't even tell you much how he looks anymore. He was a decent customer for a few years, ran up quite a tab, then never came back. Seemed he was in here a couple times a year for a while until I started asking him to pay up front."

Lester hung his head. "He hasn't been around for years?" he asked.

"Wouldn't say that, son. Just hasn't come in *here* in a few years. Seen it before with cowboys that come to town. Freshen up to find some cowgirls for a couple rodeos, then ride on out without paying anyone a dime. Common issue in cowboy towns such as these. Mining towns too, I hear."

"Sounds about right," Jack muttered.

"Any way you think we might be able to find him?" Lester asked, dejected.

"Some crisp new duds wouldn't hurt. Pick out whatever gets your coffee boiling and I'll cut you young men a deal."

Lester, even though he had recently lost his best shirt, was hardly interested in picking out a new outfit. He was feeling despondent already and it was still before noon on their first day in town.

Jack, however, was already pulling shirts from the racks and piling them over one arm, and he had seen a half dozen hats he would be happy to own.

Chapter 38

"What do you say about this?" Jack asked excitedly, emerging from the closet Howard had turned into a changing room. He spread his arms wide, letting the silk fringes hang and wave like bunting. The shirt was bright yellow silk and had front yokes that detailed western scenes on the front of each shoulder. The right showed a cowboy on horseback with an open lasso extended high above his raised hand; the left was a steer with wide, menacing horns running from the cowboy and his lasso. The back yoke was left blank but Jack imagined what the embroidered scene would have looked like and was sure it would show the steer being deftly controlled by a tight rope around his horns.

"I say," Howard shined, "I've hardly ever seen a more wonderful shirt in all my years!"

Jack turned to Lester.

Lester grimaced. "Suppose you look like a mighty pretty cowgirl."

Jack's arms fell heavily to his side. He shook his head and returned to the closet where a half-dozen more shirts were waiting.

Howard leaned toward Lester. "Didn't have enough heart in me to tell him it was a ladies' shirt."

Lester chuckled. "Wish he had sense enough to figure it himself."

Howard began to say something when the closet door once again flew open.

Jack emerged wearing a solid crimson pearl snap shirt, a simple line of black piping decorated the front and back yokes at a smooth angle, caging in an embroidered steer head on the front of each shoulder. The sleeves were just about the right length and even had four pearl buttons lining each cuff, which was three more than Jack had ever had before.

"I like it," Lester offered.

"I believe you may just have to fence in the women like cattle if you wear that fine garment around this town!" Howard glowed.

"I think I'll take it!" Jack nodded excitedly. "Your turn, Lester!"

Lester, who was decidedly less excited by the idea of trying on the decorative and expensive looking clothing, asked for a simple shirt without looking over Howard's stock. "I'd like a white pearl snap," he said simply.

Howard nodded. "Follow me, son. I have some beautifully embroidered white shirts right over here."

Lester stayed where he was. "Just a plain one, sir."

Howard turned and gave him a coy smile. "Isn't it interesting," he said, taking a white shirt from a rack and looking over Jack, standing excitedly in his beautiful, bright red shirt, "How different two brothers can be?"

Lester took the shirt from Howard, stripped off his filthy chambray shirt and tried the new white one on in the middle of the store. He snapped a few pearl buttons into place, tugged at the sleeves and nodded. "Perfect. Thank you, Mr. Rockwell."

Howard smiled at the young brothers, standing in his store with their new shirts. "Now don't forget to get yourselves some new denim jeans. And your hats and boots look as worn as your horses, if it's not too brusque of me to say."

The brothers looked themselves over in a full length mirror and agreed. They each grabbed a new pair of Levi Strausses and scoured the collection of hats to pick one that felt just right. Lester quickly and unceremoniously picked a felt silver belly one with a Gus crown. Jack, after much deliberation, decided on an inky black one after Howard casually mentioned it matched the piping of his new shirt. He asked Howard to steam the crown to a wide Cattleman crease and he happily obliged. Howard's round, flushed face brimmed with joy as the steam rose and shrouded around him. The brothers watched with interest as he worked the softened felt like a sculptor might mold a block of clay.

"And some new boots, perhaps?" Howard offered as he settled Jack's hat on his head, double checking the proportions.

Lester's toes had been crammed into the front of his boots since before his mother had gotten sick, so he needed little goading to try on new, larger pairs. He quickly became enamored with a pair of chestnut suede ones. His feet immediately loosened and unclenched. He looked himself over once more in the mirror and could hardly believe he was looking at a young Nebraska rancher who hadn't had more than a couple hot meals in the past month. As easily as his feet slid into the new boots, he could feel his confidence coming back to him, wrapping loosely around his shoulders like a Navajo blanket.

Jack was sitting on a chair near Lester, watching his brother try on stiff new boots.

Lester turned to him. "Go ahead, Jack. Pick some out."

Jack picked up a pair of black leather boots and slid his foot halfway in before kicking the boot off like he'd heard a rattlesnake hiding inside. "No way, no how. Don't want a new pair. Couldn't hardly stand to even sit in those things."

"You're joking!" Lester laughed.

Jack shook his head emphatically. "My boots are just fine. Don't need a new pair and don't want them either. Thanks anyway."

"What's got your goat, young man?" Howard asked from behind

them.

"I just like my boots. I'm good and used to them. Don't want to be walking all over town in new boots. Give me a blister the size of Wyoming."

"Suit yourself," Lester shrugged.

"No wonder Willie stole that man's old boots," Jack muttered.

"Son," Howard cut in quietly. "Hope you don't take offense to me asking, but have you ever had a new pair of anything for yourself?"

Jack looked at his ragged and faded boots, then shook his head.

Howard nodded. "I was the youngest brother too, son. Never had a stitch of clothing that was new. That's why I opened this store. Sometimes I get the notion to throw my shirts away after I wear them a day, just to spite my raising."

Jack dropped his gaze to the floor.

"Tell you boys what. I'll give you a bargain for that new outfit," he said to Lester, then turned to Jack. "And for you, I want you to have an outfit that's yours. Might as well have your name embroidered across the back. If you like those old boots then keep them, but a new outfit is the least you deserve."

"Yes sir," Jack muttered. "Thank you, sir."

Howard turned quickly and walked to the register where he played a flurry of ringing from the machine. Lester stood and collected his old clothing in his arms and followed Howard. Jack sat for a moment longer and dried his eyes before getting up and joining them. Jack was thankful to have Lester as his brother, but Jack had long wanted some clothes that were not worn through by his brother first.

Howard walked them back out onto the sidewalk where, just an hour previously, they had been walking around dazed in a cloud of filth. Now, their clothes were so new they couldn't manage to move quietly. They were certain every person passing by was silently appreciating their new clothes. Howard had agreed to keep their sordid old clothing in his back room until they returned to collect it on their way out of town. They walked down the sidewalks of Fort Collins with empty hands and on their own two legs, which refreshed them as much as a cool shower.

They'd walked a few blocks toward the center of town when a colorful poster caught Jack's eye.

"Les!" He called. "Look at this! We gotta go!"

Lester read the poster taped onto the front window of a small grocery store. *Fort Collins Players' Vaudeville and Minstrel - Three Nights Only!*

"Fine," Lester said. "We can go, but you owe me a dollar when you finally get your hands on one."

"Deal!" Jack spit into his palm and offered it to Lester.

Lester spit into his own and squelched it against Jack's, binding it into a tight handshake.

They had a few hours to kill before the show started so they kept walking the streets of Fort Collins, looking like characters in a spaghetti western, walking wide-stanced toward a saloon shootout.

Chapter 39

The show was held in a municipal gymnasium in the northeastern part of Fort Collins. A block away, when the doors of the building were just in view, Lester took off his boot and came up with a dollar he had just gotten as change from Howard Rockwell. Jack grabbed for it, but Lester snapped the bill away and gave him a disapproving look. Lester struggled to get his sweaty and swollen foot back into his new boot but when he succeeded, the brothers made their way toward the plain looking doors. They opened the doors and were immediately hit with the heavy smell of liquor-laden sweat and tobacco. A heavy man, his forehead beaded with sweat and his hair matted smooth against his head, snatched Lester's dollar, and held out some quarters and two dingy yellow ticket stubs. Jack took one and noticed it was two halves of the same ticket for a show called *The Uncommon Misery* which had played several years previously at a theater that no longer existed.

The gymnasium floor was dotted with folding chairs organized in careless rows. By Jack's estimation, there must have been three hundred of them. Lester counted eighty seven. Most of them were empty but the occupied seats held older couples, a group of teenagers, and a few families. Jack found seats near the middle of the floor plan and quickly used his new hat to fan himself.

"Reckon they turned the heat on for us tonight?" Jack asked in a huff.

"Your idea," Lester said flatly.

Jack turned in his chair as far as he could one direction, then again to the other side. "Guess it'd kill them to open a window. Can't have that damn train out there hearing the music, I reckon."

They sat in silence for a while until nearly all the chairs around them had filled and the temperature inside the echoing room warmed even further. A man taller and skinnier than their Pa sat next to Jack at some point. He sat quietly and patiently, and only took notice of Jack when he saw him staring at his pin. The man's lapel pin was a blood red circle with a white *T* in the middle, centered perfectly like crosshairs. Jack was taking in the colors and the perfectness of the lines when the man reached up and tapped it gently, causing it to plink like a coin. The man smiled to him but Jack had already embarrassingly turned his attention to the burgundy curtain in front of him. He was afraid to break his stare with it until the curtain opened and revealed a lone man standing in white tie attire, one arm held out as if he was helping a lady from a carriage.

"Welcome, welcome one and all!" The man thundered. "This," he snapped both arms up so they were parallel to the stage, "is the Players' Vaudeville and Minstrel!"

Applause broke through the crowd until Jack was certain he could feel the floor shake. After a few seconds, a young girl in an ornate, ruffled dress came onto the stage followed by a man in overalls carrying a banjo. Without much ado, the man began plucking the banjo strings slowly. The girl matched each note with a stomp of her tap shoes. The man's cadence steadily sped until he was playing a rousing, rolling banjo tune that the audience had long since given up on clapping along with. The girl, however, effortlessly kept time with her shoes, spinning and kicking without missing a beat. Just when Jack could not fathom a faster tempo, the banjo and clacking shoes sped once more before they came to a flamboyant and exaggerated end. The man with the pin sprang to his feet with applause, whistling and hooting. Jack stood quickly after, following suit. He even heard Lester let out a *yahoo*, certainly forgetting himself.

Jack felt then like he could use a good, long nap. He had never been to a real show before and had expected little. Already, the first performance had eclipsed the price of admission. Just as he was considering how much more he would be able to digest, a bearded lady stepped on stage and all previous thoughts disappeared.

The brothers thought their stomachs were set to explode after holding in their laughter for the bearded woman's entire song. They finally let loose during the applause and hollering that followed and felt much better. They bounced off each other, elbowing and bumping as they laughed. They returned to their seats in time for the next performance, their cheeks numb from smiling.

Soon, the tuxedoed man was back onstage feigning as if beckoning some place faraway beyond the edge of the curtain. "Tambo!" the man called. "Tambo, leave that skunk alone and come say hello to these fine folks!"

Stumbling onto the stage came a man in ragged, oversized clothes in worse shape than those the brothers had left behind the counter at Howard's Haberdashery. He walked in a dazed and plopping mope until he stood, facing the wrong direction, next to the interlocutor in his perfectly tailored tuxedo.

"Turn yourself around, Tambo!" the interlocutor ordered with a pat on his shoulder.

The threadbare man turned to face the audience, who broke into howls and jeers and laughter. His face was slick with black paint, except for obscene white circles around his eyes and mouth. "Don't suppose I understand all this speak of skunks," he said in an attempt at a slow, deep south accent, accentuated with hiccups between every other word. "I's just playing with that old cat! Bugger's a mean one!"

The audience broke into another round of laughter. The performers' banter continued for a few minutes before Jack understood what he was watching. He wondered why a negro like he'd seen in the oil field would wear such garish stage make up but, then again, he'd just watched a bearded woman sing a beautiful operetta.

"Say," the man said to the interlocutor, "you know this's a healthy town?"

"Why sure!" the interlocutor replied cheerily. "Nearly holds the record for clean health!"

The man nodded dumbly. "My Old Man died at 90 and my Gramma at 132!"

The interlocutor put a hand to his chest. "One hundred and thirty two years of age? How miraculous!"

"Naw," the man shook his head slowly, "at 132 Buckeye Street!"

Once more, the entire crowd roared, slapping their knees and stomping their heels until the timber floors strained and creaked. Jack heard Lester chuckle and took that to mean he could laugh as well. He did, and spun in his chair to take in the crowd, searching for a dark face in the audience, sure he would see their faces wrinkled into unrestrained enjoyment. Instead, he saw only faces that looked in one way or another just like his. His lips tightened and suddenly the impulse to laugh had vanished.

Jack turned back to face the stage and even though the interlocutor and his slapstick partner were gone the weight in his stomach remained. Even the burlesque dancers in their corsets and high-slit dresses couldn't turn Jack's thoughts from the sticky mouth of tobacco his mind was working to chew over.

After a handful of acts Jack paid little attention to, the interlocutor was back with Tambo in tow.

"Say," the interlocutor said as if they had strolled onto the stage mid-conversation, "What ever became of that brother of yours?"

"Moved back east!" Tambo said slowly, hiccuping. "Opened up a jewelry store."

"Well, I'll be. Seems to be doing well then!"

Tambo shook his head, a dumb smile plastered across his painted face. "More like doing time. Caught him wearing the goods he grabbed!"

The man next to Jack kicked and stomped the floor in glee, joining all the other sweaty white faces in the gymnasium in uproarious laughter. All besides those two young cowboys.

Jack elbowed Lester. "I'm ready," he whispered.

Lester stood and pushed their way through the rows of chairs until they emerged from the door into the street, which was mercifully cool and quiet.

They walked a dozen blocks before finding a park where they sat under a tree and fell asleep leaning against its trunk. They had been silent since leaving the gymnasium. Jack thought of long lists of questions he could ask but felt, somewhere within the lead weight in his stomach, that he already knew the answers.

Chapter 40

The next day would grow and swell into a suffocating afternoon and evening, but the morning hours were brisk and bright skied. Jack sighed himself awake and lifted his hat from his eyes. He sat up from the tree stump he'd been slumped against and stretched his back. Twisting, he realized he was alone in the park. He sprang to his feet and spun. Just as his heart began to thud in his already heavy chest, he saw Lester walking toward him. Lester made his way to the tree they'd slept under and dropped to a knee in front of Jack. He was holding two bulging packages of something wrapped in cotton rags.

"Woke up early so I went for a walk. Wanted to check the post office and found a diner on the way back," Lester said quietly.

He passed one of the cloth packages to Jack, who opened it to find two perfectly browned, steaming biscuits slathered in speckled gravy. Jack nodded in approval and dove into the food, only coming up for air when the biscuits and their crumbs were finished. Then he lifted the rag to his lips and licked the gravy from the fabric, sucking out any particles from between the threads.

Finally, Jack looked up and saw Lester was gently picking at his biscuit, pulling off small crumbs and chewing them hesitantly one at a time. He'd only eaten a third of one biscuit by the time Jack was finished and had cleaned his rag.

"What's got you wrapped up?" Jack asked.

Lester kept pinching at his food without looking up. He stared at the grass in front of his boot which was tapping an incessant rhythm.

"Reckon I'm still feeling crocky about that show last night too," Jack offered.

Lester nibbled a piece of his biscuit and shook his head. "Ain't upset about last night," he said flatly.

"Maybe we should be."

Lester looked up at his brother. "I never said that show last night was right. Wish I could get my dollar back and buy some biscuits with them instead. But it ain't our business what other folks think's funny."

Jack pursed his lips. "Why *did* all those people think that was so goddamn funny?"

Lester shook his head vaguely, like he was afraid to shake loose and awaken the heavy thoughts within it. His boot kept its rhythm. He continued nibbling his breakfast.

The boys were quiet for a few minutes until Lester had nearly finished his biscuits.

"So," Jack said, "if that ain't what's eating you then what is it?"

Lester finished his food then shook his head. "Nothing," he said flatly. "Just not hungry right now."

Jack shrugged. "I would've eaten it for you."

Lester moved only his bobbing leg.

"Anything for us at the post office?" Jack asked.

"Just a note from Mister Richard," Lester said quietly.

Jack furrowed his brows. "Who's that?"

"The man from the bank in Hayes County. Came around after Ma — with the will."

Jack nodded hesitantly and waited for Lester to go on, but his lips were cinched with disquietude.

"Well," Jack said finally, "what'd it say?"

Lester wiped his greasy fingers on his new jeans and reached up to rub his chin. He rubbed for a minute or two. "It don't matter," he said flatly.

"Aw, sure it does!" Jack howled. "If you won a prize you damn well better share it with me!" When Lester didn't laugh, or even smile, Jack could feel his chest tighten before the fully formed thought struck him. "Les," he lowered his voice, "what's the matter?"

Lester stared into the grass. "Worrying about it ain't going to make a lick of difference."

Jack realized his leg had begun to jump too, rattling his battered boot heel into the ground. "Just tell me Les," he begged.

Lester remained silent.

"Is it Pa?" Jack asked.

Lester shook his head.

Jack thought for a moment. "The ranch then?"

"Ranch is fine," Lester said flatly.

"Well goddammit then, Lester!" Jack yelled.

Lester's leg stilled and he lifted his stare from the ground to look his brother in the eyes. "It's got nothing to do with you so quit asking."

Jack huffed and shook his head. "Stubborn old ass," he muttered and sprang to his feet, wiped his mouth, and pushed his new hat down on his forehead. He set off down the street away from the park. He had no destination in mind, hoping only to walk away from his brother.

He wondered for a minute what the letter from Hayes County had said to effect Lester so heavily, but Jack could be stubborn also so he worked to leave any concern behind him. Soon enough, he could hear Lester's measured footsteps over his shoulder and he was suddenly glad for the company.

Just then, the shadows from the tall brick buildings ended and Jack could feel the morning sun on the back of his neck. They were headed west once again.

Lester's longer strides carried him to Jack and they walked the sidewalks of Fort Collins in silence, side by side. They walked without knowing which port they would anchor next, but not without purpose. Lester had felt certain he would know the right place to stop when he saw it, even though that confidence was waning after passing blocks of buildings that, in hindsight, might have held the scavenger clue that led them to their father.

A few blocks later, set aside from the square brick buildings that seemed to multiply as they walked, was a place that looked more like a lodge than a business. A couple of gas pumps stuck out from the gravel patch in front of the building like glowing fenceposts. They were painted in bright, enticing colors and topped with a decorated globe, softly glowing a light that seemed like an ethereal portal. The building's flat front had four tall windows cut through the second floor, shadowed by high peaks in the roofline like it was a gothic cathedral made of roughhewn timbers. Between the windows were perfectly white letters which, in a few hours, would shine so brightly the boys would have had to shield their eyes. Spaced perfectly between the peaks was:

JOHN'S

The apostrophe was hanging inside the last window as if it was a Christmas decoration that had never been boxed away for the summer. As soon as Lester saw the place, he knew. He'd known he would.

Chapter 41

THE BELL ABOVE the front door clanged in a celebration that welcomed the brothers into John's establishment. It took only a cursory look around the dimly lit store and its sparse shelves to know John, if that was still the name of the man in charge, was in the business of peddling fishing supplies. The live bait John was selling had, over generations, permanently tinged the humid air inside the store with the thick smell of rancid viscera. Based on the crowd of men huddled by the cash register in waders and squeaking boots, it was plain that John's supplies were only a part of the reason his patrons stopped by before each trip to the cascading rivers of cool mountain runoff.

"Sunny as all get out on the water today so that water's gonna be shinier than a silver dollar," a gentle voice said from behind the counter.

The men surrounding the voice nodded in wholehearted agreement.

"Fish's gonna see you long before you see them," the man went on, "so cast long and be patient."

The group of men shared looks of enlightenment as if they'd just heard a passionate Sunday sermon. A small faction of the men said their *thank yous* and *good days* and headed toward the door, squeezing past the brothers.

"Well come in," the gentle voice called. "No use blocking the door."

Lester and Jack took a handful of hesitant steps toward the congregation of fishermen. The men opened their loose circle and glanced at the boys, leaving a space wide enough for the man behind the counter to take them in as well.

"You boys going out on the water?" He asked. "Free fishing advice with every Coke!"

The men chuckled amongst themselves, a gaggle of men who would return home to their tired wives reeking of salty water and metallic entrails.

"Probably better luck in the Poudre Canyon than Horsetooth today if your minds aren't too made up," the man continued.

"No sir," Lester said. "No fishing today."

In fact, neither Lester nor Jack had ever been fishing. The opportunities are about as common as a vein of gold in the middle of a Nebraska dust bowl. They'd both seen enough photographs in Lester's books to know the basics of fishing; a man stands in a gentle stream with a pole and a long, invisible line of silver strand and waits until the fish miraculously becomes hitched. Lester knew bait went on the end of the line but had never considered a fish hook was for what the name implied. Jack, however, was sure the fish liked to nibble up the fishing line and could be plucked from the water like a dandelion after they'd swallowed enough of it.

"Well then," the man behind the counter called back, "Richie should've been able to help you at the pumps if you're needing it."

Lester shook his head slightly. "We're looking for someone," he said anxiously. "Hoping he might've passed through."

The man behind the counter nodded. "Damn near every man in the West's stopped by here a time or two. At least any man who plans to catch anything!"

The clique of men chuckled on cue then returned their attention to the brothers.

"Who're you looking for, son?"

"Our Pa," Jack chimed in. He had learned Lester struggled to share that information along their journey, stuttering on the words like he'd heard them for the first time only seconds previously. Jack took that to mean it was his line in the play they'd performed several times so far.

The group of men raised their brows and leaned their hips and elbows into the counter. They were listening intently now. This would surely be a good enough story to tell their companions on the water, in varying degrees of over-ripeness.

The man behind the counter sighed and looked over the men. "You fellas might as well head to the river before there's no fish left, don't you think?"

The men took the hint without argument and shuffled past the boys and toward the door. The bell above the door chimed for a minute, then stilled. A long moment after the last echo of the ringing ended, the man behind the counter stood. He was taller than either of them had expected. The worn stool he'd been sitting on, for as long as his name had been glowing out front, must have been the height of a pantry step ladder. Even though he was tall enough to get a good look at the boys, his belly forced him to bend at the waist and lean his forearms against the rickety countertop. He had a snow white horseshoe mustache and eyes as blue as a cloudless sky behind small round framed eyeglasses. All of this was shaded under a tattered St. Louis Cardinals ball cap. Altogether, the man looked enough like a picture book illustration of Santa Claus for Jack to straighten his posture.

"Are you John?" Jack asked suddenly. As often happened, the words floated out of his mouth and reverberated in his own ears before he realized he had spoken.

The man nodded heartily. "Almost like my name's up in lights out there," he laughed to himself. "So," he sighed, "looking for your old man?"

Lester and Jack both nodded.

"How long's he been gone? Since the spring?"

"Since he was born," Lester gestured to Jack.

John let out a long huff. "Just walked out on you boys then?"

Lester nodded.

"Your mother seems to be doing a job raising you boys well enough," he said tilting his chin down to look at them over his bifocals.

Jack looked to Lester, unsure what line came next now that the script had moved into an unexpected direction.

Lester hung his head and John seemed to understand.

"What's your old man's name?"

"Burke," Lester said. "Harold Burke."

John took off his cap and ran a hand over his thinning grey hair. He removed his glasses and rubbed the bridge of his nose then combed his mustache with his index finger and thumb. "I see," he sighed.

"Has he been here?" Lester asked.

John readjusted his cap and nodded. "Sure," he nodded. "Been through here plenty. Most fellas around here stop by on their way to and from their fishing spots. Tell me what's biting and what's not. Share the talk from the canyon. Then I pass anything I can onto the latecomers and the early birds the next day. Harold's been through here often enough but ain't too keen on fishing as much as gossip."

Lester and Jack could hardly contain their excitement. Lester's boots shuffled against the wood floors. Jack fiddled relentlessly with a small ball of lint in his new jean pocket. They had stalked their father's trail for weeks and had finally seen their first sets of prints, no matter how faint.

"He's — he's been here?" Lester stuttered.

John pursed his lips. "My old lady was under the weather for most of the spring so Richie was running the place for me. Couldn't tell you if he's in town anymore. But if he is, I guess he'd be staying at the Armstrong like the other fellas with jingling pockets."

"The Armstrong?" Jack asked.

John lifted an arm and pointed over their shoulders. "Armstrong Hotel. About two miles that way."

Lester and Jack both spun on their heels as if their father would be standing in the corner of the bait shop. They took a few quick steps toward the door.

"Ask at the front desk," John called to them. "They'll tell you if he's been around."

"Yes sir!" Lester was breathing heavily, keeping himself from running through the door like a trained dog. "Thank you, sir!"

"Hope you boys find what you want!" John called after them, but they were already back into the street. By the time the bell above the door rang, Lester and Jack were in a sprint toward the hotel. They only slowed to catch their breath when the Armstrong's sign came into view.

Chapter 42

"You'll need an adult to check into any rooms, boys."

The lobby of the Armstrong Hotel was more lavish than the squat brick building would have let a passerby believe from the outside. The stamped copper ceiling fractured sunlight around the lobby, casting everything in a pale blue. The floor was squared into large marble tiles that glimmered and echoed each wave of light and sound.

"I'm sorry," Lester replied to the woman behind the front desk. "We don't need a room. Just wanted to see if someone's here."

The woman pursed her lips. "I'm not allowed to share information about residents of the Armstrong Hotel," she said curtly.

Lester's eyes dropped to his new boots and the pad of his thumb rubbed along his index finger. It wasn't until that heavy moment of disappointment that he could feel a new blister, a souvenir he'd collected on his run to the hotel, pulsing on the back of his heel.

"We're looking for our Pa," Jack said. It was his line in their script and he knew Lester's crestfallen silence was his cue.

The woman looked between the brothers, sizing them up, taking in their new rodeo attire and their tired, bagged eyes.

"Right," she said quietly. "I'll help you boys but I want you to know I'm sticking my neck out to do this."

"Yes ma'am," Lester nodded. "Thank you, ma'am."

The woman gave them another long, doubtful look. "What's your father's name?"

"Harold Burke, ma'am."

The woman clicked her fingernails against the marble desktop, then sighed and lifted the thick cover of the ledger in front of her. She scanned the page for a moment then gently closed the book again. "He's staying in room 217," she said quietly.

Lester stumbled a half step backward, his boots stutter stepping against the perfectly smooth tile. In his excitement getting to the hotel, he had forgotten to remove his hat when he stepped in the cool lobby, but he removed it then and wiped his forehead with the back of his hand.

"You mean he's here?" Lester mumbled. His chest was pounding and he could feel the back of his neck growing warm.

The woman nodded vaguely. "Sure hope that's good news. You boys look more like you've just seen a ghost."

Lester shook his head quickly. "No ma'am," he said. His brain was doing its best to make quick work of the dazing news. His muscles rippled under his clothes like a racehorse in a starting gate. "It's great news!" he said louder than he had meant. He could no longer keep his excitement at bay and took off in long strides toward one end of the lobby. "Thank you so much, ma'am!" he called over his shoulder.

"Son!" the woman called after him. "Stairs are right here!" she pointed to the corner of the lobby opposite Lester's path where a wide sweeping staircase curved toward the second floor and, therefore, their father's room.

In a fluid maneuver, Lester turned on his heel and directed his steps to the staircase. He collected Jack on his way back and they began climbing the stairs, their boots snapping and echoing through the lobby.

"Boys," the woman called to them once more. The brothers stopped, both of them in the middle of skipping the steps two at a time. "If he's not in his room you can check the bar next door. Him and his pals are mostly here or there."

Lester and Jack nodded and ascended the staircase in a matter of seconds. When they reached the second floor landing, Jack yelled a *thank you* down to the woman in the lobby. It echoed like a shout through a cavern.

It would not be until much later that they would realize they'd never asked the woman her name. Her eyes, softening as she took in the boy's exhausted desperation, would be yet another reminder of the warmth and goodwill of the everyman that built and populated the cities of the West. Sometimes, it seems, the people who have shaped our lives in those unknown and unforeseen ways end up being only our memory's illustration of their likenesses.

The narrow, carpeted hallway on the second floor had a window at the far end that sent a glare of late afternoon sunlight down the corridor and shone on the brothers. Their steps were still long and hurried. They scoured the doors they passed, checking the small brass room number plaques. The numbers grew slowly until, finally, they stood next to room 216. Lester stopped short and Jack, looking at the doors on the other side of the hall, walked into Lester's back with enough force to knock his hat from his head. It was sent to the floor so he bent to pick it up. When he stood and replaced it on his head, he was staring at the glimmering plate. *Room 217.*

Jack nudged Lester with his elbow but he had already seen. He'd turned to face the door but hadn't taken any steps closer or made an attempt to knock. Jack faced Lester and saw his chest heaving. His nose whistled and sighed with shallow breaths. Lester willed himself to move toward the door but his muscles, which had been jittering with anticipation and zeal all day, were suddenly sodden with apprehension.

He spun the brim of his hat through his fingers, shuffling and wringing the silver belly felt.

Jack, once again, took his brother's hesitation to be his cue. He lifted his clenched hand and rapped his knuckles on the door. His confidence waned only when the noise thundered and echoed down the hallway. Jack was sure the doors lining the hall would open in succession and show faces of men just awoken from their afternoon naps. Instead, nothing moved. There was no sound except Lester's quick breaths, which were just now beginning to slow. Lester watched the doorknob, waiting for any indication that it was twisting to unlatch from the inside. For some time that was indeterminate to the boys and would, in later retellings, feel like minutes then sometimes hours, Lester stared at the door and Jack watched Lester.

Finally, after he began to worry his brother had fallen asleep on his feet, Jack spoke. "What do we do now?" he asked.

Lester gave no indication he had heard. Jack reached out and gently grabbed his brother's arm in the crook of his elbow. "Lester," he whispered. "What do we do now?"

Lester blinked heavily and kept his eyes closed. "I don't know Jack," he sighed.

Jack squeezed Lester's arm in his hand. The hand that had reached out and begged the door to open to reveal their father, who would cross the threshold back into the boys' lives. "We're gonna keep on getting on, cause that's what we do," Jack said.

Lester began to nod but his head only wanted to hang.

"The place next door," Jack said suddenly. They had only been half listening to the woman in their excitement, but something about the word *bar* had stuck in Jack's mind. He had never heard the word before and wasn't sure what it was, but he knew it was the direction of their next steps. "Let's go, Les," he said. "We'll find him at the *bar*."

Lester's arm relaxed and he allowed Jack to pull him a couple steps before he raised his chin and took the lead down the hallway. They descended the stairwell, their boot heels clicking a song of chagrin and dismay which echoed in the lobby just as their excited voices had, minutes before. They passed by the front desk but the steward who helped them had clocked out and was replaced by a spritely younger gentleman who seemed altogether astounded to see those young cowboys crossing the hotel lobby, their posture as heavy as a summer rainstorm but their attire as florid as an episode of Gunsmoke.

    Jack and Lester walked out of the Armstrong Hotel, whose neon sign had just begun crackling and sparking into life. The sun was warding off the low and heavy clouds that had come to oversee the slow change from late afternoon to pink tinged evening. A breeze rippled their new shirts and cooled their faces. As is often the case, changes come on the back of a smooth whisper of wind.

Chapter 43

Next door to the Armstrong Hotel was a barroom about as long but less than twice as wide as the hallway Lester and Jack had walked through a few minutes earlier. The wood slat blinds were mostly pinched shut and the lights were dimmed, which made the darkly stained wood bar and paneling appear more expensive than such an establishment could likely afford. Nearly every surface of the floor, walls, and bar were either slightly warped mahogany or mirror which had been pockmarked with handprints or splatters. Such were the trappings and decor of a watering hole.

All the men inside seemed to know each other well. The entire crowd would, seemingly inexplicably explode into synchronized laughter. Some would shake the shoulders of the men next to them, others would pound the tables and bar tops, and those of which that had been inside since opening time would lean heavily on any surface willing to hold them up. The clinking and clattering glasses kept time of the conversations, which rumbled and undulated throughout the room. A half dozen tables along the left-hand wall held circles of boisterous men. One of which at each table would take their turn leading the conversation while the others sipped, then guzzled, their foaming beers. As the glasses would clang to the table with a thin film of suds in the bottom, one of the men would stand slowly and unsteadily make their way to the bar. After a minute, they would return to the table with a dripping armful of glasses, brimmed and spilling over with cheap, honey colored lager.

Except for the smell of acrid cigarettes and yeasty liquor, Jack found the place to be exhilarating and hoped they would be able to stay and enjoy some of the bitter liquid all the other men were downing. He was so captivated by the scene he realized Lester had kept moving forward only after turning to see if his brother was as taken by the place as he was.

Lester walked tentatively toward the bar. He stood in front of the point at the corner of the bar top and stretched his back and neck until he could look down the length of it. Behind the counter was an older man with a starched button down shirt as white as his hair. His cheeks and forehead were flushed and stippled with sweat. He handled and filled the glasses with fingers as nimble as a pickpocket. Once, he slid a glass filled to the rim past a handful of men to a thirsty patron like a winning shuffleboard shot. The coasters he pulled from the front pockets of his apron, folded down and tied around his belly, were handed out in multiples with a spirited smile, as if they were a salesman's business cards.

Jack joined his brother at the corner of the bar. After a long couple of minutes, the bartender made his way to them.

"I'm sorry cowboys," he said with a wry smile. "Only thing I've got for you is a Coke and those's mixed with Seagram's."

"We're looking for—" Lester's voice croaked and caught in his throat. He coughed quietly before going on. "We're looking for Harold," he said with feigned confidence. "Harold Burke."

The bartender sized the brothers up, one of them fidgeting worse than the local boys that would come in and order a beer a dozen years before they could, and the other barely tall enough to meet his gaze over the bar.

"You're looking for Harry?" he asked. "Harry Burke?"

Lester stared wide-eyed for a moment then nodded.

The bartender took a rag from the drawstring of his apron and absently wiped the bar between them. He slung the rag over his shoulder and raised a finger to the boys before walking to the other end of the bar.

At the far side of the bar, where it turned the opposite corner, a handful of men were in the thick of a weighty conversation. The bartender stopped in front of the group and leaned his palms against the counter. The men adjourned their discussion and the bartender spoke to one of them in a sedated tone. His voice was enveloped and overtaken by the sounds of the barroom and, no matter how much they strained, the brothers were unable to decipher anything he was saying. The bartender nodded, then shook his head, then shrugged. After the man at the bar said something, the bartender turned and pointed the same finger back toward Lester and Jack. The man nodded, upturned his glass and drained it. Then he stood and walked slowly toward the Copeland boys.

When he reemerged from the throng of men crowded around the bar, he stood directly in front of them. He was tall and thin, with only a small pouch of a belly. He wore boots that were polished and shined as slick as the bar. His denim jeans were stained to such a deep indigo they looked purple in the low lighting. He wore a chestnut brown campaign hat that had four large, perfectly spaced ovals pressed into the crown. The hair underneath was as dark as the Western night sky. If not for the serape poncho he wore folded and draped over his right shoulder, his thick and precisely manicured mustache would be the first thing anyone would be likely to notice.

He removed his hat and revealed a full head of hair which had been greased straight back with a dollop of Royal Crown. Holding the hat loosely in his left hand, he extended his right.

"Howdy boys," he said chirpily, his tinny voice cut through the noise around them. He shook Lester's hand, then Jack's. His grip was strong but not as calloused as the brothers'. "How're you doing, Lester?"

Without warning, Lester let loose a torrent of information. His hesitancy gave way once the man stood in front of them and asked about them. Lester had hoped so intently, for so many days, for their father to wonder about them. So when the man in front of them asked, Lester had little hope to contain himself.

Lester told him about setting off from their Hayes County home, joining Highway 6, and riding toward the Colorado border. He mentioned the Indian boy they'd met, and the solstice celebration they watched from afar. He spoke about their time passing through Sterling, Greeley, and Loveland, painting him pictures of Mister Eli and his ancient mother. Jack cut in to tell the man about his singing and how he was just beginning to master the harmonica when it disappeared. Lester shushed Jack and went into a dramatic retelling of finding the dead man by the river, backtracking to explain who Willie was, then hinting at the existence, and their certain sighting, of a Double Face. Jack spoke up again when Lester took a second to catch his breath, sharing with him his favorite scene from Son of Frankenstein, and that they'd seen a bearded lady at the other night's minstrel. Then the brothers, in duet, spoke about Howard's Haberdashery and their new outfits before Lester mapped out their trail that day from John's to the Armstrong to the bar they stood in then, face-to-face with the man who, at long last, came forward when they called their father's name.

The man rubbed his cheeks and plopped his hat on the back of his head in disbelief of the boys' story. He remained silent for a heavy minute, digesting everything the brothers had just shared. Finally, he smiled and slowly nodded. In that moment, Lester realized he had never felt his chest grow warm and full with the pride of a father's respect.

"We knew you'd be here somewhere, Pa!" Lester beamed. "Either here or Cheyenne!" The folds at the corners of his eyes were growing damp.

The man continued nodding and removed his hat again. Then sighed, "I'm sorry son," he said. His face sank with the weight of sorrow. "I'm so sorry."

Jack looked down at his boots and stared at them, willing away the tears stinging his eyes. Lester began reaching for the man's arm. He wasn't entirely sure why. It had never occurred to him previously that sons hugged their fathers.

"Your father," the man said, "he — he just left."

Lester's arm dropped and thumped against his leg. His vision narrowed and he felt as uneasy on his feet as the men slumped over at the bar.

"Left a few hours ago," the man said. "Headed to Cheyenne for the rodeo."

Jack looked to Lester but Lester's face was blank. Exhausted.

"I'm sure you'll be able to find him there," the man went on. "But if you don't, travel safe back home." Then, after a long moment, he added, "Tell your mother I asked about her."

Then, Lester came back to himself. He met the man's gaze. "She's dead," he said and turned his back on the man. Lester walked out of the tavern without looking back, doing his best to leave the man, and his renouncement, in his wake.

Jack followed him, trotting behind his brother's long strides. Lester was stomping each step into the sidewalk and Jack knew better than to say anything. After a few blocks, Lester's strides slowed and shortened and his breathing calmed. Jack could finally walk beside him and when he did, he saw angry tears streaking Lester's cheeks. He grabbed his elbow just as he had in the hallway of the Armstrong. He held it tightly while Lester wrestled, trying to break free.

"Stop, Les," Jack pleaded. "Just stop for a second."

Lester stilled and dropped his eyes to the sidewalk, dropping splatters onto the concrete like a lazy rain shower.

"We'll find him," Jack said. "Made it this far, just the two of us. One more city ain't a big deal."

Lester was silent.

"We've got to win the jackpot soon. Can't have a streak of bad luck forever, right?"

Still, Lester gave no hint he'd heard.

"What do you reckon are the chances of that, Les?" Jack tried again. "Can you believe we missed our Pa by a couple hours?"

Eventually, Lester spoke. His voice was hushed, extinguished by heartbreak. "I'm not so sure we did."

Chapter 44

They retraced most of their steps from earlier in the day. Soon, they were standing at the boundary of the park they'd slept in the previous night. Lester's mind had been so overtaken by the day, until he saw the tree they'd slept under, that he had forgotten about the letter he'd received from Hayes County. He had felt, in the blocks between the bar and the park, that his chest could not grow emptier. Yet, inexplicably, when he was reminded of the letter, he felt it boil over like a pot of milk before sloshing and spilling over the burning contents. Staring at the tree where that day had begun, it was hard for him to imagine why he'd ever thought things would turn out any better than they did. The first step was the most important, and there were still miles to go. But how many of those steps had led to the hopeless desolation they were wrapped in?

"How much daylight do you reckon we've got left?" Jack asked. His optimism hadn't faltered — yet. He understood Lester was taking the last hours' revelations harder than he was but didn't bother to wrap his head around why. At that moment, he felt it was his responsibility to take charge. It was a role he, as the younger brother, hadn't had much practice in but, like a mother's breasts miraculously fill with milk, a boy's mind can grow clear and mature in the solemn moments such as those.

It was not at all unlike the blooming Lester had undergone, albeit in spades, when their mother had passed.

For most boys, that passage the mind and body traverse into manhood is much like when the evening rolls in on a carefree, adolescent day. The changes are easy enough to see and just as easily ignored; colors and clouds change just as sleeves and hems grow short. It happens at an unhurried pace; no amount of cussing the sun will change its direction just as limbs will stretch and hair will sprout. Until suddenly, in seemingly a blink, less than the time it takes to wipe sweat from a brow, the sun has set and the sky is purple and the things that had been sustaining are no longer of use. In the many days between the jarring sunsets, there are countless moments where the clouds cross over the sun and provide a stretch of shaded darkness. They seem inconsequential but are added to the pile of collected experiences and mettle that mold and paint each man.

"Go get our old clothes from Mister Howard," Lester ordered. His eyes were swollen and irritated. "I'm going to get our horses from the stable. I'll meet you back here and we'll set off."

Jack looked to the late evening sky. "Set off?" he scoffed. "What do you mean set off? We had an hour of daylight a half hour ago!"

Lester glared at his brother. "Did I say we'd make Cheyenne tonight?" he snapped. "I know how much sunlight we got so just do what I told you!" It had been a long, onerous day and their limbs had grown leaden and their minds refused to accept new thoughts. The boys had gotten along well enough during their lengthy journey to where they stood, but when their excitement was stripped away their weariness was laid bare.

Jack did as he was told and walked to Howard's Haberdashery. Howard beamed when he saw Jack enter. "Back already?" he called.

Jack nodded. "Our Pa's in Cheyenne," he said. "Missed him here by a couple hours!"

Howard gave a halfhearted smile, then bent and collected the boys' filthy clothes from behind the counter. "Don't believe I'd recognize you boys if you changed back into these dingy old duds," he said, raising one scruffy eyebrow.

Jack laughed and bundled the clothes in his arms. "Gotta go but thanks for everything, Mister Howard!" he called as he went through the door. Howard followed him, shuffling on his stubby legs, and watched Jack walk away into the dying sunlight. He prayed silently, a quick prayer that those young brothers would find an oasis somewhere in their desolation.

Jack made his way back to the tree and threw the pile of clothes by the trunk, then sat underneath the meaningless shade. He removed his hat, leaned the back of his head on the rutted bark, and closed his eyes.

Lester kicked the bottom of Jack's boot sole. He'd fallen asleep under the tree until only a dull shard of moonlight gleamed off the city. Lester held the reins of their horses who'd already been saddled. Larry, the old crotchety stableman, had attempted to squeeze Lester for every cent he could in various shifty ways. He argued with the stableman until his scant patience dissipated. He took a small stack of bills and shoved them onto the man's chest without a word, then turned and walked to the stables where he collected their saddles and horses. On the way to the park he found a grocer, tied the horses to a post outside, and quickly collected two saddlebags worth of canned goods. It was the same sundries they had long grown tired of.

Jack stood and grabbed his reins from Lester and followed him as they set off, out of Fort Collins. The city glittered and flared the colorless moonlight and the vibrant neon signs as they moved through it. Fort Collins, like all the other towns they'd passed through, had offered them kindness they couldn't quite return. But it had also damned them with the curse of meeting a man who shared their deep set brown eyes and seemed to know them, but was outwardly apathetic to not only their situation but to their existence.

They found a small grouping of trees a few miles outside the city limits where they made camp just as they had over many nights on the open and lightless prairies. Lester was silent for the entire ride, keeping his head down and his hat pulled low. Jack, however, offered his opinion on the situation at intervals while they walked away from the vivid city lights.

"Damn sure couldn't have been our Pa," he said once, "by the looks of his mustache compared to your measly thing!"

They unsaddled their horses and Lester worked to build a small fire. He reached into the saddlebags and took out two cans of peas and tossed one to Jack. Lester grunted a goodnight across camp as they worked to open their dinners. They were both sleeping fitfully before either of them had taken off their boots or finished their peas.

At some point in the night, with the moon flickering between low clouds, the wind whining and shuffling down the mountains and through the plains, the muted lights glowing from the nearby city, the boys continued snoring, ignorant to the shuffling footfalls drawing closer to them. The footsteps came closer to the dying campfire like moths, hushed but frantic. They stopped short of the light cast off by the fire before slinking forward again.

Abruptly, strong hands gripped both sleeping brothers by the collar and held them tightly, shoving them into the Colorado dirt.

"Howdy fellas," the voice growled, its breath sour from liquor and bitter from smoke. "Fancy seeing you two again."

Chapter 45

The boys gasped and thrashed awake. Their boot heels kicked and grappled the dusty ground looking for purchase. Lester grasped at the hands that had a hold of his starched collar. Jack dug his nails into the hands cinched around his neck. It wasn't the hands' goal to strangle him, rather to signal his control over the boys and their situation. Lester called to Jack, howling into the night, but Jack's voice was muffled by the hands and his panicked, haggard breathing.

"What do you want?" Lester screamed at the men. "We didn't do nothing!"

The man that was holding Jack laughed. "Naw," he said gruffly. "Naw, I don't believe that's true. Everybody's done something." The man slowly got to his feet, using his hands on Jack's throat to help him up. "Listen here, boy," the man said. "My pal here's gonna let go of you. But," he spat into the dirt, "if you move any more than a breath, I'll blow your brains halfway back to Nebraska. Got that?"

Lester struggled to speak but the man took his hysterical nodding to mean he understood. The man signaled to the other to let go of Lester. All the while, Jack was stammering, unable to form noises into words. Lester looked up at the men standing over them, their features glowing a mean orange from the burnt saplings and coals of their fire. The man that had held Lester was a face in the crowd, one he'd never seen before. The other man standing over Jack but glaring at Lester. He was in a battered wide-brimmed hat, a white pearl snap shirt that was bulging slightly at the buttons, patchwork pants, and a pair of roughneck boots.

"Willie," Lester gasped.

Willie tipped his flaccid hat brim and laughed. "I hoped you'd recognize me!" he grinned. The other man quietly sat on Jack's saddle. "See," Willie started, "I couldn't find a lick of work fit for any more than a slave so I bummed a ride to Fort Collins. Turns out, they ain't got much sense of humor around here. So we were just about to head south to Loveland or north to Cheyenne when we walk by this bar and figure we might's well spend our last couple bucks. And wouldn't you know it? In walks these goddamn slicked up cowboys that'd given me a hard time damn near through this state!" He scoffed then spit into the fire. "So then I get this plan stuck in my craw and I can't shake it, so we decided to follow you boys out here. Ain't too hard to find you, lighting a fire with saplings that smokes to the goddamn moon."

Willie walked backward to Lester's saddle, keeping his eyes on the boys, and removed a revolver from the back of his jeans before he sat. He worked the steel of the barrel over his fingers. He balanced it on his knee, then reached into his pocket and took out a tobacco pouch and rolling papers. He began talking again, rolling a cigarette with the same practiced fluidity the boys had seen before. "Anyway," he said, licking the edge of the paper and laying it flat then lighting the end on a smoking coal, "I rifled through your saddlebags more than a couple times so I suppose it'll be easier for all of us if I just leave here with what I want."

Lester's eyes bulged.

"Don't worry," Willie said. "I'm sure you daddy'll understand why you couldn't find him. You know, he probably never wanted you two brats to find him anyway," he said with a shrug. He took a long drag on his thin cigarette.

"Willie," Lester panted. "Please, Willie. Just leave my saddle. It's my Ma's."

Willie exhaled a blue cloud of smoke and guffawed, looking at his partner. "How'd you expect me to ride a horse without a saddle? We ain't riding double like you made me!"

"But," Jack stuttered, "you can't take our horses!"

Willie stubbed out the cigarette on his boot heel. "Oh, but son we can and we're about to."

Lester struggled to sit up. Willie grabbed the gun from his knee, cocked it, and leveled it on Lester's chest. "I said no moving!" he shouted.

Lester put his palms up in surrender. "Just sitting up," he said. "Listen, you can steal our horses, take our stuff, but leave the bible. Please. It's in my —"

"I know where it is!" Willie snapped.

Lester took a deep breath. "Our Ma left it for us before she died. Please don't take it."

Willie turned and opened the saddlebag, removing the worn bible. He flipped through a few pages until it fell open to the bookmarked page, the purple ribbon fluttering in the wind. "The mountains and hills shall break before you into song," Willie read, "and all the trees of the field shall clap their hands." He looked at the brothers, noticed the hot tears running down both of their cheeks. He held a finger up and shushed them, cupped a hand behind an ear, then shook his head. "Sure don't sound like the trees are doing much clapping for you two," he sneered.

"Willie," Jack muttered, "you taught us all those verses on our ride out here. You wouldn't really steal our bible from us, would you?"

Willie faced him. "Let his children be vagabonds and let them beg. Let them seek their bread out of desolate places."

"I've had it with your goddamn preaching," Lester spat. "We never did a goddamn thing wrong. All we did was help you. You're the goddamn vagabond. So go on and take our things and leave us here to rot. You can ride our horses all the way to Hell!"

Willie smirked at Lester then looked at the bible, open in his lap. He grabbed the marked page and ripped it from its binding, holding the tatter in his cruddy hand. He crumpled it and threw it at Lester, but it hit the ground and a breeze caught it and rolled it toward Jack. He slowly reached for the page and hid it in his closed palm before the wind could carry it back eastward in the direction it had come.

Willie slammed the bible closed and threw it back into the saddlebag. Turning to the boys he said, "What do you think of this shirt, boy?" He sneered at Lester, tugging on the seams of the white shirt. "A bit short in the arms but I reckon it's the nicest shirt I've worn in a while. Never did get to thank you!"

Lester glared at him.

"That reminds me," Willie reached into his pocket again and pulled out a shiny harmonica, the metal plates glinting off the dying fire. He cupped it in his hands and brought it to his mouth, letting loose a few whining notes. Jack stared at him with more fury than he'd ever felt in his life.

"Those are our things!" Jack shouted. "That's my harmonica!"

Willie chuckled and shook his head. "If you were raising the dead with this thing like you used to, it wouldn't have been no fun at all hunting you boys. Good thing I pocketed it before I left, ain't it?"

Jack shuffled forward onto his hands and knees, slapping the dirt, crawling in a rage toward Willie and his silent partner. Willie took the gun and blew a soup bowl sized hole into the tree behind Jack, no more than a yard above his head. Jack scrambled to his backside and retreated until his back was pushing hard against the trunk. He stammered and howled for a minute before Willie grew tired of the noise and shushed him with a threatening wave of the pistol.

Willie stood and began packing the brothers' things into their saddlebags. He paid little care to the contents, adding a haphazard layer on top of Lester's meticulously packed items. He found their old outfits and considered them, then looked to the boys and mock admired their new clothes. He looked at the two old hats, one nestled inside the other, on top of the clothing. Willie removed his beaten hat, then took the one on top and jammed it on his head, but the sweatband wouldn't budge and he could hardly cover his messy mop of hair. He threw it to his partner, who attempted the same with similar results. Then Willie took the other hat and forced it onto his head. It fit, but it was undeniably too small. The band cinched the skin of his forehead and pulled his eyebrows up into a constant look of disappointed surprise. He turned his head and regarded the new hat on Lester's head.

"What size are you?" he grunted to Lester.

Lester spit into the dirt.

"I said," Willie sneered, "what size hat do you wear?"

Lester sucked on his cheek. "I don't know," he said quietly.

Willie huffed. "Probably too small," he shook his head then looked to his partner. "You want it?"

His partner shook his head disappointedly.

Willie and his partner then worked to saddle the horses and pet them into an undecided calm. When they were done, they appraised their handiwork with smiles and hearty laughs as if they'd pulled off their enterprising plan. They hoisted themselves into the saddles, their mother and father's saddles. Willie spun on horseback to face them. He brandished the gun again. "If it crosses your mind to tattle, just remember no one'd ever believe two dirty brats like you could afford these saddles. But if I hear any whisper that either of you two said a word about this, I'll ride this poor excuse of a horse to Hayes County and find you. Understood?" Lester and Jack remained silent, glaring at the men, that harebrained band of thieves.

The brothers sat under the tree, being washed over by breezes of early morning heat but drowned and adrift in hopelessness. Just as the sky was beginning to turn oceanic shades of violet along the horizon, the boys watched them ride off, carrying with them nearly everything the brothers owned. And with it, the last thin and tattered strands of hope they had been clutching.

Chapter 46

Jack's breathing was erratic and short, like he was sucking half lungfuls of air and sputtering them out. He shook and jumped so badly he looked like an engine sorely in need of oil. His face was red and slick with a combination of sweat and tears, spittle and mucus. His eyes were draining uncontrollably, drool was seeping and foaming from the corners of his mouth, and his nose was expelling more liquid than he'd drank in nearly a day. If Lester hadn't witnessed the descent of Jack's sanity over the past several minutes as the sun rose, he might have assumed he was having a seizure. It was unlike the kicking and panting and rousing fits Jack had when he was younger. Foremost of the differences was that he was not faking this one.

The only reason Lester's face was dry was because he had saddled himself back into the role of being the big brother. He was hoping to let Jack tire himself out before he tried to assuage him into standing and taking the first step, which always appears to be a chasm in need of jumping after tribulations. When he realized Jack had no plans of stopping, Lester went to him. He took a deep breath, closed his eyes and stood. Then, before his mind could talk him out of it, he placed one new boot in front of the other and began walking. He knelt next to Jack, careful of his unruly limbs. Lester reached out and held the back of Jack's arm, just above the elbow, just as Jack had the day before when he guided Lester through his own dust storm clouds of despair. Jack struggled to free himself

"Hey," Lester whispered. "Jack, listen. Take a deep breath and listen."

Jack's breathing was still ragged and rattling but there was a hint of calm. A hitch in Jack's chest had worked itself free, then another. Lester continued speaking softly to his brother until Jack was taking deep, though still rattling, breaths.

"Good, Jack. Keep breathing. It'll be alright, buddy." Lester placed a hand between his brother's shoulder blades and patted gently. Their mother used to do the same with them when their childhood emotions seemed a pool too deep to wade. "I got a plan, Jack. It's not worth all this. It's all just stuff, remember? You told me that, remember?"

Jack shook his head slowly.

"Now you can't blame me for stealing your mouth harp anymore, huh?"

Jack took a deep breath. "It's my fault," he said hoarsely. "All of it. It's all my fault."

Lester stilled the hand on Jack's back and grabbed his shoulder, turning Jack to face him. "Quit it, Jack. Quit saying that!"

Jack refused eye contact. "It is. It was my idea to help him," he said. His face puckered when he said *him* like it had burned his mouth when it passed through. "You said he was no good and I didn't listen. I was just being stubborn, Les!" New tears, fat and heavy, worked loose from his eyes and dropped onto his cheeks. "I didn't even care that much about helping him. Just wanted to because you said no." He looked around their camp, a scattered fire and their horses' hoof prints. "And now look what happened. All because of me!"

Lester grabbed his brother's shoulders and pulled him in, wrapping himself around Jack like a sherpa coat. He clasped his hands and cinched his arms as tightly as he could, pulling Jack closer until nothing, no sentiment or sensation, could belong to one without passing through the other. "I got a plan, Jack. Let me tell you. Do you want to hear it?" Lester asked.

Jack nodded and Lester loosened his arms slowly until they stood, silently, face-to-face.

Lester sat first, cross-legged on the ground, then reached out and beckoned Jack to join him.

"Here's the plan," Lester said. "I got some money left in my boot and there's a train station here that'd probably take us pretty near to home. From there we can walk or hitch til we're back on the ranch and we'll act like this's all been a dream."

Jack was quiet, staring at the dirt in front of him.

Lester spit into his palm and held his hand out to Jack. A peace offering.

Jack didn't look up. After a minute, he shook his head. "I want to go to Cheyenne," he said flatly.

Lester dropped his hand, wiping it on the leg of his jeans. "Jack. Cheyenne hasn't got anything for us."

"Maybe it does," Jack pinched some dirt between his fingers. "Maybe it's got what we came here for."

Lester sighed. "Then what if that man we met really was our Pa?"

"What if he wasn't?"

Lester chewed his lip. "What if we got all our things stolen and walked a hundred miles to Cheyenne just to find out it was?"

"Same reason we rode all the way out here on horseback when you knew there was a train." Jack looked up and gazed at Lester. "Maybe this whole time it wasn't Pa we were after."

Lester stood and pulled his hat down low. "We keep on getting on, right?"

Jack nodded with tight lips. "Keep on getting on."

By noon, the brothers had decided they would walk back into Fort Collins and begin asking for a ride, hoping to find someone heading north on Highway 87, maybe even all the way to Cheyenne. It was only fifty miles away but, on that day, it felt to the boys that an ocean had sprung up between them and their destination.

They asked nearly a dozen people who all had various reasons why they would be unable to help. Some weren't headed north, some were suspicious of the boys, and others apologized sincerely and wished them the best of luck. But when Jack saw a couple leisurely getting into a crimson Ford DeLuxe, he went to them, sure they would be happy to give the boys a ride. As luck would have it, the couple was just heading north to Cheyenne.

"What are the chances of this?" the man said cheerfully. "Hop in the back! We'll get y'all there in no time!"

So the boys climbed into the backseat of the Ford. The bench seat was so soft and padded, Jack could jab a finger into the fabric and the dimple would take half a minute to flatten.

The man passed his hat back to Lester. "Hats off boys, there's a lady present," he said coyly.

His wife guffawed from the passenger seat. "Don't listen to him boys," she said with a bright smile. "He eats with his elbows on the table."

The man turned the engine over and pulled into the streets. By the time the brothers were settled into the plush seats, they were riding up Highway 87 and traveling faster than they had in many days.

Chapter 47

The car galloped along the macadam, rocketing north toward Cheyenne. The mountains filled most of the driver's side windows as they left Fort Collins. It had bloomed into a perfectly clear day. The only clouds were wisps of smoke hanging high and isolated like lost cattle in the azure pastures of the sky. Lester, sitting behind the man driving, balanced his chin on his fist and watched the mountains pass by. It was hard to comprehend how slowly they were shrinking back into the horizon until Lester would turn to check on Jack and, turning back a few seconds later, realize the white-capped peaks had distanced themselves once again. He felt a pang of sadness that the mountains would soon melt the insipid horizons he'd always known.

Jack placed his forehead against the cool glass window on his side of the bench seat. His vantage looked more similar to Hayes County than the Colorado foothills. The prairie stretched in lazy hills, as if the mountains had been laundered and ironed like a wrinkled bedsheet and the crags and peaks were now nothing more than a ripple. Fenceposts marked their passage every handful of yards, leaving marks of men's claim of lands that belong to no one.

The couple in the front seats chatted for a few miles, checking tasks off mental to-do lists, and scribbling more at the bottom. When their conversation waned to a sputter, the man reached forward and turned on the radio, adjusting the dials until a tinny voice spoke to them. When the dramatic storytelling of gun toting outlaws ended on a cliff hanger, with the conclusion promised tomorrow, a different voice announced the beginning of local and national reporting.

First on the docket, the cattle prices were still down but no lower than had become expected during those hard years. More heat was promised for the rest of the summer, according to the farmer's almanacs. A hearty promise that Oxydol will remove any and all stains from any and all fabrics came next. Then the voice on the radio began detailing events from places that sounded so bizarre to the brothers that they thought it might be the beginning of a new program. He reminded listeners of their duty to support the effort any way they can, then added a short quote from the president himself.

When the radio began its recount of the foreign places, the woman in the front seat turned her head to blankly watch the plains roll by. The man glanced at her, then turned the volume down until the buzzing receiver clicked off. They rode in silence for a while before the man peered into the rearview mirror at the boys.

"Excited for the rodeo?" he asked.

Jack's forehead chattered on the window. The droning of the wheels and the agreeable seats had lulled him to sleep. The gentle thumping of the road and the hissing of the radio static had almost calmed Lester to sleep when the man spoke.

"Huh?" Lester grunted sleepily.

"The rodeo," the man said. "I assumed that's why you two were headed this way with those fancy shirts."

"Oh," Lester thought for a second. "Yeah. Yeah, we're hoping to see the rodeo. And to look around."

"Well, I wouldn't say there's all that much to see in Cheyenne except the rodeo."

Lester nodded. He didn't feel the need to volunteer information about their father. He'd struggled to say the words along their trip but now he refused on principle. In his mind, they'd found their father already and he'd spurned them. Somewhere hidden in the back of his thoughts, however, was the kernel of hope that the man they'd met had not been their Pa. And maybe they really had missed him by a few hours. He did his best to keep that thought behind a closed door, refusing to peek at it in fear it would grow and catch hold like a vine and devour his more rational thoughts.

The man looked at his wife again. "Guess the competition this year won't be as tough as usual," he sighed. "You know, with all those boys shipped off."

Lester turned his attention back to the mountains, which were now so distant they looked grainy and faded, like a weathered photograph.

"Shipped off?" a groggy voice asked. Jack was squinting toward the front seat, a dull red mark on his forehead. "Shipped off where?"

"Overseas," the man smiled patiently, looking at Jack in the mirror. "Sent to fight in the war."

Jack furrowed his brows. "War?" he asked incredulously. "I thought people were just broke all of a sudden."

"Well," the man sighed, "I guess that's true too. Then add a war on top of it. Seems no one can catch a break these days."

Jack was quiet for a mile or two. "Who are we sore at?" he asked abruptly.

The man laughed. "Anyone who's not on our side, I guess. The Japs, the Germans, the Ita—"

"What'd the Japs do?" Jack cut him off.

The man turned almost completely around to look at the brothers. "Where are you boys from?" he asked, turning back but keeping a close eye on them in the mirror.

"Hayes County, Nebraska," Jack said matter of factly. "Came a damn— a real long ways."

"All that way just for Frontier Days?"

Jack looked to Lester, hoping he would answer for both of them. He wasn't sure if Lester had been listening so he reached over and smacked his arm.

Lester looked at Jack, unamused. "We were looking for someone in Fort Collins," Lester said vaguely. "And he wanted to see the rodeo before we headed back home."

"Yeah," Jack nodded. "But what'd the Japs do?"

"They bombed Pearl Harbor, son," the man said simply.

Jack shrugged. "What about the Germans then?"

"Lots," the man scoffed.

Just then, the woman in the front seat began sniffling, raising a gentle hand to brush at her eyes. The car grew silent for a few miles until they started passing signs promising the mystique of the cowboy mecca of Cheyenne.

"We have a son," the man said softly. "A few years older than you two, maybe. He's overseas."

Lester looked away from the window and studied the couple in the front seats. He stayed silent, but his face softened, and his eyes dropped with sympathy.

"Haven't heard from him in a while," he sighed. "The rodeo used to be his favorite. We'd drive up here all weekend during Frontier Days and he'd talk about it every other week of the year." He looked across the seat to his wife, who was still silently drying her cheeks. "We figured we might still go so we can tell him about if he— when he comes home."

The car grew humid and heavy then. The man cracked open his window and the breeze worked its way around the car, blowing the oppressive thoughts back out into the crystal clear day.

A few more miles down the road they passed Fort Warren, which was buzzing with training and supply flights. Planes whizzed overhead the flat, barren landscape in all directions. Jack was enamored by their glimmering wings and their tight banking turns. As he watched the planes crisscrossing the sky, they passed a sign along the highway.

WELCOME TO CHEYENNE
THE MAGIC CITY OF THE PLAINS

Chapter 48

The man pulled his Ford DeLuxe onto the gravel that ran along the roadside. In front of them was a string of parked cars stretching to, then past, the rodeo grounds. The man helped his wife from the car as the boys climbed from the back. They stretched and adjusted their stiff new jeans by the belt loops, inspecting the way they laid over their boots, then put their hats on and pulled them low. The brothers followed the couple along with a small throng of people which made their way to the gates. In the distance, the tip of the Union Pacific train station clocktower jutted like an obelisk from the featureless landscape. A low, long train whistle screamed out over the plains, blowing like a haunted harmonica. The wind bellowed its own song and carried the throng forward.

"Can hardly believe we're here already!" Jack called over the wind, twirling his head to make sure he saw their monotone surroundings from all angles. "Hardly even worked up an appetite getting here!"

Lester ignored him. But the man who had driven them turned around. "Where did you boys say you were from?"

"Nebraska," Jack said. "Hayes County."

The man raised his eyebrows. "How far's that, would you say?"

Jack shrugged and looked at Lester. "Don't know. Whatcha say,

Les? Week or two?"

"Week or two!" the man sputtered. "Two weeks? Jesus Chr—" he coughed and looked at his wife. "Did you boys walk here?"

Jack shook his head innocently. "No sir. Came on horseback."

The man took his hat off and slapped it against his thigh and howled in duet with the whipping wind. "You boys should've told me you were competing! Jeepers, our boy's going to pop when we tell him we picked up some rodeo cowboys on their way to Cheyenne!"

Lester shook his head. "We're not competing, sir."

The man stopped walking and faced the boys. He popped his hat back onto his head, askew and forward. "Then what're you doing traveling all this way?" he asked, his brows knit so far they were nearly folded over his eyes. "And where's your horses?"

Jack's mouth hung slack, unable to grasp a response. His eyes scrambled to Lester who appeared calm. He'd almost told the men about Willie and his partner before remembering their threat.

"Pawned our horses," Lester said coolly. "Things didn't go like we planned when we got out here, so we pawned them and we're using the money for train tickets home. Leaving Cheyenne on a train the day after tomorrow." Lester's face gave no indication he was lying; his eyes maintained the tepid gaze of simple facts.

Jack, however, had grown red. He was astonished with the skill and ease his brother had created and presented the lie. For a fleeting moment, Jack wondered how many times Lester had used the same skills to sneak a fiction past Jack's ears as unnoticed as wind under a drafty door.

Lester had silently impressed himself as well though. He hadn't known he could pull such convincing falsities from the summer air until his story emerged from his lips. Perhaps it was one of the only talents his father's genetics had gifted him.

The man nodded, suddenly assuaged by Lester's anecdote. "Suppose something in Fort Collins caught your fancies enough to make that trip," he said, baiting and casting a line for more answers, driven by his own curiosity.

Jack didn't need Lester's help answering and this time the truth would suffice. "We came here looking for our Pa," he said confidently. He was surprised to see the couple's heads droop like they'd heard something shameful.

"I see," the woman said quietly, her face still scarlet from the ride.

"And it didn't turn out like you wanted?" the man asked, his head still held low like a wilted flower.

"Well," Jack said, "not yet. But we think he might be here!"

"In Cheyenne?"

Jack nodded excitedly.

"Is he a rodeo cowboy?"

"He's a cowboy but," Jack shrugged, "I don't know why he's here. Someone in Fort Collins said he was. Said we just missed him!"

The man hummed, nodding. "Then no sense standing around any longer than we already have," he said, then turned and set off, grabbing his wife's hand along the way. The brothers followed them, walking in their shadows until the massive red sign came into view. It welcomed them to the Cheyenne Frontier Days.

When they reached the front gate, the woman turned and knelt in front of the boys. "Stay safe, young men. I'll pray you find your way home safely," she said quietly, her eyes set and serious. She reached a closed hand toward Jack who, by childish and innocent impulse, cupped a hand under hers. The woman dropped a five dollar bill, folded as tight and neat as origami, into the palm of his hand. She brought her head close to the boys and spoke quietly but sternly. "You wouldn't have pawned a couple horses in a town you're leaving on a train," she said soberly. Lester's cheeks flamed and he looked to his boots. "So, this money is for both of you," the woman went on. "I suppose you've cut off more than you can chew here. I'm not sure what your story is but I hope to hear it in full someday and I pray it has a pleasant ending." With that, she patted Lester's shoulder and ran the pad of her thumb against Jack's sunburnt cheek like mothers do. "So long boys," she said. "Be well."

By then, her husband was standing over them, excitedly checking over his shoulder toward the grandstand every time the crowd would grow loud with applause or jeers. When his wife stood he reached a hand toward Lester. "Wish you boys nothing but the best of luck on your travels home," he said with a wide smile, shaking Lester's hand. Then he grabbed Jack's hand, dwarfed in his grasp, and pumped it eagerly. "You're good young men and you deserve good things." He tipped his hat and turned back to the gates, collecting his wife's hand and disappearing into the herd of exuberant cowboys.

Lester and Jack found a spot along the fence between the grandstand and the judges' stand. They squeezed into a spot just big enough for two teenage boys and stayed there, captivated by what they were watching. They leaned their forearms against the rough slats of the fence, occasionally wiping the kicked up dust from their eyes, clapping and whistling every time a cowboy bested a beast.

The boys hooted and hollered loudest during the bareback rodeo. The massive horses would curl, then blast their hind end back so their back hooves were pointed skyward and their front legs were nearly four feet from the dirt. The cowboys would clench their hands, strain their arms, whip their shoulders and heads, flailing like a banner flown during a storm. They would somehow, if all went well, stay firmly on the horse's back and their hats would sit just as squarely on their heads as before, as if they'd been secured with hide glue.

Jack was nearly shaking from the hours of ceaseless excitement when they began the horse breaking competition. The young cowboys were teamed and tasked with chasing one of the penned wild horses, roping and saddling it. As the brothers watched, they began to wish they would have paid the entrance fee.

"Wonder how much the winner gets," Lester wondered aloud.

"I'm already up five bucks," Jack said with a taunting smile.

"Yeah, well you owe me a dollar from that damn show, and you paid thirty cents for us to get in here so I would check your math."

Jack went silent. He was gnawing on the inside of his lip, concentrating hard, trying to subtract sixty cents from four dollars while distracted with the braying and kicking of the wild horses.

"Three dollars and forty cents, Jack," Lester said after a few minutes, keeping his eyes on the action.

"Yeah," Jack huffed. "Yeah I know it, you dunce."

Lester's face lit into a smile and the brothers broke into the loudest, rowdiest round of laughter they'd had in many days. It worked loose the kinks in their legs and backs, the knots in their minds. They felt the easy tingle of unworried happiness ripple through their tired bodies. The cowboys around them looked them over and gave approving nods. There was, perhaps, no better place for the boys to be just that.

After their laughter faded, they watched the end of the horse breaking competition with the first sense of tranquility they'd had since even before their belongings were taken from them. They may not have had more than the clothes on their back and a couple spare dollars in their boots, but they had each other. And brotherhood, as with all blessings, cannot be stored away in a saddlebag.

Chapter 49

The crystal Cheyenne sky refracted and focused the late July heat onto the spectators, like bugs under a massive, glaring magnifying glass. The brothers' spot next to the raised judges' stand provided shade but also blocked any cool breezes that may have purled across the red dirt arena. Sweat streamed tracks down their backs, dampening their shirts where they were neatly tucked into their jeans. Drops snuck between their foreheads and sweatbands at their temples and collected in their sideburns and the corners of their unkempt hair. Lester unbuttoned the pearl snaps on his cuff and rolled his sleeves up but the relief was trivial.

The excitement of the competition distracted them from the heat for most of the day, but when the steer roping began, Lester became suddenly unimpressed. As the small steer shot in a straight line from the chutes, a cowboy on horseback would give chase, a loose lasso circling high above his head. They would cut the angle toward the steer and shoot the lasso loop from their hands like a net gun until it caught the steer around the horns. A quick pull on the rope, like a fisherman setting a hook, signaled the horse to stop short. The steer would quickly run out of line and flip like he'd stepped on a greased floor. The cowboy, who had already deftly dismounted, would then tie the steer's legs in a bastardized hogtie. They would raise their arms to signal the judges they were finished, then swagger back to his horse like he'd just bagged Rita Hayworth rather than a trained steer.

The brothers watched a few rounds before Lester lost interest.

"Wonder how they'd fare doing that with our steer," Lester rolled his eyes. His days on their ranch included a long list of things, which he worked diligently to complete with whatever brawn and skill he could muster. Lassoing and collecting ornery steer and cattle was one task which was done so frequently it hardly existed in his daily memories.

Jack nodded heartily, although he had never so much as tied his own lasso. He'd thought the cowboys were doing tricks akin to blindfolded hip shots and handstand riding. But after a half dozen more cowboys gave their best attempts, a yawn snuck out of him.

"Yeah," Lester yawned in reply. "I'm tired too. Let's head out."

"Head out where? I'm having a hell of a time!"

"I'm dog tired, Jack. I hardly slept a wink last night," Lester said. Jack noticed then the deep indigo bags under his brother's eyes.

The boys were both silent for a stretch. The luxurious car ride and the rapture of the rodeo had briefly wiped their memories of last night.

Finally, Jack nodded solemnly and followed his brother out of the crowd. They followed the tip of the train station clock tower like a beacon for a mile or two until they stood in its shadow and felt the freight trains shivering the ground under their feet. They traced the scarring black streak of the railroad line to the east until it dropped off the horizon, then turned and looked westward, squinting into the late afternoon sun. They were standing at a crossroads where the steel rails stretched in both directions until they nearly fell from the face of the earth.

The brothers walked through downtown Cheyenne. Its low, square buildings spread out to take up the expansive stretches of mundane streets. But then they passed a store selling western wear that was so massive and alight with neon that it made Howard's Haberdashery seem like a boarded up boomtown tavern. There were a few modest hotels and inns that were buzzing with the sudden increase in business and foot traffic brought on by the famous rodeo. Eventually, they wandered past a dimly lit restaurant and became snared by the deep, mineral smell of greasy meat. Their stomachs began quaking and warbling in tandem. It had been almost an entire day since they'd last eaten. Without saying a word, they turned to the door and entered the place with aching stomachs and saliva puddling under their tongues.

They sat at a small table along the far wall. The dining room was half filled with old cowboys, their skin as worn and wrinkled as their carved leather belts. They remarked and gossiped about the rodeo like men in another town might chatter about politics. A portly woman told the boys what was available to order, which was a short list of various meat and gravy combinations. Jack's eyes grew wide when she mentioned Salisbury steaks. He'd never heard of it but imagined any steak so good it was named after someone must be the most succulent offering. Lester ordered the same and, within a couple of minutes, the woman brought two hefty plates of hamburger and mashed potatoes submerged in beef gravy. The boys ate manically once the first forkful hit their tongues. They moaned and grunted quietly as they shoveled, then sat back and sighed heavily once their forks came up empty. Before either of them had burped, their eyelids grew as heavy and thick as the gravy.

The waitress swept their plates into her arms as she passed without slowing. She returned in a minute with something in her hand, wrapped in a napkin as neatly and tightly as a newborn. She dropped it discreetly on the boys' table. "Fellas ate like you haven't ate in a month. This's yesterday's bread. Might be stale some around the edges but it's good enough to pick on," she whispered and went back into the kitchen.

Lester paid the bill and Jack grabbed the half-loaf of bread. Jack turned to take another look around the restaurant and saw their waitress straightening chairs. She looked at him and winked, then gave him a tight smile.

They walked a few blocks, stretching the knot of food in their stomachs. Eventually, they found a park that had a small grove of trees that seemed as good a place as any to take advantage of the shade and sleep as long as they could. They slid their backs along the rough bark of the ponderosa pine as they sat, removing their hats and loosening their belts a notch.

"We'll take turns sleeping tonight," Lester said when they settled themselves. He knew his plan required no explanation. "If you sleep for a few hours, I'll stay awake and keep watch first."

"If you say so," Jack nodded and covered his face with his hat. "Wake me up when it's my turn."

The boys went silent and the only noise around them was the rustling of the wind through the rugged pines. Lester began wondering what he'd expected from Cheyenne and whether the city would look more colorful if things had gone differently in the previous days. He was thinking back to the glamorous feeling of Fort Collins, imagining the meals they'd had, and the film they'd seen when his tired mind surrendered.

"Hey!" Jack shouted. "You're goddamn sleeping!"

Lester fumbled awake, his eyelids fluttering. "Was not!" he lied.

"Oh, guess it was this tree that was snoring then!" Jack quipped.

"Reckon so." Lester shook his head to spike himself awake when Jack wasn't looking.

"Aw, go on and sleep," Jack said after a few minutes. "I ain't tired anyway."

"I wasn't sleeping."

"And I won a rodeo buckle today. Just go to sleep."

Lester took his hat and covered his eyes. He was willing to lose the argument for the sake of sleep. He was just beginning to float off when

Jack spoke.

"Thinking about what that man said about the war," Jack said. "Got stuck in my craw."

Lester tried to ignore him.

"Just hard to think they'd ship guys like us off to some godforsaken place to get shot at."

Lester took a deep breath. He readjusted the hat balanced over his face, uncovering his mouth. "I'm going," he said wearily.

"Going where?" Jack asked.

"Over there."

Jack was quiet for a moment. "What do you mean over there? You can't go over there!"

Lester took his hat and jammed it over his bent knee. "I got to," he said. "I got drafted."

Chapter 50

"What the goddamn are you talking about?" Jack sprang up from the three.

"I got drafted, Jack. I have to go fight. Got a letter from home the other day saying so."

Jack shook his head in wide, sweeping motions. "Got a letter from who?"

"From Pa."

"He ain't our Pa," Jack hissed.

Lester shrugged. "Closest we've got."

Jack thought for a while. "What're you going to do?"

"Nothing I can do," Lester spit between his boots. "I've got no choice. Far as I know any boy over eighteen can get sent over there if they get drawn." He worked the brim of his hat between his thumb and forefinger. "Only lottery I've ever won," he said.

Jack's head was still shaking slowly like a pendulum. "But you're not eighteen!"

"I am according to my birth certificate. Ma changed my birthday in her will so I could get the ranch."

"So then just tell them!"

"And what?" Lester snapped. "Lose the ranch? Leave you with nowhere to go home to? With three dollars in your boot a thousand miles from home?"

Jack desperately worked over the situation in his mind. He was sure they could work to find an option that didn't include Lester being shipped off into the middle of a war. But the more he thought, the longer he looked over the card that'd just been laid on the table, the clearer it became that Lester would soon be donning camouflage.

"None of this would've happened if Ma didn't — if Ma wasn't," Jack stuttered then stopped, swallowing his words. "This ain't fair!" he yelled finally.

"Fair," Lester repeated like he had never heard the word before. "Reckon fair never was a tool we had in our shed."

The sky, for the first time that day, began to show a trace of color other than topaz. The evening redness moved across the sky like wildfire, mourning the passing of another faultless summer day and, perhaps, one of the last days the brothers would spend together before things changed once again.

"When did you find out?" Jack asked. He was calmer but was still unwilling to accept the circumstances.

"Other day. Checked the post office in Fort Collins."

Jack wasn't able to place the day in his memory. "What'd we eat that day?" he asked. It was a trick he used often to remember one day from another.

"Had biscuits for breakfast."

"Aw hell!" Jack screeched. "So that's what you were all sore over? I knew something was eating you."

Lester was silent. He continued rubbing his hat brim until there was a faint circle, as large as the pad of his thumb, left behind. "I'm sorry Jack," he said. "I'd never mean to leave you like this."

"Leave me like what?" Jack asked warily.

"Here. Like this. With all our stuff gone. Without our Pa. This was my great idea and now we got nothing to show for it," he said. He wiped the collection of tears that had welled in the bags under his eyes. "We got less than nothing. Now you've got to go back home by yourself with all our stuff gone. You don't deserve that and it's nobody's fault except mine."

Jack inhaled deeply, then stood on legs that were stiff and unstable. He pulled his hat onto his head and faced Lester, extending his hand to him.

"Where're you going?" Lester asked.

"To get a beer," Jack said with a smirk.

Lester clasped onto Jack's hand and let himself be pulled to his feet. They stretched their legs for a moment then set off in the direction of the fiddle music they'd heard on their walk to dinner.

They followed the string sawing until they came to a white tent a hundred yards from the road. It was as if a revival had sprouted from the dry weeds of the Wyoming dirt. The bacchanalia crept under the white canvas and through the small slit in the entrance that wove in the breeze like a flag. The brothers stepped through the threshold and abruptly found themselves in their own great awakening. It *was* a revival of sorts. One where salvation was found in the plucking of a hidetop banjo and drawing a bow across fiddle strings. Under that white tent, the devil was driven out one beating, clacking foot stomp at a time.

They stood at the edge of the crowd, just outside the throng of dancers. They gyrated and spun, sweat dripping from their chins and swinging elbows, stamping their heels into the dance floor on the off beats. They appeared to be thoroughly possessed by the fiend of bluegrass music. The brothers watched the dancers, men and women, young and old, with delight as the music caused their hearts to beat faster until it matched the driving tempo. They stood and watched it all with wonderment for a half dozen songs.

"Let's try it," Jack yelled over the band then walked onto the dance floor. Lester followed him without argument. They joined the horde hesitantly at first, but by the second song they were tossing their limbs and boots haphazardly in an attempt to mimic the people around them. They saw a few couples clasping both hands and squeezing together and apart like an accordion. Then they'd throw the lady so she'd spin like a top before starting again from the beginning. The brothers watched one couple for a few cycles before facing each other and grabbing hands, giggling to themselves. They did their best to match the military precision of the couple's feet. When it was time to spin, Jack volunteered. To him it was clear the spin was far and away the most amusing part of the entire choreography. He pushed off of Lester's hand and went into a spin that looked more similar to an automobile on an icy highway. His boots spun him as fast as they could but also covered more ground than he'd expected. Wide-eyed dancers parted and watched as he pirouetted across the floor, nudging their partners so they could cackle together.

On the opposite end of the dance floor, Jack finally stopped spinning. Perhaps he would have spun all the way back to Hayes County had he not bumped into her. She was dancing with a group of her friends. Jack made contact with her elbow to elbow. Both were immediately withdrawn from their gleeful dancing.

"Ow!" Jack howled. "Watch where you're going!" Then he looked around and saw the top of Lester's cowboy hat on the other side of the tent with nearly a hundred heads in between. It took him a second to work out what had happened. He turned to apologize to the girl but she was already scowling.

"Ow yourself! I've been in the same spot all night!" she scolded.

"Well," Jack said, "you should think about moving around some then!"

The girl rolled her eyes and turned back to her friends. Jack stood, watching her dance until the song ended.

"I'm Jack," he said. "Jack Copeland."

The girl turned to look at him again, with only an ounce less disdain. "Copeland?" she asked. "I haven't heard of any Copelands around here."

Jack nodded proudly. "Cause I ain't from around here!"

The girl turned to face him full-on just as the band began a new song.

"From Hayes County, Nebraska!" Jack shouted over the music.

She nodded knowingly. She'd met more than enough of his type passing through Cheyenne. "Here for the rodeo?"

"Nope. But we did go today and boy howdy those boys could really throw a lasso. What are you doing in Cheyenne?"

"I live here," she said.

Jack nodded, interested to find out anyone lived in the city during the other fifty one weeks of the year. "We rode all the way out here on horseback," he boasted.

The girl smiled. Showing Jack, for the first time, something besides toleration. "Well," she said, "I guess that makes you a real cowboy then."

"Reckon so," Jack nodded. "That, and I live on a cattle ranch in Hayes County." He left out the part about how he fell from the hayloft and hadn't done a day ranch work in years.

"My name's Henrietta," she said. "Henrietta Takoda. But everybody calls me Hen. Like a chicken," she smiled coyly.

Jack shook her hand heartily. "What's that mean?" he asked.

"Hen? It's my nickname. It's short for Henrietta."

"No, the other one."

"Takoda," she said. "It's Indian."

"Are you an Indian?" Jack looked her over again.

"I don't know. Maybe a little."

"What's it mean?"

"Means friend to all," she said.

"Ha!" Jack roared. "Weren't a friend to me when I bumped you!"

Henrietta pursed her lips and considered turning her back on the cowboy and rejoining her friends. Instead, she asked, "What does Copeland mean?"

"Don't have the slightest," Jack shrugged. "But I'm named Jack after my grandpa. His name was Grandpa Jack."

Hen smiled. "Did you ride all the way to Cheyenne by yourself?"

"No way no how," Jack scoffed. "Rode here with my brother. Follow me, I'll bring you over to him!"

Jack set off to the other side of the dance floor where he'd left Lester a couple of songs ago. He weaved through the cavorting crowd like a cat through thickets. He turned to make sure Henrietta was following him twice before reaching back and grabbing her hand and leading her through. Her fingers were as cold as a bolt of electricity on his callused palms.

Henrietta clasped Jack's hand, warm like proofing dough, and gave it a quick squeeze. Jack wasn't sure if she had meant to, but his breath caught in his throat either way. At that moment, he was glad she couldn't see his face.

Chapter 51

Jack and Henrietta surfaced from the crowd like they'd broken free from a riptide. They were dazed and dizzy from the twisting crowd and no longer knew which direction they had been heading. Jack stood and craned his neck, searching for the crown of his brother's silverbelly hat. To his right, he caught a glimpse of the hat and also saw there was an older man standing with Lester. They were in the middle of a conversation. Their enunciation was so exaggerated due to the music, Jack may have been able to stand where he was and understand all that was said. But he pulled Henrietta along by her hand toward them, wondering if the man might be the missing link between them and their father.

When they neared Lester and the man, Jack saw that the man was built like Lester. He was tall and slim with a flat brimmed cowboy hat, making him look altogether like a nail. He was taller and a bit pudgier than Lester but the likeness was uncanny. Jack stood by, eavesdropping before he coughed to get their attention. When the man turned to look at Jack, it was as if he'd seen his reflection in a calm, clear-watered stream. A mirror image it was not, but the deep brown eyes and the serious mouth but enduring smile looked so comparable to his own that he would have been pleased enough had it been a painted portrait. His chest cinched and his breath reversed back down his throat. He could feel the back of his neck grow cold and damp.

"Jack," Lester said. "We were just about to come looking for you."

Jack still hadn't taken his eyes off the man. "Are — are you?" he stuttered. "Are you our Pa? Harold Burke?"

The man dropped his eyes and removed his hat. He faced Jack and dropped to one knee in front of him so he could speak to him intimately. "You must be Jack," he said kindly.

Jack nodded haltingly. "Yes sir."

"I'm so sorry to meet you like this," the man said.

This is him. Our Pa, Jack thought. *We did it after all.*

"Well, my name is Thomas. Tom Burke. And I guess I'm your uncle."

Jack could feel his insides roil. "You're not our Pa?"

Tom shook his head gravely. "I'm sorry, Jack. I understand you're probably disappointed that I'm only your uncle. But I'm your Pa's brother. Younger brother, just like you and Lester here. I was only a few years older than you are now when he married your Ma." He put a gentle hand on Jack's shoulder. "Your brother told me about your mother. And I'm very sorry."

Jack shrugged with counterfeit toughness.

"Lester was just telling me about how far you boys came. I'm proud of you. And I'm sure your Pa was too, even if he didn't say it."

Was. Didn't say it. Realization clicked into place inside Jack's head.

"So," Jack furrowed his brow, "that really was our Pa we met the other day?"

Tom nodded soberly. "I'm sorry Jack. I ain't about to make an excuse for him. For anything he's done to you boys. I don't have any kids of my own so I can't think how he felt when you boys showed up all the way out here, but he had no right turning you away. You came all this way and he turned you onto a fake scent like a bunch of mutts."

Lester wiped his cheeks.

"You've got nothing to be ashamed of, boys. And I want you to always keep that somewhere in your minds," Tom said then looked from Jack to Lester and back again. "Listen here. I don't have much money and I can't just up and quit on my ranch work here, but if you boys ever need anything, I want you to write a letter or send a telegram and I'll be there by the next sunrise." He looked to Lester. "That's my word and I know you've got no reason to believe me but it's the least you two deserve."

Lester nodded sharply. He took a step forward and, surprising even himself, wrapped his lanky arms around Tom, tucking his face into the man's shoulder. Tom grabbed the back of his shirt and held him, saying something softly that only Lester heard.

Jack took a deep breath and looked around, unable to bear the sight of his brother falling apart. There, by his side, with tears in her own sorrowful eyes, was Henrietta. Her hand was still holding his.

Lester and Jack held open the slit entrance of the canvas tent. Lester emerged with a scrap of paper, on which was written: *Thomas Burke, CMC Ranch, Cheyenne, Wyo.* He held it tightly. Jack held Henrietta.

"This is Henrietta," Jack said to Lester's back as they walked away from the rowdy sounds of the hoedown. "But call her Hen, right Hen?" he turned to her.

Lester stopped as quickly as a steer roping horse and faced her. "Hiya, Hen. It's nice to meet you. Are you Jack's new friend?"

"Yes," she said shyly. "I guess I am."

Lester smiled at her then continued off. He had no direction, but the act of crunching miles under the sole of his boot was the closest he had to riding on horseback. It didn't ease the cogs of his mind as well, but it would do in a pinch. On one hand, their journey westward had turned out to be nothing more than a dismal failure; a defeat that was dealt to the brothers, hand after hand, like a joker card that inexplicably came up three, then four times. They had set off from their ranch hoping for aces. Instead, they were dashed and swindled into betting the house on a high card.

The other hand, however, had just been dealt a jack. It was not the face card they had hoped for, desperately looking for a trail then praying they'd followed the wrong one. But, in this case, close had to be close enough. That man was not their Pa, but he was a man who had offered them paternal goodwill in a time when the vacuums of their chests needed it most.

When their father left them as children, he made no promises. Perhaps he had made faint oaths to himself, along with the unspoken covenant that his sons would grow up without their father. Now, walking away from their uncle, they were the ones leaving and they held with them the vow that, although distant, they would never be left on their own again.

The sun had set over Cheyenne, taking with it the translucent blue sky that can only be brought to mind in color by travelers who have stood under it. The boys were growing tired, but Jack was beginning to worry he may never see Henrietta again after they said their goodnights. They walked back to the park they'd attempted to sleep in earlier in the evening.

"What are we doing tomorrow?" Jack asked, hoping both Lester and Hen would answer similarly.

Instead, they both shrugged.

"Like to go to the rodeo?" he asked Henrietta.

She thought for a moment. "Sure," she smiled. "But I ain't allowed to go on a date until I turn sixteen."

"Well, when do you turn sixteen?"

"Next week," she giggled.

"By next week I'll be back in Hayes County, so maybe I can get one early. Les won't tell anyone, right Les?"

Lester ran pinched fingertips across his closed lips.

"Fine," Hen said. "But don't get any ideas about necking."

Lester let out an explosive laugh which caught Jack and Hen so off guard they ended up joining him. It saved Jack from what had almost escaped his mouth impulsively: *Too late for that.*

After a few minutes of standing by the pine tree, staring at the trunk where the boys would sleep, Hen shivered and said she was getting cold and had to get home.

"Night, Hen," Lester said. "See you in the morning."

Jack attempted to play coy until she began walking away. Then he scrambled after her. "I'll be waiting right there under that yonder tree for you," he promised with a wink. Then he took a half step toward her and kissed her cheek. It was much warmer than her hand had been, but the same cool electricity pulsed through his limbs.

Hen tried to act perturbed but the corners of her mouth ticked up.

Jack walked toward the tree. "I pecked ya," he called over his shoulder. "Get it? Peck! Like a hen!"

Henrietta rolled her eyes and began making her way home. It was late and she would find herself in the shade of that ponderosa pine again in a few hours. But until then, it would be a restless night for all of them.

Chapter 52

THE FRONTIER DAYS grandstands were filled early the next day. The entire day's schedule was consigned to bull riding and word had seemingly traveled far into the stretches of the Wyoming and Colorado badlands. Their group found a space high on the bleachers, realistically large enough for two people, but Jack wasn't going to complain about the tight accommodations. Henrietta, as she'd promised, met the brothers at the tree they'd slept under. She'd walked into the park around sunup and found the two cowboys slumped under the pine branches, still asleep. She considered kicking Jack's boots to wake him but instead sat cross-legged under a neighboring tree and quietly watched the sun finish its rise into the flaming turquoise sky.

They watched the cowboys, *real* cowboys as Lester remarked, wrestle the massive horned beasts into the chutes. Their snouts dripped swinging chains of heavy snot and spit. They kicked and butted anything they could reach along the fenced path to their temporary pens, where the kicking and butting continued with renewed earnest and fury. As soon as the bulls seemed to calm in a waspish resignation, a cowboy would climb aboard their burly backs spur first. Hand-holds and ropes were tied and retied, rosined and sapped, before the cowboy would give a nod exaggerated by their massive cowboy hat brim and the gate would swing open, spewing the battle into the dirt arena. Like gladiators, they would wrangle for the upper hand in a rage of stubborn tussling. It all happened in slow motion like a sluggish film reel. The man and beast would scuffle for what felt like hours, until a man in the judges' stand would reach for the knotted rope and pull, ringing a large bell as loud and piercing as a church steeple's. It was, if all things went according to plan, just over eight seconds from start to finish.

Henrietta had seen the entire process since she was a young girl, when her father would walk with her from across town to sit on the same grandstands. The bulls were different, only a smattering of riders were the same, and now the company she kept was a change as well. As soon as she was old enough to know the difference, she had turned a cold shoulder toward the riders who would appear in Cheyenne as quickly and fleetingly as a summer rainstorm. She detested the spit shined buckles they so proudly wore, and how they watched women's eyes, not to see if they were looking at them but at their buckles. Their boots would click along the usually quiet streets of the city, their musk and overly righteous colognes would waft from the train station like sinew from a slaughterhouse. Those men were not cowboys to her.

Her father, a ranch hand with a measly ownership stake, worked long hours on a wide open stretch of plains in the shadows of two moderately sized, mountainous outcroppings he called the Sister Peaks. He would be gone before she woke in the mornings, no matter how early she'd will herself awake. Sometimes, she was convinced he would close his eyes at night only until she fell asleep, then slip silently into the cool nights to ride to the ranch. He would return, spent and matted with dirt. No matter how late Hen decided to start cooking, dinner would have inevitably gone cold by the time her father walked in. He would open the squeaking screen door of their home and kick his leather boots into a corner. The thumping would bring Hen shuffling from the kitchen and her father would pull her into a suffocating hug, the dust from his work clothes leaving an imprint on her blouses. Then he'd land a scruffy kiss on her forehead.

Henrietta had been cooking since she could reach the stovetop. She'd learned how from walking into town to request and read cookbooks and cooking manuals (among stacks of other books) from the Cheyenne Library, an imposing columned building which stuck from the ground nearly as sharply as the Sister Peaks. She had never known her mother, other than the pieces of herself she couldn't fully attribute to her father. Helena Takoda died on an unseasonably cool August morning at the age of nineteen, shortly after giving birth to her first daughter, Henrietta May Takoda.

Her father never returned to the ranch he'd been hired to that year, sending only a quick scribbled note saying *Things to look after at home, my apologies.* He lived on discarded produce and day old bread for a year to be able to afford milk for his newborn daughter. As Hen learned more of the world, she realized that most men would have sent their baby girls off to be cared for. For the first year of her life, Kenneth Takoda's daughter rarely left the nest of his rugged arms. Henrietta grew up quick and, by some divine chance, she grew up well. She was a soft natured and responsible woman by the time she turned five. Her father had been working short and sporadic days when he could find a rancher willing to allow it for a few years. But by the time she was preparing to go to her first day of school, her father was working long hours, and she was serving rudimentary meals which her father would praise every night.

So, Henrietta did not think very highly of the cocksure cowboys who swaggered into town once a year. She didn't even call those men cowboys. Her definition of the term had been skewed toward humility and devotion by her father.

"Now *that* is a cowboy!" Jack smiled, looking at the man that had just perfectly ridden a bull so large it could have fed an entire town for a winter.

Hen shook her head. "That isn't a cowboy. That's a boy with a buckle."

"Well," Jack shrugged, "I ain't got a buckle."

They watched a few more rides in silence, the morning sun beginning to tickle their cheeks.

After one cowboy was flung from the back of a bull nearly over the fence, Henrietta nudged Jack. "I always wanted to read a cowboy story," she said. "A *real* western."

"Like those gunslinging ones next to the soda fountain?"

Hen shook her head. "I've read those and I don't think any of that is close to what things were like back then. Or now."

"Well sure, but that's what makes them fun to read, I bet!"

"I think the stories people want to hear are the ones from genuine cowboys camping miles away from the closest town's reach." She thought for a minute. "Maybe I'll just have to write it myself then."

"I've been all the way out there," Jack scoffed. "And there ain't a thing about it that'd make a good story. Besides the bad luck we ran into."

Henrietta shook her head again. "No matter how it turned out, I think you've got a story to tell and I'd like to hear it. And I'd say it's a long way from being turned out anyway."

Jack watched a rider best a rust colored bull. "I don't know," he sighed. "I can't reckon anybody'd want to hear our story. It's too damn sad."

Henrietta and Jack fell silent, their breathing synchronized into long sighs and their shoulders rubbed with the ebb and flow of the crowd's cheers. Jack blankly watched the bull riders, thinking back on the tale he and Lester had lived.

"Jack," Henrietta said, "you're still a long way from the ending."

"Yeah," Jack blinked hard. "Yeah, I reckon so."

Chapter 53

At some point in the afternoon, when the backs of their necks were patently angry with sunburn, they climbed from the crowded grandstands and walked into town. Along the way, Henrietta shared the history of the buildings and their owners, past and present. It was information she'd picked up like dandelions over the years. She walked the brothers to the state capitol building, where they stood in its shadow and squinted up at the gold domed rotunda rising high above the city like the sun itself. It glinted and shimmered in the summer afternoon light. They stared in wonderment for so long, their necks grew stiff and their vision took several minutes to readjust.

Henrietta, after a short time, had shifted her attention to Jack and, instead, watched his eyes dart over the precise masonry and gilded panels of the building. "I'll send you a postcard, Cowboy Jack," she said playfully.

Jack blinked; his eyesight was bleached by the golden reflection. "I think I'd like that, Hen. Never got a postcard before."

They found a bench near the bus depot, just across the square from the train station, and sat, watching the trains rumble away slowly before picking up steam and rolling into other faraway places.

Lester coughed. "Guess I'll report tomorrow," he said.

"What do you mean?" Jack asked.

"Report. To the Army. See what they want to do with me, I guess. Reckon that's how it'll be for a while."

"Tomorrow?" Jack said, panicking. Just like that, on a day when Jack's heart was brimming fuller than it had in over a year, he could feel the familiar emptiness in his chest where the small pile of hours he had remaining with his brother collected. Jack had felt alone, in one way or another, since his mother passed. But now he was less than a day away from being more alone than he'd ever been.

After a stretch of silence, Lester offered to buy them all a hot lunch. They walked the wide sidewalks of downtown until they found a place that looked quiet. A long, linoleum countertop extended nearly from the door to the opposite wall. The place smelled thickly of onions and salt, a promise of a hearty meal. They found three stools along the counter and ordered slopping plates of shallow fried foods, which they cut into tiny pieces and nibbled on. The brothers' stomachs were churning, and the oil slick food felt regrettable as soon as it touched their tongues. Henrietta pushed her green beans around her plate, wondering why she'd allowed herself to make a friend so quickly, knowing she'd soon be back in the cycle of her mostly solitary day to day.

She asked the brothers about their trek; why they'd decided to leave, what had happened along the way, the people they'd met, how they'd come to be possessionless, what their father had said to unknowingly send them away to another state. The boys, happy for the opportunity to speak about the past, rather than the dreadful present or unknowable future, shared their tale with Hen. They spoke lovingly of their mother, doting on her memory, carefully allowing someone else to have a spoonful of the mental souvenirs they had of their mother, as small as the bites they'd been taking from their plates. The story's cadence picked up once they rode from their Hayes County ranch into the western sunsets, and hardly slowed enough for a breath until Jack recounted meeting a girl, sharp as a tack and cute as a bug's ear.

Then, as if the mention of his mother was enough to quell his fears, Jack asked how he was supposed to get home. And what he should do once he got there.

Lester reached into his pocket and pulled out a sheet of scrap paper, torn from a pamphlet promising eternal life to any sinful cowboys. He'd written scant directions on the back then slid it across the countertop to Jack.

"A train leaves tomorrow at 12:03, just after noon, from the Cheyenne station," Lester explained. "Heads east on the Union Pacific line which'll take you nearly to home. Closest station I could see on the map is in Hershey. It's not a stone's throw but it's better than walking."

Jack nodded in agreement. "How am I supposed to get home from that station then?"

"Walk," Lester said flatly. "Or hitch a ride, but I suppose you won't see many cars out that way. You remember how different it is in Hayes County."

Jack nodded and carefully folded and pocketed the paper. The boys went back to silently poking their food with their dull forks.

Lester chewed his lip, then offered to write Pa to see if he would be able to help at all. Both brothers shrugged, knowing the chances were slim.

Henrietta had the patience of a schoolmarm, but soon after the silence resumed she noticed the sky outside was growing darker. She would need to rush home and hope the pantry held enough flour for biscuits and gravy. She pushed her beans in a circle around her plate once more while rallying the gumption to tell Jack she had to leave and wouldn't see him before he left.

"Jack," she said softly.

"Yeah," Jack sighed. "You gotta go too. I know."

Hen leaned on her stool and landed a kiss on Jack's sunburnt cheek.

"You boys sure were nice to meet. And I'll be praying for you, Lester."

"Thank you Hen," Lester smiled faintly.

She could tell Jack was busy fighting within himself. His eyes had a faraway stare and his cheeks were sunken in the most somber expression she'd seen from him. He refused to cry, but it seemed the rest of his body was leaking despair instead.

"Yeah, well go on Hen," Jack said shakily. "And don't forget to write that postcard."

Hen squeezed his arm and nodded to Lester, then walked slowly to the door. She turned to take another look at Jack, but he'd refused to watch her walk away. He'd had his share of leaving and it wasn't over yet.

Under the same tree they'd slept against the previous night, Jack fell into his old habit of sighing and huffing until Lester gave in and asked what he wanted to say. He'd grown since the time their mother had first gotten ill, but that night, just before Lester was going away for the first time, he was only comfortable being a little brother in need of counsel.

"What is it?" Lester asked from under his hat.

Jack let out a long, hissing sigh like a leaking tire. "We saw a lot out here but — I don't know, Les — I reckon I'm still afraid of Pa."

Lester tipped his hat back away from his face and looked at his brother, who was struggling to work through his swirling thoughts.

"He never took a liking to me and I can't imagine he did since we've been gone. He'll be up a goddamn wall that I'm back and you ain't. At least if it was you he'd have some help around the ranch."

"If you think you're not cowboy enough to help on the ranch after you rode all the way out here, then I don't reckon I've ever met one."

"I don't know," Jack shrugged. "It's strange enough being home without Ma and now I gotta be there without you too. Just me and Pa doesn't sound much like a family to me."

Lester breathed heavily. "Maybe not," he said. "But it won't be just you and Pa forever. I'll be home soon enough. Maybe," he teased, "we'll find ourselves some cowgirls one of these days."

Jack wiped his eyes. "I wish you didn't have to go," he said quietly. "If I'd known my Ma'd die and my brother'd get shipped off, I don't reckon I would've ever picked to be born in the first place."

"Then I'm glad it wasn't up to you," Lester said. "Cause I could've never done this without you. And I wouldn't have wanted to either."

Chapter 54

Like all dreaded hours that are wished to be delayed, the brothers' restless night under the tree blew eastward on the Wyoming wind as quickly and easily as wisps of smoke. The morning sun broadened the horizon, growing a blaze of orange flames which whipped between the high clouds. Jack opened his eyes after a fit of sleep to see the change in the sky and was awed until the weight of the day crashed into him. How easily a flaming western sunrise can feel like raging wildfire when your fate has seemed to turn its back against you.

Lester brushed the legs of his jeans and stood slowly. "I could use some coffee," he said. "You want one?"

Jack shrugged. He'd never had more than a sip, which he'd stolen from Pa's chipped ceramic mug.

"Alright, well I'm going to find some. I'll be back in a few minutes." Lester pulled his hat on and walked from the pine tree.

Jack watched him walk away until he reached a street corner and turned right, disappearing behind a stone building. Jack's breath felt hot in his nose when his brother went around the corner. He stood quickly and sprinted toward him. He ran out and across the street, down the sidewalk and around the corner. He looked down the street Lester had just turned onto but it was deserted. He jogged forward, his heart rumbling anxiously in his chest, until he saw a business with the lights on. It was a tavern that had opened early to serve rodeo cowboys a hearty breakfast before their competitions. Jack stood in the door and saw Lester standing at the counter, carefully reaching for two steaming paper cups. Lester held them and walked gingerly to the door. Jack went to him and took one of the cups.

"Thought you were waiting at the tree," Lester said.

"Yeah, I —" Jack struggled, "I figured you might need help."

Lester nodded knowingly. "Come on," he said, walking down the streets of Cheyenne. "We got a few hours left."

Time that morning, like last night, slipped and leaked away like water from a rusted pail. The boys found a seat near the shade of the capitol building. From there, they could hear the distant crowd cheering at the rodeo, feel the thundering train cars rumbling in and out of the depot, and the clanging church bells signaling the expiration of each hour. The brothers sat and talked about things that hardly extended beyond the surface of their thoughts. They were afraid to reach their fingers into the murky, treacherous waters that lay deeper within their minds. When Jack realized he had only a small collection of minutes to ask the questions he'd worked to push down, he asked them. He knew Lester was not likely to have the answers, but he felt the need to ask anyway. He quizzed Lester on reasons for a draft, locations of faraway lands like Germany and France, and what exactly he would be doing there.

It would be years until Jack realized those hours tolled on Lester's own mind. The journey back home to a lonely ranch was not what Jack had imagined when they set off toward the setting sun, but the solitary ride home was still favorable over the long trip overseas in a ship overcrowded with terror-stricken young men. When they made landfall, they would be told when and who to shoot. Any man their age would have much preferred a mean Pa over the sight of an Axis army gaining ground.

Lester wouldn't feel homesick for a few more days. The nervousness needed to erode away first, like topsoil being blown away in a dust bowl storm to reveal the arid surroundings of a place far from home. His withdrawal would creep in and grab hold of him, keeping his heart and lungs from expanding fully. Any thoughts of his brother or the ranch would cinch tightly around the same places as thoughts of his mother wilting in her bed.

The church bell pealed eleven times over Cheyenne. The brothers counted them, their throats growing tighter and drier with each chime. Lester removed his hat and rubbed his forehead. He bent in half and pulled his boot off. He reached in, rifled around, and removed the last of his cash.

"Take this," he said, handing it to Jack. "It's all I've got but I don't suppose I'll need it."

Jack pocketed it slowly. "Is it time?" he said quietly.

Lester nodded. He put his boot back on and took a long breath. "I know you're upset but I want you to listen to me for a minute," he faced Jack. "I want you to know I'm proud of you. When we left, I guess I didn't really suppose we'd find him. I didn't know if we'd make it and I didn't think you could do it. But these were the best couple weeks of my life. I don't want you to think this was for nothing. We found our Pa and we gave him every chance to be our old man. We haven't done a damn thing to hang our heads over. Luck just wasn't on our side. But we were on our sides."

Jack nodded. Tears rolled down his cheeks.

"Only thing we didn't do was see a herd of buffalo."

"Bison," Jack corrected with a wet smile.

"Right. I'll write you as much as I can."

"Okay."

"And I'll be back home before you know it."

Jack nodded, doing his best to keep the heaving sobs inside.

Lester knelt in front of Jack. "Look at me," he said and Jack's red, glinting eyes met his. "We've been by each other's side when nobody else was. I couldn't have done this without you and I wouldn't even have wanted to try. If you feel alone, remember I'm thinking about you. I'm proud of you. And Ma would be too."

Lester pulled Jack into him. They grasped each other tightly for a few minutes, breathing together, their eyes clenched shut. They imagined times that, in the moment, had seemed dark and desperate but would be a respite from this afternoon.

Lester stood and gave his brother a last look. "Be safe, Cowboy Jack," he said grimly and turned toward the street. He walked away, toward Fort Warren, refusing to look back. He did his best to keep his shoulders from showing his breathing, which had grown ragged and whimpering. He knew Jack would be watching him, so he waited until he turned a corner to drop to his knees on the sidewalk and cry.

After Lester disappeared around the corner, Jack closed his eyes and buried his head in his hands. He sat until his breathing slowed and his eyes dried. His chest was still tight, but like he'd learned from Lester during those solemn times, he took the first step. He walked to the train station and stared up at the clock tower. He had forty minutes until the train that would carry him back to Hayes County left Cheyenne. He walked along the outside of the building, following the ragged stonework and peering inside through the massive windows. Eventually, he found himself near the rail yard and watched the trains shuffle their cars like a deck of cards. They would disconnect from one then shudder into another and be pulled along to a new station.

Jack watched a few lines of cars disappear westward until he could see to the far side of the yard. There, he saw a man sitting with his back against a utility pole. The man wore a faded cowboy hat he'd seen many times. A beautiful leather saddle laid next to him and his shirt was blinding white in the noon sunshine.

Chapter 55

"Son of a bitch," Jack muttered. His heart buzzed into action, freed from the muscles of sadness, for the first time all day. The heat from his sweaty and sunburnt neck froze into an icy glaze. He squinted at the man across the tracks. It had to be him. It was Lester's old hat and his white shirt. He couldn't see the saddle clearly enough but he was sure it had once hung in the barn of their ranch. He squatted in the shallow ditch alongside the outermost pair of railroad tracks and removed his hat. Only a small tuft of his cowlick emerged from the top of his hiding spot. He popped up stealthily every half minute to make sure the man was still where he'd been. Between those times, he worked through his options.

The safest of those was to hide until just before 12:03, when he eastbound Union Pacific train would leave the station. This decision would also mean a lifetime of recalling the time he could have fought back and did not. He had just watched his brother willingly walk toward a destination that would likely end in a battlefield so hiding, now that he was two hundred yards from the only man on earth he could summon hatred for, seemed spineless. He hadn't ridden across the western prairies on horseback to become a weak-kneed young man.

The option Jack almost immediately chosen was to fight. Perhaps he would have considered for a half hour longer on any other day but on that one, he felt he had little to lose. The thoughts he worked through while crouched in the ditch were, therefore, working on his cunning plan. He was no longer deciding what to do but, rather, how.

He crawled over the jagged rocks until he was safely behind the line of sight. Along the way, he found a rusted and bent metal pipe, half the width of a flagpole, which he grabbed and slapped against the palm of his other hand a few times. He had considered sprinting into town to buy a gun but he wasn't sure the bills Lester handed him would cover the cost or, even, if the man would still be there when he returned. The small pole would have to be enough. He craned his neck to check the clock. A half-hour until his train departed.

Jack removed his boots, figuring he could walk more quietly in the uneven stones with socked feet. He held his boots by the shaft in one hand. In the other, he hid the length of the pipe against his leg. He waited until a train moved somewhere down the line, sending a loud vibration through the tracks that would drown his footfalls. When two cars would latch in an explosion of noise, he would sprint twenty feet before the echoes ended. It took a while, but eventually he was close enough to the telephone pole and the man leaning against it that any doubts he'd had dissipated. It was Willie.

Jack stepped gingerly toward him, becoming more cautious with every inch he gained. When he was just outside of the drifter's reach, he realized Willie was sleeping and still hadn't stirred. But Jack, who'd been fooled by him before, remained vigilant. He took two steps closer and reached the end of the pipe toward Willie's head. He pointed the end of it at his temple, an inch away from dimpling the skin. In a sudden roar, he screamed and jabbed the end of the metal into him.

"Don't move!" Jack screamed. "*Don't even think about moving! I got a pistol to your head and if you so much's reach for your gun, I'll blow your head back to Colorado!*"

Willie scrambled and kicked awake. Looking back, Jack would smile slyly thinking it was akin to how the brothers might have looked when they were woken up by the barrel of his gun. Willie muttered groggily, asking incoherent questions. He reached up to grab the pole pressed to his head, but Jack pushed it against him harder until Willie placed his hands on to the legs of his ratty pants in defeat.

"Where's your gun?" Jack asked sternly.

Willie was silent.

"Last chance," Jack said. "Where's the gun?"

"Pawned it."

"You pawned a gun but not that saddle?" Jack asked incredulously. "Tell me. Where's the gun?"

Willie huffed. "Waistline."

Jack dropped his boots and slowly reached between the wooden pole and Willie's back. He kept the metal pipe pressed against him and watched Willie's hands intently. Tucked into Willie's waistline was the same gun that had shot a crater out of a tree trunk just above Jack's head. He rolled the cylinder and saw it was half loaded with three bullets, then cocked the hammer slowly, close to Willie's ear. Only then did Jack take the pipe from his temple and chuck it into the ditch where it skittered out of reach. Jack rounded the pole, keeping the gun leveled on Willie.

Willie's eyes widened to the size of a castrated bull when he saw the boy, who he thought he had bested, standing in front of him, and pointing his own gun at his chest.

"I'll be," Willie scoffed. "I thought we left off on pretty good terms. Don't suppose there's any reason for another visit."

"Where's the horses?" Jack asked.

Willie gave an unsettling smile. "Why don't you just shoot me?"

"Answer me."

"Young man, I believe I'm ready for my great reward."

"Only reward you're getting is to see my face once more time. Now tell me where the horses are?"

Willie's smile broadened. "Well, see, we rode them all the way from your dinky camp in Fort Collins. Didn't have money to feed them so they hardly got us here in the first place. Those old girls were looking mighty rough so we thought it best to just put them out of their misery."

Jack thought about the half empty cylinder. One shot above his head and one for each horse. He uncocked the gun and slid it into his waistband quickly, then took a step toward Willie and hit him across the mouth with the first punch he'd ever thrown. He could hardly believe the pain shooting in bolts up his fingers, but the pain subsided when he saw a red stream flowing from Willie's bottom lip.

"Keep your hands where they are," Jack ordered.

Willie reached up to wipe the blood from his chin.

Jack swung again, hitting him in the same spot. "I said keep your hands where they are."

Willie's eyes raged at Jack. His mouth streamed blood. He was certain if the gun was in Willie's possession, Jack would have a hole clear through him.

"Where's the rest of it?" Jack asked.

"Rest of what?"

"All our goddamn things!"

Willie shrugged. "Gave half to my partner. Pawned some, sold some."

Jack warned him not to move once again, then stepped toward the saddle. He opened the saddlebag and saw his family's bible shoved inside. He took it out and rubbed his thumb over the cover.

"Nobody wanted to buy that from me. Got pretty damn cold last night though. Should've just burnt it then."

Jack opened the other saddlebag and found a dented can of butter beans. "Where's the harmonica?" he asked.

Willie shrugged. "Probably pawned it."

"I hardly paid a quarter for it. Nobody would've given you a penny for it."

Willie was quiet.

Jack patted Willie's front pant pockets. "Reach in there and pull it out for me," he said.

Willie did, slowly, and held his hand open to show the tarnished and beaten harmonica. Jack grabbed it from his palm and turned it over in his hands. He looked at Willie — really looked at him. He saw him for who he had always been. Jack took the revolver from his belt and crouched in front of Willie, just beyond his roughneck boots.

"Never avenge yourself," Willie said, "but leave it to the wrath of God. For it is written, 'Vengeance is mine.'"

Jack laughed. "I don't care what the bible says. This vengeance is mine." He watched thick droplets of blood cascade down Willie's chin and collect there before falling and staining his brother's shirt. His blood was a red carnation blooming on the fabric. Seeing the desecration of Lester's shirt by Willie's wretched blood filled Jack with a wrath that even retribution would do nothing to satiate. "Remember when you asked if I believed in God?" he asked.

Willie stared.

"Well, I said I wasn't sure. But now I reckon I am. Way I see it, I guess there is a God. Not that he's done much good for me or my family. But if there is a devil then that means there's got to be a God." Jack stood and spit between Willie's boots. "And you, *boy*, are the fucking devil."

Jack put his harmonica in his pocket and pinched the bible under his arm. Then he grabbed his mother's saddle by the horn and lifted it, carrying it to the Union Pacific train that was waiting to take him home.

CHAPTER 56

THE 12:03 EASTBOUND TRAIN steamed and hissed just behind the stone walls of the station. The line of canary yellow cars stretched in a line that seemed to unfurl all the way to Laramie. The titanic engine growled as it sat in the shade of the clock tower, as riled up as a penned rodeo bull. Below the massive ocular headlamp was the Union Pacific shield, flanked by blue wings that looked like a mustache on the face of the locomotive.

Jack stood proudly at the ticket counter and bought his fare for a trip to Hershey Station. The man gestured toward the large arching door that lead to the loading platform. Jack went through and came face-to-face with the hulking yellow machine. He walked alongside it until he found a man in a peaked navy cap who offered to help with his meager luggage.

"We'll need to stow that saddle," he said with a smile.

Jack handed the saddle to the man. "Please be careful with it," he said.

"Yes sir!" the man nodded heartily. "Of course!"

Jack watched the man gingerly hoist the saddle and carry it into a windowless car. When the man climbed down, he beckoned Jack further along the line of cars until they came to an open door.

"Any seat in this car, sir," the man said.

Jack thanked him and climbed aboard. The car was mostly empty, save for the random travelers in wide-brimmed cowboy hats that had traveled into Cheyenne for the business aspects of the rodeo; to inquire about rodeo bull prices, or place bets on the cowboys that rode them. He found an empty row near the back of the car and shuffled into the window seat. The seats were as plush and padded as that Ford Deluxe. The revolver in Jack's waistband dug into his back but he refused to move it until the train pulled away from the station and left Willie in its wake. He placed his mother's bible on the seat next to him, then took off his hat and put his forehead against the cool glass window to watch a handful of people milling around the loading area. Jack could feel the engine's cylinders vibrating the floor beneath his feet.

He thought about the miles covered by the soles of his boots over the past weeks; about how the dust that rippled over the ground like a bedsheet had changed, like paints mixed from ochre to cinnamon; how the wind grew and whipped in a fury over the sweeping badlands of Wyoming just as it had years ago in the dust bowl of Nebraska. He reflected on the warm, kind-hearted people Jack and Lester had met across the parts of the West they had seen; how they had treated the boys, who were hundreds of miles from their home, like neighbors. Yet, he felt how easily a couple snide characters can shadow those acts of goodwill as if they were blanketed under layers of earth. Jack remembered Lester saying every man has a battle inside them where God and the Devil struggle for the upper hand. He figured that was true enough. They'd looked on enough faces to fill a village that had won the war, but the conflict continued for some.

Jack realized then that the world is filled with Double Faces. They walk among us, just as the Indian boy had promised. Life is full of beasts that don't wait until dark to show their wicked faces. Most of the bogeymen we meet are much better at hiding their second faces than the brothers had been led to believe. Their eyes won't kill you with a single stare. Instead, they'll draw you in so close you'll wish yourself dead.

Most people are good. Jack knew this, and their journey solidified that idea in his mind. But those where the dark was winning the battle inside them are the ones that will make you lust for the end before you see their second face.

The train sputtered into motion, slowly rolling past the depot. Jack watched as the pillars and stones of the station slid out of view. The train horn signaled its departure. The noise roared over the rolling landscape of Cheyenne as easily as the wind. It was a heavenly harmonica tune played for the drifter named Willie, as a final reminder of the young cowboy that bested him before riding away.

The horizon stretched for miles outside Jack's window, a razor sharp demarcation between dust and sky. In the distance, he saw a bluff that looked like the one he and Lester had ridden up during their first ride together. The sight of the striated rock reminded him of something. He reached into his jean pocket and removed a balled up sheet of paper. He carefully opened it and flattened it on his thigh until the wrinkles resembled the gently rippled ground outside. Grabbing the bible from the seat next to him, he opened it and flipped through the pages until he found where it had been ripped from its binding. He matched the edges of the tear and smoothed the page again. Then he read the circled verse and closed the cover, holding it securely on his lap.

Jack looked out the window and saw dark boulders jutting from the ground. Dozens of them stretched as far as he could see to the east and to the west. As the train trundled by, they grew more dense. Only after picking one, and observing it closely as he passed, did he notice they weren't boulders. They were bison. An expansive herd of bison. Jack's jaw went slack and he stood almost completely out of his seat.

He cupped his hands over his eyes so he wouldn't miss a single one. A mile or so down the track, the herd thinned until the landscape became lifeless once again. Jack turned to the seat next to him, his smile wide and his eyes sparkling. He had expected to see his brother's stoic face when he turned, nodding knowingly at Jack's excitement.

Jack turned back to the window and watched the Wyoming plains roll by. The landscape warped and waned as his eyes brimmed over with tears.

He had been yonder and he had been west. Now, it was time to go home.

INTERLUDE

Letters

Dear Jack,

I hope you made it back to your ranch safely. Here is the postcard I promised. I hope you enjoy the photograph of the Capitol. Cheyenne is quiet again now that all the rodeo business is over. Looking forward to getting a letter back. Unless you have postcards from Hayes County. Hope you write back soon. Think of you often.

Hen

WEST OF WANTING

Lester & Jack,

I just wanted to make sure you boys got back to your ranch. I wrote your father to tell him I met you boys but I haven't heard back. I'll write if anything changes here. Hope you both are doing well. Best of luck on the ranch. Like I said before — if there's anything you need, please send a note and I'll do what I can.

Sincerely,
Thomas Burke, Your Uncle

WEST OF WANTING

Dear Jack,

I don't have much time to write but I wanted to let you know what is going on here. I prayed you made it back home okay but I guess I would have heard by now if you didn't. I called Mister Richard at the bank in Hayes Co. and asked him to tell Pa you were heading home by train as soon as I could when I got to Fort Warren. He said he would pick you up if Pa couldn't. But I guess you know that by now too.

I'm leaving basic training tomorrow morning so this address won't be able to reach me by the time you get this. Training went okay. Lots of running and climbing but not much harder than days on the ranch. I'm not sure where they're sending me but I heard something about other boys from my troop going to France. They gave me a nice haircut when I got here. Better than what you did last time with the barn shears.

Anyway, I hope everything is going well with Pa and the ranch. Wish I was home but I reckon I'll be home soon. Write soon and cross your fingers for me.

Lester

WEST OF WANTING

Uncle Thomas,

Everything is going well here at the ranch. I am here with Pa — that's not our real Pa but the one we grew up with — and the work is hard but the days are getting cooler and shorter. Think about that night at the hoedown often. I'm writing a pretty girl from Cheyenne and maybe I'll visit there to see her and you soon. Now I know it's only a day's train ride away.

Lester was drafted into the Army and left training a couple weeks ago. I haven't heard from him in a while but I don't think he got shipped off yet. Hope he comes home soon.

We don't get mail out here often, but it's nice to get letters when we do. Write soon, if you want.

Jack Copeland

WEST OF WANTING

Dear Hen,

I still have that postcard you sent. It's in my dresser drawer and I take it out most nights before I lay down. Some mornings when I'm tired from nightmares I read your other letters and they help me get up and going. My nightmares are mostly about Lester but I've been having them less since the last time I wrote you. I wish I had more good dreams like ones where you would come and live with me and we could have this whole ranch to ourselves.

Write soon. Miss you too.

Love,
Jack

WEST OF WANTING

Jack,

Writing you from France. We got in a little over a week ago. It's going okay so far, but I'm not sure I'm cut out for it. Sometimes I forget what we're over here fighting for but then I reckon it doesn't much matter. When you're getting shot at, what else can you do but shoot back?

Sorry to sound so down. Just haven't slept much in a few weeks. All this makes the ranch work seem like a ballgame.

I was real happy to hear Pa came to the station to pick you up. Sounds like a pretty fancy automobile he bought. One of the boys here said his old man used to drive a Chevrolet too. Guess the ranch is doing well enough. Soon winter's going to roll in and you'll be wishing for the heat again.

Could hardly believe your story about getting our things back from Willie. He deserved more than what you gave him for what he did to our horses. First thing I'll do on my way home is give him a swing of my own. Can't imagine your harmonica playing sounds any better than it used to but maybe it will by the time I'm home.

Glad to hear about Hen too. I hope she keeps writing you. I'll write as soon as I can too. Pray for me, I'm praying for you.

Lester

WEST OF WANTING

Jack,

I sent a telegram along today, too. Not sure which will reach you first. Sorry to say my father passed away the day before yesterday. It was a ranching accident. He was kicked by a mare he was breaking, as far as I've heard. His funeral was this morning. Not much to say about that. His boss from the ranch and a couple other hands came to see him buried but we haven't got any family left to tell. We buried him next to my mother.

I'm not entirely sure what happens next. He hardly had anything in his pockets when he died and even less saved away. I guess soon enough the bank will come and ask for something I don't have. I could look for a job here, waitressing tables or washing linens at the Hotel Albany. Maybe if you're still sweet on me I'll pack my things and move to Nebraska.

I'm sorry this note is so short. I don't have much to say right now. Maybe soon I will. I know you know how it feels to be alone. Write soon. I could use the smile.

All my love,
Hen

WEST OF WANTING

Jack,

I'm real glad to hear you and Pa are getting along since you've been back. He said he'd quit drinking when we left for Cheyenne so maybe he kicked his mean streak too. Always figured he must have been nice enough for Ma to let him stay all those years. Lots of boys I'm with drink any time we march into a new town. I don't mind the beers they have here but that other stuff isn't much for me.

I'm still somewhere in France. I would tell you where if I ever figured how to spell it, but I don't suppose it'd do you much good anyway. Me and all the boys here are praying this will be over soon and we'll be home by Christmas. You might as well pray for that too.

It's good to know Ma's room will be full again. I hope Hen gets there safe. I bet she'll be real impressed when you pick her up in the Chevy. Maybe you and Pa could paint the room before she gets there. If you pest her enough, maybe she'll be there by Christmastime too.

Lester

WEST OF WANTING

WESTERN UNION TELEGRAM

Mr. Jack Copeland
Hayes County, Neb.

I REGRET TO INFORM YOU PRIVATE LESTER COPELAND WAS ON SIXTH OF NOVEMBER WOUNDED IN ACTION IN FRANCE. YOU WILL BE ADVISED AS REPORTS OF CONDITION ARE RECEIVED.

ULIO THE ADJUTANT GENERAL

EPILOGUE

Home

I ARRIVED IN NEBRASKA by train the same day as Lester. It was identical to the journey Jack made by himself earlier in the year. Like him, I made the trip with almost nothing; my scant possessions were hardly enough to warrant packing. As promised, Jack met me at the station in his Pa's waxed and shined Chevrolet. It must have been the shiniest thing in the entire state. If I'd been looking, I might have caught the afternoon sun glinting off it from Cheyenne.

Jack's face was a storm of emotion when I stepped off the train car. I saw him long before he spotted me and those moments as I watched him, sitting on the hood of the Chevy, eagerly scanning the faces on the platform is still, after all these years, how I picture my Cowboy Jack. He'd grown into himself by the time I moved to Hayes County. His shoulders had broadened. The long days on the ranch had chiseled his boyish cheeks. He was a boy when we met but he'd seemingly long since become a man before the next time I saw him.

He finally spotted me and ran toward me. His excitement was exactly what I remembered and loved about Jack from our short time in Cheyenne. Our first kiss was standing on the rickety wooden loading platform of Hershey Station, in the shadows of a Union Pacific locomotive. He wrapped his arms around me and cinched them with strength that must have surprised even himself. Jack clasped my hand in his and lead me toward the rear of the train to find his brother. Only then did his shining smile fade.

Lester came home in the luggage car, like he was a suitcase or a saddle. Jack stood proudly next to the train, waiting for his brother, his hand beginning to tremble in mine. His face was stoic and hard to read. He'd learned that, as I've come to believe, from his brother. Three men in Army dress uniforms brushed by us and climbed into the train car. Soon, they brought Lester with them. They loaded his flag draped casket into the back of the Chevrolet and stood at attention while we drove away.

Lester Harold Copeland was buried in the early months of 1943. He lies, still, next to his mother.

I only met Lester briefly, during those summer days at the rodeo, but I feel I know him almost as well as anyone. I came to know him through Jack. And I suppose I know Lester only as Jack knew him, but I cannot imagine a better way to become acquainted. Lester exists to me in the ways Jack felt necessary to speak of him. In turn, you know Jack only in ways I have spoken of him.

Jack would say his brother's name any chance he could, as if it were an elixir that brought the youthfulness of their adventure back to him. He would share the stories of growing up with Lester, their adventures on the ranch and their rides beyond, and especially the apogee of their brotherhood — their journey westward in search of their father.

I've known Lester, in some way, for most of my life now. Although he passed before I made Hayes County my home, I could feel him in the house he and Jack grew up in, in the expansive reaches of the ranch, on top of the bluff he would ride to. I've heard Lester's voice only in Jack's, so what you've read is Jack's memories echoing through me and onto these pages. Jack, for his entire life, continued to give Lester a voice — for me, for our children, and for our children's children. When he would speak of his Lester, his voice was as brave and clear as a harmonica tune, no matter how much the Nebraska dust tattered his throat.

Jack and I lived on the ranch in Hayes County for the remainder of our time together. It was sacred land to the Copeland family, and they worked as hard as necessary to keep it through two wars and a depression. Times were never easy, but the work wasn't either. By the time our children were grown, the cattle became corn and the ranch became a farm. Jack still thought of himself as a cowboy and would walk the rows of crops with jingling spurs.

Jack mentioned, vaguely, a few times that Pa was once as mean as a bull, but by the time I met him he was as gentle as a calf. I believe Pa appreciated having a woman in the house again as much as Jack. They spoke about Ma nearly every day. It seemed every breeze, every song, every smell reminded them of her. When she passed, Caroline left a void in those men's hearts that they desperately attempted to fill in with loving words of her. If a blade of grass grew every time Jack told me his mother was the best woman he'd ever known, the dusty ground would have waved like a green ocean.

A few years later, sitting at the dinner table when one of those hard winters had turned to spring, I heard Pa tell Jack he was glad I was there and that I reminded him of Ma. The next morning, Jack asked me to marry him and we were married within a month. Less than a year later, we had a baby boy. We named him Lester Thomas Copeland.

Every odd year after that, for the next six years, we had another child. Andrew, Helena, and Nicholas all slept in a crib in Jack and Lester's childhood bedroom. We gave each of them a patch of land on each corner of the ranch. They helped on the farm as much as they could and joined us for dinner almost every night. They all, in time, had children of their own. Our table grew as our family did.

Nicholas, our youngest, took over the farm when Jack's knees grew too stiff. Helena was as stubborn as her mother and grandmothers combined, but eventually married a young man that had gone to the college in Fort Collins, and together they had a litter of kids that were as free-roaming and energetic as puppies. Andrew was sent to Vietnam; he returned home to Hayes County with his limbs still attached but he was changed somehow and was never altogether the same. Our Les left the ranch for Texas the day before his eighteenth birthday where he joined the rodeo circuit and scratched out a living until the bull he was riding fell sideways and crushed his leg; he was twenty three and walked with a hard limp for the rest of his life.

Pa, Sybil Andrew Hodge, passed away in his sleep a few months before our youngest son was born. Even though our family knew the story well enough, our children called him Grandpa. Jack called him Pa from the day he returned from Cheyenne to the day S.A. passed. If anyone were to ask who Jack's father was, he would have surely pointed across their ranch to S.A.

As for Harold Burke, the catalyst for this entire tale, Jack got a letter from his Uncle Thomas in 1961 that he had died. Jack, over all those years, only mentioned him as a minor character in these stories.

When I sat to write this account, the cowboy story I dreamed of when I was a young girl, I wondered who this tale's main character would be. To me, this is Jack's story. But after hearing his retellings so often, Jack certainly feels everything I've written is Lester's tale. Although I suppose, like all good stories, this one belongs to no one in particular. I've come to believe the brotherhood that cinched Jack and Lester together under the western skies is the part in this tale that matters most.

The story changed very little over the decades Jack told it. Perhaps our lineage will warp and expand the tale, but when Jack would close his eyes and begin his story again, he would be lost in an open plain with his solemn brother beside him. There was no need to ornament the story and Jack never did. The only sprigs of spice he would add would be songs, played on his battered harmonica, or sung with his high lonesome voice. As a coda, he would often sing his favorite Tex Ritter song.

WEST OF WANTING

My foot's in the stirrup, the rein's in my hand. Goodbye, old friend, I'm a-leaving Cheyenne.

Jack could have surely conjured a happier and more fantastical story to tell his children and grandchildren, but he hardly considered it. The tale they heard was his story and, most importantly to Jack, it was Lester's story. One night, our youngest son sat and listened to Jack tell his granddaughter the story. He asked Jack if he would have still set off westward knowing how it all ended. I expected him to breathe heavily and blink slowly, as he often did when thinking. Instead, he nodded confidently. "Yes," he said. "And with the same smile I wore the first time." It was that lesson which Jack wished to teach our children: Failure is not a tragedy and is very often just the opposite. "Remember," he would tell them, "the sad songs are the ones we sing most often."

Every now and then, Jack and I would return to the places he so often spoke about. By the time we welcomed our youngest child, the journey was only an afternoon's drive west on Interstate 80. Sometimes we would go for the rodeo, one time to spend a night at the Armstrong Hotel, but other times simply to gaze at the mountains and fill our lungs with cool western air.

Jack's mind held meticulous paintings of the scenes he and Lester rode through. He could return himself to the prairies between here and there at will, and often did. In his last days, while his family sat by his bedside, we could hear him speaking to Lester. "Oh, now I see the mountains!" he gasped the morning he passed away. I can't say for sure, but I believe Jack reunited, at long last, with Lester and their mother that day under the vast skies of the West.

My husband, Jack Copeland, is buried next to Lester and his beloved mother. A headstone stands at his grave, but this story is his true memorial.

Acknowledgments

To say this book would not have been possible without my mother, and my partner, Heather, is not in any way hyperbole. My other half and best friend, my 'Heddi' listened to this story one chapter, one line or paragraph at a time. Sometimes it was the same passages written in a dozen ways only I could have known were different. You were the first line of defense, and I am so grateful for your honesty, your unwavering support, and your bottomless and unfathomable patience. You are a good confidante, a better woman, and a great partner.

And my mom - who never let me leave the house without a book (or a snack). You saw these chapters one at a time, like a path of breadcrumbs, for almost a year before you found out how it all shook out for the Copeland boys. I'm sorry I did that to you. The pages you saw were hardly smoother than my scribbled notes, but you still saw the glimmering pieces of the story that this book became. The lessons Jack and Lester find along the plains were ones you and Dad worked hard to teach Nik and I, and I hope this book is a testament that you both have taught us well.

The brotherhood that litters these pages is lifted mostly from the only source I know on the subject. My brother was the stoic one, the one that always had a plan, and, most importantly, the one who always just seemed to know right from wrong when it mattered most. If reading about that solemn cowboy named Lester is like looking in a mirror for you, Nik, it's because when I think of brotherhood, I think of you.

Abundant thanks are due to Carol Kressley, who read the earliest full drafts of this book and found mistakes that had slipped through my tight sieves several times. Your keen eye and meticulous notes were a tremendous help in adding another layer of polish to this story. I'm glad I could share it with you. To that end, if there are any mistakes anywhere between these covers I take full credit for them.

Lest I forget my comrades, Huma and Amanda. You both are phenomenal friends who always make time for honesty. I appreciate all of your listening, kind words, and critiques. Tori Simmons deserves thanks as well for her candid notes on one of the later drafts of this book. You're a voracious reader and it shows. I hope you all can see how the effects of your suggestions and compliments are peppered throughout these chapters.

There is nothing fictitious about the Western kindness that became such a pervasive theme during the Copeland's trek. My time living in the West showed me that goodwill is permeating. It is contagious and, above all, it is necessary. Thank you to the band of characters that offered me simple kindnesses, like I was a young cowboy in desperate search of something. I was.

Lastly, to you. Thank you for making it this far. I hope you came to enjoy the Copeland brothers and the landscapes they traversed as much as I did. Being able to share this story with you has made this all worthwhile. I hope to see you again sometime with another tale. And I hope I have many more to tell.

J. R.
May 8, 2020
Worcester, Massachusetts

About the Author

Born and raised in rural Pennsylvania, JARED REINERT is an eye doctor and a writer. He lives outside Boston with his partner, Heather, and their dog, Ellie.

jaredreinertbooks@gmail.com

jaredreinert.com

CPSIA information can be obtained
at www.ICGtesting.com
Printed in the USA
BVHW031112010821
613365BV00011B/430/J